this novel. A truly astonishing survival tale of ministry and marriage will keep you from putting this book down.

~Pastor Wayne King
48 years of pastoral ministry and church planting

If you are looking for a spine-tingling novel that touches on the reality of spiritual warfare in the church today pick this up! Great warnings of dabbling in the darkness are arrayed against the faithful preaching of the gospel. Don't miss [*Presence in the Pew*].

~Art Ayris
Kingstone Studios

[*In Search of Felicity*] gives voice to those of us who find inspiration and insight into our own lives through great works of literature. Rizzo's work will resonate with Rawlings fans and even those who will take up her books for the first time.

~Florence M. Turcotte
literary manuscripts archivist
George A. Smathers Libraries
University of Florida, Gainesville

Truth be told, I am not a novel guy. But I have to admit, Marian Rizzo's *In Search of the Beloved* drew me in from the first page. I love how she weaved her characters in and out of the search for the Apostle John. Great read.

~Dr. Woodrow Kroll
Creator of The HELIOS Project
Radio host, *Back to the Bible*

Time Capsule

Also by Marian Rizzo

Angela's Treasures
Muldovah
In Search of the Beloved
In Search of Felicity
Presence in the Pew
Plague
O Holy Night: A Christmas Gift Book
The Legacy of Mrs. Cunningham
In the Boat with Jesus
The House on Maple Street
The Shepherd's Walk
Silver Springs (with Dr. Robert Knight)

Time Capsule
a novel

MARIAN RIZZO

WordCrafts Press

Time Capsule is a work of fiction. All references to persons, places, or events are fictitious or used fictitiously.

Hardback ISBN: 978-1-967649-34-1
Paperback ISBN: 978-1-967649-35-8

Cover design by Mike Parker.
Author photo by Doug Engle Photography. Used by permission, all rights reserved.

Published by WordCrafts Press
Cody, Wyoming 82414
www.wordcrafts.net

To my grandchildren, Scarlet, Zelda, and Korbin,
and all the young people of Generation Z.
As they lead us into the future,
may they trust in God's guidance along the way.

Chapter One

April 23, 2058

A distant explosion woke me from a sound sleep. I untangled my legs from my quilt and managed to slide out of bed. The hologram on my bedroom wall said Tuesday, 7:45 a.m.—15 minutes short of my normal wakeup call at 8.

Another distant rumble drew me to the window. The horizon lit up with a flash.

Next came another rumble, kind of the way thunder follows a lightning strike. I knew the truth. It wasn't a storm at all, but military drones setting off electrical discharges several miles away. We hadn't expected our neighborhood to get targeted until next weekend. Another flash—closer—told me they were already near our doorstep.

Weeks ago we'd received the warning. The new regime was annihilating everything that had been built by the old administration. The Chinese wanted to rebuild America using their own materials and design specifications. They had done what they always wanted to do. They had taken over America.

Over the last forty years, Chinese immigrants began to filter into the United States. They came legally, with all the appropriate papers, first as college students, then by entering the medical field, then by filling the nation's workforce, soon outnumbering all other ethnic groups in the nation. Ultimately, their offspring, born legally as American citizens, entered the political realm and created a third party, the People's Republic, which led to the ousting of President Harmon Brooks and his cabinet. Brooks vanished from Washington, leaving no trace of where he went, and President Ming Yu moved into the White House. Though full-blooded Chinese, Ming Yu was born in the United States after his parents emigrated here. He had all the legal credentials to run for the highest office, and once elected, he turned his allegiance to the nation of China, brought in more immigrants and the Chinese military.

Meanwhile, the Russians, North Koreans, and Iranians also had aimed at targets throughout the world, and had even threatened to battle the Chinese for dominance over America.

Then, last year, attack drones began moving across the North American landscape, hitting capital cities, downtown areas, and suburbs. Now they'd reached my hometown, Carter Springs, Pennsylvania, and they were closing in on my neighborhood. We thought we'd have plenty of time to get our things in order. Now we were getting ready to move into a time capsule, where we will remain until after the war.

I just celebrated my 17th birthday last week. I wasn't ready to go into hiding, to live among the chosen few—those who possessed useful skills for the rebuild. Thanks to my father's work in electromagnetics, my family had been chosen. But chosen for what? I was about to live hundreds of feet below the surface of the earth, and this was moving day.

I was standing at the window, captivated by the display of fireworks in the distance, when suddenly my bedroom door flew open. Mom appeared in the doorway. All color had drained from her face, and her chocolate brown eyes, usually sparkling with interest, now flashed with panic.

"Olivia, you need to hurry," her voice broke. "Your father's already loading our Tesla X-6 with our luggage."

Another blast went off, closer now. Mom's eyes shot toward the window. She shuddered. "Hurry," was all she said, then she spun away.

The click of her heels resounded in the stairwell, sounding

much like rainwater on the metal dome over our house. The front door squeaked open, then shut with a loud click.

I sprang into action, dressed hurriedly, then grabbed a large traveling bag from beneath my bed and flung it on top along with my backpack. I raced about the room, grabbed handfuls of clothes from the closet, and unloaded my dresser drawers into the traveling bag. In the end, I tossed in a jacket and my hiking boots. Though we'd be entering a climate-controlled environment with no need for outdoor apparel, I'd been nurturing a plan of escape. No way was I going to live underground for a year or more.

I shifted my attention to my backpack. The antiquated tote had served me well over the years. Though I no longer needed to carry school books in it, I sometimes packed it with power bars and water for my hikes with Zaq. I'd also found it useful for quick trips to the corner market, when the food delivery service fell short on supplies. Plus, it made a terrific hiding place whenever the authorities decided to make one of their surprise inspections.

I packed it now with my FlexPhone, grooming kit, several power bars, pens and pencils, and my journal, its cover etched in gold lettering with my name: *Olivia Jackson.* I didn't mind my old-fashioned name. In honor of Grandma Jackson, I was dubbed Olivia from birth.

Unlike most of my peers, who preferred to record everything digitally, I still wrote my thoughts in a journal like I did when I was a little girl. With all that was happening in the world, I feared electronics might fail us one day, and I wanted to offer a message to those who might come after me many years in the future. I could leave them an account of what life was like during World War III, kind of like Anne Frank did in her diary during the Holocaust, more than a century ago.

I read *The Diary of Anne Frank* three years ago, just before the new regime confiscated all of the books in our homes and town libraries. I watched with my heart in my throat the day a contingent of soldiers marched into town, piled the books at the town square and set them ablaze. The conflagration reminded me of Ray Bradbury's *Fahrenheit 451*, bringing his fantasy to life.

The memory of having watched the burning of books and Bibles drew my attention to the secret panel behind my desk where I kept Grandma's Bible. Those fragile pages had survived years of being passed from one generation to the next. They contained more than the word of God, for Grandma and her mother before her had scrawled their personal thoughts in the margins. I carefully settled the Bible inside my backpack and gave the zipper a tug. Though Gram been gone for several years, I could take a part of her into the time capsule with me and hope none of the authorities would decide to check my bags.

Leaving my backpack on the bed, I grabbed my heavier traveling bag, and stumbled down the stairs. Dad was waiting by our car, one of the latest electromagnetic powered models he designed for the Tesla Company. He stood there like a statue, his hands on his hips, his forehead lined with impatience. I handed my bag to him and spun back toward the house.

"Get in the car," he called after me.

I hesitated for only a second. "I need to get my backpack," I shouted over my shoulder, and I raced toward the house before he could stop me.

I passed Mom on the front walk. My heart leaped. She was staring off in the direction of the distant bombings, her lips parted in a silent scream. Ignoring the nervous flutter inside me, I charged into the house and up the steps two at a time. I grabbed my backpack and gave my bedroom one last look. Never again would I sleep in that bed or sit at that desk or gaze out that window. I blinked back a sting of tears, then turned away and left, closing the door behind me, sealing up everything familiar, forever.

Downstairs again, I rushed past Mom who was still standing on the walk, unmoving. I paused for one more glimpse at our neighborhood. Our house blended in with an entire row of identical two-story dome homes modeled after the monolithic dwellings that withstood Category 5 hurricanes on the Florida coast twenty years ago. My own father had played a role in the design, installing his electromagnetic technology within the framework and making each house energy independent with numerous AI automatic functions. It was almost as if the house could read our minds, or at least anticipate our needs and desires.

From what my dad told me, we should appreciate Michael Faraday, an English chemist/physicist, for discovering electromagnetic induction in 1831. Now, more than 200 years later, my father was involved in the further development of that powerful source of energy, not only in transportation, but in daily living. More evidence of Dad's labor now stood before me in a meticulously organized row of identical dome-homes that reminded me of the tiny game pieces on the *Monopoly* board Grandpa used to pull out of his hall closet. But unlike the red-roofed miniatures that ended up safely packed inside the box, our real-life houses would not survive the game we were about to play.

My eyes drifted next door to the Spencers' home, and my heart broke. Old Mr. Spencer had been ailing for months. He could barely walk and had not made arrangements to leave. Mrs. Spencer stood at their front window. She offered a sad smile and lifted a feeble hand to wave at me. I was about to respond, when she backed away and let the curtain fall across the pane.

The Spencers, like many older Americans, had been surviving on government subsidies. Despite the growing shortage of food in America, we'd been more fortunate than the third-world countries already devastated by famine and slowly surrendering to the invasions by super powers like China and Russia. Over the decades, famine, disease, and wars had shrunk the earth's population of nearly eight billion to six billion, then to three billion, and the latest numbers were closer to two billion or less.

I pulled my gaze away from the Spencers' home and watched in horror as other neighbors loaded up their vehicles and sped away. Unlike my family, not everyone had been chosen for preservation. Hopefully, our neighbors and friends would find shelter, perhaps in one of the abandoned Pennsylvania mine shafts or in the caves common to the Southwestern states. I turned toward the house across the street. My friend Matt Ellison and his parents had left the day before. Prior to their departure, I stood at my bedroom window and shivered as the government's Restoration Team barged into their home and loaded a panel truck with Charlie Ellison's blueprints and 3-D models. He was behind the design of the dome houses. Perhaps the Chinese had reconsidered and simply wanted to rebuild with more of the same.

Charlie's outer shells, combined with the clean-and-green power grids my father designed, must have impressed the authorities. Otherwise, why would we have been chosen if not to recreate more of the same?

Yesterday afternoon, the same Restoration Team came back to the neighborhood and confiscated Dad's holographic electro-magnetic charts, his drafting table, and his three-dimensional computer system. Dad stood helpless in the doorway, a troubled wrinkle creasing his brow.

"Don't worry," the workmen called to him from the street. "You'll get it all back after the war."

At that moment the truth hit me like those flashes on the horizon. While hundreds of people were facing annihilation, my father's career had saved our lives. We'd be living inside a time capsule, underground and safe, until the war ended. Meanwhile, millions would fight for their lives amidst one of the most destructive attacks to hit our nation since the Civil War of 2028. Like the enemy had threatened for years, the third world war would be fought on American soil.

I stared off in the direction of the attacks. The drones had moved beyond the edge of town. A flash erupted a few blocks away, followed by a thud and a puff of smoke. A cloud of ash drifted over the rooftops, swirled around us, and tickled my nose with the odor of a school science experiment. I blinked against the sting, then I escaped into the backseat of our car and peered out the window.

My little brother, Peter, walked onto the front lawn and picked up his laser gun. He raised his eyebrows at Dad, who frowned and shook his head at him.

"Leave it," Dad commanded.

Peter's face fell. Poor kid. He was only ten. And that gun? It was a toy, for goodness' sake.

Peter turned toward Mom and contorted his face in a silent plea for help. She stared right through my brother, not seeing him at all.

Reluctantly, Peter lowered the rifle to the ground, but he held onto his helmet and night vision goggles. He slunk over to the car and slid into the backseat beside me. I slipped my arm around him.

"Don't worry, Peter. You'll have plenty of virtual games to keep you busy. And think about it, if the war lasts more than three years, you'll get to train with a *real* gun."

As soon as the promise slipped from my lips, I regretted having said it. The truth was, in three years Peter's name would appear on the roster for military training. At 13 he'd face several months of grueling drills. Then, one day, someone would thrust a laser grenade launcher in his hand and send him out with a team of young fighters. Though much of the warfare would take place with remote controlled drones and long-distance missile attacks, ground fighting continued to lie in our future, and my brother would take part in it. The question was, would he be fighting as an American soldier or as a Chinese legionnaire?

I pulled Peter closer and breathed in the scent of my strawberry shampoo he must have used that morning. He lifted his chin and looked up at me, his innocent blue eyes floating in tears.

I forced a smile. "It's gonna be all right, Peter." But, even as I said those words, I didn't believe them. We were leaving our home, our friends, our life as we knew it. And there'd be no going back.

A series of pops erupted at the north entrance of our street. The armed drones were almost overhead. My dad fastened the restraining bars holding our luggage on the roof.

Peter leaned toward the window and straightened. "What's the matter with Mom?"

Our mother's feet seemed glued to the sidewalk. She was still gazing off in the direction of the gunfire. Her forehead knotted up with distress. Her lips moved but no words came out.

Dad slipped behind the wheel. "She's behaving like a Lot's wife," he sneered. He tapped the horn and stuck his head out the window. "Clarisse! Let's go!"

She didn't budge. I released my hold on Peter and reached for the door handle.

"Clarisse!" The agitation in Dad's voice stirred her to life. She took halting steps toward our car. I let go of the handle and settled back in my seat, but I kept my eyes on Mom as she slid into the front passenger seat and pulled the door shut with a gentle click. Dad looked her over, frowned with disgust, and activated the car's energy system.

As always, it was a clean, silent start. Multiple lights flashed across the console. It had been ten years since America scrapped all the pipelines and went to an electromagnetic source of power. Our brilliant scientists—my dad among them—had developed a geothermal energy system that was able to access the explosive energy boiling 4,000 miles inside the earth's core. Until ten years ago, the deepest hole ever drilled was less than 8 miles deep. America's clean, cost-effective source of energy had left Chinese scientists salivating over the rich source of power, while nations in the Middle East were scrambling for a market for their worthless oil resources. Though other nations tried to get their hands on America's energy design, their failure to do so only served to fuel their bitterness against the West. The prospect of owning it all had increased China's desire to take control of America.

Dad punched in the coordinates on the car's satellite

navigation system, and we moved soundlessly upward and floated out of our driveway. We headed south, away from the attack. From the time I was little, my dad had explained the process of magnetic levitation to me, but the concept escaped me as we left the home where I'd grown up. I had only one thing on my mind. Having to leave all that was familiar so I could live beneath the ground for an undetermined amount of time.

Through blurred vision I stared out the side window. We sailed past our neighbors' empty houses, past a deserted playground, the swings suspended in eerie silence, past the corner market, now shrouded in darkness. A lump came to my throat. Our entire neighborhood was dying.

Peter tugged at my sleeve. I turned to face him and frowned with concern at the lines of terror etched on his young face. He was staring out the rear window. I followed his gaze and let out a gasp. Houses were tumbling like dominoes into the street. Sparks shot upward. There was an explosion followed by another puff of black smoke. The ground quaked as fire bomb after fire bomb went off, toppling more houses, the playground equipment, the corner store—and, amidst the rubble, the Spencers' home, the Ellisons'—and our house along with everything we had left behind.

Chapter Two

Ａs we drifted farther away from our neighborhood, I pulled my journal and pen out of my backpack. Time for my first entry.

April 23, 2058, 9:30 a.m.

We're on our way to the time capsule. I don't know what to expect, can't imagine what it will look like or how confining it will be. I shudder at the thought of being locked up in a hole in the ground. And for how long? No one can say.

Threats of a Third World War started two years ago on June 1, 2056. Millions of people in third-world countries had already died from famine, disease, and enemy invasions. Much of their land fell under the control of despots who blocked the humanitarian efforts of the Red Cross, the World Health Organization, and Doctors Without Borders. Rescue groups were unable to enter areas where they were needed most. Their supplies were confiscated and passed among the surviving powers. Ebola went unchecked. So did malaria, cholera, and a new form of the Covid epidemic. Though scientists had discovered more cures, the ruling powers reserved them for established nations and allowed people in third world countries to perish, like worthless baggage.

Earthquakes, hurricanes, and tsunamis completed the devastation of those faltering nations. Then, the normal course of events took place. The strong overcame the weak, and the weak died off.

Recently, the leaders of the surviving nations called for a temporary cease-fire. They met for a G-10 conference in Berlin, and during negotiations, they divided the world into ten separate power zones.

We live in Zone Three, which, before the Chinese takeover, included the United States, Canada, the Caribbean islands, and Mexico, and still did. Our allies lived in Zone One, a united force of Israel, Jordan, and Egypt; also Zone Two, a unification of several European nations; and Zone Nine, a composite of South America and Central America.

Zone Seven: India, Japan, South Korea, Taiwan, and several other islands in the Pacific, were so war-torn they fell under the control of Zone Four's combined force of China and North Korea.

Zone Five's Muslim nations of the Middle East and North Africa; and Zone Six, Turkey, which has become more powerful over the last twenty years. There also was a neo-Nazi segment of Germany, which left the European Union, started its own Zone Eight and took its own stand against Israel.

But the greatest threat to Israel generally came from Zone Ten, which included Iran, Iraq, Syria, Afghanistan, and Russia, plus all of the Soviet Union's annexations. Our pastor, David Getz, often referred to Zone Ten as "Gog and Magog" from the book of Ezekiel. It wasn't long after that when Pastor Getz's virtual church sessions ceased. Then, he and his family disappeared, and no one knows where they are.

In the midst of the cease-fire, the zone leaders halted all conflicts to discuss the inevitable annihilation of the earth's population. They agreed to gather in Moscow to decide how they might preserve a useful remnant to rebuild after the war. Zone One's leader, Benjamin Kesler, premier of Israel, came up with the idea of time capsules. In addition to preserving documents and artifacts, like traditional time capsules did, he recommended constructions capable of holding people and supplies. Kesler's plan called for huge underground fortifications, equipped with all the essentials to keep the residents safe and well. His idea was well-received by the other leaders. They agreed the time capsules should be stocked with professionals in various fields, a flawless section of humanity who could create a perfect world.

With everyone in agreement, construction began on time capsules in all ten zones. The cease-fire had to continue until all time capsules are ready for habitation.

No surprise, Chinese troops moved onto American soil long before the cease fire was lifted. With Ming Yu's approval, military officers took over the government seats in every state of the Union. In most countries, except for bunkers to house their top government officials, only one or two time capsules were deemed sufficient for the population. In America, workers were encouraged to excavate a time capsule in every state in the union. Fifty time capsules housing what will be a remnant, and my family is about to settle in the one in Pennsylvania.

Over the last four decades, the Chinese population in the U.S. grew to 60 percent of the population. They became citizens, ran for government offices, and elected their own leaders, including Ming Yu, the despot who ran President Brooks out of office. The same thing happened in Canada, where Chinese immigrants swept through the land and took over the government seats in every province. It troubles me that while most of the other nations honored the temporary cease-fire, the Chinese simply continued invading wherever they chose. What I couldn't understand was why American citizens qualified for time capsule preservation when their own people did not.

Similar takeovers had taken place in other parts of the world. Russia moved beyond its annexations and overtook Ukraine, most of Europe, and the Scandinavian nations. In the Middle East, every nation except Israel and Turkey are being threatened by the control of a huge united Iran and Afghanistan coalition. There's no telling who will survive when the war ends and the time capsules are emptied.

To anyone who reads this in the future, this is the state of the world I live in today. Those of us who hope to survive the war have been relegated to confinement in time capsules. We are supposed to be the chosen few.

Though I have been awarded a safe place, my heart is breaking. I can't go back, and I don't want to go forward. I worry constantly about my boyfriend, Zaq. He's out there somewhere. My one hope is that I'll be able to leave the time capsules and find him.

I keep looking out the window in search of familiar landmarks where the two of us used to walk together. I just spotted the stone entrance to a park and the trail where we spent time together only a few days ago. Somewhere beyond the tree line is the abandoned mine shaft where Zaq and I took shelter from the rain. I'm certain I could find it again.

Tears filled my eyes, and I had to stop writing. I closed my journal and slipped it inside my backpack. I reached for my FlexPhone, flipped it open, and brought it close to my lips, my eyes on the back of Dad's head. Though the X-6's automated system had taken over, he appeared to be watching the road ahead.

I whispered into my phone, "Call Zaq."

My boyfriend's holographic image rose before me, along with the word, *Unavailable,* and my heart sank. The light streaming in the side window ignited a gold spark in Zaq's chocolate brown eyes and brightened his cocky grin. With a wink of his eye and a shift of his head, Zaq sent a wave of relief through me, reassuring me that my boyfriend was still all right.

I thought about sending him a message, but we'd already said everything that needed to be said, including a tearful goodbye. I kissed my forefinger, then pressed it to his lips. As I folded the two sides of my phone together, Zaq's image shimmered and disappeared. For the moment, I had to accept our fate. He would remain out there, and I would continue on to the time capsule with my family.

A depressing silence had settled on the inside of our car. Mom wept softly into a tissue. Dad sat rigid with his eyes on the line of cars ahead. The traffic came to a halt, then inched along at a snail's pace. Aware that the firebombs were creeping closer behind us, I feared we might not reach the time capsule ahead of those attacks. We should have left days ago, but for some reason, we'd received the wrong information.

I looked at my brother. At 10 years old, he couldn't possibly have known what danger we were facing. He was fiddling with his night vision goggles, oblivious to what was going on outside our car. His young mind must have seen it all as one big adventure. The day Dad informed us we'd been chosen to live in a time capsule, Peter leaped from his chair at the table and shrieked with joy. I could only imagine what images were running through that kid's brain.

I dug inside my backpack, unwrapped and ate an oatmeal power bar, then I pulled out my virtual music stick, inserted my ear buttons, and selected an instrumental album by The Steampunk Trio. Their electronic vibrations blended with a holographic display of colored lights hovering just out of reach before me. The music and the vision provided a temporary escape amidst the colors and an aura of peace.

Still, I looked past the images and continued to gaze out the window. Months ago, winter left its death-grip on the landscape, and all that was green and lush disappeared under patches of snow, barren tree limbs, and wet leaves. The forest spoke of loss. Then, annihilation crews moved in and plowed away what was left of the greenery. They destroyed so much of the woodlands, I couldn't imagine what kind of world we might find when we emerged from the time capsules in months or years to come.

Gone also from the landscape were the numerous billboards we used to see along the way, psychedelic displays advertising everything from chiropractors to cryogenic freezing. Their bright colored lights eventually flickered out and all that remained were 10- by 12-foot dilapidated frameworks that once held works of art. I didn't miss them because they obstructed the natural scenery I shared with Zaq. As the strains of a synthesizer swirled within the imagery hovering before me, I blinked away the reality of a world I was losing and tried to relax.

Not very long ago, Zaq and I strolled together along one of those wooded paths. He led me to an abandoned mine he'd claimed as his own special retreat. Overhead, gray clouds converged amidst a haze rising from the broken earth. We had planned to meet that day for only one purpose—to say good-bye.

I remember gazing at my boyfriend with concern. His skin had turned from its usual bronze tone to a paltry gray. His chocolate eyes, once sparkling with flecks of gold, had turned dull and lifeless. Even before he said the words, I knew I wouldn't see him again for a long, long time. Maybe never.

"My family wasn't chosen," he said, confirming my fears.

"There must be some mistake." My insides were tightening, I stepped closer to him and pressed a hand over his heart. I wanted to prove him wrong, but I didn't know how.

Zaq offered a wry smile. "Think about it, Olivia. Your father has something to offer in the new build. He's a talented engineer. My dad sells life insurance. Life insurance, Livie. Who's gonna need life insurance in the new world?"

"Surely, people will buy insurance. Not just life, but medical, accident, and insurance to cover their homes and cars."

His snicker drove a knife in my heart. "That's what I wanted to believe. Apparently, the government will provide everything the population needs, including its own insurance program that will cover any losses. They want the survivors to depend on the government for everything." He shrugged. "Anyway, who knows? Chances are, nobody will be around to buy life insurance. If the war is as devastating as I think it will be, we'll all be gone. All of us, Livie. Even those of us lucky enough to be inside the time capsules."

I trembled at the thought of complete annihilation. Tears filled my eyes. Zaq's face dissolved behind the blur.

His voice softened. "I could be wrong, Livie. I don't know what will happen. Nobody does." He placed a hand on my shoulder as though to offer a little comfort. "I'm praying for you, that you'll be safe."

I allowed the tears to spill. "I'm not fearing for my own safety. I can't stand the thought of maybe never seeing you again."

His smile vanished. He drew closer and wrapped his arms around me. I pressed my cheek against his wool jacket, a worn remnant from his grandfather's closet. It carried with it the residue of pipe tobacco and the woodsy hint of the old man's labors in the fields. Visits to his farm had left me with many sweet memories of freshly picked vegetables, apple pies, and three dogs welcoming me at the door. After his grandparents died, Zaq inherited the old guy's clothes. Instead of the more fashionable jumpsuits young men of our day were wearing, he preferred his grandfather's flannel shirts and denim trousers. He claimed they made him feel closer to the old man. In a way, Zaq had turned into his grandfather, or at least the man's clone. The rugged, sun baked lines on Zaq's face, his warm brown eyes, and the mass of hair flowing in waves to his shoulders made him a duplicate of the wrinkled photo he carried in his pocket. The wool jacket made the image complete.

"Look, Livie," he said, resting his chin on top of my head. "At this moment, I have only one concern—that you'll be safe inside the time capsule. That's all that matters."

I lifted my face and gazed at him, my eyes pleading. "I want you to be safe too," I said, my throat tightening with emotion.

"Don't worry about me." He straightened his shoulders and raised his chin with boldness. "I'm not going down without a fight."

I backed away from him. "What? Tell me you won't get involved in the fighting, that you'll find a place to hide until it's over, like lots of folks are doing. It's nothing to be ashamed of."

He took my hand and led me beside him on the path. We followed the winding trail, sidestepped ruts and stones, and suddenly ran out of woods. A terrible sadness rose up within me. One more forest was dying amidst the devastation. I knew at that moment that even if we were able to stay alive, the world we knew would be gone one day.

"I've joined a militia." Zaq shocked me with the news. While I felt myself crumbling, he stood tall, his face brightening with courage. Color set his sallow cheeks afire, and his eyes sparked with renewed passion. "We call ourselves The Vindicators," he said with an air of pride that frightened me.

I couldn't speak, could hardly breathe.

"There are about two dozen of us—all guys—with more coming from different parts of the state," he went on, his voice rising with emotion. "We've banded together, like brothers—and vowed to protect, to encourage, to look out for one another." He let out a little laugh. "I guess that could be our motto, right? *Brothers to the end.*"

Clouds parted overhead, and a ray of sunlight fell on my boyfriend's face, lighting the brown of his eyes. He'd come back to life, and a ray of hope entered my heart, though it had little to do with my boyfriend rushing into battle.

He reached for my arms and held them fast. "I'm gonna survive, Livie. I've got to if I want to see you again."

I pulled back from his grasp. "The Vindicators?" I shook my head. "Are you insane? What can a small band accomplish against an invading army? The Chinese and the Russians use drones. You and your friends will be sitting ducks."

He sputtered a laugh. "It's okay, Livie. We won't be alone. There are other groups, similar ones, all over Pennsylvania and more across the nation. We're already establishing a web of communications, and we're using technology that can't be hacked. We're gonna unite into one big force. We have weapons. Drones of our own. And hiding places." He gestured toward the mine shaft just beyond the woods.

I pressed my hands against my face and allowed another flood of tears to flow.

He stroked my back. "Please, Livie. Don't cry. We have a good chance of surviving. At some point, they'll have to run out of drones, and then it'll be mostly hand-to-hand combat. We can do that."

"And you believe this?" I was incredulous.

"Yes, I do. The Chinese and the Russians don't want the earth to dissolve to nothing. They're as much against radiation poisoning as we are." He cocked his head and gave me one of his half-grins, which I'd found attractive in the past, but now feared its foolishness.

"There's going to be nothing left," I moaned.

"Come on, Livie. You couldn't possibly think they're gonna wipe out *everything*. They have to leave some of the vegetation, some of the wildlife, some of the people even."

I shook my head slowly. "I'm afraid, Zaq. Afraid I'll never see you again. Don't you see, this could be the end of everything?"

He frowned and squeezed his lips together, like he was thinking or perhaps growing even more stubborn. I knew the look. Determination. Unwavering faith, but not in God. Not even in any well-organized army. Zaq was trusting in *himself.*

"It's not the end," he insisted, stomping his foot. "One day I'll come for you. I've already been able to find out where your time capsule is located. I can get there in minutes."

I stepped back in shock. He raised a hand. "I have ways of finding things out. Believe me, Livie, I won't be far away."

Inside I was trembling. Outside, I was weeping.

He leaned close to me for a kiss. I lifted my chin, welcoming—

The car lurched forward, and I sat upright with a start. The memory vanished as quickly as it had appeared. The haze outside my window swallowed up Zaq's image, and reality struck. I was not with him on the trail. I was not close to the mine shaft. I was in the car with my folks and Peter, traveling toward the time capsule, and Zaq was back there somewhere, out of reach.

I pushed the button on my player, stopped the music and the swirling lights. I removed the ear buttons and tucked them away. The traffic had picked up. We glided along, keeping our place in line, picking up speed when another vehicle veered off in a different direction. Everyone, it seemed, was looking for a place to hide. Then, there were the select few who would continue along the highway to the time capsule. The thought of what lay ahead evoked a whole new set of questions.

"Dad?"

My father swiveled his seat around and faced me. "Yeah?"

"What's it gonna be like? You know, living in the time capsule. I'm beginning to feel claustrophobic already."

My problem with close spaces was no secret. It started when I was five years old and a group of neighborhood bullies shut me up inside an old, abandoned freezer. Though I'd pushed with all my might, I couldn't force the door open. Thankfully, Matt Ellison happened to walk by and heard me screaming. He opened the door and pulled me into his arms.

"Dad?" I persisted.

His jaw pulsed as though he was considering an answer. He knew my problem, had tolerated my nightmares, had soothed me out of them only to watch me submit to them again and again, night after night.

The lines on his face softened. "Olivia, trust me. You won't be caged up like an animal. I checked out our time capsule two days ago. It appears to be quite spacious. We'll have our own living quarters, separate bedrooms for you and Peter, and one for Mom and me. We'll be eating communal meals in a huge dining hall. And you'll be glad to know, the time capsule won't be completely underground. It has a roof consisting of a large dome made from two-way, bullet-proof glass. The outside looks like solid metal, but inside the transparent shield allows for a 360-degree view of the forest surrounding the time capsule. It won't feel at all like we're closed in."

"But, it's going to be boring, Dad. What will I have to do besides my virtual studies? As far as I know, none of my girl-friends' families were accepted. I'll be all alone."

"Don't worry," he said, compassion filtering into his voice.

"Believe me, you'll be kept busy enough. For one thing, we'll all have jobs."

"Jobs?"

"That's right. Every resident will have a job. I already told you that, didn't I?"

"No." I shook my head. "Maybe you did. I just don't remember."

"I'll be meeting daily with Charlie Ellison to draw up plans for the rebuild. The two of us will also fix things that break—inside and outside our capsule. Your mom will work with the kitchen crew."

He swiveled his chair back around and faced the road ahead, a move that told me our conversation was over.

I glanced at the back of Mom's head. Doubt overcame me. She sat frozen, just staring out the front window. Concern washed over me. How useful was my mother going to be? When we left home, Dad called her a *Lot's wife*. If that were true, then what was she trying to hang onto? All of our grandparents were gone. Mom was an only child, so she had no one else. Was she trying to hold onto our house? I snickered. It was a boring replica of everyone else's. Her friends? There'd be others. Our family dinners? Most of the time, she used an instant-meal electro-convection oven, the world's replacement for the microwave. I would hardly call them gourmet meals. Nothing like Grandma's home cooking. After my grandparents died, their farm went to pot. That's when Dad invested in one of those geothermal vertical gardens. An entire wall of our kitchen became a greenhouse. If we had been able to stay there, we would never have gone hungry. And with his talents, Dad could certainly replace everything that broke.

"What about Peter and me?" I ventured to ask.

"You'll have jobs," Dad said, his voice matter-of-factly. "Besides your school work, you'll help out in the kitchen, watch over Peter, and keep our living quarters tidy. And Peter will pick up trash and concentrate on his studies."

Then, my dad added one more bombshell. "One more thing,

Olivia. In the new build, you'll be a procreator. What an honor. You have been chosen along with other young, healthy teenagers to repopulate the earth. You'll be kind of like Eve."

My heart felt as though it had stopped beating. Did my dad really approve of that insanity? His last words gave me one more reason to work on a plan of escape.

Chapter Three

My situation had gone from bad to worse. Not only had I left my home, my friends, and my boyfriend, the leadership was about to match me up with some young guy, and we'd play Adam and Eve with no regard for our own feelings.

I couldn't believe my father had agreed to such a plan. Decades ago the Chinese were killing the unborn in an effort to reduce their population. Couples could have one child, no more. Now they wanted to force teenagers to copulate with complete strangers. It made me sick.

"Why didn't you just say no?" I complained to the back of my father's head.

He didn't turn, merely shrugged, and replied. "I couldn't. We could have been left behind."

"But sex without love?" I shrieked. "I'm already in love—with Zaq—the two of us can repopulate the earth. I don't need to hook up with a stranger."

Dad let out a long sigh, but said nothing.

"Exactly when is all this procreating supposed to take place?" I sneered.

"Don't worry, Olivia. You won't have to obey that part of the deal until it's certain the war is coming to an end and we can expect to leave the time capsule. Until then, you'll do your other jobs, including one more I hadn't mentioned yet."

"One more?" I slumped back in my seat.

He kept his eyes fixed on the line of vehicles ahead. "You'll be a caregiver, honey."

"What? Not just Peter? Other kids too?"

"No, someone a lot older," he said, chuckling. "You'll sit with a Mr. Crenshaw for an hour or two every day. The guy's 110 years old, but his mind is as sharp as a two-edged sword."

"Are you kidding, 110 years old?" I tried to picture an aging man in the midst of the rest of us younger, more able-bodied chosen ones. "And he was chosen? What use will *he* have in the rebuild?"

Dad turned his head to look at me, his eyes narrowing. "Look, Olivia. Mr. Crenshaw is a decorated war veteran. He's a history buff and world traveler, a literal filing cabinet of the way life was decades ago. That man can spout statistics and historic details without having to search through digital files. What's more, he's considered an expert in biblical prophecy. He's memorized much of the Book of Isaiah, portions of Ezekiel, and Daniel, and he's correlated those passages with the symbolic references in the Book of Revelation. I'm not really sure if the leadership is depending on Crenshaw to fill in the gaps when things start happening, or if they're keeping him on to satisfy their own amusement. Whatever the case, he's been accepted."

"And I'm supposed to babysit him?"

Dad chuckled. "More than babysit, Olivia. They want you to record everything Mr. Crenshaw says, no matter how trivial. If he should die before we're released, he'll leave a legacy of data that could be useful in the rebuild. And you'll be the one who's recorded it all. That's a pretty important job, wouldn't you say?"

Dad kept his attention on the road ahead, but he continued to press me. "Olivia, tell me you'll at least try."

I didn't respond.

"Hey," he said. "I've seen you scribbling away in that journal of yours. You can do the same thing with whatever Mr. Crenshaw tells you, only you'll use the journal the leadership provides, not that little book you keep hidden away. " He laughed softly. "The good news is, Mr. Crenshaw isn't the type to hide in an underground apartment. He'll want to spend much of his time where he can see outside and enjoy the daily sunshine, which means he'll want to meet with you in the dome."

"The dome," I mumbled. I shook my head. We hadn't seen sunshine in several days. Noxious fumes from the drone bombings had painted the sky a dull gray and filled the air we breathed with a toxic haze. From inside the dome I'd be looking out at much of the same. I was about to be closed up in a metal tube with people I'd never met, including a doddering old man who would fill my hours with historical facts and predictions that might never happen in my lifetime. Then another thought struck me.

"Why can't I train to fight?" I blurted out. "I'm old enough."

"We've already gone over that, Olivia. You know why."

"Yeah. I'm a *girl*."

"Now, you know that's not the only reason. Lots of young women have been inducted into the military. They've been training for months. But the leadership chose you for something special. You should be glad. Proud even. They looked at your genetic makeup, your health records, your level of intelligence, and your physical stamina, all prerequisites for one of the most important jobs in the rebuild."

"Right." I scoffed. "I'm a *procreator*." I spit out the word like it was laced with poison.

My dad huffed in frustration. "Look, honey, this life is better than sending you out with a weapon in your hands. Think about it. You're going to help repopulate the new world. The leadership has placed a high honor on girls who are willing to do their part. There will be compensations. A fresh start with everything you need to set up house. Maybe a scholarship through a virtual college of your choice. There's no limit to the honors that will come to you."

"And if I refuse?"

"Well, they could artificially inseminate you. I don't recommend it. The only other option is, they could harvest your eggs and fertilize them in the lab. But you would never get to know your offspring, never know the joy your mom and I experienced in raising you kids. What's more, you may never give us grandchildren." He shook his head. "Get used to the idea, honey. You're already slated for reproduction. There's no turning back." He glanced at me before returning his attention to the front. "You know, Matt Ellison would be a great match for you," he said, like he hadn't been listening to me. "He already likes you. I can see it in his eyes whenever you come into the room. Remember how he used to hang around our house? He behaved like a hopeless puppy-dog."

"Matt Ellison?" I shook my head. "Not a chance, Dad. We're friends. Nothing more. If the leadership wants me to take part in this insanity, they're gonna have to chase me down and tie me up. First chance I get, I'm out-a there."

My plan had slipped out. I could have kicked myself. I'd pretty much exposed my hope for escape to my father. It wouldn't take much for him to figure out I wasn't speaking hypothetically. I sighed in defeat. I hadn't even entered the time capsule yet, and already I was planning to leave it. Desperation flamed up within me. I needed to find Zaq and make a life with him. The truth was, I could still fulfill the leadership's need as a procreator, only it would be with Zaq, not with Matt.

I shut my mouth and settled back in my seat, hoping Dad was too busy tracking our location to pursue the conversation any further. Perhaps, he'd already forgotten what I'd said, if he'd even heard my protest at all.

Thankfully, Peter perked up about then, leaned toward the front of the car, and squeaked out his own concern. "What about me, Dad? Will I have a job?"

Dad's eyes crinkled at the corners. "You'll have a few chores, Peter, mostly bussing tables in the dining hall and picking up trash around the hallways. And you'll have homework. Lots of it. They'll be preparing the best students for leadership roles. If you do well academically, as I believe you can, you won't have to fight."

Peter dropped back in his seat, a frown on his little round face. There went his dream of traipsing through the woods wearing a vest with pockets full of ammo and an AK-94 strapped over his shoulder.

"Crud! I don't want a cushy job. I want to *fight*. I want to wear a real military helmet and night-vision goggles that work better than the toy I got for Christmas."

"You don't know what you're asking," Dad cautioned. "Believe me, Peter. We already have the best plan for you. Mom and I want you to be safe. You'll be wise to put all your efforts into your schooling."

"But, Dad—"

"No more arguments, Peter. Your future has been mapped out. The leadership has agreed. No military training for you. Now, let me pay attention here. Our turn will be coming up soon."

With an air of defiance, Peter slumped in his seat and crossed his arms in front of his chest. His face had turned a bright red and his breath escaped in short, exasperated puffs. I loved my little brother, but sometimes he acted like a spoiled baby.

Dad ignored my brother's brooding, punched in a few more coordinates, and sat back to let the X-6 do the driving. The vehicle's cameras, radar, and lidar systems had worked well enough to get us this far and would likely locate the time capsule in record time.

The X-6 was a far cry from Grandpa's old farm truck. I was a little girl, about five years old, when he gave in and agreed to trash the thing, but I still remember the overpowering odor of gasoline and the sharp, rusted creases on the truck's body. Grandpa used to let me ride in the bed while he bounced around the fields looking for crops to harvest. Back then, he insisted on doing things the old way, hadn't yet grasped the technology that eventually wiped out everything familiar to him.

The rest of us accepted the changes. They came so gradually we hardly noticed. Dad especially. Being an electromagnetic engineer, he was always looking for something new and different, never looking back. Now we were getting closer to another change in our lives, and like always, Dad not only had accepted the fact that we were moving into a time capsule, but he obviously welcomed the change. I wondered how the authorities had been able to brainwash him so easily.

Peter was still fussing. He turned to me with a pout. "I won't do it," he mumbled. "I'll show Dad. I'll fail my courses. I won't do the work. I'll—I'll find a way and sign up for combat. I'll do it on my own."

I peered down at him and had to chuckle. He was just a child resisting authority. And the truth hit me. He was just like me. A wave of guilt settled on my heart. Hadn't I moments ago done the same thing? Hadn't I defied my father and made my own plan?

"I know just how you feel," I whispered.

For a while I rode in silence, my eyes glued to the back of Dad's head, resenting him and loving him all at once. He'd been the best dad, firm but kind, and handsome as a film star, even at his age. I had inherited his full mane of honey-colored hair and maybe a little of his stubbornness too. I had Mom's willowy frame, but I hadn't inherited her need to please others. A people pleaser. That's what she was. And now a different life had been thrust upon her, and there was no telling how she was going to handle it.

I gazed down at my little brother. Somehow Peter had ended up looking like neither Dad nor Mom. He had shiny blue eyes, freckles, and copper red hair, like Grandpa Jackson. Perhaps he'd also inherited Grandpa's inclination to put on military gear and go fight a war. Isn't that what my grandfather did during the conflict with Afghanistan so many years ago? Every photo in Grandma's album were of her husband in uniform, proudly posing with a rifle or some other symbol of war in his hands.

What an incredible mix of genes in our one household. Shaking my head, I turned my attention again to the lifeless terrain outside my window. It was supposed to be springtime, but there were few buds on the trees. We'd had almost no rain and very little sunshine for a long while. The gnarled branches lining the road triggered another memory. That abandoned mine. Zaq holding my hand, leading me inside. Enveloping darkness. Me, catching my breath. Zaq's voice in my ear, soothing me. Then total submission while I took in my surroundings. With Zaq holding onto me, the walls of the cave didn't seem as close. The darkness didn't overwhelm. I was surprised that I could breathe the air inside the cave, air that seemed to rise from glowing crevasses. I hadn't experienced a single tremor or fluttering of my heart. It was as if I had instantly conquered my claustrophobia, if only for the moment. Such was the power Zaq had over me. He could calm me like no doctor or medicine had ever been able to do. No lecture. No numbing. Just a quiet walk inside a cave with my boyfriend.

I scanned the forest, peered through the spindly oaks, and caught sight of a familiar path running past a crumbling stone wall. I smiled at the memory. I straightened in my seat and trained my eyes to look beyond the trees. The abandoned coal mine stood back there somewhere. I was certain of it.

"Dad?"

He tilted his head in my direction.

"What is it now, Olivia?" He fiddled with the dials on the dash, punched in fresh coordinates, then returned his gaze to the road ahead.

"I was just wondering, what's gonna happen to the people who didn't get chosen? Some of my friends are out there."

"Who knows? They'll have to fight, I guess. Or find someplace to hide until it's over. Just thank God we'll be safe inside the capsule."

Peter stirred to life and poked my arm. "You're worried about Zaq Myer, ain't ya?" he said, loud enough for Dad to hear. "Forget him, Ollie. He's a goner."

Dad's piercing blue-green eyes shifted to the rear-view mirror.

A surge of heat rushed to my face. "Shut up, Peter. Zaq can

take care of himself. And don't call me Ollie." I elbowed his ribs, but not hard enough to hurt him.

Dad's eyebrows shot up. "If it'll ease your mind, Olivia, I heard through the grapevine that the rebel groups have been hiding in caves and in those abandoned fallout shelters of the 1960s. Maybe your friend will end up in one of those."

Only one word stood out in all he'd said—*Rebel.* "Zaq is *not* a *rebel*," I growled.

"Didn't he get arrested last year for spreading anti-government propaganda?"

"Well—yes—but he only spent one night in jail." I squirmed a little, then I regrouped. "He didn't do anything wrong."

The incident reminded me of the shift in government leadership that had taken place. I hadn't yet recorded any of that in my journal. Perhaps, this was the time to do it.

I pulled out my book and pen and started to write.

April 23, 2058, 11:00 a.m.

For two years the United States was governed by President Harmon Brooks, a legitimately elected man of God who made right decisions for our country. Brooks took a strong position on issues that had bothered the dwindling Christian community for years. Abortion was at the top of his list. He wanted to do away with the killing of unborn babies with no restrictions. He also favored a reversal of the laws that supported trans-genderism and homosexuality, often reminding his constituents about what happened in Sodom and Gomorrah and supporting his decisions with scriptures. He relied on men like my own pastor, David Getz, and others who'd taught from the Bible and had become quite popular. Getz had written several books on the threats of end times philosophy—books that had long since been destroyed by the leadership. He'd also traveled all over the country presenting his ideas to other churches.

Then he'd mysteriously disappeared, about the same time our president had. As we should have expected, Brooks and his followers were outnumbered by proponents of the People's Republic Party, and the new regime put in their own rules and regulations. First thing, they condemned the Bible as an antiquated book of fantasy and ordered them destroyed. They ordered church services to cease, and gatherings of all kinds were condemned.

Brooks was ousted in the middle of his term, and Ming Yu was selected through a special election. Though the overthrow bore undertones of illegitimacy, Brooks and his cabinet left Washington, and no one has seen him since. Even the vote of evangelical Christians, now a minority, couldn't reinstate Brooks. An underground movement attempted to gain support through peaceful rallies in Washington, D.C. and at government capitals throughout the nation. Followers wrote and distributed pamphlets. They created virtual documentaries that were eventually banned by the opposition. Still, they continued to join together in secret prayer meetings, their main goal to bring Brooks back to the White House. Zaq was among the most outspoken among those who sought restoration of the former leadership. Was it any wonder he'd been arrested? He'd simply taken a stand much like the early apostles did before they were martyred.

Dad let out a grunt. "Your young man has been labeled, darlin'," he said, as though he'd been reading over my shoulder. "You don't want to be associated with someone like Zaq Myer. You need to forget him. He's nothing but trouble."

"Yeah," Peter blurted out. "Nothin' but trouble."

I glared at my brother. "Shut up, Peter. You don't know anything." I narrowed my eyes at him and sent him a silent warning.

He shrank down in his seat. "Sorry," he whispered.

Peter and I had had a difficult relationship for most of his young life. I resented having to babysit him, and he resented my being placed in authority over him. I tried not to get bossy, but sometimes he needed a strong hand. I never spanked him, never hollered. When needed, I simply dragged him by his ear and let him know I meant business.

At that moment, Dad turned toward Mom and patted her hand. She didn't respond. He turned slightly and cast a smile at the two of us in the back seat. The car came to a halt.

"Well, we're here," he announced. "Home at last."

Chapter Four

W e'd stopped in front of a huge metallic dome, a monstrosity of a structure that glowed more like an alien spacecraft than a place of refuge. And beneath the dome? A huge underground pit where I'd be expected to spend the next year of my life—or longer. The outer structure looked a lot like one of those 1940s Quonset huts I'd read about in my virtual studies. Back then, Quonset huts were used for everything from housing soldiers and storing military supplies to serving as makeshift hospitals during World War II. The black-and-white photos depicted galvanized steel domes with only one access door and no windows. I shuddered at the thought.

Then there were the fallout shelters people constructed in their backyards in the 1950s and '60s during the Cold War with Russia. People filled them with canned goods, water, and other non-perishables, but they never needed to live there. When the threat of war lessened, they simply removed everything.

I gazed at the monstrosity before me and had to admit our time capsule appeared to be a lot more streamlined than a Quonset hut, and a little more promising than a fallout shelter. Before me stood a seamless glistening shell. I couldn't see what lay beyond the bubble, but I was uncomfortably aware that the people standing inside could see me.

"It's an amazing structure," Dad enthused. "It's hard to tell by just looking at it, but that dome is an entire wall of radon-tempered glass, an impenetrable shield that allows daylight in while able to keep shrapnel out. From out here, it looks like reinforced steel, but peering out from the inside you will be able to enjoy a spectacular view of the surrounding forest." He turned toward me and Peter. "You'll be perfectly safe in there, kids." Then, with a wave of his hand, "Let's go."

I opened my door and an icy chill rushed through me. I shuddered, then sucked in a long breath of outside air. I stepped out of the car, still shivering, though the air wasn't cold.

Dad began to unload our luggage. He piled it on the ground at our feet, then he tossed his security key on the driver's seat and slammed the door.

"We can say good-bye to this old heap," he snorted. "When we get out of here, we'll have lots better means of transportation. The auto people who've been chosen will be working on new concepts in a special, climate-controlled shop somewhere inside the capsule, and the minute we get out, they'll put their ideas to work."

I frowned in disbelief. "How can you be sure, Dad?"

"Sure of what?"

"That things are gonna change for the better."

He raised his eyebrows and smiled down at me. "Olivia, do you think we're gonna be sitting around twiddling our thumbs in there?" He tipped his head toward the dome. "Professionals from all walks of life will be gathering with their peers to make plans for the future. Automobile executives, clothing designers, makers of household products, everything you can think of, plus Charlie and I will be drafting a plan for future constructions— houses, office buildings, stores. By the time we get out of here, there's no telling what wonderful new world we'll have waiting for us. Don't you remember all the futuristic concepts displayed at the last world's fair we attended? We should be able to work those ideas into our designs."

My dad's enthusiasm should have spilled onto the rest of us. My mom just stood there, still in shock. Peter crinkled his forehead in confusion. And I simply shook my head. As far as I could see, my dad had been brainwashed by the leadership, and there was nothing I could do about it.

"Grab your stuff," Dad ordered and marched off ahead of us, juggling three large suitcases and Mom's tote.

Releasing a grunt, I flung my backpack over my shoulder and picked up my own suitcase, then I followed my father along the path to the entrance. My mother hadn't grabbed anything. She merely glided submissively along the walk behind him. Peter came up beside me dragging his one large bag, the metal wheels clattering over the stony path. With his free hand he gripped his precious helmet and night vision goggles.

As we approached the entry, waves of claustrophobia swarmed over me. I was going inside an underground pit, this time without Zaq to calm me. A massive steel entry door stood waiting between two marble statues resembling America's new President, Ming Yu and his Vice-President, Chen Li. They looked like Siamese twins—fat and squat with clean-shaved faces, pointed eyebrows, slick black hair. The two icons sent a chill through me. Though the new leadership had promised peace and prosperity, they had delivered the opposite. They had removed leadership we trusted and had installed their own warped system of control. Ever since they'd assumed office, I hadn't seen a single American flag anywhere. Only the flag of China was raised on the 12-foot pole, a symbol of the power that now ran the United States of America.

My anxiety building, I lagged behind. Peter moved ahead and marched up to the door—a brave warrior eager to embark on a new adventure. I laughed to myself at his innocence.

I looked at Mom. She hadn't said a word since we left home. A terrible knot formed in the pit of my stomach. I needed her now more than ever. She would understand my fears. She could comfort me and tell me everything was going to be all right. But she was lost to me for the moment.

I drew closer to the door. My breathing came in short gasps. My entire body began to tremble, and I felt like I was about to faint.

Dad must have noticed my distress. He set down the bags

and placed a firm hand on my shoulder. Then, guiding me to the door, he reached out and pressed his fingers to a scanner on the wall. Though composed of metal, the door melted soundlessly into the side wall and exposed a large entry. Dad hoisted the bags and passed over the threshold, followed by Mom, who continued to glide silently behind him. Peter barged ahead of me, then stopped in his tracks as he took in the big receiving area.

I hesitated long enough to gulp a final breath of outside air. Then I moved forward and drew up beside the rest of my family. The opening to the outside shut with a click behind me. The rotunda was constructed of a blend of silver and brass. As part of the dome, it was illuminated with light from the outside. Still, the circular receiving area gave off a cold, lifeless feeling, like one might encounter in an ancient mausoleum. A wave of claustrophobia engulfed me.

I searched the rotunda for signs of life. A few people mingled about, conversed for a few minutes, then departed down several hallways that radiated from the rotunda, like the arms of a giant octopus. My eyes settled on a uniformed attendant behind a large desk equipped with three virtual monitors and a huge keyboard. She busily fingered the controls and appeared to be intent on her entries. Dad approached the desk and set his bags on the floor. We did the same. She reluctantly left the project she was working on and stared at us through half-open eyelids.

"Names?" she said, her voice clipped and as expressionless as her blank stare.

Dad pulled our family chip from his wallet. "We're the Jacksons," he said, holding it out to her. "Rave, Clarisse, Olivia, and Peter." He smiled at the attendant. She did not return his smile.

Dad handed her our chip. She plugged it into one of the monitors, then swept her eyes over our family as though matching us to the names. While eyeing us, she moved her fingers over the panel of buttons. Her cold gaze lingered on Mom, she blinked with concern, then she punched a few keys and set off a series of beeps and flickering lights.

"You're in pod number 12," she said at last, and handed the chip back to Dad. "Second floor down." Her words were clipped, almost robotic. "I've summoned your host family. They will be here in a minute."

No welcoming smile, no kind inflection in her voice, no hint that she was a living, breathing human being. I began to wonder if she might be one of those experimental hybrids I'd read about. They could perform nearly every service known to man, as long as they were confined to one place, one room, and programmed for one specific duty. They looked human, possibly were infused with human genes, had a brain of sorts, but did not have a heart.

Without saying anything further, she swiveled her chair away from us and returned her attention to whatever she'd been working on before being interrupted.

In two minutes our identity had changed. We were no longer the Jacksons, family of four, educated and desperately needing to go back to our suburban lives. Now we were simply the people in pod number 12—nothing more.

The sound of footsteps drew my attention to the hall on my right. I caught sight of a crop of copper-colored hair reflected in the metallic walls of the hallway. My friend Matt emerged, smiling and with a gleam of anticipation in his eyes. I breathed a sigh of relief, happy to see a familiar face and a pair of smiling blue eyes. Behind Matt came his parents, Charlie and Jeanine Ellison. Matt's father still looked the same—balding, with a short, stocky build, conservatively dressed in expensive khaki pants and a polo shirt. Upon seeing us, smile lines burst at the corners of his eyes, and he extended a welcoming hand to my dad.

One look at Jeanine, however, caused my jaw to drop. She was wearing a skin-tight, black body suit, far too youthful for her aging, out-of-shape figure. Like some of the teenagers did at that time, she'd shaved her hair on one side. The other side was dyed red and hung down to her chin. She had painted her fingernails a metallic gold, and she wore platform heels that put her a foot taller than her husband.

Matt drew close to me. "You can shut your mouth now," he whispered.

I blinked and tore my gaze away from Jeanine.

"Sorry," I mumbled. "What on earth has happened to your mom?" She'd noticeably changed from the apron-clad home-maker with brown curly hair, flitting about her state-of-the-art kitchen. The woman who once greeted Matt and me to her table for cookies and milk had morphed into something from the 2057 Comic-Con.

Matt shrugged. "Some sort of mid-life crisis, I guess. I hope it's temporary."

I giggled. Matt had a knack for saying something humorous within the most dire circumstances. Like the day he pulled me out of an abandoned freezer and saved my life. He'd immediately made a joke.

"Hiding from the mob?" he'd said, his eyes twinkling.

I actually laughed. Out loud. And then I fell into his arms, crying.

Seeing Matt there, in the time capsule, the first familiar face, assured me that everything would be all right.

Matt's dad possessed a similar demeanor. Standing there in that cold rotunda he was grinning with such enthusiasm you'd think he'd invited us to his house for one of his famous barbecues.

"We got settled yesterday," Charlie said, still smiling. "We offered to be your host family."

Dad nodded and returned Charlie's smile. Mom just stood there. Charlie's smile faded slightly. He eyed my mother with concern. Then, he blinked and turned his attention to the pile of bags at Dad's feet.

"How about we escort you to your quarters?" he said. "You and I can set a time when we can meet to discuss the new build. I've got lots of ideas about construction, and I'm eager to pick your brain."

"I'm looking forward to it," Dad said.

Their behavior puzzled me. The two of them were acting like they were planning one of their fishing trips instead of setting up residence in an underground pit. To make things worse, my mom hadn't budged, but was standing apart from the rest of us, like a manikin in a department store window, unmoving, unblinking.

Jeanine broke from our group and hurried to my mother's side. "Clarisse, are you okay?" Her high-pitched voice echoed off the rotunda walls. Except for a few benches along the far wall, there was no furniture and no carpeting or wall decorations to muffle the woman's screech.

Mom didn't even blink. Jeanine looked her up-and-down, then snickered. "Listen, Clarisse, I was scared, too, when we came here yesterday. But, it's really not so bad. You'll see."

Mom flinched and took a step back. Her face was drained of color, like those expressionless marble statues standing outside the entry door. I stepped toward her, but Jeanine cut me off and took hold of Mom's hand.

"Come on, dear. Let's take the elevator down to our level."

Mom stiffened. "I–I can't—" Her eyes wide with fear, she yanked her hand free.

Dad interrupted his chat with Charlie and rushed to Mom's aid. "It's okay, Clarisse," he murmured. "The kids and I will go down to our floor and get settled. You can stay up here as long as you need to. I'll come back in a few minutes."

I shot a look at my dad. "I can stay with—"

"I'll keep her company," Jeanine said. Ignoring my frown, she took Mom by the arm and led her to a padded bench by the far wall. "C'mon, Clarisse," her voice echoed. "Let's sit and rest awhile. We don't have to go down in the elevator just yet."

I stared after them. I was the one who should have been helping Mom. Instead, I stood helpless, not knowing what I should do. I turned to Dad. He was smiling with what looked like relief. *Fine. The responsibility for Mom was off his shoulders.*

The two mothers had settled on the bench. My mom was now in the control of a teenage wanna-be, my dad was intent on getting us settled, and I had to look after Peter.

For a moment, my attention drifted to another bench about ten feet away from my mom. A young woman had settled there alone. She placed a hand on her abdomen and stroked the unseen baby inside. She looked about ready to deliver, but she didn't appear the least bit happy about it. A pang of sympathy seared my heart What did Jesus say about the last days? *"Be careful that you're not with child in that day."*

That day. Had the world drifted so far from God? Pastor Getz said it had. He preached Sunday after Sunday about the coming fall of mankind and how we should watch for the signs and be ready. He encouraged us to stay strong in our faith. Then one day, just before the final invasion, he was gone. We then had no one to guide us, no one to show us the warnings mentioned in the scriptures. No one to prepare us for what could be the end.

Jeanine wrapped an arm around Mom and turned her dark eyes on Charlie. He nodded with understanding, lifted two of our heaviest suitcases, and headed down the hall to a bank of elevators. Matt grabbed my bag. I hung onto my backpack and stepped up beside him. Peter juggled his own luggage and stumbled along behind us.

Charlie paused before one of the elevators and pressed his fingertips to a scanner. The door opened with a whoosh. I hesitated in front of the opening. That metal box looked an awful lot like an abandoned freezer. Dad followed Charlie inside. So did Peter and Matt. The four of them stood there, eyeing me with impatience.

"It's okay," Matt said, his voice soft.

I swallowed the lump in my throat and stepped inside, but remained close to the door. The cubicle was barely big enough for three people, but there were five of us, plus all our luggage. The door shut with a *squish*, like it had just sucked all the air out of my lungs. I struggled to take a breath, reached for the steel bar on the wall, and hoped the ride down would be quick. Charlie faced the control panel and gave a voice command, "Number Two." A scattering of lights flickered to life.

"We lucked out," Charlie said with a lilt in his voice. "Our individual apartments are on the second level. Many of the other guests are on levels three and four, much deeper inside the capsule." I supposed I should have been happy to hear that. I wasn't.

The elevator lurched into a descent. I gripped the bar like my life depended on it.

"At this level," Charlie continued. "We'll be close to all the ground floor facilities, but deep enough underground so we won't hear the fighting."

"How many levels are there?" Dad wanted to know, and so did I.

"Six," Charlie responded. "Enough room for 200 residents, plus staff, leadership, and a storeroom containing everything we need to survive for several years, if necessary."

I shuddered at the thought of being interred in a huge grave constructed of metal and plastic with nowhere to go but down, plus enough supplies to keep us going for several years, like there was no end in sight.

When the elevator door hissed open, I lunged out ahead of the others and surveyed the area. Three hallways extended from the elevator pod, and each hallway contained four doors on either side. I assumed they led to individual apartments.

Charlie started down the center hall, and we trotted after him like a bunch of dumb sheep following their shepherd.

"There are two dozen families on levels two, three, and four," he explained as we walked. "The apartments were built to accommodate a variety of family sizes, plus operations staff. The fifth level contains a medical clinic and pharmacy, plus one entire wing of labs and workrooms for design projects, including the auto makers and the two of us," he said directly to Dad. "To help us out, they installed drafting tables and overhead lights. I'm expecting we'll spend a lot of time in there." He continued his spiel as we progressed down the center hall. "There's a chapel, an exercise room, a kitchen and dining hall, plus a study area for the kids on the main floor. Best of all there's the dome where residents can sit and enjoy the outdoors without leaving the capsule. The sixth and lowest level is used for storage. That's where they've housed all of the energy components that keep this place running." He looked at me. "That level is off limits, but you can tour the rest of the capsule at your leisure. If you like, Matt can show you around."

Without waiting for me to answer, he turned back to my father. "It's past noon now, so you missed lunch. I put a basket of fruit and snacks in your compartment. Enjoy it. It's the last you'll see of fresh fruit. All of our meals and snacks are rehydrated, like the astronauts dined on when they took long trips around the moon and that one journey to Mars a couple years ago." He released a chuckle. "The coolers contain plenty of cultivated meat products, including the edible animal protein the agri-scientists grew from cells using a bioreactor. They've proven to be a taste-satisfying and nutritional way to provide the necessary proteins without having to raise and slaughter live animals."

Dad nodded his approval. "That ought to make the animal rights people happy."

The two fathers laughed together, then moved on to another subject that had nothing to do with food.

Meanwhile, I was dreading the thought of having to eat a lot of processed foods that would probably taste like paper. Call me spoiled, but I had gotten used to Charlie's barbecues, Grandma's home cooking, and Mom's cookies. At that moment, I would have even welcomed the instant meals Mom prepared in her electro-convection oven, if it would bring her back to us.

Charlie stopped at the first door on the right. "Here you are," he said. "You might want to rest up a bit. The dinner bell will ring at six o'clock. If you miss it, you won't get fed until morning."

"What time is breakfast?" Dad said with a little concern.

"Eight a.m. Don't be late."

Chapter Five

Dad pressed his fingertips to the scanner, and the door to our apartment opened. I stepped cautiously across the threshold. Immediately, an invisible veil dropped around me, and the walls began to close in. I doubted I could tolerate being shut up in that small space for very long. I stared at my dad, my eyes pleading. His smile faded to a frown of concern. I turned away from his sympathetic eyes and studied the tiny apartment with its vinyl furnishings and tile floors. The air reeked of recycled plastic.

I tried hard to find something redeeming about the place I'd be living in for what could be a long time. The sitting room contained a two-seat sofa and a small table with four chairs. Everything was done in brown and gold. A media screen hung high on a wall across from the sofa. I snorted. The leadership would likely stream in whatever newsreels and documentaries they decided we should watch. Sadly, such technology also had a reverse capability. Most likely nothing we said or did in that sitting room was going to be private.

I looked beyond the immediate space to the only area that might offer privacy. Our three sleeping quarters. They were small, yet far away from the notice of *Big Brother*, as George Orwell had referred to the all-seeing eyes of leadership. It troubled me how many of the man's predictions had come true, like voice-activated gadgets, dependence on leadership, and government control through surveillance and propaganda. It was a sad day when the powers that be confiscated and burned all of Orwell's books along with many other classics. Had I not already read

1984 and *Animal Farm,* I might have been surprised by the changes that had occurred over the years. We lived through the burning of books and every version of the Bible. I thought smugly about my Grandma's treasure, packed safely away in my luggage. What would the authorities do if they found out it had made it into a time capsule?

Charlie dropped the heavy bags to the floor with a thump. He walked farther into our unit and opened a side door, exposing a sink, a commode, and a shower stall with barely enough room for one person to turn around.

"We'll be sharing this bathroom," he said, and a tightening came to my throat. I'd expected to at least have a private bathroom. Now I had to share that crawl space with Matt and his parents? "Our living quarters are on the other side." Charlie gestured toward a door at the other side of the bathroom. "When you're using the facility, be sure to lock both of the inside doors." He gave me a wink. "We'll have a shower schedule, of course."

So, the seven of us would be living like one family. How wonderful. The plan to unite Matt and me had started to take shape.

"Well," Charlie said, striding back toward the hall. "I'll see you later for supper. Don't worry about your wife. Jeanine will bring her down in a little while."

Charlie never mentioned his wife's new look, as if he had accepted the change or perhaps was embarrassed by it.

I stared at Matt, and a surge of pity swelled over me. His parents did not seem normal. One of them was trying to relive her teenage years, and the other was walking around like he'd taken charge of the new transfers, including my family.

Matt gazed back at me and raised his eyebrows. "See ya later?" he said, a hopeful smile on his lips. When I didn't respond, his face dropped. Then he followed his dad out the door.

I let out a sigh. Matt had been a good friend since we were little kids. This uncomfortable situation wasn't his fault.

He turned around in the hall and stared back at me, an anxious sparkle returning to his eyes.

I nodded. "Later, Matt." My response, though brief, returned the smile to his lips.

Matt and his dad walked away toward their room down the hall. I stepped back and held my breath as Dad pushed a button, and the door shut with a resounding *click*, sealing us inside.

Already perspiration had broken out on my forehead and the back of my neck. Like the *Time Machine* Eloi going back inside their cave, I drifted to my sleeping cubicle and began to unpack my bags. I thought I would suffocate in that small space. Sure, we had a climate controlled air system, but it didn't help that there were no windows. A framed window box hung on the wall next to my bed. It displayed a landscape of rolling hills, flowers and trees, a sorry attempt to give the feel of the great outdoors.

My bed resembled one of those old-fashioned MRI machines, a long, narrow tube that could swallow up your entire body. Inside were plenty of plush cushions and a thick comforter, plus an overhead arc of LED strips that made it seem less confining. The remainder of my tiny bedroom included a plush chair, and a wall of cupboards. I vowed right then to spend the majority of my free time in the dome.

I shoved my socks and underwear in a drawer, stashed the rest of my clothes in a tiny closet to be sorted later, then I carried my grooming kit to the bathroom and placed it inside the cubby marked, *Jacksons*.

I inhaled a deep breath, surprised by how that simple act calmed me. With my confidence building, I walked over to my parents' cubicle—a larger version of the one I'd been assigned. Their sleeping tube was double the size of mine, and they had several more cupboards. Dad was folding clothes and laying them carefully in the drawers. He lifted one of Mom's nightgowns, pressed the soft material to his cheek, and breathed in a whiff of her perfume.

I tapped on the doorframe. "Can we go check on Mom?"

He started, then hung the nightgown in their little closet. He turned toward me, and I got a better look at his face. He didn't have to tell me how worried he was. I read the truth in the way the lines on his forehead came together and because dark shadows had settled beneath his eyes.

"She's being ridiculous," he said. "Your mother wants to hold onto a life that no longer exists, and she just—won't—let—GO."

"Maybe she *can't* let go," I said in Mom's defense. I recalled her look of desperation as she stood in my bedroom doorway that morning.

He grunted and deposited a neat stack of his shirts in a drawer.

"Dad, I understand how she feels. I didn't want to leave home either." I searched for the right words. "Maybe it's a female thing. We need to feel secure. We're not like you guys. You're always up for another adventure. You can move from one place to another without giving a thought about what you left behind. Did you notice how fast Peter adjusted to this place? He's in his room right now playing war games."

Dad had paused in his unpacking. He seemed to be listening intently, so I went on.

"We females can't bear having everything familiar taken away all at once. Coming here was traumatic enough. And we can't be sure what awaits us in the new world."

He raised open palms toward me. "Olivia, we've known for weeks we'd been chosen. Your Mom had plenty of time to adjust. And, by the way, so did you."

He stepped closer to me, his jaw firmly set, his eyes hardening with determination. I'd seen this look on him before, when another engineer applied for the same job he wanted. He fought for that job and won. But when Pastor Getz challenged the congregation to protest against the new regime, Dad sided with the government. The rebellion fizzled out, and he acted like he'd won the lottery. His stubbornness surfaced again two weeks ago when Mom told him she didn't want to go into a time capsule. He silenced her with a glare I would never forget and continued making arrangements for our family.

Now he was hanging Mom's bathrobe in the closet.

"We'll be safe here," he said, still trying to convince me. "Your Mother will understand, in time, and so will you." His brow wrinkled, and he stared at me as if to read my thoughts. "Would you rather we hadn't been chosen? Would you rather be out there—" he gestured toward the ceiling and beyond, "roaming around with nowhere to hide, defenseless, and waiting for the next attack? Remember, Olivia, our house is gone. Everything is gone."

I stared back at him but didn't speak. *Yes, I'd rather be out there, with Zaq.*

Dad turned back to his suitcase, like he'd assumed the matter was settled. He pulled out more clothes, arranged them in a drawer, then hung Mom's blouses in a neat row in the closet, taking his time with each one.

"I need to see Mom," I pressed. "I need to make sure she's okay."

Dad dropped more clothes in a drawer and shut his suitcase with a loud *click*. He shoved their bags inside the closet and turned to face me. "Okay, Olivia, let's go."

We found Peter in his room with the light turned off. His layout was the mirror image of mine. He was wearing his helmet and virtual reality goggles, and he had ducked behind his bed like a soldier on a reconnaissance mission. Chuckling, Dad tip-toed over to my brother, pulled the helmet off and tossed it into the chair.

"Let's go, little soldier," he said, and he started for the door.

Peter shed the goggles, and dragging his feet, he followed our dad. The three of us took another claustrophobic ride in the elevator. We were heading for the first floor and the lobby. I had hoped each subsequent ride might feel less confining. But when the doors opened on the first floor, I burst out ahead of my dad and Peter, and I sucked in air as if I had just risen from deep inside a swimming pool. We went directly to the lobby, expecting to find my mom there. I scanned the area. The pregnant woman was gone. Jeanine sat alone on the bench where she had taken Mom. But there was no sign of my mother.

Dad took three brisk steps toward Jeanine. "Where's my wife?"

She leaped to her feet. "A couple of medics took her to the infirmary." She extended her hands in her defense. "They said she needs twenty-four hours of observation. I'm sorry, Rave. I couldn't stop them."

Sure, I thought. If I had been there, no one would have been able to touch my mom. We'd entrusted her care in the hands of a woman who didn't seem to be in her right mind, and now my mother had been taken away.

Dad narrowed his eyes. "She's *my* wife," he growled. "They had no right." He looked around and settled his eyes on the bank of elevators. "We need to go to the infirmary."

I remembered Charlie's explanation of the various levels. "It's on the fifth level down. At least, that's what Matt's father said."

Dad spun away and stomped down the hall toward the bank of elevators. Peter and I scrambled to keep up with him. Jeanine remained behind. The last elevator bore a sign that read, *"Level Five. Infirmary. Medical Staff Only."* Dad punched in a series of numbers on the keypad. I set them to memory, in case I might need them one day.

To my amazement, the doors separated. I stood there, stunned. Apparently, my dad held far more authority than he'd revealed to me.

"I don't like this one bit," Dad snarled, stepping inside the elevator. "Not one bit."

Peter followed him. I held back. The fifth level down—deeper inside the core of the earth. It was like being buried alive. I inhaled deeply and once again passed through the open door into the 4-by-5-foot box, suppressed a swell of claustrophobia and grabbed for a handrail.

Dad checked the panel's cluster of lights and buttons. "Infirmary," Dad said, and keyed in that same set of buttons.

"How are you able to do that, Dad? How can you go where no one else can?"

"I told you, I checked out the time capsule a couple of days ago. They gave me special clearance." And I knew *they* referred to the leadership.

A sniffle rose from my brother. He was wiping his nose while a flood of tears seeped from his eyes. The brave soldier was gone. In his place was a frightened little boy. His anxious eyes mirrored my own anxiety. I couldn't blame the kid. Everything about the time capsule had me trembling. While gripping the rail with one hand, I managed to wrap my other arm around Peter's shoulder. I pulled him close to me. To my surprise, he didn't resist.

He turned his face up at me. "I'm worried about Mom."

I didn't know what to say. He was definitely a mama's boy. I simply offered him a sad smile.

As soon as the door opened, Dad bolted out ahead of us. Peter and I followed close behind. We immediately met up with a uniformed guard who glared at us from behind a desk. Dad was about to go through a set of double doors, when the guard raised a hand to stop him.

"State your business," he said, his tone harsh.

Dad stepped up to the desk. "We were just getting settled here and already you people have taken my wife away. I want to know where she is. I'm gonna take her out of this place. We'll care for her in our apartment."

The guard rose and leaned across the desk, his scowling face inches away from Dad's. He was tall and muscular, and his black eyes narrowed with intensity.

Dad stood firm. "I demand to know where Clarisse Jackson is." He balled up his fists.

Peter and I stood back. Though I'd never seen my dad in a brawl, I suspected he was on the verge of one.

To my surprise, the guard backed off and dropped into his chair. The frown hadn't left his face, however, and without saying a word he pressed a button, then mumbled something into a communications device. Seconds later, a white-robed medic burst through the double doors. He was a frail looking guy with a pasty face. He peered at us through horn-rimmed glasses. He didn't look like a man who could burst out of anywhere, but there he was, looking like someone who had authority.

"Mr. Jackson?" His tone was high-pitched but friendly.

"Yes." Dad relaxed his fists, but the scowl remained.

"I'm Doctor Timothy Rand."

Dad shook the medic's outstretched hand. "Where's my wife," he demanded. "I want to see her. Now!"

"Come with me." The medic gestured with one hand, and guided us away from the scowling guard and through the double doors.

We passed several curtained cubicles. Dr. Rand turned into the last one and spread the curtain. At the far end was a narrow bed where my mom lay encased in a jumble of tubes and wires running from various parts of her body to a console of flickering lights and resounding beeps. The room smelled like our bathroom did the time I dropped a bottle of antiseptic on the floor while attempting to medicate Peter's scraped knee.

Mom's eyes were open, but she was staring at the ceiling. She didn't move, didn't even seem to notice us.

"She's dead!" Peter cried, and rushed to her side. "Mama!" He flung himself across her chest.

"No, she isn't dead, Peter," Dad assured him. He placed a hand on my brother's shoulder and eased him back.

Dad was right, Mom wasn't dead. Her chest rose and fell with each pulse of the machine. I moved to the other side of the bed and reached for her hand. "Mom. It's me, Olivia."

She didn't acknowledge any of us.

"Mom, please." I choked out my plea. "It's Olivia. And Peter. Please look at us. Talk to us. We need you." Hot tears escaped from my eyes and fell on my mother's bed sheet. I held my breath and waited ... but there was no response.

Chapter Six

W e should have noticed what Mom was going through weeks ago. We could have worked together to help her adjust to the relocation. Now it looked as though we'd lost her and might never get her back.

Whimpering, Peter laid his head on Mom's stomach and sobbed his heart out. Dad leaned close, like he was listening for her next breath.

"Clarisse," he whispered. "Say something. We miss you. We want you with us. Come on, honey. The kids need you. *I* need you."

He straightened and looked at me. "I don't know how to help her," he said, his desperation evident. He turned his attention to the doctor, who'd been standing quietly nearby.

"What's she on?" Dad said, his tone sharp. "I want to know what you people gave her."

Dr. Rand crossed his arms and raised his chin, his demeanor cool. "Nothing. We've given her nothing yet. We've done the basic tests, and we're monitoring her vitals, but we have not started her on any meds." He took a step toward my mom and placed a hand on her shoulder. "Nothing's been prescribed, Mr. Jackson. She came in here in this condition. We're going to need more of her background information before we can prescribe any drugs." He released his hold. "That's where you come in. Tell us if she's been on any medications. Describe her demeanor over the last few days or weeks. And give us her complete medical history, particularly noting if she's ever reacted this way before."

Dad breathed a sigh of resignation. The anger drained from

his face. "I'm sorry," he said. "I'll help in any way I can. As for medications, she's not taken anything I'm aware of, has actually avoided drugs for as long as I've known her. And she's never behaved this way before. Regarding her medical records, I'll transfer them to your personal device." He took a step back, like he was about to leave the room. Then paused and added, "But I expect a complete report in return."

"Agreed." Dr. Rand said, nodding.

But I had questions of my own. "Please, Doctor, do you have any idea what's wrong with my mom?"

The medic scrunched his lips, like he was trying to decide how much he should tell me. He breathed a long sigh. "It appears to be a form of PTSD, Post-Traumatic Stress Disorder," he said at last. "Several women who came into the capsule displayed similar signs, though not as severely as your mother." He grunted. "Only the women, never the men. This sudden lifestyle change can be quite a shock to women, while most men find it challenging, even adventurous. Some, like your mother, simply need to slip into a safe place for a while. Your mom's case is one of the worst I've seen. She's practically catatonic. I'm guessing the trauma must have started several days, or perhaps weeks, ago. It may help if you could tell me when the change began."

Dad pondered this quietly for a couple seconds, then he nodded. "It was gradual. I guess I was preoccupied with making our arrangements, and I didn't notice."

Peter wiped a tear from his cheek. "She stopped playing games with me about two weeks ago. And she kept making the same stuff for dinner. Night after night."

I searched my memory, but could only come up with, "A few days ago I saw her on her knees beside her bed. Praying, I think. After that, she just got more quiet."

"I see." The medic appeared to ponder all this. "Here's the good news," he said, brightening. "Most of the ladies responded well to an anti-depressant I ordered for them. Mrs. Jackson may need something a little stronger. With proper treatment,

I'm confident she will come out of this soon. But we have to be patient. Some people simply need more time."

Dad turned toward Mom, bent close and mumbled something in her ear. I saw a broken man, helpless to do anything for his wife, but hoping. It was obvious how very much my father loved my mother. Other than the death of his parents, the only other time Dad looked so lost was two months ago when he learned his closest friend wouldn't be going into a time capsule. Now he was crumbling to pieces over Mom's condition, and there was nothing he could do. For a man who appeared to have his whole life in order, a man who took command of every situation and had adjusted well to the new regime's control, he looked desperate.

Moved to compassion for him, I stepped closer and placed a comforting hand on Dad's shoulder. He slid his arm around my waist. We stayed like that for several minutes, father and daughter sharing a moment of anxiety. Then he grabbed Peter with his other hand and pulled us both close to him. I found comfort there, against my father's strong frame. Peter trembled like a dry leaf and wept with childlike abandon. My own eyes stung with fresh tears.

The medic never said a word. He simply allowed us to grieve without interruption. Though my mother was still with us, it was as if she had died. That's how heavy my heart felt at that moment. After a while, we separated, each of us wiping away tears. Dad pulled out a handkerchief and blew his nose. The medic flicked a tear from his own cheek, which surprised me. And I knew, the Time Capsule staff were not simply cold-blooded robots, like the guard at the desk. Some were real people with sympathetic hearts and a desire to help. My confidence in Dr. Rand had improved.

Dad tucked the handkerchief away. "So, what's next?" he said.

The medic thrust his hands in the deep pockets of his white coat. "Her medical records will give us a place to start. We'll monitor her condition over the next twenty-four hours." He kept bobbing his head as he spoke. "I'll notify you, step-by-step, and we'll decide—together—what treatment we should follow. Then—with your approval, Mr. Jackson—we'll administer the appropriate meds."

"That sounds reasonable," Dad agreed.

Dr. Rand pulled a business chip from his pocket. "Here's my contact information. Just insert it in your FlexPhone. You may call me anytime, day or night. And please send me your wife's medical records right away."

Dad accepted the doctor's chip, then shook his outstretched hand. We had nothing more to do but to leave.

Dad drew close to Mom's bedside, leaned past the wires and tubes, and planted a kiss on her forehead. Then he straightened and faced the doctor again. "Notify me of any changes," he said, the sound of authority returning to his voice. "Day or night."

"You have my word," Dr. Rand assured him.

Spreading his arms around Peter and me, Dad guided us out of the infirmary.

I dreaded returning to our apartment. Those four walls were already squeezing the life out of me, though no one else had noticed.

Months ago, I had several sessions with a therapist to discuss my claustrophobia. Dr. Green was making great progress with me. When she learned we had qualified to go into a time capsule, she recommended that I try to think of it as a place of refuge rather than confinement. She suggested I close my eyes and think pleasant thoughts.

"Or recite scripture," she said. "You know some Bible verses, don't you?"

She narrowed her eyes at me. I nodded. Verses of scripture had worked for my grandma, hadn't they? So why not for me too?

After leaving the clinic, I headed straight for my cubicle and pulled Grandma's Bible from its hiding place. I lay back inside my climate-controlled enclosure and turned to the Book of Psalms.

There shall no evil befall you, I read, then turned to another page. *The Lord is my defense.* Another flip of the pages. *I will lift up mine eyes unto the hills, from whence cometh my help.*

From memory, I recited one of my grandma's favorites from the Book of Isaiah. *Thou wilt keep him in perfect peace whose mind is stayed on thee: because he trusteth in thee.*

I felt myself relaxing amidst those ancient promises. They had helped my grandma through tough times. When she and grandpa lost their farm. When they had to go on government assistance. When Grandpa died. When Grandma became ill with cancer. Always, she opened her Bible and sang out one of her favorite verses of the day. When I saw her comforted, I felt comforted too. Now I was depending on Grandma's scriptures to bring me through a tough time of my own.

Exhaustion eventually took over. I did some deep breathing exercises, drifted off, and the next thing I knew, Dad was calling my name.

"Olivia. It's time for dinner. We don't want to miss another meal."

It took me a few seconds to focus. I'd forgotten where I was. I rubbed my eyes, still blurry from sleep. I scanned the enclosure around me. There was a faint glow of tube lighting, beyond stood a closet with built-in drawers, a cozy chair, blank walls that begged for some colorful art to brighten them.

One word came to mind. Sterile. That's how I could describe my new environment. *Sterile.* There was no window. *No window.* Only a fake one that didn't comfort me. The room began to shrink. A familiar coldness came over me, like when I was trapped inside that freezer. I lurched upright, and the walls immediately receded, but the momentary suffocation left me trembling.

I could taste the oatmeal power bar I'd eaten in the car that morning. I leaped off the bed, lunged past my dad through the open door, and ran into the bathroom. I splashed cold water on my face, and the nausea subsided. I looked in the mirror and winced. Dark circles framed my eyes. My face was drained of color, and I looked far older than my 17 years.

"Olivia, it's almost six o'clock." The sound of Dad's impatience got me moving.

"I'll just be a minute." I locked the door—softly, not defiantly.

I made sure the adjoining door was locked, then I freshened up for dinner. Assured I looked more like a living, breathing soul, I took a deep breath and emerged to face Dad, standing there with his arms crossed and a scowl on his face. Peter was sitting on the sofa, dangling his legs, his toes poking at cracks in the tile floor. When I approached him, he leaped to his feet and headed for the door. "I'm starving," he said, and he eyed me with disgust.

"Don't expect too much," I told him on the way to the elevator. "We'll be eating prepackaged, freeze-dried cardboard. They'll probably feed us pressed sawdust harvested from the Global Seed Vault in Norway, anything to make our time here even less enjoyable."

"Global Seed Vault?" Peter screwed up his face and gave me one of his looks that said, *Sure. Like always, I don't believe you.*

I raised my chin. "That's right. Once again, man's answer to feeding billions of people with as little ingenuity as possible."

As soon as the elevator door opened, I moved ahead, my confidence growing. Though I'd given Peter the worst of my impressions, I really had no idea what to expect when we got to the dining hall.

During the ride in the elevator, Dad checked for messages on his FlexPhone.

"Any news about Mom?" I asked.

Dad shot me a look of annoyance. "It's too early, Olivia." He read a text, typed an answer, then turned back toward me. "That was Doctor Rand. They've started IV fluids and will be adding some meds. They're gonna use Medafinil. Apparently, it will stimulate her brain without increasing her anxiety. And Sunosi, which hopefully will give her a boost of energy. Together, they might bring her around and help her to accept her new situation. Once she starts coming around we'll need to watch her closely."

"I can sit with her tomorrow," I offered. I wasn't looking forward to spending time with the old man I was scheduled to meet.

Dad hesitated. "We'll see," was all he said.

We arrived in the dining hall to a noisy hubbub of clattering dishes and an undulating ebb of conversations. Complete strangers moved around the serving tables. I didn't see anyone I knew. Then I spotted a familiar face in a far corner of the room. Matt Ellison was there with his parents. He waved me to an empty seat beside him. Though I would have wanted to be anywhere else, I acknowledged with a nod.

I couldn't help but notice Jeanine. She had changed into a skin-tight, bright red jumpsuit that accentuated every curve, and she'd adorned herself with enough rings and bracelets to fill a jeweler's case. I drew up beside my dad at the food line. "Do we have to spend every minute of every day with them?" I lifted my chin in the direction of the Ellisons.

"Let's just join them tonight," Dad said. "They're our host family. It would be rude to ignore them after the kind way they welcomed us today."

I glanced around the room, now filled with families just like us. "So, where's the leadership? Don't they eat with us commoners?"

Dad snorted. "We're not commoners, Olivia. But since you asked, the leaders and their families will eat their meals inside their living quarters. Though those particular apartments weren't part of my tour, I've heard they are far more elaborate than our meager holes in the wall." He caught the disgust on my face and smiled. "It's all right, Olivia. They earned it. They made the new President's short list. Anyway, as long as they don't mingle with us, we can relax and just be ourselves. No need to put on airs."

He gave a little laugh, like he was kidding, but I knew better. The new administration not only controlled my dad's salary, they also had charge of his equipment and would divvy it out to him only as they saw fit, and for one purpose—to follow their orders for the rebuild. There was a time when men like my father owned their own businesses, made their own plans, drew up their own blueprints, and took charge of each project to the end. Things were better back then, when President Brooks was in office. After the take-over, the government gradually usurped everything, and within a short time, they had taken control of Dad's business, our house, our car, everything, right down to the books I read and the toys Peter played with. In the end, all that was left was what we took into the Time Capsule with us.

As I looked around the dining hall at the people who would live in close contact with us for the next year or more, I began to see them as pathetic robots who mindlessly followed orders. Sadly, my dad had become one of them.

It also struck me that there were a lot of teenage girls in our midst. *Procreators*, I thought with a sour taste in my mouth. A lot of young women—like a harem—to be matched with a few young men who'd also been selected. Matt was one of the lucky ones.

I picked up a tray and moved past the options at the serving station, surprised to find behind the Plexiglas shields an array of pre-made salads, slices of roast beef and turkey, and casseroles of steamed vegetables. There was a pot of potato soup, an assortment of fresh baked breads, and an entire table dedicated to desserts, including chocolate cake and donuts. I frowned in confusion. Where on earth did all that food come from? What had become of the astronaut menu I had expected?

"You lied," said Peter. "They've got real food here." He scurried down the line, grabbed enough meat and cheese to make a sandwich and headed straight for the dessert table.

I selected a salad, a cup of the soup, and a slice of whole-grain bread. I avoided the dessert table altogether. I'd recently become more conscious of my calorie intake. Our home scale didn't lie. The last time I stepped on it a couple days ago the numbers had me cringing. At five-foot, five-inches, I now weighed 132, an increase of three pounds since my weigh-in at the clinic in January. This could be the beginning of an even bigger weight problem. After all, I was going to be confined inside a metal tube with no chance to do my daily 5-K run. If I didn't get out of that place soon, I'd have to find some way to exercise, or I'd have to starve myself.

From the instant I passed along the food counter until I reached the Ellisons' table, I felt Matt's eyes on me. I squirmed with discomfort. As kids we'd played together without any thought about our different genders. We were just two friends having fun.

But now, with mandated procreation hovering over us, I cringed with distaste. Matt didn't seem to share my concerns. Over the last couple of years, his treatment of me had changed. He'd started opening doors for me. He'd bought me gifts, like the virtual puzzle he'd ordered through a games database. He'd even let me beat him at chess a couple of times. Matt had been our neighborhood chess champ since he was ten. I'm not nearly as good a player. But somehow I won. Twice. There was no reason for it except that he was trying to win my approval, though he knew that I knew he was the best player.

Didn't he know I'd given my heart to Zaq? I must have told him. Now, with this whole procreation business looming over us, Matt's interest in me seemed to have increased. Somehow, I had to tell him we never would move past the friend stage. Leadership rules or not.

I settled in the chair Matt had saved for me, bowed my head, and waited for Dad to mumble his usual blessing over our food. For the moment, at least, Matt had to shut his eyes. I'd begun to feel self-conscious, like I was being scrutinized whenever he was around. Somehow I had to tell him. And soon.

I started shoveling the food in my mouth, winced from the hot soup on my tongue, and quickly took a bite of bread, followed by a long drink of water. I just wanted to finish supper and get out of there.

"Have you checked out the exercise room?" Matt broke through my icy wall.

"Not yet." I slid a few inches away from him and kept my attention on my soup.

"It's a small gym, but it's well-equipped." He took a bite of his sandwich. "It has all the usual stuff. A couple of treadmills, an elliptical machine, five stationary bikes, and several sets of free weights. I'll take you there after we finish eating."

I didn't want to give him false hope, but he *was* my friend, and he *had* saved my life once. And I figured it might help me to get an idea of the layout of that pit, maybe even find a possible way to escape. "Okay," I said with resolve and downed the rest of my soup.

Meanwhile, my brother completely ignored his sandwich and was enjoying a large piece of the chocolate cake. I stared in disgust at the brown stains on his chin. Dad was so busy talking with Charlie he didn't notice that his son was filling his stomach with sugar. If Mom had been there, Peter would have had to make quick work of his sandwich, and then he'd have to settle for a much smaller piece of cake.

"Peter, you're going to ruin your teeth," I told him. "And you will get soooo fat."

"Like you?" He stuck out his chocolate-covered tongue.

I wrinkled my nose at him, then I scooped up a forkful of salad, surprised to find the lettuce crisp and the tomatoes ripe.

My Mom's name came up in the conversation, and my attention was drawn to Charlie, who'd asked about her.

"There's nothing new," Dad told him. "It's gonna take time, I guess. Just keep her in prayer."

"We will," Jeanine said, though she smirked with indifference.

I couldn't help but stare at her. Almost overnight, she'd gone from an apron-clad, cookie-baking homemaker into a freak of nature. Her left ear had a long row of diamond piercings, and her right earlobe boasted one small gold hoop. She'd penciled black eyebrows beyond where her real ones ended. And what was that on her cheek? A fake beauty mark?

She stopped eating and turned her attention to my dad, a half-smile on her lips. A shiver crept up my spine. I frowned. Was she flirting with him?

Several of my mom's women friends had referred to my dad as handsome. I couldn't help but notice the upward tilt of their chins or the subtle spark in their eyes whenever he came into the room. He had a full head of honey-colored hair, the same color and thickness as mine. I also shared his blue-green eyes that darkened to cobalt, almost black, when troubled. The smile lines at the sides of his eyes didn't age him but merely added to his masculine appeal. I could see why Mom's friends swooned a little and spoke to each other behind raised hands, whenever Dad was around.

Then there was Charlie, a fairly good-looking guy, though no competition for Dad. Bald has been beautiful for decades. And, though short, Charlie had a muscular physique that had him looking like he could deck a far younger man. Plus he had a laid back personality most women found non-threatening and even attractive.

Didn't Jeanine appreciate what she already had? I decided to keep my eyes on that woman. My own mom lay strapped to a hospital bed. She was a decent woman who wouldn't think of looking at another man the way Jeanine was eyeing my father.

I pulled my attention away from her. The conversation at the table faded amidst the clatter of dishes in the dining hall and the hum of other voices throughout the room. In much the same way that I dealt with my claustrophobia, I separated myself from what was real and escaped to a safer place. In my own secret sanctuary I could picture Zaq and imagine the cave in the woods where he probably had gone.

In a perfect world, I could wander into the clinic five floors below, where my mom lay in a stupor. I could say good-bye to her, and then find a way out of the time capsule, run into the woods, and find my one true love.

"Are you ready?" Matt's voice drew me back to reality.

"Huh?" I looked him in the eye. "Ready for what?"

"The tour of the capsule," he reminded me, frowning, but with an amused smile on his lips. "Haven't you been listening?"

"Oh, yeah," I said, blushing. "Let's go."

Chapter Seven

That night, before I went to sleep, I settled inside my lighted cubicle and recorded the days events in my journal.

April 25, 8 p.m., written inside this closet of a bedroom I live in.

This is an account of the tour of the ground floor with Matt:

We had finished dinner. Matt had convinced me to take a walk through the time capsule, and Peter begged to go too.

We kept to the areas where we were allowed to go, but I didn't find them the least bit exciting. I may take a tour on my own sometime. Without Matt, and without my snoopy-nose brother tagging along.

The workout room had a pathetic collection of free weights, two old-fashioned treadmills, and a workout station that had a line of teenagers waiting to use it. In fact, every piece of equipment was tied up. I don't guess I'll ever work out in there. On one wall hung a large diagram showing a quarter-mile track circling around the hallways. I could run the circuit twelve times and maybe get three miles in. But the workout room? I don't envision myself wasting precious time waiting in line so I can use a piece of equipment for a few minutes until someone tells me my time's up.

Peter had a different reaction. "Yes!" he shouted. Then, he rushed inside and grabbed a pair of five-pound weights.

I shook my head in disgust. "Do you believe this?"

"It's not so bad," Matt assured me. "Just come at odd hours,

say 6 a.m. or 10 o'clock at night. Then you can have the whole place to yourself."

"C'mon Peter. We're moving on," I called out. He frowned back at me and kept making curls. I practically had to drag him out of there.

We followed Matt down a long corridor that ended at a student classroom. Multiple stations lined one wall. Desks were equipped with virtual screens with voice controls. There was a cupboard labeled "Manual Arts," which piqued my curiosity. Beside a far wall stood several two-seat cubicles, which, I assumed, were used for tutoring sessions.

We left the classroom and went around a corner, came up to a wall of plate glass that gave a view of a combination nursery/pre-school filled with crying babies and over-active toddlers. Two teenage girls were hopelessly trying to maintain order. I left with a knot in my stomach. They could give that job to someone else. Sitting with old Mr. Crenshaw began to look like a better option for me.

As we circled back around to the dining hall, one room grabbed my attention. The kitchen. The cleanup crew was just finishing up. One man, wearing a soiled leather apron, carried a bulging trash bag through a door that led to the outside.

The outside!

I didn't see a security panel. The door opened with a simple turn of the handle and appeared to be the only door in the time capsule that opened to the outside without a fingerprint coding system.

I took one last look at that outer door, filed the image in the back of my mind, then I followed Matt down another hall.

This one led to a tiny chapel, a real surprise. Most church buildings were gone by now. To find one in the time capsule had me thinking the new administration either missed something or they had ulterior motives. Maybe tricking us into thinking everything was all right when it really wasn't. I couldn't help being suspicious. Even when the new regime allowed services, *they selected them and streamed them into our living rooms, with approved pastors appearing in holographic images so realistic I felt as though I could reach out and pinch their noses. You could join in the singing—or not. No one would know the difference. And if the sermon sounded like more propaganda, oh well.*

I sure miss our former pastor, David Getz. His words of wisdom must have come straight from God. Like the time he warned of the "coming reversal of powers." It happened just like he predicted, only the turnover was so subtle most of us still couldn't believe it when Ming Yu moved into the White House.

I followed Matt inside the chapel and stopped to catch my breath. A rack of votive candles filled the air with the scent of vanilla and seemed to eat up all the oxygen.

"Are there any windows in this place?" I said, backing out the door.

Matt simply smiled and said, "Come on." Then he took hold of my hand and ushered me away from the chapel and down yet another hall. Peter kept close at our heels. We entered the dome, the only place in the entire time capsule that had a view of the outside. The 180-degree see-through wall gave us a transparent view of the landscape surrounding the capsule. But this was daytime, and there was no sign of a lighting system to illuminate the grounds at night.

"Are these windows enough for you?" Matt chided me.

I'm sure I was blushing. "I feel like I could step right through the glass and disappear into the forest."

"They're bullet-proof," Matt said, tapping the glass-like wall. "We'll be able to watch the fighting from here and stay safe. The gunfire can't touch us."

Peter let out an excited whoop, but I froze. As I stared through the glass, I imagined Zaq running around out there, fiercely defending himself. I pressed my hand against the glass, then jerked it back, startled that a small part of me had disappeared to the other side.

"It feels like you can pass right through the glass, doesn't it?" Matt said, grinning. "Well, you can't. It's simply an illusion."

I gawked at him. "How were you able to tap the glass when my hand went right through?"

He just shrugged. "It has something to do with the amount of pressure you use."

"I was able to enter the glass, and I wasn't really trying."

He laughed and pressed his fingers to the pane. They also momentarily disappeared. "I told you, it's an optical illusion," he said, drawing his hand back. "It's something to do with refracted light—a trick of the eye to make us feel less confined."

I stared daggers at him. "Believe me, Matt. Nothing can make me feel less confined. I know where I am, and no trick-of-the-eye can convince me otherwise."

He reached out and gently stroked my arm. As always, I backed away from his touch.

"Time to hit the books," I said. Then I spun away from him and headed for the door.

"Let her go." Peter snarled. "Let's you and me go back to the workout room."

"Okay, little man," I heard Matt say.

I picked up my pace and trotted off in the opposite direction, their voices diminishing behind me.

I suppose I should feel sorry for Matt. After all, he did save my life that day, long ago, when he opened that freezer door and helped me get out. But that one act of rescue didn't give him ownership over me—did it? My heart belongs to Zaq. That is never gonna change. Matt needs to get used to the idea. He needs to move on and find someone else to procreate with.

I shut my journal, fell into bed, and began to dwell on the possibility of escape. I mentally retraced my steps along the route Matt had taken us, all the way to the kitchen and the door that opened to the outside. I thought about clothing. Black for sure. A hoodie, hiking boots, and gloves. Of course, I'd stuff my backpack with a grooming kit, clean underwear, pens, and my journal. Plus Peter's night vision goggles. I'd leave at night, when everyone else was asleep. But I couldn't leave until I made sure my mother was going to be all right. Then I'd move.

I was awakened in the middle of the night by a gentle tapping on our entry door. I opened my FlexPhone. It read 2 a.m. I sat up in bed and leaned to one side for a better view of the sitting room. Dad's shadow swept past my cubicle. He tiptoed toward the front door.

"Who's there?" he whispered.

A woman's voice mumbled from the other side, and for a moment, my heart surged with excitement. Had Mom returned to us?

Dad unlatched the lock and opened the door a crack.

More whispers. A woman giggled. An electrified prickle ran through me. It wasn't Mom.

Curious, I slipped out of bed and crept into the sitting room. Still too far away to discern what was happening, I tiptoed closer to Dad and drew up behind him.

The murmuring voice on the other side of the door sounded familiar. *Jeanine!*

"Just for a little while?" she murmured.

Dad firmly held the door open, but only a couple inches. "Sorry," he whispered. "I can't. You know my wife is in the infirmary. Have a little respect, Jeanine."

"Clarisse? She's a zombie."

How ironic that Matt's Mom was calling *my* Mom a zombie. If anyone looked like death-warmed-over, it was Jeanine with her dark eye makeup and pasty skin.

"Clarisse is doing better," my father said a little louder and a little more forceful.

"But, she's not here, and *I* am."

"It's late."

I had to give him credit. While some men might crumble

under such persistence, Dad had stood firm, and he hadn't yet discovered that I was standing behind him.

"I just want to talk," Jeanine whined from the other side of the door.

"Maybe you should talk to your husband."

She let out a sarcastic laugh. "Charlie? He's in his own little world."

"Nevertheless, he's your husband, Jeanine. And I'm married. I love my wife. In sickness and in health, like the marriage vows say."

My dad's words sent a wave of comfort through me. I was so proud of him. He was living up to every vow he'd made at the altar. I would like to have a husband like him one day.

He started to shut the door, but Jeanine stuck her foot through the opening and prevented it from closing.

"Stop it, Jeanine." Dad's impatience should have been evident. "Go home."

"All right then," she moaned, sliding her foot back into the hall. "I'll see you at breakfast?"

"Maybe," was all Dad said before shutting the door.

He turned around, and his eyes grew wide when he caught me standing there only two feet away. I frowned and crossed my arms. "What did *she* want?"

The lines on Dad's forehead deepened. "Nothing important," he said with an air of disgust. "That woman is nothing but trouble. Don't know what happened to her, but she sure has changed."

He flung his arm around my shoulder, and edged me toward my cubicle. "Go back to bed, Olivia. The witch is gone."

For the first time in my life I was trying to see my dad the way other women did. He was ruggedly handsome and had the most tantalizing blue-green eyes. They glowed like sapphires when the light hit them just right. He had a firm jaw, slim build, sinewy arms, and broad hands that could break a wooden beam in half, and once did. To me, he'd always been just Dad, the master of the house who kept the rest of us in line. But moments ago he'd turned into a chick magnet. Who knew?

"I guess you know that was Jeanine at the door," he said a little sheepishly.

"I don't like that woman," I told him.

He smirked. "Don't worry, Livie. I love your Mom. I love you kids. I would never do anything to ruin what we have."

I relaxed and snuggled up to my father's side. He wrapped an arm around me. It felt strong and secure. "I know, Dad," I murmured. "But what's the matter with Jeanine? Do you think you should mention this incident to Charlie?"

"Nah." He leaned away from me, his eyes searching my face. "What good would it do?"

"Well, for one thing, he could keep an eye on his *wife*."

"I doubt that would change anything. Charlie's no dummy. He probably already knows she can't be trusted."

I raised my arm and made a fist. "She'd better stay away from my father."

Dad chuckled and, gently pushed me toward my cubicle, then he said, "C'mon, Olivia. Let's forget about our neighbor and get a good night's sleep. You're going to have a busy day tomorrow. You'll get to meet Mr. Crenshaw."

Chapter Eight

Morning came sooner than I was ready for it. Dad was standing by my bed. "You missed breakfast, Olivia." He was holding a spiral notebook in his left hand.

I tried to focus. "What's that?"

"The leadership wants you to record Mr. Crenshaw's words on paper," he said. "Remember? Whatever he says. Past, present, and future."

I let out a frustrated sigh. "Why can't I just use virtual recordings like everyone else? They're faster and more accurate."

Dad gaped at me like he couldn't believe I'd just said that. "Have you forgotten? I told you before, they don't want his words recorded electronically. In case—" He stopped short of giving me a full answer.

"In case of what?"

A silly grin tugged at his lips. "I don't know. In case the system fails and we lose everything."

"Okay. So we blindly obey whatever they tell us?"

"We need to cooperate. Please, Olivia, try to comply with the rules. We'll all be better off. Now, come on. It'll be like writing in a journal, like your grandma taught you. You already do that. I've seen you with that leather-bound journal of yours, the one you keep in a secret place and never let anyone else read. This will be just like that, only you'll eventually turn it over to the leadership, and they'll be able to read it, or store it away, or whatever they want to do with it. If you ask me, it's one of the most important jobs in the time capsule."

I gazed at the book in my hand. It was smaller than my journal, about four inches square, but it had a lot more pages to fill.

"Look at the first page," he instructed me. "There's a list of questions they want you to ask Mr. Crenshaw."

I sighed and opened the notebook. Just like Dad had said, a list of questions filled the first page.

He handed me a couple pens. "Try not to stray from their list, but if something strikes you—say, if one question leads to another—you may go ahead and ask him. Just make sure you make a note that it's *your* question, not theirs."

I was starting to feel the pressure. I looked at Dad, challenging him with eyes that resembled his own, but darkened to cobalt blue with resolve. "Why don't they use one of their androids for this job?"

"Two reasons. An android would electronically record Crenshaw's answers with phonetic alterations. They don't want that. The leadership is hoping for a human connection, maybe an emotional bond between you and the old man. It makes sense, Olivia. Crenshaw would be more willing to spill everything he remembers if he learns to trust you. The man has lived through a couple of wars and he's one of the last living experts on biblical prophecy. Whatever he has to say could make a world of difference to us after the war."

"They shouldn't have gotten rid of the old textbooks in favor of the propaganda they feed us through the virtual programs," I snapped. Then, suddenly aware that the room might be bugged, I clamped my mouth shut.

"Now, Livie, you're just going to have to trust them."

"Why should I?" I boldly replied, this time hoping the room *was* bugged. "The new President doesn't think our people could record accurate historical events. And he doesn't believe in God or the Bible. So why would he want that information now?"

"So they can explain it away, I guess," Dad said with a shrug. "It's like a lot of people do. They check out the opposition to their own doctrines. Then they formulate arguments against whatever they discover." Dad shot a look at the corner of the room as though concerned about the possibility of a listening device.

I smiled to myself. So Dad was just as uneasy about the takeover as I was. "I wish Grandma were still here," I said. "*She* wouldn't give in to their demands."

The mention of my dad's mother brought a pained reaction to his face. His eyes blinked a couple times, like a light going off, then came back blue and bright.

"Help me out here, Livie." His face turned to stone. "I have to cooperate with the leadership. When they chose our family for the new build they saved our lives. They have positive plans for us. And remember, I'm trying to keep things going around here without your mom to help. Until she comes back to us, I have to take care of you kids and do my own work too."

I caved, mostly because his pitiful eyes had lost their sparkle. "Okay, Dad. I'll try."

"Good. I knew I could depend on you." He blinked and the sparkle returned, if only for the moment.

"So, when do I start?"

He glanced at the automatron timepiece on his wrist. It was much larger than the watch Granddad used to wear. This one was covered with icons—a digital clock, a red button that, when pressed, revealed a list of jobs Dad was expected to complete each day. There also was a port for entering people's business chips and other data. Dad started wearing the leadership's expensive gadget two months before we moved. I stared at him with increasing interest. What was so special about my dad? He was a talented electromagnetic engineer, but so were a lot of other men. What did he have to offer the leadership that the others didn't? I hated to think it was me, but none of the other men in his company had daughters my age. They either had sons or their daughters were grown women with families of their own.

"You start in ten minutes," Dad said, jolting me back to the truth. He was grinning. "You'll find Mr. Crenshaw inside the dome on the main floor. He'll be sitting in a high-backed wheelchair, the type that reclines when the person in it wants to take a nap. This is where he sits during the daylight hours. Apparently, Crenshaw likes to enjoy the outdoor scenery. Maybe he's waiting for the fighting to begin. Whatever his reasons, he prefers to use the dome for your meetings."

"I'm glad," I said with relief. "I can't imagine what it would be like to be cooped up in a tiny room with an old man who smells like mothballs and coughs into a handkerchief every five minutes."

Dad gave me one of his "I can't believe you said that" looks, patted my behind, and sent me off to get ready.

I dressed quickly and used the bathroom—making sure the door was locked to the Ellisons' side. On my way out of our cubicle, I grabbed a bottle of water and a handful of dried fruit from the bowl on our dinette table. I headed straight for the dome, consuming the fruit on the way, assured it would satisfy me until lunchtime only two hours away.

Sure enough, I found Mr. Crenshaw seated in a padded wheelchair, a cup of coffee in his hand. He'd turned down the lip so he could drink from it easier. I glanced around the huge glass bubble at the separate groupings of tables and chairs. There also were three loveseats and an assortment of potted plants, giving the place an even more outdoorsy feel. I turned my attention away from the artificial setting and settled my eyes on Mr. Crenshaw.

He was really old. Had snow-white hair—a good crop of it—watery blue eyes, and his body was practically skin and bones. He'd parked across from a metal folding chair—my seat, I presumed.

He took a sip of his coffee, then looked straight at me. "You're Olivia." He said it more like a statement than a question.

"And you're Mr. Crenshaw." I accepted his handshake, recoiled slightly from the knobby feel of his bony fingers, then I settled into the folding chair, opened the notebook, and poised ready to write.

He almost smiled. "Before you pelt me with the leadership's idiotic questions, why don't you tell me a little about yourself?"

Already he'd caught me off-guard. I was prepared to *ask* the questions, not *answer* them. But he cocked his head and eyed me with interest. To be honest, he reminded me a little of Grandpa. So, I figured, why should this be any different from the times I used to spend chatting with my grandparents? The job would go a lot easier if I could think of Mr. Crenshaw as just one more grandparent.

"C'mon, girl," he prodded, and his tired eyes came alive with anticipation.

I chewed my bottom lip. "What do you want to know?"

"Tell me about yerself."

I kind of liked his folksy way of talking. "I'm not sure what to say," I admitted.

While I hesitated, he lunged ahead with what sounded like a reasonable description, though we'd just met only a minute ago.

"What I see sitting before me is a very pretty teenager," he said. "She's tall, slim, with long, honey-colored hair, wide blue-green eyes that are wise beyond her years, and beneath the surface, a strong, determined character that won't bend under the pressures that are sure to come."

I gawked at him. "Beneath the surface?"

He smiled, and the wrinkles nearly disappeared from his face. "I have a gift," he said.

"A gift?"

He chuckled for the first time. "I figure people out before they say a word. I watch how they carry themselves, the expression on their faces, whether or not they make eye-contact. You strutted in here like a person who knew where she was going and what she was going to do. Orders or no orders, I can tell you have your own agenda. Your questions might not always jive with what the leadership is trying to force down our throats. I'm guessing that we'll be able to move beyond the canned interview and really have a nice talk. What do you think, Olivia?"

He paused and studied me with those silvery blue eyes. "Olivia, huh? That's an old-fashioned name. I'm guessin' you were named for someone."

I nodded. "My grandma. And my mother was named after her grandma, Clarisse."

"Well, do you mind if I call you Livie? That's your nickname, isn't it?"

I couldn't help but smile. "Yes, it is. My boyfriend calls me Livie. He was the first."

Though I didn't want to give him the satisfaction of knowing he'd already figured me out, the truth was, he'd piqued my interest. That old guy—110 years old, Dad had said—already had me in the palm of his hand, and I began to wonder who was going to be in charge of the interview. Him or me?

I gazed into those shimmering blue eyes and summoned a little boldness. "Tell me, Mr. Crenshaw—and I'm not writing anything yet—what exactly is the purpose of our visits?"

He giggled, and it sounded out-of-place for a man of his age. Yet, I liked the sound of it. "Ours is not to question why—" he began.

"I know. Ours is but to do or die." I laughed. "That saying was drummed into me before I could walk."

"Comes from 'The Charge of the Light Brigade,'" Mr. Crenshaw quipped. "May be a fitting slogan for the two of us. We can charge ahead."

We both started laughing, and it was obvious the ice had been broken.

"Now," Crenshaw said as though resuming control. "Tell me what I don't see sitting in front of me. What are your dreams? What kind of education have you had, so far? And what do you hope to accomplish when you get out of this place?"

At that moment, I realized our first interview was going to take a lot longer than I'd expected. Except for that little bit of fruit I'd grabbed, I'd missed breakfast, and if I couldn't speed things along, I was also about to miss lunch. I needed to keep track of the time, but I suddenly noticed I'd left my FlexPhone back in our apartment. I looked around the dome. Not one clock. My eyes fell on Mr. Crenshaw's bony wrist. He was wearing one of those huge multi-purpose watches exactly like my father's.

I began to see the old guy in a whole new light. There was something really special about him, and I couldn't wait to start asking the questions. But for now, he wanted to know more about me. Okay then, I decided to open up to him.

"My main dream is to get out of this place," I said, my tone serious. "And my education? I've completed my virtual studies through all the required grades. I'm about ready to graduate and start my college courses."

"College? Sounds right for someone who just turned 17."

"How did you know my age?"

"They told me."

"They?"

"The leadership. You don't think I'm here because *I* planned this, do you? They commanded my cooperation the day they told me I qualified for the time capsule. Then it was up to me. But I had to agree or be kicked out if I failed to give you what you need. Now that I'm here, I'm in charge."

"Sounds like you have a lot more gumption than most of us."

He raised his furry white eyebrows. "Gumption, huh? Is that a word you learned from your grandparents?"

"Yeah."

"Hmmm. Gumption," he repeated. "That term hasn't been bandied about for decades. I suppose I have some of that gumption." He gave a little shrug. "The truth is, they *need* me."

"But why?" I asked him with sincere interest.

"Don't you know? I'm a bundle of information. I have it all up here—" he tapped his temple with his forefinger. "I'm loaded with data they couldn't find in any of the electronic archives."

"And that's why *I'm* here," I confessed. "To collect it all the old-fashioned way—on paper."

We both laughed again, and I thought, *Maybe this isn't*

going to be such a tough job after all. I leaned close and gave him a pat on the shoulder. The guy didn't smell like mothballs, as I'd expected. In fact, a pleasant scent of musk rose from his shaved chin, and he was wearing blue jeans and a freshly laundered shirt with a crisp collar. If I didn't already know his age, I'd swear he was only about 75.

"So," I said, taking a breath. "Are you gonna cooperate? Or will this turn out to be another of those ridiculous jobs they're shoving at me?"

I leaned back in my chair and poised with pen and pad, ready to go.

He grew serious then and set his blue eyes on me for several long seconds.

"Hmm," he said, stroking his chin. "You're a procreator, aren't you?"

I blinked hard against the telltale rise of tears.

"No wonder the first thing you told me about yourself was that your main dream was to get out of this place."

I pressed my lips together, afraid he might pass the message on to the leadership.

Instead, his next remark caught me totally off guard.

"We may be able to put that dream of yours to good use," he said, nodding thoughtfully. "Yes, we just may be able to make it happen. And soon."

I searched the old man's face, "What do you mean?"

He set his coffee cup on a little side table and reached for my hand.

For some reason I found comfort in those gnarled fingers. His grip was gentle, but firm. The penetrating gaze of his eyes conveyed a sincerity that set me at ease.

"Tell me, Livie, what would you do if you *could* git out of here? Where would you go?"

I already had an answer. "I'd find Zaq."

"Zaq? Is he your boyfriend?" I nodded. "And he's out there?" Crenshaw tilted his chin toward the wall of windows.

I continued to fight back tears. "His family was rejected from the reorganization plan. He told me he was going to join a rebel group and—" I stopped short, aware that I might be saying too much.

I darted my eyes around every part of the dome—the curved ceiling, the metal strips dividing the panes of glass, the framework around the entry door, even the potted plants. "Do you think the leadership may have planted hidden cameras or listening devices in here?"

Crenshaw shook his head with what appeared to be confidence.

"What about some other hi-tech surveillance equipment? They could be listening to us right now."

Crenshaw raised a hand. "Believe me, we're safe," he said. "There's a good reason I chose the dome for our visits. The authorities may have bugged individual cubicles. But this place? And the dining room—the acoustics are too poor for hidden mics to pick up anything. Didn't you notice how every sound echoes? It's nerve-wracking!"

That was something I hadn't considered. I relaxed and offered him an appreciative smile.

Crenshaw drew up proudly like an old teacher who'd finally gotten through to his student. "As for the windows," he said. "They absorb and smother every sound." He patted my hand. "We couldn't have more privacy if we were to walk out of this place and disappear into the woods."

He lifted his coffee cup and took a sip. "Bah, cold," he snorted and returned the cup to the table.

"Do you want me to get you a fresh cup?" I offered.

"Nah, let's move ahead with your interview. I'm eager to get started. Got a few ideas of my own."

Encouraged, I lifted my pen.

"Okay," I said, opening the leadership's record book to the first page. "Here's Question Number One. *From your vast knowledge of the past, what would you say is the main event in the world's history that set the stage for where we are now?*

To be honest, that was something that had been troubling me, as well. What started this disgusting ball rolling? I was eager to hear his answer.

Crenshaw stroked his chin. His eyes drifted off toward the outside, then back at me.

"I'd say," he said, still stroking his chin. "The one event in history would have occurred when our leadership started bowing to the demands of China and Russia." He stopped stroking and narrowed his eyes. "It happened little by little, you see, long before Brooks took office. The former administration made this deal and that deal until we lost a good part of our authority in world relations. The United States became a puppet, controlled by powers on the other side of the world. Americans blindly accepted the decisions of the previous administration. Then, when Brooks was voted in, they thought he would fix everything. The representatives put the entire burden on that man's shoulders. But it was too late. You know the result. A complete takeover."

"I grew up with it," I admitted. "Never thought much about all that until recently. Then came wars and more wars, the embargoes, the tariffs, the dramatic increase in the price of food, the subsidies, the lack of them, and the resulting downfall in our economy."

"Brooks tried to straighten it all out, but the Chinese didn't give him a chance." A bitterness had entered Crenshaw's voice. "They installed their own people in Congress. Brooks didn't git the support he needed. They cut him out of office halfway through his term, before he could put anything in motion."

I jotted it all down, unconcerned that the leadership might take offence to Crenshaw's remarks. The old man must have known the consequences. I was recording everything he said for them to read. But he just rambled on like he didn't care. So why should *I* care? I was just doing my job.

"Okay, here's question Number Two." I moved on. *What lessons from the past will help us establish a more peaceful society in the rebuild?*"

Crenshaw shut his eyes. For a second, I thought he had fallen asleep. But then, he opened those baby blues and leaned toward me.

"A peaceful society?" he said, chuckling. "What a pipe dream." He raised a hand and stopped my pen. "Don't write that, Livie, but here's what you can write. There is no hope for a peaceful society. Until Jesus returns, we will remain in socialist hell. We will continue to live life the way it's been dealt to us. Everyone gets equal treatment—except for the leadership, and they live high off the hog. While they own ten times more than anyone else, the rest of us will continue to work hard and be grateful for the handouts."

"Was it better when you were young?" I ventured to ask him. "That's *my* question."

He shifted in his seat and cocked his head to one side, like he was pondering an answer. I rested the pen on the open book and waited.

"Years ago," he said, his eyes seemingly trapped in the past. "Years ago, America was the land of opportunity." The old man's voice had become soft and pensive. "If a person worked hard, he or she could accomplish great things. I personally knew a couple self-made millionaires. My own job as a professor of history put me in the limelight. I was sought after by companies on the verge of new development. They trusted me."

I picked up the pen and started scribbling again. Crenshaw cleared his throat and went on. "Then everything changed. Society morphed into two main classes—the elite and the struggling—much like had already taken place in India, Africa, and other countries on the verge of self-destruction. They don't exist anymore. Still, America followed the same path, gradually allowing the elite to get stronger and the rest of the population to dwindle into servitude. With the influx of illegals, the government robbed from the working class and gave free benefits to the new arrivals, again making everyone equal. It was a very sick version of a neighborhood Welcome Wagon. As a result, there's been no middle class for decades. Mind you, it's not my favorite scenario. I still prefer capitalism that had people who work hard being rewarded with promotions and higher pay. But most of our population, these days, can't get along in a capitalistic society. Such a scenario demands that people work hard to better themselves." He leaned to one side and looked sideways at me. "Think about your dad. A highly educated man who now works for the government, is compensated by the government, and wouldn't *dream* of going against the government."

I frowned at the image, but I had to agree. There were times when I'd seen my dad as nothing but a servant, bowing to the demands of whatever government official called on him. Each time I lost a little more of the respect I'd held for him since my childhood.

Crenshaw patted my knee. "Poor guy had no choice," he said with a touch of compassion. "It was that or put his family in poverty. And," he added waving his hand at the dome, "you're here."

Crenshaw continued on. "The days of honest competition are over, Livie. Whoever is not in leadership is a member of the working class. Ever since the government approved free college, free childcare, and free medical benefits, we became totally dependent on big brother to provide everything we need, kind of like a newborn baby depends on its mother."

He sat back. My fingers gripped the pen with surprising force. I had mentally soaked up everything Crenshaw had said, and now had to decide how much of it I should write down.

"Tell me this," he said, his eyes focused on my face. "What are you planning to study when you get to college?"

"Digital communications," I responded with confidence.

"Ah, another tool of the government." I winced at his remark. "And what will you communicate?" he added.

"I don't know. I'd like to think up ways to make everything better. You know, in medicine, in technology, in social trends."

He snickered, a response that offended me. He didn't have to say a word. I suddenly was aware I was becoming one of the government's puppets, like my dad. My virtual teachers had recommended my course of study based entirely on tests *they* administered to me. They claimed my answers would reveal my strong points. The truth hit me like a bolt of lightning. The teachers also were controlled by the government. They, too, were pawns in the leadership's hands. Somehow the powers that be had been able to direct my path into the course of study they thought best for me, and it had little to do with my test answers or my own desires and everything to do with what they knew about my life—the past and the present. If I entered the world of digital communications, any ideas I might come up with would still be subject to government approval or dismissal.

A flash of heat rushed to my face. I felt like a fool. I was no different than my dad or anyone else who'd been chosen for the new build. I had submitted to a government that would determine how I'd spend the rest of my life. They had even made me a procreator.

"I don't like it," I admitted to Crenshaw. "The government has been controlling my life since the day I was born. I didn't know it till now. They got to me by getting to my father first. I don't know how to take the control out of their hands and into my own. My only hope is to escape from the time capsule."

Crenshaw slumped back in his chair and set his eyes on me. "Don't give up, Livie dear. Don't ever give up." He leaned toward me and lowered his voice. "I have an idea, but I can't share it with you yet. For now, let's git on with the interview. You'll need to show the leadership *something* from our visit today. Even the negative stuff I said."

"Okay," I told him. "Here's Question Number Three. *What type of leader will America need in the future?*"

"That's easy," Crenshaw said. "Forget the narcissist. We had too many of them in the past. Still do. If they don't like the way things are going, they don't simply pick up the ball and go home, they destroy the whole playground. And the flip-flop candidate? You never know which way they're gonna go. If someone keeps changing his mind, how can he lead? Then, there's the figurehead. They had one of those in England for centuries. All they did was hold parades and celebrations and get their pictures plastered all over the news. They didn't do anything worthwhile for the population. Someone else, behind the scenes, made the real decisions."

"So what do you recommend, Mr. Crenshaw? Do you have a particular type of leader in mind?"

He rested his elbow on the armrest and propped his chin in his hand. "Well, aside from electing myself, I would want any man who puts God ahead of everything else, a man who falls on his knees before he stands at a podium, a man who communicates vertically before he speaks horizontally. Or, for that matter, a woman who does those things. Believe me, we'll never have a worthwhile government order if we keep cutting God out of the equation."

I raised my eyes from the pad and gazed at him. I'd heard similar words from the pulpit before they closed my church. Pastor Getz used to say much the same thing. Then he disappeared. A surge of fear rose inside me, and I stared at the old man with concern. Couldn't he be accused of treason, too? Might he also disappear?

"Mr. Crenshaw, are you certain you want the leadership to know all this?" I pointed to the book.

He emitted a little laugh. "Look at me, Livie. I'm a hundred and ten years old. If they don't like what I say, they would probably shrug it off as coming from a demented old man. No, dear, I'm no threat to the government. Or at least they *believe* I'm not."

"Then, if what you say is true, what hope do we have?" Again, I asked a question from my heart rather than from the words printed in the leadership's book.

"I don't know about the rest of the world, but America hasn't had good leadership since Harmon Brooks was deposed," Crenshaw said with an air of pride. "Look at what we have now, a self-serving President and his hand-picked followers—a group of people who don't even agree with each other. They get us into a third world war and then they decide who's going into these pods and who's gonna stay out in the cold to fight for their lives and probably lose."

Again I was reminded of Zaq, and my heart broke all over again.

"I just need to know for myself, Mr. Crenshaw—I'm not writing right now—is there any hope for us?"

He bobbed his head and a weariness shrouded his face. "Hope? Chances are, I won't be here to see it."

"Please, Mr. Crenshaw, give me something positive."

He scratched his head. "Okay. You wouldn't remember this. It was a little before your time, but we once had a document called the Constitution. You've probably read about it in your virtual studies."

"I have. A former President back in 2038 decided it was obsolete and revised it. Then members of Congress didn't like the new wording, so they proposed to get rid of the document altogether. The Senate approved, and here we are. No Constitution. No Bill of Rights. Just rules thought up by the current administration, subject to change."

Crenshaw leaned toward me and lowered his voice. "If I were to raise up something positive from the past, it would be the Constitution. Then we'd once again have a government constructed of the people, by the people, and for the people. They could elect their leaders instead of having a coup take over. We'd have a government that promotes advancement of even the poorest of the poor, based on their motivation and talents and not on government control and free gifts. Look what you have now. A government that tells us who will have children and how many. Do you want *that* to be your legacy?"

"Of course, I don't want that. Not long ago, the leadership prevented my mother from delivering her third child. They whisked her away to a hospital one day, and she returned home no longer pregnant. She hasn't been the same since."

Mr. Crenshaw was shaking his head. "Such a pity. Government controlled family planning."

"It's barbaric," I acknowledged. "Now they want to repopulate the new world. I really don't want to be a government-controlled baby-maker. That's their plan, and they are determined to use young girls like me to accomplish it."

Crenshaw patted my hand. "There's more at stake than the size of families," he said tenderly. "Americans have lost the ability to plan any aspect of their lives. There was a time when people had the freedom to buy a plot of land and build any type of house they wanted. They could design their own homes, pick out their furnishings according to their own taste, and make it all theirs. Forgive me for saying this, but those cardboard cutouts your dad got involved in just don't measure up to what we had before."

I gave a little shrug. "I don't really like living in a house that looks exactly like the one next door. But I grew up with it. Call it comfortable ignorance, if you want." I paused and gathered my thoughts. "My grandparents used to tell me stories about the early days. After a while, I began to think that was all they were. Stories."

"I'm certain they were not," Crenshaw said.

"Okay, then. Tell me some more things that changed over the last hundred years."

"Well," he said, placing a gnarled finger to his lips. "Years ago, kids walked to an actual school building or they rode a yellow school bus. They had real classrooms, not virtual ones where there's little or no interaction with other kids. The children sat at desks all lined up in a row and a teacher stood at the front of the class and wrote on a white board. Before that, when I was a kid, we had blackboards with chalk and erasers that let off a cloud of dust when we banged them together."

I chuckled at the image, and even felt a little envious. Life was obviously a lot simpler back then.

"They had a thing called recess," Crenshaw went on. "Kids ran outside screaming happily to the playground. They teamed up for games and sports, and developed lasting friendships. Some got awards for their athletic abilities. I won several medals in swimming competitions myself. I had my own set of thrills. For one thing, when I got to my teenage years I rode a motorcycle to school, and later to college."

I tilted my head quizzically. "A motorcycle?"

"Surely you've read about them. Two wheels, loud, flies like the wind."

Then a sadness crept into Crenshaw's eyes. "Such thrills were short-lived. Virtual schooling kicked in sixty years ago. In the beginning, when people home-schooled their children, it was by choice. Then, in 2019, a terrible virus spread around the world. Covid-19, they called it. People died. Businesses closed down. Churches stopped holding services for a while. And here in America began the biggest political upheaval of all."

Crenshaw pulled a handkerchief from his pocket and wiped perspiration from his brow, then he tucked it away and settled back in his chair again.

"People wore face masks whenever they left their homes. For a long time, social gatherings ceased." He gazed at me. "Your virtual classes—" he said, raising his eyebrows. "They caught on big time during the pandemic. Even after things got back to normal, a lot of folks said they liked the virtual system better. Eventually, the government leadership found it was more lucrative to shut down all the training institutions. They didn't have to run those school buses anymore, they didn't have to maintain the buildings or cover the cost of heat and air conditioning, and they could reduce their teaching staff by more than half. For a while the homeschoolers planned their own activities and sports. Eventually, the leadership started restricting where they could go and what they could do. So here we are—everybody from pre-school to graduation stays home and gets pre-programmed courses on an electronic display screen, and there's no interaction with other kids, no sports, no playground recess, no *fun*—and definitely, no independent thinking." He looked directly at me. "Livie-dear, you are slowly being indoctrinated into what the government wants you to be."

"I still have my friends," I challenged. "Lila Duggers, Rhoda Wilkes, and Matt Ellison. He's here, you know. His dad's an architect."

Crenshaw looked sideways at me and shrugged those bony shoulders of his. "I guess what they say is true, what you don't know won't hurt you," he said, softly, but those words were like daggers piercing my heart. "Why, you've been barely bruised by all the changes," he said, adding more pain to the wound. "Some people—your parents maybe—have suffered a great deal from it. It sure sounds like your mother has."

"My dad told you about her?"

He nodded, a sad wisdom entering those blue eyes.

I thought about my mom, recuperating in the clinic. She seemed to have lost the life that once brought her joy. She may not remember everything Crenshaw was describing, but she certainly *had* experienced some of those changes.

Although Grandma and Grandpa had told me lots of stories about how things were when they were young, Mom and Dad hadn't shared much from their own past. I always assumed life was going on the way it always had. Now Crenshaw had me believing that things had changed. Drastically. Sometimes every decade. Sometimes every year. Sometimes every day.

Crenshaw let out a sigh, gazed at me with those sad, crystal blue eyes, and said, "What do you think, Livie? Shall we continue?"

I moved on to question Number Four. *"What role will leadership play in the new world, after the war ends and people emerge from the time capsules?"*

"If things go the way man expects them to, it will only get worse," Crenshaw said, frowning. "But if things go the way the Bible predicts, we're in for a huge upheaval," he added with a smile. "Pretty much everything has happened that the Word of God predicted would take place before the Rapture and the Great Tribulation."

I frowned and searched my memory. Pastor Getz had spoken about such things, but they were lost to me now.

"Are we close to the end?" I ventured to ask.

Crenshaw shook his head. "Lots of biblical prophecies still need to happen first." He gave a little chuckle. "You've asked the same question most of us asked over the years—yours truly included. Every time something major happened in the world, I wondered if we'd gotten close to the end. Of course, we hadn't."

Crenshaw stared at me with such intensity, I almost couldn't breathe. "You think you've seen it all?" he went on. "Let me tell you, you ain't seen nothin' yet."

"I'm afraid I haven't read much about the end times," I admitted. "My virtual instructors don't allow it. They insist the Bible is merely a book of literature, that we shouldn't let it control our lives. As you know, they've gotten rid of most of them. But for some reason I can't explain, I held onto Grandma's Bible when they came around collecting them. I hid it in a safe place."

Crenshaw flushed with anger. "I did the same thing. Had to. The leadership was courtin' trouble from above. Think about the ministers who preached the Bible and stood up to the government. They're all gone now."

"My pastor, David Getz, was one of them," I said with sadness. "He disappeared."

The creases on Crenshaw's brow deepened. "Can't be the Rapture. Not yet. After all, *I'm* still here." He let out a little laugh. "And so are you," he said, soberly.

"Somebody needs to come along soon," he added, his blue eyes swimming in tears. "The right man can make a difference. I can only think of one person. Harmon Brooks. He's a good man. He was my son's best friend. He's smart. And fair. I can't think of a better person to get this country back on track." Crenshaw smiled like he was remembering something. Then he added, "And he can play a mean game of chess."

Our first session ended, leaving me with a whole new set of emotions. Crenshaw had given me a ray of hope, but then he had added a challenge, and I didn't know how I could fulfill it. He said my escape could be useful. Useful for what? I began to look forward to our next meeting.

Chapter Ten

We'd been inside the time capsule for several days, but it seemed like years to me. Whenever I left the dome and returned to our tiny apartment, the walls closed in on me, and the air became more dense and harder to breathe. I had to get out of there, but I couldn't leave until I knew my mom was going to be all right. I needed to see her again, to reassure myself—and my brother.

I found my father in the sitting room watching one of the leadership-approved news programs. The 38-inch monitor swirled with images. The speaker read from a pre-written script. Dad leaned toward the screen, his elbows on his knees, as though he were transfixed by what he was hearing. I grunted in disgust. Little by little, Dad had given in to the brainwashing. The leadership had taken complete control over a man who once had charge of every situation at home and at work.

"Whadda ya say, Dad? Can we visit Mom again?"

Reluctantly, he pulled his attention from the screen and settled hard eyes on me. I caught my breath. It was like looking at someone I hardly knew anymore.

"The medic suggested we stay away for a while and wait for the treatment to work," Dad said, his voice a monotone. He sounded like a robot repeating a programmed message.

"But, Dad—"

He raised his hand and cut me off. "Stop it, Olivia. We don't want to interfere with what they're trying to do. It might set her back even more." He leaned back. "I've already approved the meds Dr. Rand recommended. Now we just have to wait."

As though dismissing me, he turned back toward the screen and raised the volume.

I stomped my foot. "Dad, please. I read somewhere that people who are in a coma can hear voices. We won't be interfering if we break through her subconscious and let her know we love her and need her. We'll be helping."

Heaving a sigh, he muted the sound and turned toward me. I fought the trembling in my gut and fell to pleading. "Please, Dad. *You're* supposed to be in charge of Mom's care. Not *them*." I pointed toward the virtual screen, where Ming Yu's mouth was still moving.

A glimmer of awareness flashed in Dad's eyes. He lifted the remote and turned off the program.

"Okay, Olivia. You're right. I think we've given them enough time." He beckoned me with a sweep of his hand. "Let's go."

I couldn't believe the transformation. It was as if my dad had returned from the dead. Relief flooded over me. I glanced toward my brother's bedroom. "Where's Peter?"

Dad shrugged. "Don't know. Last I saw of him he was pickin' up trash in the dining hall."

"Okay. It's probably better if he doesn't go with us to see Mom again. He's doing pretty well. We don't need to upset him. Right, Dad?"

My dad released a little chuckle, then headed for the door with me close at his heels.

We took the elevator down to the fifth level, another thirty or forty feet underground. Once again I gave in to those demons that kept me paralyzed in close places. But the thought of seeing Mom again helped. As soon as the door opened, I flew out of the elevator and inhaled a deep breath.

By the time we got to Mom's bedside, the pressure inside my head had begun to ease. I stared at her, lying there, chalk white, her eyes half-open, and another wave of anxiety swept through me. Was I about to lose my mom?

Dr. Rand was affixing medical patches to Mom's arms. He looked up, and his eyes widened in surprise.

"We need more time," he said. "She hasn't responded to the treatments. And—" His discomfort was evident. "She had a seizure this morning."

I let out a gasp.

"Don't worry," he quickly added. "We got everything under control, cut back on some of her medications, and she hasn't had another."

At that moment, the outer door burst open and three attendants wheeled gurneys into the infirmary bearing young men who appeared to be unconscious.

"Three more," one of the attendants called out.

They passed by us and hurried into a side room. One of the patients, a young man about my age, had a shock of red hair. Aside from that, none of them had any color at all. Their faces had turned a pale green, and their eyes had a vacant stare. Before the door shut behind them, a horrible wail erupted from one of them. Then there was silence.

Dad and I looked at each other, the shock on his face mirroring my own anxiety.

"What's *that* all about?" he asked the medic.

"We're not sure." Dr. Rand shifted uncomfortably, then went back to adjusting the patches on my mother's arm. "They've been bringing people in all morning. We think it might be food poisoning."

He continued to work on my mom, but his demeanor had definitely changed from the confidence of a physician intently at work to that of a man who was hiding something.

"Food poisoning?" I could hardly believe it. "Here we are, prisoners in an underground pit, and now we have to worry about the food? Does that mean we need to be careful what we eat?"

"No, not at all." Dr. Rand straightened and stepped away from Mom's bed. "We're working on it. We—"

"The same way you're working on my mom? Look at her. She's no better than yesterday."

Scowling, he stared down his nose at me. "Your mom's situation is different."

"And how is it different, Doctor? You've had her down here for several days, and she hasn't gotten any better. Now, the rest of us might get sick—with what? Food poisoning?"

"Olivia!" The sharpness in Dad's tone cut through my outburst.

I approached him, my face pleading. "Dad, look. We're stuck down here in an underground tomb. Mom's condition hasn't changed—maybe she's even worse—and now more people are showing up sick."

Dr. Rand turned away from us and fumbled with the tubes and wires. It was as though he might be avoiding the truth. He couldn't help my mother or anyone else.

Meanwhile, my father—once, my hero—had succumbed to the will of the leadership and now was giving in to the excuses of a quack. Less than a week ago he'd been strong. He'd insisted on having control of my mom's care. But little by little, he'd given over control to the leadership and their appointed drudges. There was nothing more I could do. I planted a kiss on Mom's forehead, flashed an angry glance in Dr. Rand's direction, then I walked away, determined to get out of the time capsule, and soon.

✝✝✝

That evening, I managed to eat another boring supper with the Ellisons. Immediately after, I snuck off to my apartment before Matt had a chance to suggest some other activity. Far too many troubles circled around in my brain. I longed to leave the time capsule, but I couldn't go as long as Mom was confined to a hospital bed. Mr. Crenshaw had offered a sliver of hope when he said my escape might be a good thing. Now I needed to know what he meant. I wouldn't be able to find out until our next meeting in the dome. He'd sent me a text suggesting 10 o'clock in the morning.

I slumped on the edge of my bed and pulled Grandma's

tattered Bible from my bag. I carefully turned the fragile pages and stopped at the part of the book where Grandma camped out most of the time, the Book of Psalms. The margins nearly disappeared beneath her multiple pen scratchings.

I had reached Psalm 31, one of Grandma's favorites, which spoke about trusting God, deliverance, and guidance. My finger came to rest on verse 4, *You will pull me out of the net which they have secretly laid for me, For you are my strength.*

How fitting. The leadership had arranged for this incarceration, had tried to make it look like a rescue, when all it did was give them more control over a remnant of the population. My father had given in without consulting the rest of our family. Now I've been forced to look within the pages of a worn, old Bible to find a ray of hope. The Psalm said God was my strength. I needed to trust that promise.

My grandma's notation in the margin caught my eye. Though barely legible, her script revealed the broken spirit of a woman who'd found herself in a different kind of confinement.

Dear Lord, they made the decision for me. Not one word, not one question about what I might want. Here I am, living in a house I didn't choose, married to a man I don't love.

Then, she'd underlined the words, *For you are my strength.*

Shocked, I read the text again, then reviewed Grandma's inscription a second time. I had a vague memory of my grandfather. He died when I was twelve. He and Grandma were married for 32 years. I strained to recall how they treated each other, but I only remembered a quiet resolve had settled on their home. Theirs was not an excited kind of love, like my parents displayed, but more of an acceptance. I never saw them touch each other with affection. Never saw them kiss, except for a peck on the cheek or a brush of one's lips against the forehead. Could it have been an arranged marriage? Not in that day—what was it, around 2005 when they married—nothing like the arranged marriages that took place a hundred years before. But an arrangement must have been possible, and I could only imagine it had something to do with business. There was money involved. Lots of it. A lucrative blending of family farms had taken place.

I read the text a third time. It seemed Grandma had found her own little prison, though not exactly like mine. This hole in the ground had been meant to be a shelter, but it had become a prison to me. For Grandma, perhaps a marriage planned by her parents had bound her to a life she hadn't chosen for herself. Like the Bible passage said, Grandma wanted to break out of a particular net, but the strength she found in God helped her to stay. I, too, wanted to break out of a net. I wanted to leave the time capsule and find Zaq and happiness. I was not afraid of what awaited me on the outside. I only knew I needed to go.

I turned my ear toward the door of Dad's cubicle and listened for his rumble of sleep. As for Peter, he typically dropped off like a rock after 9 p.m. It was nearly 10 now. I couldn't simply sit in my cubicle and flip through Bible passages. Couldn't just read Grandma's written comments and try to apply them to my own life. I had to *do* something.

I set the Bible aside, and holding my breath, I slipped out of my cubicle and tiptoed into Peter's room. He lay sprawled on his bed, deep in sleep. I crept around, checked the chair, the desk, under the bed, and opened a couple drawers, searching for his night vision goggles. I spotted them, half hidden under a pile of Peter's clothes in a corner of the room.

Slowly and quietly, I slid them free of the pile, tucked them under my arm, and tiptoed out the door. As I passed Dad's cubicle, he let out a snort. I froze. Then there was the ruffle of bedding, like he'd rolled to his other side, followed by the long, heavy breathing of a man in the throes of sleep.

Instead of going back to my room, I slunk through the sitting room and headed straight for the front door. Carefully, I managed to disengage the lock without making a sound, then I slipped out in the hall. It was empty, quiet as a tomb. Except for a single, faint emergency light bulb over each apartment door, the way ahead vanished into darkness. I put on Peter's night vision goggles, and immediately, the hall became illuminated as bright as day. It amazed me that a simple toy could work as well as something the government might issue. I looked around, could see every seam in the paneling of the walls, every crack in the floor tiles, every print where someone's dirty fingers had touched the door frames.

Something else showed up that didn't under normal lighting. The mark on my right hand. The leadership had sent their tattoo artist to our house several days before our departure. My whole family, including Peter, received a mark on the back of the right hand. Each person received a different number. Up close, the leadership's special lasers could read the markings. At a distance the marks served a different purpose. They were part of a tracking system the leadership could use to follow their subjects' movements. At the time I received the mark, such a purpose didn't concern me. Now I feared if I actually *did* escape, it wouldn't take long for the authorities to track me down and bring me back.

There was no way to remove the tattoo. I could only hope that when I carried out my plan, it would be at a time when the leadership was asleep or too busy to notice. For the time being, I wouldn't risk it. My venture out in the hall with Peter's night vision goggles had proved a worthy experiment. But I had something else to consider. If the kitchen door didn't turn out to be a suitable exit point, I'd have to search for another way out.

I moved from one level to the next, taking the stairwell instead of the elevator and exploring each floor. The third and fourth floors were arranged exactly like the one I lived on—nothing but apartments lining each hallway.

I bypassed the fifth floor, which, in addition to the medical clinic, accommodated the leadership offices and lavish apartments, plus a separate section of crew barracks. At least, that's how Matt had described everything during our tour. I wondered if he'd actually seen any of those compartments or might be just guessing.

After an hour, I reached the sixth floor at the very bottom of the time capsule. The elevator jammed shut. I began to panic, then I recalled the numbers my dad had entered on the fifth floor, the day we went to the infirmary to find my mom. I took a deep breath and punched them in. The door opened with a hiss. I stepped out and looked around. Though decidedly more frigid than the other floors, the sixth floor had an adequate supply of breathable air.

I moved forward. On one side of the hall was a big storage area with floor-to-ceiling shelves that held many years worth of non-perishable foods. Labels revealed a variety of dehydrated fruits and vegetables, bread products, desserts, and cooking staples. Stacks of boxes contained rice and pasta, cans of gravy, and bottled juices.

Toward the rear of the storage area was an entire wall of refrigerators and freezers. I peered through frosted glass and looked closely at the labels.

If everything was freeze-dried and frozen, what could have possibly caused the food poisoning? If it wasn't because of the way the food was being stored, could it have been the result of how it was being prepared? Or, God forbid, perhaps someone was intentionally contaminating the meals after they left the kitchen.

Determined to fine out the truth, I headed back toward the stairwell. I'd nearly reached the door when my attention was drawn to the wall on my left. From somewhere on the other side came a rustling sound, then a series of muffled squawks, and a vicious growl that reminded me of wolves I'd seen in a film about Alaskan wildlife. But this was no movie. No screen showing a documentary. All those sounds were coming from behind that wall, and they were alive. I searched for a door. There was no access—no door, no passageway of any kind to the other side. I followed the wall from one end to the other, up and down and back and forth, like a painter giving the finishing touches to a painted wall. I was almost to the end when my fingers found a hidden indentation. Holding my breath, I inserted my fingertips, activated a button, and the wall separated, revealing a vast compartment. I caught my breath. Both sides were lined with cages. And in those cages were small animals of nearly every species—cats, dogs, monkeys, birds, rabbits, rodents of every kind, and inside the larger cages around the perimeter, baby goats, horses, donkeys, and calves. At my arrival, the entire room erupted in loud screeching and wailing, growling and howling. A noxious odor struck my nostrils with hints of urine, feces, and some type of mash—corn maybe.

I peered closely at the cages. It was like someone had selected a chosen variety of creatures to preserve for the new world. My head spun. Bile surged into my throat. I swallowed, but tasted it again. Then, slowly, I backed through the space in the wall to the other side. As soon as I stepped clear of the door, it automatically slammed shut and blended with the outer wall with no apparent access, sealing the animals on the inside and me on the outside.

All I could think was that I had stumbled on a sick version of Noah's ark. Renewing the earth wasn't going to be just about people. We were going to need animals, too. Some for food. Some for protection. Some for testing new drugs. But hardly, I conceded, for pets.

My head clearing, I went straight to the elevator, paused to catch my breath, and stepped inside. The howling and snarling became a distant memory. I bypassed the residential floors and went all the way to the top, then I headed for the dome. Once inside the giant glass bubble, my claustrophobia subsided, and I breathed a whole lot easier. Though darkness had settled on our part of the world, a nearly full moon cast a beam on the forest outside, giving off a feel of normalcy. I stayed perfectly still until my body stopped trembling.

After leaving the dome, I revisited every part of the first level where Matt had taken me—the exercise room, the nursery and daycare, the schooling facility, the chapel, and, last of all, the dining hall. Nothing had changed, except now it was all dark and lifeless. Nowhere else did I see a way of escape.

As I had planned, my last stop was the kitchen. The shiny steel counters stood barren of cooking implements and small appliances. Except for the soft purring from the refrigerators along the far wall, there was no sign of life, not even a rat or a roach or even a tiny ant looking for a crumb. My attention strayed to the trash door leading to the outside. I noticed the keypad by the door. Could it be that Dad's numbers might work here too? I stopped and looked behind me. There was no surveillance. No cameras, no listening devices that I could see. And nobody was there.

I stepped closer to the door and pressed Dad's numbers from memory, aware that I might set off an alarm. Then, I gave the trash door a gentle push. No siren. No flashing lights. No loud bells. Nothing—unless a signal sounded somewhere else. I had to trust that it didn't.

I slipped outside amidst the piles of garbage. The stench was overwhelming. Beyond it all was what looked to be a fire pit. Whoever was in charge obviously hadn't bothered to burn the last batch of trash. I surveyed the piles, astounded that all that garbage had come from the meals we'd consumed that day. Then, of course, there was a pile of hazardous waste from the medical unit. I started to turn back toward the kitchen when, under the light of the moon, a white object stood out amidst the rubble. I stepped toward it, squinted for a closer look, then gagged. It was a human hand!

Chapter Eleven

Acid rushed to my throat. I swallowed hard in an attempt to keep from vomiting. I had just seen a human hand. My skin turned cold, and I found myself trembling. I wasn't inside a locked freezer. I was outside. I took a deep breath and blew it out slowly. I had to find out the truth. Trembling, I leaned over the bag and tugged at the string. The black plastic fell away, and out spilled the rest of the body.

I backed away, stumbled against something behind me, and nearly fell into the pile. Straightening, I stood in shock, just staring at the corpse of what once was a vital young man. He looked to be about 20 or 25 years old. His skin color was a sickening blend of green and yellow. His eyes were open. His mouth drooped as if it had frozen that way during his taking of one last breath. But, the one feature that jumped out at me and gripped my heart like a clamp was his shock of red hair. Only a few hours before, I had seen that same young man on a gurney being wheeled into the infirmary. I had assumed the medical staff had been able to save him along with the others who came in at the same time. But they hadn't healed him. The truth hit me like a jolt of electricity. He wasn't brought in there for treatment. He was there for disposal.

Vomit rose again from the pit of my stomach. This time I wasn't able to suppress it. My last meal erupted onto the lifeless young man. The odor of my own puke brought on another eruption. And then another. My eyes watered, and I could no longer see the mess for the blur. I wiped my mouth on my sleeve.

I took one last look at the poor, lifeless young man and then forced myself to look over other bags of the same size and shape, certain they held more victims. I didn't have to open any more bags. At least a half-dozen more appeared to be holding dead bodies. There was a foot, and over there another hand, and one open bag revealed the top of someone's head.

I was broken-hearted over that senseless loss of life. Like me and my family, those people had found shelter in the time capsule. And like me and my family, they had expected to live throughout the war and then be released. But they didn't last more than a few days. So what was to become of the rest of us? I thought of my mother, still captive in the medical clinic where sickness paraded through at any given time. Would the next black bag contain her body?

I turned away from the trash heap and passed through the door into the kitchen. The specter of death followed me inside, down the stairwell, along the hall, and back to our apartment. I was surprised to find I could place my fingers on the scanner and the door opened, just like my dad had done. We had all received some type of clearance.

I removed Peter's goggles. Except for a small nightlight in the kitchenette, I found myself in the throes of darkness. I tiptoed through the sitting room and went directly to the bathroom, grabbed a bottle of mint-flavored mouthwash and rinsed the filth from my mouth. I splashed cold water on my face, then I buried my face in a soft towel and released the trauma in a flood of tears and sobs.

Before that night, I hadn't thought much about what might become of people who died during our time in the time capsule. Though that question had never come up, not even concerning Mr. Crenshaw, I knew the truth. The dead were thrown out with the rest of the garbage and would be incinerated by the cleanup crew, perhaps sometime during the night. The corpses would soon be forgotten. No memorial services. No proper burials. No words of acclamation for the dead. I wondered who might be missing the young man with the red hair. Did he have a family in that place? Were they to grieve the loss in the solitude of their cubicles?

I lowered the towel and stared at my image. I hardly recognized the girl in the mirror. A stranger stared back at me. I didn't look anything at all like a 17-year-old—innocent, eagerly planning a future. Gone was the animated sparkle in my eyes. Gone was my unwavering posture, back straight, shoulders back. Gone was the flush of my cheeks, the plump of my lips, now pressed tightly together.

I suddenly felt very much alone. Who could I tell about what I found outside the kitchen? My father would want to know why I'd ventured outside the time capsule in the middle of the night. At one time, I might have shared what I'd seen with Mom. She listened without judging. But she was inaccessible to me. Then there was Matt. We were close friends. I used to talk to him about everything. But something had changed between us, and I no longer trusted him. He wanted more from our relationship than I could give him. I'd told him about Zaq, but that hadn't mattered. No, he was the last person I could talk to about what I'd seen that evening.

Forget about sharing that information with my blabber mouth brother. He'd already immersed his brain in video games that had the player running from zombies and leaving a trail of dead bodies behind. What I stumbled on behind the kitchen would merely feed his imagination. He'd want to check it out for himself.

I fell to weeping again. I had no one I could trust. No one. Then, a face came before me, the image of an old man with pure white hair and piercing blue eyes. Mr. Crenshaw. He already knew my darkest secret, that I wanted to get out of there. Like me, he didn't trust the leadership. I was scheduled to meet with him the next day. Ten o'clock, he'd said. In the dome. I could hardly wait to tell him what I'd seen.

†††

I spent a fitful night, tossing and turning and hardly getting a wink of sleep, as my grandfather would have said. I awakened to crumpled sheets and no pillow. I flipped on the light and reached for Grandma's Bible, once again turned to the Psalms and settled on Chapter 23. The verses spoke of a Shepherd who was watching over me, green pastures where I could lie down in peace, still waters to replenish my soul, goodness, mercy, and a safe dwelling place. My grandma had penned a big heart around the entire passage. How I wished she'd been there to read the verses aloud with me. She always had something positive to say, something of value she'd gleaned from the passage. For now, I'd have to depend on my own interpretations. I'd hang onto the Shepherd, and if I were able to leave, I'd have to trust him to guide me and watch over me, like a Shepherd with a wayward lamb.

I set aside Grandma's Bible and went to get ready for breakfast. Once again, my father had seated us with the Ellisons. Matt's eyes were on me the whole time. I set my attention on my plate of scrambled eggs that looked disgustingly like the intestines I'd seen in a medical book. They reminded me of the bags of horror I'd seen outside. I lost my appetite and shoved the plate away.

I tried not to look Matt's way, but he was sitting right across from me, his brow wrinkled with interest. He stared through me, like he was trying to read my mind. I ignored him, finished off my toast, and took a drink of juice.

Meanwhile, Peter dug into a pile of pancakes that nearly blocked his face from the rest of us. He'd doused them with something gooey, probably a time capsule version of maple syrup. Still, my brother moaned and smiled and smacked his lips, like he was actually enjoying his breakfast.

As usual, Charlie and Dad plunged into a conversation about the new build. Neither of them noticed that Jeanine hadn't taken her eyes off my father for one second. Like Matt penetrating me with a steady stare, she also had focused on her own subject of interest. Though I didn't approve of her behavior, I couldn't say anything about it short of sounding disrespectful. It saddened me that Mom wasn't there to defend her territory. I tried to think of a way to draw that woman's attention away from my father.

"So, *Mrs.* Ellison," I began, putting emphasis on the Mrs. "What are you doing to keep busy while we're in here?"

Jeanine jerked her head in my direction, annoyance clouding her eyes. She fumbled with her fork, then heaved a sigh. "Busy?" she sneered. "What else do I have to do in this hole in the ground except style and restyle my hair, paint my fingernails and toenails, and sort through my wardrobe for something to wear to no place in particular?" She waved her ten daggers at me. Then, she raked them through the tangled strands that framed one side of her face. "I suppose I could learn some new dance steps," she said and glanced in my dad's direction.

He didn't notice, just kept his attention on Charlie. I smiled to myself.

Jeanine turned cold eyes on me. She puffed out another sigh and rolled her eyes. "If you must know, Olivia, I spend lots of time flipping through stations on the virtual screen in my apartment. I check out the news and watch the leadership's approved documentaries. Boring, boring, boring." She slid her left hand down her sequined bodysuit and shot another glance at my dad. He still didn't notice.

My dear father was a genius living in a cloud. Most of the time, he was consumed with plans for the new build. He wouldn't have noticed Jeanine or any other woman who came into the dining hall. My mom didn't need to worry about him.

I'd had enough. I picked up my tray and rose to leave. "I hope you feel like you're doing something constructive, Jeanine. While you're busy primping and grooming yourself, my mom is lying in a hospital bed. She can't do any of those things. Nor can she dance or watch any of your virtual programs. But she can be a good wife and mother, and she will be back with us soon. I guarantee it."

I turned away, but not before I caught Matt gawking at me with his mouth open, too stunned to say anything. It was coming up on 10 a.m. I hurried from the dining hall, and went directly to the dome. I arrived there ahead of Mr. Crenshaw.

Inhaling a deep breath, I gazed through the tempered glass, the scene outside so realistic it was like we weren't confined at all. The landscape on the other side of the dome beckoned me to a place where I couldn't go. I strolled around the perimeter, amazed at how close the outdoor setting appeared. I pressed my hand against the glass and gasped as my fingers disappeared to the other side. Quickly, I drew back my hand to a sucking sound emitted by the glass.

Though shocked by the experience, I needed to know if a person could pass through to the other side. I was about to step closer when I caught Mr. Crenshaw's reflection on the glass. I turned, amazed to find him on his feet, this time hobbling into the dome with the assistance of a walker. He took baby steps, wobbled a little, and paused to catch his breath. I looked around. There was no sign of his wheelchair.

I pulled away from the glass and rushed to his side. Slowing my pace, I ambled alongside him and helped him get into a padded chair.

"Thank you, Livie-dear," he said, feebly.

"Should you be moving around like this without your wheelchair, Mr. Crenshaw?"

He chuckled. "I felt pretty good this morning. Guess I was wrong." He nodded toward the glass. "What were you doing over there, Livie?"

"Do you think a person might be able to step through the glass to the other side?" I smiled like I expected him to say yes.

"What do you mean, *glass*? You think that's glass?"

"Well, y-yes, I guess so."

"It's not glass, dear girl. It's a poly-fission barrier. It's impenetrable."

"But, my hand—"

He chuckled again. "The consistency of it gives the illusion that we can cross over to the other side. I'll bet that's what you thought, right?"

I smiled sheepishly. "Yes, I did.

"It's one of the many tricks the leadership uses to make us feel less confined." A whimsical sparkle lit up his blue eyes. "It's a protective shield. Brilliant, isn't it?"

"I'm not sure I'd call it brilliant," I said with disdain.

I thought about Zaq and the battles that were sure to come. "Are we really going to be able to watch the fighting from inside the dome and not be able to help?"

"That's what they say."

I frowned and pressed my lips together.

"What's the matter, Livie? You'll be safe in here."

"Yes, *we'll* be safe. I just don't want to watch other people get killed. When the fighting gets close, I'll stay away from the dome. I don't want to stand safely behind this poly-whatever wall while people on the outside try to defend themselves. I know someone who is out there. And I won't be able to help any of them. Do you really want to watch people being slaughtered?"

I grabbed the chair beside Crenshaw and brought my hands to my face, hiding my grief. The two of us retreated into a pronounced silence. It was as if my old friend understood my distress. I was already grieving the loss of a dear friend and nothing had happened yet. I raised my head and connected with Crenshaw. He was sitting very still, his darkening eyes bathing me in sympathy.

"Mr. Crenshaw." I leaned toward him and lowered my voice. "You do care what happens to the people who weren't chosen, don't you? I can hardly believe those of us who are in this place might have to watch the battles going on mere feet away, and we won't be able to help them. How I wish things would go back to the way they used to be—before the Chinese took over, before they went to war against the Russians to decide who would rule America. And definitely before all of this..." I swung a hand toward the wall of glass.

Crenshaw smiled, but his eyes filled with moisture. "Of course, I share your concerns," he said, and he patted my hand. "I'd like nothing better than to be able to protect our fellow Americans." He breathed a sigh and slumped back against the padded chair. "You have to understand, Livie, it's been a long time since things were good. Whether I'm inside the time capsule or out there—" He gestured toward the glass. "I don't have the power to change anything." Then he stared at me in that penetrating way of his. "But you can," he said.

I was stunned. "*I* can?" I laughed aloud.

Ignoring my outburst, he cocked his head and looked directly at me. A spirit of mischief entered his eyes turning them silver blue again. "Yes, you can," he said, grinning. "I have a plan of my own, and you might be the very one who can carry it out."

I sat up straight and gave him my full attention. This was it. This was the idea he didn't finish telling me the day before.

"Livie, I need to pray about this, to see if it's what God would want and not merely the wish of a delusional old man." He raised his hand, a sign he would not be rushed. "We'll discuss it at another time."

I frowned with annoyance, but he remained firm. "When I'm ready," he concluded.

The man kept dangling an idea in front of me but never revealed what it was. The more he did this, the more I wanted to know exactly how he thought I might be able to help. Already I knew it had something to do with my wanting to escape.

"Let's get to the leadership's questions," he said, directing my attention to the record book.

I lifted the book. But first, I wanted to tell him about what I'd encountered the night before in the garbage heap outside the kitchen. Choosing my words carefully, I talked about my personal tour of the time capsule, my visit to the basement and the shock of finding animals down there. He listened without comment, so I moved quickly to the rest of my excursion and described my escape through the kitchen garbage door and the horror of what I'd found outside.

Except for an occasional raising of his eyebrows, Crenshaw showed little emotion. No frown, no laugh, not even a flinch when I told him about the dead bodies. When I finished, I collapsed against the back of my chair, exhausted from having relived it. He sat very still and stared straight ahead. I assumed he was rehashing everything I'd just told him. He blinked a few times. Then an intense sadness filled his eyes, turning the deep blue almost gray. He shifted his gaze to my face.

"So *this* is what they've come to," he said at last. "This is what happens when a new leadership places less value on human life. Olivia, I'm afraid people have become disposable. *We* have become disposable. Like someone's old clothes. When they fall apart, just throw them away."

His frown went deeper. "You say that red haired young man had been brought into the infirmary earlier in the day?

I nodded. "That's right. Possibly because of food poisoning, someone said."

Crenshaw pressed his gnarled fingers against his lips, like he was trying to make sense of it all. "So, people are getting sick and dying," he said. "And they're throwing their corpses into the garbage."

He shifted his gaze to the glass and beyond. Tears ran like wax down the old man's wrinkled face.

A terrible panic seized my heart. "What about my mom? Those medics have her strapped to a hospital bed. And the sick are being carried through the clinic right past her."

He turned to look at me. "I doubt she's in any danger. How long has she been in there?"

"Several days, since we arrived."

Mr. Crenshaw couldn't have known any more than I did concerning what was happening in the clinic. Though he was the kind of man who cared about what happened to the sick and the dying, the frustration on his wrinkled face showed me he could do nothing about it.

"What's wrong with your mom?" His eyes flashed with interest.

"She went into some kind of trance. The day we left home she withdrew completely, like she couldn't cope with what was happening."

Crenshaw's eyebrows went up. "I've seen it before. Other women came into this place with similar reactions. They suffer from catatonic stress. Maybe not as intense as your mom's, but something to be concerned about. It must have something to do with a woman's innate need for security."

"That's what I tried to tell my dad."

The lines on Crenshaw's face eased a little. "There's no doubt your mom's security has been threatened, and she's going to need to go through a period of adjustment. I'm confident she'll be coming back to you soon."

"What about the people who ended up in the trash? If people have so little value, why bother with time capsules? Why preserve us at all?"

He shrugged a bony shoulder. "Someday, they'll have to repopulate the world. The leaders will need survivors, people to do their bidding, to bring wealth to their coffers, trained to function under their new rules."

His intense gaze sent a shiver up my spine. I shuddered. "What are you saying, Mr. Crenshaw?"

"Don't you know, Livie-dear?" he said with mounting sadness. "We're not only being preserved, we're being reprogrammed."

Chapter Twelve

I shifted uncomfortably in my chair. *Reprogrammed? Exactly how?*

I hadn't written much in the leadership's notebook. Crenshaw had said some things he might not want the leadership to know. Slowly and precisely, I had penned only what was common knowledge, his relatively safe remarks, while storing his accusatory statements in the back of my mind. A surge of excitement rushed through me. I had been given a power I never expected—unequaled control over what I wrote in that notebook. Like those virtual reporters did on the government's authorized programs, I also could bend the stories to fit whatever scenario I wanted. I was beginning to understand what Mr. Crenshaw called *reprogramming*. Such a tactic could work both ways. I had the ability to reprogram what the leadership understood.

The old man's eyes glowed like he was reading my thoughts. He leaned close to me and lowered his voice "You, young lady, have been handed a tremendous power."

I smiled in agreement. "Yes, a power I never wanted." I whispered. Then I let my smile fade. I leaned close to him. "Please, Mr. Crenshaw. Tell me what to do. I don't want to put my family in danger, but that's exactly what can happen if I misuse this so-called power. I never wanted to be the leadership's messenger girl, and I definitely don't want to be a procreator. I need to know, Mr. Crenshaw, what can I do now?"

He sat back in his chair. He stared off through the glass.

The wrinkles on his face came together, like he was straining to find the right words. I found myself holding my breath.

"Those animals you encountered in the basement," he said at last. "They're also procreators. They're meant to repopulate the world's wildlife, but I think something more sinister is going on down there. It seems the leadership also brought in America's top biologists. They live on the fifth floor with the other officials. Who knows what kind of experiments they're doing? Not only on the animals, but maybe on some of us, too."

"The guys I saw in the trash—when they came into the clinic the medic suspected food poisoning."

Crenshaw gave me one of his knowing smiles. "Don't let them bamboozle you, girl. They may have died from food poisoning, or they could have ingested something concocted in the lab."

I shuddered. My hands trembled, and I dropped the pen. "I want to get out of here," I said, picking the pen off the floor. I straightened and faced Crenshaw. "And soon."

"You already told me," he said. He paused, stroked his chin, and stared again through the wall of glass. Then, he brightened, like he'd come up with an answer. "You told me about the way out through the kitchen. What do you plan to do about it?"

I hesitated. I hadn't yet decided if I could trust this man. I shook my head. "I may have said too much already," I told him.

"Your secret is safe with me," Crenshaw assured me.

He gazed at me with eyes like my grandfather had. Sky blue, clear as glass, guiltless. I had no reason to mistrust him. I plunged ahead and spilled the rest of my story. "I want to find my boyfriend, Zaq. I want to make sure he's all right, maybe find a way to sneak him inside the capsule, or stay with him in his hiding place."

Crenshaw let out a grunt. "Impossible. He can't enter the capsule. The leadership will detect his presence. We all have a numbered chip." He nodded toward my arm, then turned his attention to his own hand. "Their high-tech equipment will send out an alert that an alien has entered the capsule. Every siren will sound and every security light will flash. They'll send guards into every hallway and crevice. Your friend will not be safe, and neither will you."

"Then I'll stay outside. I'll join his militia and fight alongside him. To the death, if necessary."

Crenshaw chuckled at my lame attempt to sound courageous. Then a watery sadness filled his eyes. "Such gumption in one so young," he said with a shake of his head. His remark, *gumption*, brought my grandparents to mind. They used that word a lot.

"I respect your courage, which may come in handy with *my* plan," Crenshaw went on, piquing my curiosity.

The way he was looking at me, with a sparkle in his eye and a quirk of his eyebrow, I couldn't tell if he was feeling compassion, amusement, or a desire to be young again himself.

Once again, Crenshaw had stirred my interest. I ached to know what idea had been going around inside that head of his, but I knew I couldn't push him. He would tell me in his own time.

I gazed into those wise blue eyes, and I immediately knew why the leadership chose to save this decrepit old man. Not only was he a bundle of information of the past, he seemed to have figured out a few things about the future. Though he was openly opposed to what the leadership was doing, he didn't have the physical strength to resist them. But wisdom often can be more powerful than bodily might. My grandparents had read Bible stories to us kids that talked about one man standing up to a giant, a small group of Israelites defeating a much larger tribe of attackers, one woman risking her life by agreeing to be the mother of the Savior. Those stories had instilled in me a courage I couldn't have had without them.

"Tell me what I need to do," I boldly declared. I gazed into those intelligent blue eyes and waited.

"You can go to the kitchen and ask the attendant for another cup of my coffee."

I breathed an exasperated sigh. Now, I'd become the old man's personal servant.

"You can order coffee whenever you want it?" I said, stunned by his audacity. "And everybody jumps?"

He grinned and his eyes sparkled with mirth. "Not everyone. But I do have some clout around here." His smile grew wider. "If you tell them it's for the old man, they'll know what to do. No problem."

As ordered, I left him sitting there, went to the kitchen, and requested Crenshaw's coffee. To my surprise, one of the workers leaped into action. I suddenly realized I hadn't asked how the old man wanted his coffee, but it didn't seem to matter. The attendant was already adding cream and sugar. I laughed to myself. Crenshaw had the staff eating out of his hand. And me too, for that matter. I had to admit, there was something fascinating about the old guy, something that made a person want to be close to him, to fulfill his wishes, no matter how outlandish. I returned to the dome, Crenshaw's steaming coffee cup in one hand, the leadership's journal in the other. Before handing him the cup, I turned down the lip the way he liked it.

As soon as I settled into my chair, he took a hardy sip and then fell into a reminiscent of the past. "You are too young to have seen it happening," he said, and took another sip. "China and Russia became more powerful over the last twenty or thirty years, but it was such a gradual change, few people noticed when America began to slip off its pedestal. Now the nation lies mostly in ruins. Those two superpowers brought us down. Once allies, now they're fighting against each other. Sad to say, once rich and prosperous, our country is no longer the greatest power in the world."

I scribbled away in the journal, trying to catch the details. I finished the last few words and looked up at the wisdom-lined face, aware that those wrinkles had deepened with every journey the man was taking into the past.

"You were just a little child when the great tsunami wiped out several miles of the east coast and inundated all of the islands in the Atlantic Ocean and Caribbean Sea. Scientists had warned us for years that a fragile undersea shelf on the edge of the Iberian Peninsula could break away and create a huge tidal wave across the Atlantic. They predicted it could reach the U.S. coast and wash away entire cities—homes, businesses, beaches, and nearly the entire state of Florida."

I nodded. "That's why Pennsylvania has become a coastal state. So much land has washed away."

"That's right, Livie. And don't forget, a similar catastrophe happened on the west coast mostly because the San Andreas Fault severed a great land mass and left the western half of California, Oregon, and Washington State underwater. Several years before that, a great wild fire destroyed much of the northern part of California. Those catastrophes reduced America to three-quarters the size it once was. America could no longer be called the land of plenty and was a few steps from becoming a third world nation. If not for our deep core power supply, we would have been completely lost."

I frowned in disbelief. Was this man telling me we were doomed, that we would lose the war and ultimately submit to the greater power of a foreign nation? With China already encroaching on the capital cities, plus taking over the White House and Congress, such a scenario was starting to look more feasible.

"My pastor, David Getz, preached about the fall of America, but none of us wanted to believe it."

Crenshaw pursed his lips thoughtfully. "I remember Getz. The man made a lot of sense. Sadly, his time of service was short-lived. But he was right about one thing. For a long time, America was the leading nation in the world, both economically and commercially. This great nation was once *clothed in purple and scarlet,* with *gold and jewels and pearls*, just like Babylon is described in the Bible. And just like Babylon, this great land of ours has been reduced to rubble—burned up for the rest of the world to overtake. But a semblance of America still stands. Though we're currently under enemy control, there is hope."

He stared at me, his blue eyes scintillating with secrets. I poised my pen.

Crenshaw leaned back in his chair and went on. "Several decades ago, our nation started losing its importance in the international market. Other nations produced more cars, household goods, and electronics, using cheap labor and poor quality materials. Commercial power then shifted to Asia, and people living in third-world island nations provided their workforce. Though the resulting products didn't measure up to America's standards, buyers stopped caring whether something lasted less than a year. If something broke, they could simply go out and buy a new one."

Crenshaw pulled a handkerchief out of his pocket and mopped beads of moisture from his forehead. I was instantly aware that the topic had touched him deeply.

"The only thing we hung onto until the end was our amazing energy supply," Crenshaw repeated, tucking the handkerchief back in his pocket. "No other nation had developed the technology to tap into the earth's fiery core. But instead of our accomplishment keeping us a superior nation, it made America a sitting duck. It wasn't long before every power in the world came after us. They wanted what we had."

I shuddered. My own father had a job because of that electromagnetic power. I looked to the old man, expecting him to tie everything he'd said to my plan of escape.

Instead, he continued his monologue. "Our government leaders—including President Harmon Brooks—never saw the attacks coming until it was too late. The steady invasions wore us down, and the political power struggles finished the job. Instead of working together to restore our power, the Republicans and Democrats set out to destroy each other. That's when the People's Republic Party capitalized on the internal conflict, overthrew President Brooks, and put Ming Yu in the highest office in the land. It happened so fast, no one could stop it. Then, Yu instituted an immigration system that brought more Chinese pouring into America. And Brooks had no recourse but to flee into hiding."

I sat upright. "You think Brooks is still alive!?"

Crenshaw's eyes filled with tears, and though he blinked them back, more rose up and blurred his vision. Again, the handkerchief came out, this time to stem the flow that spilled from his eyes. "I'm positive Brooks is alive and well, and I have a good idea where."

My heart went out to him. It was obvious he had suffered a great loss during America's collapse. Friendships, perhaps, and maybe his own position of influence.

"Mr. Crenshaw—" I began, and placed a hand on his shoulder. I recoiled in amazement. A mere skeleton lay beneath his shirt.

He tilted his head to one side. "Let me be clear," he said. "I'm trying to decide how much to tell you, Livie. You're so young—maybe too young for the mission I have in mind."

"I can do it, Mr. Crenshaw. Whatever it is, I can do it."

He shook his head. "My dear, we could be closer to the end than we think."

"Is there no hope for us then?" I was beginning to panic.

"Only one hope that I can see. And that hope may lie with your friend, Zaq, and his army. They may be the key to America's deliverance."

My doubts crumbled beneath a surge of pride. Could my boyfriend and his militia really save what was left of America? And could I help?

"I need to get out of here, Mr. Crenshaw. I need to find Zaq and make sure he's okay. Please, tell me your plan."

He raised a hand like a stop sign. "Patience, Livie. When the time is right, I will share my thoughts. Now, shouldn't we keep doing the job we've been assigned? I will spout off any bits of useless information I can pull from my memory, and you can write it all down for the leadership to mull over and decide whether they already knew all that."

A mischievous glimmer set off the blue in his eyes. It was true, he hadn't said anything worth reporting. Everything he'd told me could be found in any archived news reports. But his opinions? That's what the leadership wanted. I was certain of it.

"I doubt the leadership will appreciate what you said about the decline of America," I said. "Maybe you'd better give me something they don't already know."

"Okay then," Crenshaw acquiesced. "Let's feed the monster."

I filled two pages of the notebook with Crenshaw's recollections about yellow school buses and black-and-white movies and ice cream parlors. I, of course, was fascinated. My grandparents had shared similar stories from their youth, and I often found myself thinking I'd been born in the wrong era. Sometimes I fantasized about walking into an actual schoolroom, carrying a book bag filled with completed homework assignments, and being able to express my own thoughts on thesis papers for teachers who supported free thinking.

But I was born at a later time when brainwashing had become an accepted method of controlling a population. They all did it, whether Communist or Socialist or plain old down home country Americanism. There was a time when the classic writings of the past were banned, books burned, and Bibles deemed worthless. Thank God, my grandparents showered me and my brother with principles from their youth, that they didn't let the positive lessons of the past die out. Perhaps that could explain my current attitude of rebellion. Every day I found myself fighting against the indoctrinations that had become a way of life for us. I felt a strong urgency to hang onto the teachings of my grandparents, to continue to secretly read Grandma's Bible, and to continue with my plan of escape, perhaps not to save America, but to save myself.

That morning I parted with Crenshaw feeling like I had grown up a little more. We had bonded in a special way. I had learned to trust him the way I trusted my grandparents. We both cared about America. And we both wanted to do something about the current situation. In time, he would share his plan, and I dreamed of carrying out my own plan to escape. Perhaps, at some point, both desires were meant to come together as one.

Chapter Thirteen

I was on my way to my family's cubicle when I ran into Matt Ellison.

"Hey, how about a game of Pawns?" he said, referring to one of his favorite chess games played only with pawns and a king and queen.

I hesitated. I didn't want to give him any encouragement, didn't want him to think he had a chance with me. He had to know I loved Zaq, yet he kept wanting to spend more time with me. I suppose I should have been flattered. I wasn't. I needed to keep my distance. I didn't care what the leadership had decided about us repopulating the earth, I had no desire to share that responsibility with Matt Ellison.

I was about to walk on without saying anything. But his sad eyes pricked my heart. Anyway, I had nothing else planned, so why not?

"Okay," I said. "Let me get rid of this notebook." I held up the leadership's journal. "I'll meet you in the virtual room in ten minutes."

I left him standing there, opened the door to our cubicle and went directly to my little closet of a room. I tossed the notebook on my bed, then rushed back out to meet Matt in the virtual room. The environment was perfect for a casual encounter. Matt rushed around and pulled out my chair for me to sit.

Always the gentleman, I thought.

We spent the next hour in front of a large screen that displayed a traditional chess board, but with only kings, queens, and pawns arranged for play. The game proved challenging. I'd become dependent on rooks, knights, and bishops to complete my strategies. I expected to lose, because Matt had perfected this unusual and difficult version of the game We played until lunchtime, and I was surprised when Matt let me win. Though he attempted to make it appear that I had legitimately beat him, I knew better. For someone who claimed the city championship two years in a row, he played like a loser this time.

"You threw that one my way." I flashed him a sly wink. His face flushed a bright red, almost as bright as his hair, and I knew I'd caught him.

"No, really," he protested. "You won, fair and square."

I smiled, and rising from my chair, I gave him a mock curt-sey. He reached for my hand and like a gentleman might when about to kiss the hand of a lady, he puckered his lips, also in fun.

"We're friends, Matt," I reminded him.

"You know what they say, don't you? Friends sometimes get to be more."

Sighing, I turned my back on him and hurried out the door. I headed toward the dining hall with Matt plodding along behind me. I picked up my pace, but his footsteps remained close. The poor guy was never going to give up.

To my dismay, my dad and Peter were already sitting with Charlie Ellison, which meant I wasn't going to be free of Matt for a while.

"Where's Jeanine?" I said to Charlie, though I really didn't care where she was.

"In bed." He lowered his gaze to his bowl of chili. "She must have eaten something at breakfast that didn't agree with her."

I thought about the three young men who were wheeled into the infirmary. "Food poisoning?" I said.

Charlie stared into my eyes, his own eyes hard like stones. "We don't know. If she gets any worse, we'll have to take her to the clinic."

A part of me wouldn't have minded seeing that woman

wheeled into the clinic on a gurney, like those young men who'd died. But another part of me—the compassionate part—hoped she'd be okay. With my mom lying on what could be her death-bed, I had all the more reason to pray that everyone could be safe. Those young men had contracted an unknown illness. Now Jeanine was sick. I couldn't mention my concerns to Dad. He'd been involved with plans for the new build. He'd become more obsessed each day, like he expected our time in the capsule to be short. The truth was, we could be confined for a year or more.

I thought about Mr. Crenshaw—my one ray of hope. I loved spending time with the old guy. Not only was he a wealth of information, he'd given me a sense of peace while staying in that hole, at least until my mother was well.

The truth was, the old man intrigued me. His mind was like a computerized filing cabinet. He remembered things about the past that most adults had forgotten or perhaps never knew at all. And, he had a fairly good idea about the future, as well. Like a prophet. Many of his warnings came straight from the Bible, some from passages many preachers have claimed are symbolic. But Crenshaw seemed to be taking much of what the Bible said literally.

I was thinking about my next visit with him when Dad reached across the table and handed me a sheet of paper.

"What's this?" I said, perplexed.

"Read it, honey."

I unfolded the paper and discovered a list of duties. My *duties*. First, I needed to spend a couple hours babysitting in the kids' room, and I was to do so immediately after lunch. *There goes my meeting with Crenshaw.* I'd be trading him in for a room full of wailing brats.

The news hit me hard. I crumpled up the paper and shoved it in my pocket. Of course I lost my appetite. I took my half-eaten lunch to the dumping bin, then obediently slunk off to the kids' area.

Somehow, I got through all the diaper-changes, feedings,

and rocking—not really my idea of a fun day. With so many families in the time capsule, I couldn't believe the leadership wanted procreators. I had to admit, though, I enjoyed the toddlers most of all. They were like tiny little sponges, soaking up every word I said. Briefly I thought I might be a teacher in the new build, but that idea was lost amidst government controlled virtual lessons. There'd be no chance for personal interaction, no opportunity to mold those young minds as I might see fit. No. They were to become little robots, just like the rest of us.

I left the children's area, and as I walked the hall, the electronics went down and plunged the time capsule into utter darkness. I looked around in a panic. Dim emergency lights flickered to life over each doorway. But the virtual monitors went dark, the locks on the doors snapped open, and the circulation motors stopped putting out fresh air.

A voice came through the overhead speakers, directing everyone to the dome. I followed the human flood to the one place where daylight filtered through the glass.

Peter was already there. And Matt. So was Mr. Crenshaw, now sitting in his high-backed wheelchair. The dome soon filled with all of the residents and staff. I looked around for my dad and spotted him coming down the hall swinging a flashlight. He took a position in the center of the dome and held up his hand. The buzz of more than a hundred people diminished. All eyes were on my dad.

"Everybody, stay calm." His voice reverberated against the glass walls. "I'm gonna try to start things up again. You're safe in here. Stay in the dome and wait for the guards to give the all-clear."

He came over to Peter and me. "You heard what I said. Stay here, kids. I'll come back for you."

"What about Mom?" I said, panic in my voice.

"The clinic has an emergency generator. The doors will automatically lock. She'll be fine."

Dad left with a uniformed guard. Peter grabbed my arm.

His face was all screwed up, like he was about to cry. The last time he reacted that way, we were in the back of the car leaving our neighborhood. My heart went out to him.

"Don't worry," I said, taking his hand. "Let's walk over to the glass and look outside." He clung to me with both hands. We edged closer to the glass wall. Then he gave my shirt a little tug. "Let's leave this place, Ollie."

"I wish we could, Peter. And don't call me Ollie." I pulled my arm from his grasp.

If I had been ready, I would have gone in a flash. But there I was, trying to comfort Peter and wondering how my mom was. I couldn't go anywhere.

Right about then, a blood-curdling scream cut through the air. Two uniformed guards rushed inside the dome and bolted the door.

People surrounded the two guards and demanded to know what was happening.

The guards stared back at the crowd, their eyes wild with fear. "The baboons!" one of them yelled. "They've escaped their enclosure, and they've already killed someone!"

"Baboons?" someone in the crowd shouted. "What baboons? Nobody said anything about baboons."

The other guard rushed over to the man and talked quietly to him. I already knew what no one else did. There were animals in the capsule, and all of them were on the bottom floor. Those beasts shouldn't have been a threat, right?

Peter lunged at me and wrapped both of his arms around my waist. I stroked his mop of sandy hair. I couldn't let on that I was just as terrified as he was. I remembered my trip to the basement and the horrifying screeches and snarls that erupted down there. The horror had stayed with me long after I returned to the main floor.

Despite the guards' quick action to quiet the man, the entire dome dissolved into a state of panic. The tension in the air was so thick, I couldn't breathe. Not surprising, a woman fainted. Children started crying. A mob of people circled the guards and pelted them with questions.

One of the guards broke away, climbed onto a chair, and raised his hands. "Please! Calm down, everyone. Be quiet, and we'll try to explain."

The entire dome settled into a hush. But before he could say anything, more screams erupted on the other side of the door, followed by an eerie quiet, then more screams, fainter and farther away. Peter continued to cling to me. I thought about my dad, somewhere inside the capsule, and I trembled. How could I keep Peter calm when *I* was about to fall apart?

People continued to surround the guard on the chair. He spread his arms and began to speak. "My name's Walter," he said, a nervous tremor in his voice. "I work on the bottom floor in the science lab, the area where they keep the test animals—mostly rats, dogs, cats, and, yes—baboons."

"What do you mean, *test* animals?" one man shouted. "Nobody told us we'd be sharing this capsule with dangerous test animals."

Walter looked around nervously, as though he was trying to decide how much he should say. With everyone crowding around pressing him, he heaved a sigh and then continued.

"All I know is, they're part of the plan for the new build," he said, his eyes darting toward the entry door. Sweat poured from his brow. He pulled out a handkerchief and mopped it away. "When the power went down, so did our security system. The cages all had a backup system, old-fashioned padlocks, but the lab workers had taken a couple of the baboons out so they could draw some blood. When the lights flickered, the lab crew headed for the elevators, and the two baboons broke free of their restraints. Those beasts followed the men to the elevators and made it to the top floor. They're out there now, destroying everything in their path, including—" He started to choke and his face contorted. "Including anyone who gets in their way."

"What about the lab workers?" a woman called out.

Walter stared back at her and didn't respond. He shook his head. "The baboons tore them apart," he conceded. "The rest of us were able to get away."

"Then who's still out there?" another man shouted.

"A few workmen and more guards," said Walter. "They're protecting themselves—with guns, lasers, and pepper spray."

Panic surged through me. As far as I knew, my dad had none of those protections.

I rushed over to the guard. "What about my father? Rave Jackson? He's out there."

Walter paused, then stepped down off the chair. " He's the electromagnetic engineer, isn't he?"

"Yes. That's right. Where is he?"

"I don't know. I didn't see him. He probably went down the stairwell to work on the power compartment."

"That's on the bottom floor, isn't it, the level where the animals are?"

"Yes, but someone is with him, someone who is armed. He should be safe."

"And the people in the clinic?" I pressed, still thinking about my mother.

"They're safe, too. They're on a different floor, and there's a manual lock on the entrance to the medical ward. Nobody can get in or out."

He swallowed, and a look of dismay engulfed his face.

"What's wrong?" a woman cried. "What aren't you telling us?"

Walter wet his lips, like he was trying to find the right words. "Sadly, one of the baboons found a way outside the capsule. The other one is still inside, but guards are trying to trap them both."

I trembled at the thought that one of those beasts had gotten outside. Not only would I have to worry about the leadership tracking me using the tattoo on my hand, but once I got outside I might have to face a killer baboon. As much as I wanted to see Zaq, I didn't want to be torn apart by a beast that had already killed a couple of lab workers.

Gunshots rang out in the hall. Peter and I jumped. Then all went silent. A few seconds passed, and the door flew open. In walked Matt's father carrying a small handgun.

"I got him," Charlie shouted. His flushed face glowed with the announcement. "I killed the baboon. Now if Jackson can get the power going, we'll be back in business."

Matt's mother stumbled into the dome behind her husband. She clung to Charlie's arm with both hands. She gazed up at his face, like he'd become something of a hero to her. I was amazed at the transformation in that woman.

I moved closer to Matt. "I didn't know your father had a gun."

He grinned. "Yeah, he's full of surprises. Brought it home a couple years ago when things started heating up. My mom was against it back then. Now look at her."

Jeanine was still clinging to her husband, her eyes glistening like those of a star-struck teenager. I chuckled softly. *So much for her interest in my dad.* Maybe she'd leave him alone now.

Charlie approached us, dragging Jeanine with him. "You kids all right?" he said.

"We're fine." Matt placed a hand on my shoulder, like he presumed he could be my protector.

Charlie was looking at me, his face glum. "Listen, Olivia," he said, and his serious tone frightened me. "Your dad has an idea, but it's going to involve a huge risk."

"What do you mean, a risk?"

"There's a storm brewing on the horizon. It's a big one, and it's heading this way. If it generates a good amount of lightning, your dad believes he will be able to harness some of that power to spark our electromagnetic system back to life." Charlie shook his head. "Our complete system has failed, no backup, no alternate solutions. Your father's a real genius, honey—a kind of modern day Ben Franklin, except he doesn't have a kite and a key. He's going back in time, in a sense, and using old-school methods. He's going to rig a twenty-foot power probe out there, then run the wires inside to the control box in the bottom level. He needs to get it done fast—before the storm reaches us. But he's gonna have to go outside to do it."

Peter tugged on Charlie's sleeve and lifted anxious eyes at him. "Will we be able to watch him from in here?" He gestured toward the wall of windows.

"Yes, and I'll be right out there with him," Charlie assured us.

"You're going out there?" Matt said, a tremor in his voice.

Charlie nodded. "Don't worry, son. I'll be fine." He lifted the gun.

My heart was pounding. "What about the baboon that got out? Those animals are vicious."

Charlie pursued his lips and drew a breath. "I'll keep an eye out for him," he said.

"No, Dad, you can't—"

Charlie raised a hand and cut Matt off. "I have to go out there. I can keep the baboon at bay while Jackson works his magic. He won't be able to finish the job and watch his back at the same time." Charlie lifted his gun. "I've already killed one baboon. I can get the other one."

Jeanine, still clinging to Charlie's arm, turned her face up at him, anxious tears ruining her makeup. "Don't go, Charlie."

Charlie backed away from his wife and son. "Listen, you two. I have to do this. We won't have any power otherwise."

Matt straightened and jutted out his chin. "Then, let me go with you, Dad. I can help—"

"No, son. I need you to stay here and take care of your mom. Do what I say. I need to go now. Rave is waiting for me."

Charlie headed for the door and was gone.

For a few seconds I just stood there staring at Matt. Then I noticed Jeanine was about to drop to the floor.

"C'mon, Matt. Let's get your mom into a chair."

We guided Jeanine to the far wall and settled her into a loveseat. Then Matt and I joined Peter at the window. A desolate landscape spread out before us. Oak trees had begun to develop a hint of green amidst their brown and gray limbs. Darkening skies lay several miles to the west, and as Charlie had predicted, a roll of dark clouds tumbled toward us. The sky turned gray. Flashes of heat lightning lit up the sky. In the distance, a bright bolt struck the earth and sent a resounding tremor across the ground. The wall of glass rippled briefly but remained intact.

I kept my eyes on the clearing and waited for my dad and Charlie to emerge from the capsule. They staggered into view, straining against a powerful wind. They wore work gloves, and Dad was dragging a long rod that sparked whenever lightening lit up the sky. Together, they positioned the rod in the ground next to a flag pole where a Chinese flag showed off its red and yellow design. Dad pulled it down and continued to set up the rod. Charlie backed away and pulled out his pistol.

My dad moved with amazing dexterity, his hands grasping at wires and lines, working to brace the rod upright. Frustrated, he ditched his protective gloves, and barehanded, he inserted four pegs into the ground stabilizing the rod, then ran a long wire toward the base of the time capsule.

I scanned the trees for any sign of the escaped baboon. My dad kept working, intent on getting the probe in place. He didn't notice when two red eyes peered at him from a clump of shrubbery near the edge of the clearing. Nor did Charlie see the animal, though it was only a couple of yards away from him.

I shouted at the glass. "Dad! Look behind you." But my voice bounced back at me.

Not only was the glass wall impenetrable, it also appeared to be sound-proof. Matt and I waved and shouted. Others rushed up to the window and begin to scream at our two men. Not a sound reached them. Nor did they notice the frantic waving or hear the pounding of fists against the glass.

Out of the corner of my eye, I caught sight of Walter, who'd frozen in the center of the dome.

"Walter!" I shouted. "Can't you do something?"

"I'll try," he said, and he ran toward the door, drawing his pistol.

My dad had gotten so involved with setting up the probe, he never saw the animal lurking in the bushes. Without warning, the baboon lunged into the clearing. A loud gasp filled the dome, and we stood frozen, helpless to do anything to save him.

Chapter Fourteen

I turned away from the glass, unable to watch the slaughter. Tears ran down my cheeks. I was about to lose my father, and my mother lay helpless in the medical clinic. What was to become of Peter and me?

Then, someone by the window shouted, "Look!"

I dared to turn around. Walter had left the capsule and stepped into the clearing. There was a flash of gunfire.

"He shot him!" a woman screamed. "The guard shot the baboon."

Walter's quick action awakened Charlie. He aimed his own gun, but didn't fire it. I held my breath.

"Why isn't he shooting?" I looked at Matt. "The baboon is lying there, but it's still breathing. Shoot it, Charlie. Shoot!"

Matt shook his head, his eyes on his father. "I don't know why he's just standing there."

Of course, Charlie didn't hear me shouting at him. He just stared at Walter, who was reloading while the baboon struggled to it's feet. Though bleeding, it was still very much alive. Charlie had a clear shot, but he never fired. He could have killed the beast, but he didn't even try.

I stood in horror as the wounded baboon limped off into the woods.

I considered what awaited me if I escaped with a wounded animal prowling around out there. If I wanted to stay safe I could not leave the time capsule unarmed. But what could I use? A knife from the kitchen wouldn't offer enough protection.

Charlie had a gun. Somehow, I had to get hold of it. I was going to need Matt's cooperation, of course, whether he knew he was helping me or not.

For now, I kept my eyes on my dad and watched him finish up the last of the ties. The storm was building. The sky grew darker. Lightning flashed a couple miles away. The job completed, Dad and Charlie hurried back inside. Charlie came straight to the dome, his shoulders back, a satisfied smile on his face. What did he have to be proud of? He never fired a shot, and he let an injured beast escape. If not for Walter's quick action, the baboon would not have been injured at all. I could only hope the animal would bleed to death. But if it didn't, it would pose an even greater danger to anyone who made it to the outside.

I rushed toward Charlie. "Where's my Dad?" I scowled at him, didn't try to hide my disgust. "Is he all right? You should have shot that animal, Charlie. My dad could have been killed out there."

Charlie flinched and took a step back from me. "Your father has gone to the control center to adjust the electrical components."

"No thanks to you," I snapped.

Charlie ignored my accusation. "All we need now is a good blast of lightning, and we'll have our power back."

His use of the word *we* had me fuming. Charlie hadn't done a thing to help out there. He'd left everything up to my dad, and then he didn't even stand guard.

"Sure," I said.

Matt drew close to me. "Think about it, Livie. There's a major storm coming our way. If your dad's correct, one good lightning strike will reboot our system and get things running again."

I did trust my father. No one else had the kind of expertise he possessed. My heart pulsed with pride. He was the reason we qualified for the time capsule in the first place, and he was the only one who could get things running again.

I joined the crowd at the window. A sudden gust stirred leaves and debris into the air. Sand rose in tiny spirals from the earth. Trees bent nearly to the ground from the force of the wind, it was so strong. The sky exploded with several flashes of lightning. A brilliant glare was accompanied by a loud crash, and the time capsule's power flickered to life. LED lighting glowed around the perimeter of the dome. An open door revealed hallways glowing with brilliance. The power was back on.

Residents erupted in cheers. Mr. Crenshaw clapped his bony hands, and others picked up his beat, joining him in a rousing celebration of hand clapping, stomping of feet, whistles, and shouts of joy. Several men surrounded Charlie and patted him on his back. Tearful, Jeanine threw herself in her husband's arms.

Matt also beamed with pride. "You did it, Dad," he said, and he gave Charlie's arm a gentle punch.

I was appalled at the accolades being showered on Charlie, the man who did nothing to protect my dad, the man who had a gun in his hand and never used it.

About that time, Walter returned to the dome. Several men rushed to his side, patted his back, and praised him for his bravery. He responded with a modest shrug.

The dome began to empty. People streamed into the hall, bound for their individual quarters, I assumed.

"Hold on," Walter shouted after them. "Give the guards a few minutes to check all the levels. We need to make sure no other animals got loose. And we've sent workers to pick up the dead."

I knew where they would take them—the trash heap outside the kitchen to be incinerated with the rest of the garbage. The dead baboon also would be disposed of, along with the two lab workers the animal killed. A terrible sadness washed through me. I don't know if it was the thought of human life being reduced to trash or if I feared this was merely a sign of more apathy to come. It seemed the new regime had little regard for human life.

Walter rushed into the hall. "Stay put," he commanded, holding up his hands. "We'll make an announcement when it's safe to go back to your cubicles."

The crowd quietly drizzled back inside the dome. Mr. Crenshaw rolled his wheelchair to a far corner. I left Peter with Matt and hurried over to check on the old man.

"Are you all right, Mr. Crenshaw?"

He appeared to be trembling. He looked into my eyes and forced a smile.

"PTSD," he informed me. "I'm afraid I served in far too many battles. All the noise and activity kind of set me back. But don't worry about me, Livie. You need to go and take care of your family."

I knelt beside him. "Mr. Crenshaw, I won't leave you like this."

In the short time I had grown fond of the old guy. He was nothing like the decrepit airhead I first imagined I'd be working with.

"Listen," he said, peering deep into my eyes. His gravely voice was reduced to a whisper. "I have a good feeling about you—and your friend Zaq. I think you should keep on with your plan to leave this place. You have something many of us lost a long time ago. You have faith in God and faith in yourself. And you've got gumption."

"Gumption?" I had to laugh. My grandma used that word with me. When I was only 10, she placed her hand on the crown of my head like she was about to bestow a blessing. "I can see your heart, Olivia," she choked. "You won't sit around while the rest of the world moves on without you. No sir. You've got gumption, my dear. Lots of it. And it's gonna come in handy someday."

Crenshaw's use of the same word had sparked more than a memory. Two people had believed in me. How could I not believe in myself? Baboon or not, I was determined to leave the time capsule. I only needed Crenshaw to share his plan.

"I trust God will protect you and Zaq," he said. "You're our only hope, Olivia. Now that the world powers have come onto American soil, we could use a couple of heroes."

"You said you could help us, that you have a plan."

He set his watery blue eyes on me. "I will and I do. Come and see me tomorrow. After breakfast, as usual. And bring the leadership's notebook. I have some things I want to say to them, too."

A thought came to mind, something my grandma often talked about near the end of her life.

"Are we drawing close to the end of the world, Mr. Crenshaw?"

He snickered, but he didn't smile, and the light had gone out of his eyes. "It's too early for that," he said, a certain sadness filtering into his voice. "Tonight, take out your Bible and read Matthew Chapter 24. Lots of things still need to happen before the end. God has a plan, and it's orderly."

I tilted my head quizzically.

"Just read it," he insisted. "You'll understand."

That was all I needed. I left him sitting there and went back to Peter. The all-clear alarm sounded, Walter opened the door, and everyone filed out of the dome.

I got into the hall and almost shrieked with joy. Dad was coming our way, moving against the flow, dodging the surging crowd to get to us.

He wrapped Peter and me in his arms.

"I'm so proud of you, Dad," I gushed, fresh tears spilling down my cheeks.

He brushed them away and smiled down at me. "Let's go check on your mom."

Peter and I walked beside him, one on each side. I picked up my step, eager to see my mom again. But when we arrived in the clinic, we found her bed empty. My dad hollered for the medic. A nurse walked in.

Dad rushed toward her. "Where's Clarisse? Where's my wife?"

The nurse held up her hands. "Hold on. We released her."

"What?" Dad's face turned beet red. He was ready to blow up. "Without checking with me? Where did she go?"

The nurse took a strong stance and crossed her arms,

determined not to allow him to intimidate her. She breathed a long sigh.

"She must have overheard the nursing staff talking about you and how you went outside to get the power going. We couldn't believe the transformation in her. It was like someone lit a fire under her. She sat up in bed, threw off the blanket, and said she wanted to go to you, to help you."

"Where is she now?" Dad snarled.

She cowered under his steady gaze. "I don't know, Mr. Jackson," she murmured. "Your wife checked herself out. As far as we know, she went to your residence. I'm pretty sure Doctor Rand was trying to reach you."

Dad and I exchanged a look. Without saying a word, we both turned away and hurried out the door and back down the hall to the elevator. Several people were milling about. A few cornered an attendant and pelted him with questions about their loved ones. Some feared their relatives had been victims of the baboon attacks. The attendant assured them they were not.

In the midst of all the weeping and wailing, I wrapped an arm around Peter and pulled him along the hall behind Dad. With all the people in front of us, I grew impatient waiting to get on the elevator. We were too far inside the capsule to use the stairwell.

Then, a place opened up, and we were able to squeeze into the tiny box with a crowd of other people, all of us crammed together like sardines in a can, as the saying goes. My claustrophobia returned with a vengeance, though I tried to fight it. Heavy perspiration and cheap perfumes filled the elevator. I squirmed against the bodies to get closer to the door. Our ascent began with a jolt. Someone's elbow pressed against the small of my back. A large man slipped between me and Dad. I held my breath. When the door opened, I burst out ahead of everyone. Without waiting for Dad and Peter, I took off down the hall toward our apartment, pressed my fingers against the entry device, and charged inside.

I couldn't believe what I found. Mom was sitting on the sofa, smiling and humming a tune. It was as if she'd been there all along. Like she'd never left us, never had an emotional meltdown, never spent the last few days in a hospital bed.

"Mom," I shouted. Tears came. I knelt before her and grabbed her arms. "I can't believe you're here. I missed you so much, Mom. I'm so glad you're back."

I bowed my head to her lap and sobbed out my relief. She stroked my hair, pressed her lips to my forehead, and sighed. Peter lunged into us, shrieking with relief. Then Dad's long arms encompassed us. And the four of us stayed that way, in a tangle of arms, weeping and laughing. My family was together again for the first time in days, and it felt so good.

I thought about how lucky I was to be part of this family, each one loving the others. I thought about the leadership's ridiculous plan of reproduction, two complete strangers producing offspring to populate the new world, and I cringed at the idea. I didn't want to give myself to a stranger or even to a friend. Nor did I want to have my eggs harvested and fertilized in a lab, never to know my own children. I wanted to be like Mom, married to the man I loved, bearing his children the right and proper way, raising them, loving them, and being loved back. I wanted all of that, and what's more, I want it all with Zaq.

After all that had happened, my plan of escape had become even more necessary.

We spent the rest of the evening together. After Dad showered and changed his clothes, the four of us went to the dining hall in time for supper. We sat alone this time, didn't even look for Matt and his family.

Afterward, I went back to our apartment and straight to my cubicle. I did what Crenshaw had suggested, I pulled out Grandma's Bible and read Matthew 24. The verses came alive, and I saw the old man was right. Though we'd had wars and rumors of wars, earthquakes in diverse places, and lots of other phenomena, there were still a lot of things that had to happen in our current world before the end would come. The one positive that came out of my reading that passage was that I developed a greater understanding of God's power, and I had more confidence in what the Almighty planned for believers. My faith was strengthened, I determined to read more of God's word, perhaps the Book of Revelation and look forward to what was yet to come.

✝✝✝

A definite plan was beginning to take shape. Now that my mom was back and seemed well, I wanted to meet with Mr. Crenshaw, record his messages to the leadership, and insist he share his plan with me. Sometime during the day, I needed to get with Matt and convince him to take me to his apartment, hopefully while his parents were out. While there, I had to figure out a way to get hold of his dad's gun. Once I had a weapon, I could go ahead with my plan to leave.

Excitement bubbled inside me. Nothing could keep me in the time capsule now. I could walk out of there without any misgivings. I could leave, satisfied that my mom was okay, that Peter and my dad didn't need me around, and maybe wouldn't even miss me until I was long gone. I could at last breathe fresh air and feel free again. I'd have to find Zaq, and together we could decide what to do next.

Instead of all four of us going to the dining hall the next morning, Dad suggested he go there alone and put together a tray of food we could share in our apartment. This was a special time for our family. We didn't want Charlie or Jeanine interrupting our time with Mom.

While we waited for Dad's return, Peter and I filled in Mom with our experiences since coming inside the time capsule—our tour with Matt, the layout of the different floors, our school work, the virtual screens in the study lab, my visits with Mr. Crenshaw, Peter's job cleaning up the dining hall, and his workouts in the weight room. I didn't mention my discovery of animals on the bottom floor, and none of us talked about the baboons' escape and the death of those individuals who were attacked. Peter and I raved about Dad's work on restoring the power at great risk to his own life.

When Dad returned, we gathered around the little table in our sitting room, and Dad dished out our selections. We kept the conversation light and tried to focus on what we might expect when the day of our release finally arrived. Though I was anxious to go to the dome and find Mr. Crenshaw, I forced myself to eat slowly and enjoy my time with my family. These were moments I needed to remember. Once I left the capsule, I might never get them back again.

Chapter Fifteen

The next morning didn't come fast enough for me. It was like I'd gotten a fresh boost of energy, partly because Mom was back and seemed fine, but also because I now could move ahead with my plan to get out of that place and find Zaq. With Mr. Crenshaw's words of encouragement, I believed an escape was possible. But what did the old man expect me to do once I found Zaq?

I hurried through breakfast, grabbed the leadership's notebook, and ran to the dome, surprised to find Mr. Crenshaw already there waiting for me. Did the guy ever sleep?

Crenshaw spent the first hour of our visit dictating information for the leadership, mostly military remembrances from his deployment to Iraq and Afghanistan many years ago. He complained about China taking over our clothing industry and how Japan sold more cars to Americans than Ford and Chrysler put together. He ended his spiel to the leadership with advice about how to avoid making the same mistakes in the future. The advice he poured out revealed an expert in nearly every kind of industry. The man was a genius.

As Crenshaw cited an unreal number of statistics, I marveled that his mind had stored up data like an intricate computer system. He rattled off facts so fast, I could hardly keep up. At the same time, I was learning details about the past I had never read about in my virtual classes. He talked about former political upheavals and government resolutions that might be helpful in the new build. I doubted the Chinese would pay much attention to his suggestions, but I wrote them out exactly as he dictated them to me.

At one point, I quit writing and heaved a big sigh. "Slow down, Mr. Crenshaw, I'm trying to get it all." I cocked my head at him and laughed. "Do we really need to record so much in one sitting?"

"Sure do," he said, sticking out his chin in that resolute way he had of taking control. "That way the leadership won't suspect we're talking about anything else."

When he finally stopped dictating, he took my hand in his and leaned close. The smell of mint escaped from his dentures and the odor of rubbing alcohol rose from his neck. The poor guy must have had a lot more aches and pains than he complained about. He hunched his bony shoulders and tightened his grip on my right hand. Looking around the dome rather surreptitiously, he pulled a small metal plate from his shirt pocket and placed it over the spot where the leadership had etched my tracking tattoo. His arthritic fingers moved with amazing dexterity as he wrapped a bandage over the metal plate and bound it to my wrist. I gazed into his eyes, my own eyes questioning.

"They won't be able to track you now," he explained. "That metal plate is made of lead. It'll block their signal."

I froze—and smiled. Crenshaw had just eliminated one of my greatest concerns—that the leadership could track me down.

"Of course, that won't stop 'em from lookin' for you," Crenshaw noted. "Once they've combed the entire time capsule and determined you'd left, they'll send a small army out after you— probably a special forces unit with trained bloodhounds. If they succeed in following you to your friend, that will be the end of both of you—and anyone else who's teamed up with Zaq." He straightened and looked me in the eye, his own eyes piercing mine with a warning. "It's for this very reason I held off telling you my plan. I didn't want to put you young people in danger. Now tell me, Livie. Do you want to forget this whole thing?

Should we simply go back to what the leadership instructed and leave saving the country to someone else?"

I didn't have to think twice about it. I responded with an emphatic, "No. Let's keep going."

"Okay then. Tell me this, how do you plan to camouflage yourself?"

I mentally ran over my initial plan. "Black. I'll wear mostly black," I said. "I'll leave after dark. Not only will that give me a terrific head start, but by wearing black I'll disappear into the darkness of night."

"How will you find your own way, if it's dark?"

"I'll have my brother's night-vision goggles," I said, grinning. "They're just a toy, but they work really well."

"That's all well and good," Crenshaw said, stroking his chin. "But, the trackers also will have night-vision goggles—serious ones like those in the military. They'll be able to see greater distances than your little brother's plaything." He puffed out a concerned sigh. "You'll have to move fast, Livie-dear. Tell me, do you know exactly where Zaq is, or are you just guessing? It's important that you have a definite location. It will save you lots of time."

I frowned with unease. "I have a very good idea," I said, my voice soft and less certain. "We passed an abandoned mine shaft on our way over here. I recognized many of the landmarks. Zaq took me to that hole in the ground when he was trying to help me overcome my claustrophobia."

"Claustrophobia?" Crenshaw's furry eyebrows merged with concern. "You didn't tell me you have a problem with claustrophobia."

I decided to give him a condensed version of the time I was trapped in the freezer. "My friend Matt got me out. He saved my life."

The lines on Crenshaw's face gathered, and I feared he had changed his mind and was about to tell me not to go.

"Don't worry, Mr. Crenshaw," I quickly added. "Right now, that mine shaft seems far less threatening than *this* place."

He grew quiet, like he was rethinking what I'd said. "Are you sayin' you can handle close quarters, but only if Zaq is there?"

I gave him a sheepish smile.

He scratched his temple, then searched my face with those piercing blue eyes of his. Finally, he relaxed against the back of his chair.

"Okay then," he said. "Don't let anything keep you from reaching that mine."

"That's my plan." I said. "Your support means the world to me, Mr. Crenshaw. And thanks for the metal plate. I never thought of trying something like that. It's genius."

We exchanged a look that bonded us as allies, maybe for life.

"Now, let me have that notebook," Crenshaw said, and he reached for the leadership's record book.

While I waited, he flipped to a blank page, and with trembling fingers he sketched what looked like a map. Then he made an X and showed me the page.

"Okay. This is where we are," he said, pointing. He drew another line, shorter than the first, and marked another X. "And this, we can assume, is Zaq's hideout." He made still another X, this time near the bottom of the page. "Way down here is White Sulphur Springs, West Virginia."

I straightened my back and eyed the mark with interest. "White Sulphur Springs? Never heard of it."

"You have now." He gave me a smile that piqued my curiosity. The old guy was about to let me in on the rest of his plan.

"You need to go there," he said. "You and Zaq. That's where you'll find Harmon Brooks. I'm positive when everything started to go down, and Harmon's position in Washington was threatened, he most likely went to White Sulphur Springs. And he would have taken with him his own family, members of his administration, and undoubtedly, a number of brilliant scientists."

"I don't understand."

"Think about it. We're in this time capsule simply because, for now at least, we all have a purpose. For now, we're nothing but slave labor. Your dad included. Once the workers accomplish everything the leadership wants done, there's no telling what will become of us. We have only one hope. We need President Brooks. That man and his followers adhered to the Constitution as it was written. If he can resume his presidency, he'll restore that important document along with the Bill of Rights. We *can* survive this upheaval. We *can* rebuild our nation, and we can do it the way our forefathers originally established it."

"So you want us to find Harmon Brooks?" I shrank beneath what seemed like a daunting challenge.

"I do." He'd responded with such confidence I couldn't help but feel encouraged.

Crenshaw then slipped a ring off his finger and placed it in my palm. The circle of gold had a square black onyx gemstone and in the center the outline of a fish engraved in gold leaf.

I peered at the image. "This is one of those old Christian symbols, isn't it?"

Crenshaw's lips broke into a proud smile."Yes, it is. I've had this ring for fifty years. It once belonged to my son. When my Johnny passed away, I slipped it on my finger. Harmon Brooks has one exactly like it."

I turned it over in my hand and admired the workmanship. I'd rarely seen anything so meticulously crafted.

"This had to have been handmade," I remarked. "Nearly every piece of jewelry comes from China these days. But they're cheaply made. Even with my untrained eye, I can tell this is not from China."

"You're right, Livie. It costs the Chinese very little to produce most of their merchandise. Then they charge Americans top dollar. It's what's become of our failed trade agreement, which happened once they got rid of the tariffs."

The old man's eyes filled with tears, but instead of weeping, he pulled himself together and scrutinized.

"Now, listen up," he said. "What I'm going to tell you will help you on your journey." He held his breath and glanced around the dome. "Haven't you been just a little suspicious about all the things that have been happening in here? The sicknesses. The power outage. The escape of mutant baboons. Do you think they were mere coincidences?"

"I'm not sure," I said with a shrug.

"I believe a saboteur has infiltrated the capsule—someone from Russia perhaps." He lifted an index finger to his lips to silence me. "I'm guessing similar invasions have taken place in all the other time capsules in America and maybe around the globe. The Chinese and Russians are bitter enemies, and they both want to rule the world, beginning with America."

"Why don't we include that information in your report to the leadership?"

Crenshaw adamantly shook his head. "Big mistake. They already know it. They just don't want the rest of us to know." The lines on his face deepened, and he narrowed his eyes. "This whole thing with you writin' down everything I say, they're just trying to find out how much we really do know. Now, if you want to save your family—and the rest of us—you need to find Brooks. He'll know what to do."

I shrank back in my seat, unable to suppress the fear bubbling up inside me.

Crenshaw released a sigh. His brow furrowed, and he blinked several times, like he was reconsidering his plan.

"I don't know, Livie," he said with sadness. "Maybe I'm putting too much on your young shoulders." He shook his head. "We should forget the whole thing. I certainly don't want to put you in danger. This old man remembers a day when the youth had all the courage. A day when young soldiers marched into danger without concern for their own safety. Forgive me, child. This isn't that day. We're fighting against a far more menacing adversary. I don't want you to go."

I straightened. "Don't say that, Mr. Crenshaw. I'm going, whether you want me to or not."

"Of course, that's what got me fired up to help ya." He

seemed to shrink inside his shirt. "I wasn't thinking straight. I heard you say you wanted to get out of here, and I thought this might be the chance I'd been waiting for, the chance to reach Brooks."

"I can do it, Mr. Crenshaw. Zaq and I can do it together."

He nodded, slowly at first, then with more emphasis. "We have to survive—to be part of the believing remnant that will rule the world when all of this is over. And we need a leader who will bring us back to what we used to be, only stronger and wiser."

"Harmon Brooks," I acknowledged.

I few seconds of silence passed between us. The conversations of others in the dome and the strains of piped-in music swirled in the air. Crenshaw and I had been communicating in our own little world, unconcerned about the others. We'd entered a tiny bubble of intimacy apart from everyone else. Without intending to, Crenshaw had incited me to take action. The plan was set.

"Okay," I said. "So where do I find Harmon Brooks?"

"I told you. White Sulphur Springs, West Virginia."

"And where exactly is White Sulphur Springs?" I nearly burst out laughing.

Crenshaw was chuckling. He pointed at his hand-drawn map where he'd placed the last, much larger X.

"I'm guessing Harmon Brooks is hiding out in the Greenbrier Bunker. It was a top secret underground shelter, built back in the 1950s. Very simply, it's a time capsule to beat all time capsules, a remnant of the Cold War between the United States and Russia. It's far larger and better equipped than the one we're living in. When the cold war ended, it hadn't been used and kind of faded into anonymity."

I sat up straight and stared with wide-eyed interest at Crenshaw.

"Greenbrier Bunker?" I mused. "Tell me more."

He settled more comfortably in his chair, cleared his throat, and appeared to be organizing his thoughts. When he opened his mouth again, I was hardly prepared for all he had to tell me.

"That thing was built more than a hundred years ago," he said. "Since then the government has constructed other underground facilities. Politicians and their families can hide out in any one of them. Maybe some are doing that right now. That first one, though—the Greenbrier Bunker—was meant to be an underground shelter for President Eisenhower and his cabinet, plus all the members of Congress and the Senate, and their families, too, I suppose. They built it beneath the west wing of the Greenbrier Resort, a vacation retreat for the rich. Funny thing though. Eisenhower never got to use it.

"For years, the Greenbrier Bunker remained a government secret, until thirty years after its construction, a savvy Washington Post reporter caught wind of it and wrote an article exposing it to the entire country. The government capitalized on the exposure and opened up the bunker for public tours. Then, a half-century passed, the cold war was forgotten, everyone felt safe, and the Greenbrier Bunker fell into oblivion."

Crenshaw chuckled mischievously. "The so-called leaders we have today don't even know it exists. But Harmon Brooks knew. He did his homework. That's why I think that's exactly where he is hiding out."

I crossed my arms in front of me and narrowed my eyes at Crenshaw, not altogether convinced the Greenbrier Bunker fit into my own plans. All I wanted to do was leave the time capsule and find Zaq. Period. Now, it looked like the old man was sending me on an even more complex mission, one that I might not be able to complete. The big X was miles away from the mine shaft. How was I supposed to find that place and get inside? Still, my curiosity had been aroused, so I figured I'd give the old man a chance to explain.

"Okay," I surrendered. "Exactly how far away is White Sulphur Springs?

"Three hundred miles," he replied, a bit sheepishly.

"And how am I supposed to get inside the Greenbrier Bunker?"

"I'm glad you asked."

Chapter Sixteen

I had posed a challenging question, but Crenshaw wasn't the least bit intimidated. He merely tilted his head to one side in that whimsical way of his, moistened lips, and began to fill in the blanks.

"They carved the bunker in the side of a mountain in the Appalachian range, directly below the Greenbrier Resort. The high-class getaway served the politically and socially elite of that day. The bunker was furnished with the finest materials and was stocked with the kind of foods the Washington aristocracy enjoyed. It could easily house 1,100 people."

"And you believe the bunker is still there?"

"Yes, ma'am. As long as the resort stands, the bunker has to be there. Far as I know, no one has ever torn down the resort, so it has to be there."

"What about the Chinese invasion? Could they have found the bunker?"

"I doubt it. Some of their troops may have taken over the resort—you'll have to watch out for that—but there's no way they can be aware of what is lying directly below them. They couldn't possibly have found the secret passageways or the outside access."

A nervous tremor struck my insides. "So, if the enemy has taken over all the state capitals, as well as whatever was left of the White House, doesn't it make sense that they would move in on most of the well-equipped resorts, including the one in West Virginia?"

Crenshaw nodded and I caught a spark of admiration in his

cool blue eyes. "You're a smart girl, Livie. Of course they'll move their people in wherever they can. The Russians too. But chances are, they haven't figured out there's a huge shelter underneath the Greenbrier's west wing and probably never will."

My curiosity was growing. "What's the bunker like on the inside? Have you ever seen it yourself?"

Another nod and a flicker of memory. "I went there many years after it was finished." Crenshaw turned his gaze away from me. He stared off past the wall of glass and into the woods, and he pulled on his chin, like he was remembering.

When he looked back at me, his entire face lit up. "The pit measures 112,544 square feet," he said, spreading his arms. "It was outfitted with eighteen dormitories that contained enough beds for more than a thousand people." It surprised me that he could spew statistics like he was reading them in a book, another sign of his sharp computer brain.

I was now perched on the edge of my seat, my own mind imagining the details Crenshaw was feeding me.

"In the event of a nuclear attack, the government officials were to rush from their individual offices straight to White Sulphur Springs," he said, his voice ticking with excitement. "They couldn't stop for clothes or precious items of any kind. But they must have had their families with them. The bunker was well-fortified with whatever they might need for a lengthy stay. Except for the President, the Speaker of the House, and the head of the Senate, few people knew the bunker existed back then. I imagine the rest of 'em would have been in complete shock when all hell broke loose, summoning them to safety with only the clothes on their backs. As it turned out, the cold war ended, and they never had to use it."

I couldn't restrain a little snicker. "Seems like a waste of money to build something they never would use."

"It's called *being prepared*." Crenshaw said with a smirk. "If a nuclear attack had been imminent, the Washington elite would have had a place of refuge."

"So they would have entered the bunker. Then what?"

"They would have passed through a 25-ton steel door into an entry where they had to remove all their clothing before entering a decontamination chamber. Then they were given new coveralls and a grooming kit, and they'd be ushered into the main bunker and stay until there was no further threat of radiation poisoning."

I tried to imagine people in a high-speed exodus from offices and homes into an underground pit, unprepared for what they'd find there. I couldn't help but compare their rush to safety with the move my family had made—one day, safe at home, and the next, heading for a time capsule for an indefinite period of time.

"Picture it," Crenshaw said, his cracked lips breaking into a silly grin. "Those folks would leave their mahogany desks and their high-rise offices. They'd shed their expensive black suits and put on government issued coveralls. They'd trade their briefcases and portable phones for gas masks and Geiger counters. Then they'd sit underground and wait for the attack."

I shook my head in disbelief. "So the government leaders and their families would remain safe, and the rest of the Americans would be sitting ducks," I mused. "Kind of like us."

Crenshaw chuckled. "Yes, and like us, those few chosen ones would have had everything they needed to survive underground for a year or more. The bunker also was equipped with an advanced communications system, a twelve-bed medical clinic, a pharmacy, a cafeteria, and several well-appointed meeting rooms, just like what they'd been enjoying on the surface. They'd sleep on cots stacked on top of each other, much like in an army barracks but with a few more frills. The storeroom was stocked with enough non-perishable food and water to keep them going for months. I have no doubt Brooks and his team took the same pains to get well supplied."

A horrifying thought struck me. "What if a bomb were dropped directly on the resort? Wouldn't it also destroy the bunker?"

Crenshaw frowned at me like I'd touched a nerve. He scrunched his lips and gave a nod. "I'm afraid the bunker wasn't built to withstand a direct attack. It was meant as a fallout shelter, nothing more. Again, like this time capsule."

I did some calculating of my own. "You said the bunker was built in the 1950s. You couldn't have been more than two or three years old at the time. How do you know so much about it?"

He released a little chuckle. "My father worked on the construction. For years he talked privately to us kids about the secret hole-in-the-ground nobody knew about except for a few special people. I got to make a tour of the place when the government offered them. I was around 50 years old by then."

I looked into Crenshaw's sparkling blue eyes, and I caught my breath with another realization. "You're certain Harmon Brooks is still alive? He wasn't killed like the news reports said?"

He nodded. "I'm not positive. But the Greenbrier Bunker is still there, and I'm guessing if Harmon Brooks survived the attack on the White House, he and his people are holed up inside that place just waitin' for a chance to win the country back. As long as the enemy doesn't know they're in there, they'll be safe. I hope Brooks will take back his position as President and that his military will be able to defeat the Chinese and the Russians. We need to get America back like it used to be, the most powerful nation in the world." His voice escalated, and his enthusiasm sent a flutter of excitement through me.

"But where is Brooks' military? They certainly can't be inside the bunker with him."

"The armed forces have their own fortresses. I have no idea where, but I'm sure they're safe somewhere and just waiting for the opportunity to fight back."

"Mr. Crenshaw, even if Zaq and I are able to find that bunker, what good can we do?"

The old man straightened in his seat. "Remember what I said. The bunker contains an advanced communications system, capable of not only sending messages but intercepting them.

Harmon's team of technicians could easily adjust the system to operate off the many satellites that are circling the earth. It makes sense. Before he turned to politics, Brooks worked for NASA. Believe me, he knows how to adapt the equipment to send out a warning to the pockets of militia, including his military, and the group your friend Zaq joined. Brooks can organize them to deal with the final threat that's sure to come."

I shrank back in fear for my boyfriend. "What final threat?"

"As I mentioned, I believe saboteurs may have infiltrated the time capsules, most likely Russians who want to overturn the Chinese. That puts us all in danger."

I caught my breath. "Do you mean a Russian spy might be living among us right now?"

Crenshaw turned even more serious. "And whoever it is—man or woman—that person is already planning to destroy the capsule and everyone in it. That's why your mission is so important."

My heart was in my throat. I swallowed hard. I thought about my parents, how my mom had already escaped death. My dad too. And what about Peter. He was so young, had his whole life ahead of him. Somehow, I had to be brave enough to follow through with the plan, get to Brooks, and help get the word out, no matter what it took.

Crenshaw remained quiet, like he was giving me time to absorb it all. An overwhelming discouragement settled upon me. I hadn't left the time capsule yet and already I felt as though I'd failed. I kept thinking of my family, Matt and his parents, and Mr. Crenshaw, and I surfaced with newfound courage. I inhaled deeply, sat up straight, and looked Crenshaw in the eye.

He tore another sheet from the leadership's notebook. "I'll sketch a more detailed map for you." He went to work, included route numbers and approximate mileage from one checkpoint to the next.

I looked at the map and sputtered out a laugh. "It's 300 miles? Mr. Crenshaw, I'm gonna be on foot."

"Maybe your friend Zaq will figure something out. All you need to do is get to Harmon Brooks and tell him about the unexplained deaths we've had and the power failure. If my suspicions are correct, someone is trying to destroy us from *inside* the time capsule, and it's only a matter of time before they end us all. That's why you need to find Brooks. He needs to know this is going on, perhaps in all the time capsules across the country."

I tore another blank page from the leadership's journal.

"Now, sketch the property around the bunker and show me how to get inside."

He took the page and kept talking as he made more notations. "There are four entrances. The main one inside the resort has a steel door. It's located inside the Exhibition Hall behind a fake wall. If the hotel is unoccupied, you can access the bunker through that door. But if it's occupied by either the Chinese or the Russians, you'll have to move around to the west side of the building." He made a check mark and continued speaking. "Search for a sloping driveway that may be covered over with grass. The drive was once a way in for supply trucks, but it hasn't been used in years. You'll be able to spot it where the lawn dips down between two walls of lush shrubbery. At the bottom is a large door encased in green panels that stand as high as the hill on both sides. There should be a *High Voltage* sign there, but don't worry. It's a dummy, meant to keep out the curious."

He stopped writing for a moment and locked eyes with me. "You won't be able to open the door from the outside. It's made of reinforced concrete, is impenetrable, and has a special lock. It can only be opened from the inside. At that point, you'll have to get in touch with Harmon Brooks. Call him on your FlexPhone. Here's his contact information." The old man scribbled another notation. "Text him, and use the code words *Chess match* in the subject line. He'll know it's from me."

Crenshaw sat back and smiled. "As soon as he answers, mention my name and hold up my ring so he can see it." His face lit up, and his eyes sparkled with excitement. "I'd go with you if I could." He gazed into my eyes, and I felt his passion. "I've been wanting to go, but these old legs will never make it. When you said you wanted to get out of here, I knew I had an emissary of my own. You need to do this, Livie. But you also need to protect yourself. The leadership is going to be looking for you. And that wounded baboon is still on the loose. There's no tellin' what other dangers might be lurking out there. You may come across bears, coyotes, raccoons, and all of them will be hungry."

Despite the sudden fear that welled up inside me, I forced an encouraging smile. "I'll be fine, Mr. Crenshaw. Do you remember the man who stood there like a dummy while my father was working on the electrical probe?"

"I did."

"He had a gun, but he didn't use it. He should have, but for some reason he froze."

"I remember him."

"That man's son is a friend of mine. I'm pretty sure I can get a hold of his father's gun."

Crenshaw heaved a big sigh. "I don't know."

"Trust me. I can do this."

"Okay. Just stay safe. Take a knife from the kitchen. Get the man's gun. Arm yourself as much as you can."

"I will. Don't worry, Mr. Crenshaw. I've thought everything through. I know what I'm facing, and I'm not afraid."

I was lying, of course, but I couldn't let him know I was trembling inside. All I could do now was move forward, one step at a time, and hope to make it to the end.

After leaving Crenshaw in the dome, I ran off to find Matt. I searched several rooms including the workout room. Then I located him in the study lab inside a simulated operating room. He was wearing a white lab coat, just like a real doctor, and he was holding a metal instrument that glistened beneath the glare of an overhead light. I chuckled to myself. My friend wanted to be a medic one day, kind of like Dr. Rand, the man who was in charge of my mom's care. In Matt's pretend operating room he leaned over a half-naked holographic test patient. Matt had already made an incision in the guy's right side. A ripple of bright red oozed out. Matt mopped it away with a swath of gauze, then, meticulously, he stitched up the wound, and when he was finished, he stepped back and smiled with satisfaction.

I waited through the entire process. I said, "Good job," and I pointed at the tool in his hand. "What's that?"

"It's a laser cutter." He waved the arc-shaped blade in front of me. "Someday, I'll be able to do this for real." He gestured toward his fake patient. "And I'll do more than cut him open and close him up. In my next lessons I'll learn how to utilize robotics to take out a faulty organ and replace it with a bionic one."

"Nice work, *Doctor* Ellison," I said, boosting his ego even more.

"Thanks, Livie. So, what do you want?" He removed his surgical gloves. "Another chess game?"

He seemed surprised that I'd come for him. I had to admit, I rarely went looking for Matt anymore. He was usually the one who came for me. But there I was, seeking him out. If he thought I'd be interested in him because he wanted to be a doctor one day, he was sadly mistaken. I loved Zaq, and I didn't care if he sold insurance like his father or picked up people's garbage. He was the one I wanted to spend the rest of my life with.

"I thought maybe we could play a game of regular chess," I told Matt. "In your room, away from all the activity up here." I made a face and gestured toward the room full of students working in their own virtual labs. The clamor was unbearable.

With a flick of his fingers, Matt shut down his holographic operating room. The microputer sucked up the image, including the patient, like a genie going back inside its bottle. Matt arranged his medical tools inside his personal kit, removed the lab coat and placed everything in a private locker. With a bob of his head, he beckoned me to follow.

"Let's go," he said. "I haven't beaten you at regular chess in a while. I think it's time."

Matt didn't know the real reason I wanted to play chess with him. His father's handgun was somewhere in their apartment. If I wanted to get my hands on it, I needed to get inside that room.

We walked together to the elevator, then traveled the hall in silence. Matt paused outside my door. "Do you want to leave your backpack in your apartment?" He said, gesturing toward the pack I'd flung over my shoulder.

"Nah. It's not heavy. Just a couple journals and some pens, that's all."

He led the way to his door. We entered the Ellisons' place, a mirror image of our own. I made a quick scan of the living area.

"Where are your parents?"

"My dad's working on a design plan with your father, and I don't know where my mom is. They took off when I left for the virtual room."

We settled in the sitting area with an old-fashioned chess board positioned between us on the little table. Though we had multiple playing options—a virtual screen, a holographic display, or—the most challenging of all—a three-tiered hologram—I still preferred the old-fashioned way of playing like my grandfather had taught me. I enjoyed moving the little ceramic figures into action. Matt arranged them like miniature armies ready for battle. He allowed me to have white, so I could make the first move. As always, I advanced a pawn. He did the same. After a couple more moves, I figured enough time had elapsed for me to casually mention his father's gun.

"That was so brave of your dad," I said, as I moved my knight. "You know, the way he went out there to protect my father."

"Yeah." He slid his bishop. "Too bad Walter shot the baboon before my dad could take aim."

"I didn't even know he had a gun."

"Pay attention, Livie. You just lost your knight."

"Oops." I studied the layout of the board, then swept in to take his rook. "I'd sure like to see that gun."

He straightened and eyed me with curiosity. "Really?" Then, he frowned. "I thought you wanted to play chess, Livie. But, you're more interested in my dad's gun."

Embarrassed, I waved a hand at him. "Just curious, that's all." I raised my eyebrows and managed a flirtatious smile. "You're not afraid of it, are you?" I challenged.

"Okay," he said, heaving a sigh. "Come on."

I grabbed my pack and followed Matt into his parents' cubicle. He pulled open a drawer and withdrew a metal strongbox. He punched in a code and glanced at me over his shoulder. "I got the code one day when my dad didn't know I was watching," he admitted. I held my breath as he flipped open the latch and lifted his father's handgun out of the box. I had to laugh. He was gripping the gun tenuously, with two fingers.

I reached out to take it, but he pulled it back. "It might be loaded."

"I'll be careful." I reached out again. This time he let me take it.

Now that I had my hand on that gun I didn't want to let it go.

"Is there any ammo?" I asked.

"Yeah, lots of it."

He reached inside the strongbox and grabbed a palm-sized case. I peered through the clear top. It was full of shells.

I examined the handgun, turned it over in my hands, and took aim. The question was, how could I get rid of Matt for a few minutes? My mind scrambled. I faked a cough.

"You okay, Livie?" Matt said, patting my back.

I coughed again and pretended to gag. "Say, Matt. Can I have a glass of water?"

He puffed out a sigh. "Sure. I'll get it. Return this stuff to the safety box and put it back in my dad's drawer. And hurry up. I'll get us some snacks too."

While Matt was out of the room, I jammed the gun and bullets inside my pack, then I resealed the lock and put the empty strongbox back inside his father's drawer. I headed back to the sitting room at the same time Matt came along with his hands full of snack bags and two bottles of water.

I plunged back into our chess game and discovered Matt really was playing his best. He wasn't going to let me win this time. It didn't matter. I could leave the time capsule with his dad's gun, and I'd be miles away before Charlie ever noticed it was gone.

Chapter Seventeen

I could hardly wait for the darkness of night, got more antsy by the minute. Still, I tried to keep calm as suppertime dragged by. There was no sign of the Ellisons. Instead, sitting at our table were two other families—people I hadn't met till now. The conversation between the men centered around Dad's repair of the capsule's electrical system. Dad graciously described the whole process, giving details that meant nothing to the rest of us women and children, but seemed to enthrall the men at our table. They soaked up his account like they were starved for adventure.

The children—all of them younger than 12, played table games. The women griped about having few opportunities for social activities like those they enjoyed before coming to live in the time capsule. They tried to come up with ideas for gatherings but failed to rouse interest. Their conversation then settled around tips for getting their children to eat the food being served there, balancing their kids' studies with playtime, and planning for their future release into the new world.

Meanwhile, between bites of bland vegetables and a watery soup, I counted the minutes until I could get back to my family's cubicle and prepare for my escape. I was able to sneak a couple sandwiches and some snack foods into my backpack, sustenance for my upcoming journey. As the anticipation grew within me, so did the fear of not being able to accomplish what I was about to set out to do.

There'd been times when I'd wished we hadn't been chosen at all. Then I wouldn't have had to come up with a plan of escape.

I could be out there with Zaq, dealing with life on the outside, both the good and the bad.

After supper ended, I went to our cubicle with my parents. While Peter played soldier in his room, I paced up and down the hall, like a caged panther, from my bedroom to the front door and back, thoughts of my escape swirling around in my head. Dad helped Mom settle into a chair in the sitting room and flicked on the virtual screen. Images of waterfalls and distant mountains appeared, backed by orchestral music. I stopped pacing, walked over to Mom and gave her a hug. She appeared rested, like she'd simply gone to sleep for a while and now had awakened. I couldn't believe she'd come back to us in such good health. Whatever they gave her must have worked. Or maybe it was just time.

Smiling up at me, Mom reached for the remote control and skipped though the few channels the leadership had made available. Sadly, she settled on propaganda about what we could expect in the new world. The war-torn countryside melted away and in its place surfaced green fields, vast flower beds, animals roaming in pastures, and cities with skyscrapers made of glass and steel. Storefronts displayed the latest in household novelties, autonomous vehicles floated above the highways, and a variety of amusements and parks appeared out of nowhere. I stifled a snort. Where did the leadership expect to get the materials for all of their projects?

Dad pulled up a chair and sat beside my mom. He casually crossed one leg over the other and flung an arm around her shoulder. They looked like a happy couple planning their next vacation. Delusional was the word that came to mind. They'd fallen for the propaganda. It was as if someone had drugged them.

Smirking, I checked my FlexPhone for incoming mail. Nothing from Zaq, but then, Dad had warned me that once we got inside the capsule, we'd be outside the range of communications. In my mind, it was one more proof that the leadership controlled everything we did, including conversations with people on the outside.

My nerves were like stretched-out rubber bands. I needed to keep from snapping, had to stay busy or I'd go nuts. I called up a virtual game on my FlexPhone, passed through the easy levels, and soon became bored with that too. With not much else going on, I went to my cubicle, pulled out my journal, and I begin to write.

Journal Entry, May 3, 9 p.m.

I'm waiting for my folks to grow tired of the propaganda machine and go to bed. Until that happens there's no way I can make it out of here without being seen.

My parents are spending an unreal amount of time in the sitting room. If I join them, I'll have to watch more of the leadership's fairy tales.

It wouldn't surprise me if Dad asked about my meetings with Mr. Crenshaw. I couldn't tell him much except that I'd grown fond of the old guy. He'd already taken me back to the early days of what life was like in America. The old guy could describe everything as clearly as if he'd experienced it yesterday.

I couldn't help but wonder what it would be like to attend a real school and carry my backpack and a lunch box with me to class. I could picture myself figuring math problems on a white board, playing soccer and baseball on a grassy athletic field, and dressing for a prom. And what about those shopping malls Crenshaw mentioned? Dozens of stores, all linked together with a big hall between them and all of it under a protective roof. Escalators to a second floor where more stores were linked together and a variety of clothes and shoes you could actually try on before buying them. Nothing like the government issued jeans and Tees we young people had to wear.

Crenshaw's descriptions left an indelible mark on my brain. They reinforced what my grandparents told me about the world they grew up in. How I wish we could reclaim those amazing remnants of a simpler life, before computers, electrons, holograms, and visionics.

> *One thing I know for sure, even after I get out of here, I may never be able to shake the nightmares I've experienced—the power failure, the feeling of claustrophobia, the tasteless food, Matt's persistence, and the dead bodies. I can't discuss any of it with anyone except Mr. Crenshaw.*
>
> *The pressure is getting unbearable. I can't breathe. It's getting late, and Mom and Dad are still snuggling in front of the virtual screen. I don't want to wait another day. Tomorrow Charlie will probably discover his gun is missing, and Matt will figure out that I took it.*
>
> *I'm glad my mom is back with us. I can leave knowing she's back to normal. I haven't seen her this happy in a long time. I can't write much more now. I'll take my journal with me, and I'll record everything that happens during this wild escapade. When I find Zaq, I'll have plenty more to write about. Maybe someday, when I'm old and gray, like Mr. Crenshaw, I'll relive my own adventure.*

I tucked away my journal, then I took a chance and peeked at the living area through the narrow opening at my door. My folks were still cuddling there. A wave of comfort flowed through me. I had two parents who loved each other and their kids. It was good to see them so contented, but why didn't they just go to bed?

I filled the next 15 minutes laying out the clothes I'd picked out. Black cargo pants, black T-shirt, black boots and socks, plus a black cap to hide my honey blonde hair.

I peeked through the door again. It looked like my parents might spend the entire night in the sitting room. I turned away and began to fill my backpack. I would need my journal, a couple pens, my FlexPhone, a change of underwear, the food I'd swiped from the dining hall, and most important, Charlie's gun and ammo. I loaded the gun and set the safety off.

With everything ready, I only needed to wait for the right moment. I flopped down on my bed and must have drifted off, because when I opened my eyes, the sitting room had gone dark.

I sucked in a long breath, then I checked the hologram clock on the wall. The time glowed red. It was 10 o'clock.

Struggling to my feet, I went to my door and peeked through the opening. My parents had left the sitting room. The virtual screen had been silenced. I tiptoed into the hall and snuck a look inside my folks' bedroom. They were huddled together under the quilt. Dad had flung a protective arm over Mom. I held my breath and listened. Their steady breathing told me they were asleep.

I drew back, careful not to make any noise, and headed for Peter's room. His night vision goggles were not where I had last seen them on the chair in the corner. But then, hadn't he been playing soldier? He could have dropped them anywhere before falling into bed.

I checked the floor around his bed, rummaged through his closet and ran my hands in the drawers of his bureau. He moved slightly and moaned. I froze. He fell to deep breathing again. I moved about the narrow room. Then I spotted a pile of his clothes, which he'd probably shed before going to bed. I searched through the pile. The goggles weren't there.

I didn't want to leave without those goggles. They weren't just a toy anymore. They would help me find my way in the dark woods.

I bit my lower lip and left Peter's cubicle. On a whim, I searched the sitting room, found nothing, and returned to Peter's tiny box of a room.

As I passed through the door, a blinking red light drew my attention to Peter's pillow. I stepped closer. The kid had gone to sleep wearing his goggles. They had slipped to one side, half on and half off his head. I needed to get them without disturbing my brother, but how?

I edged closer. Taking care not to jostle Peter's bed, slid close to him and carefully lifted the goggles, first one side, then the other. Suddenly, Peter turned toward me and let out a sigh. I held my breath, then I peered closer. He was still asleep. I backed away and put a little distance between us. He rolled to his other side and faced the wall with his back to me. I clasped the goggles to my chest and tiptoed out.

Back inside my own cubicle, I set the goggles on my bed and started to go for my pack beneath my bed, when I sensed a presence at the door. I turned to find my dad staring at me, his arms crossed.

"May I ask what you're doing?"

"Oh–uh–I–"

"Can't sleep, huh?" The lines on his forehead relaxed, but he was looking at the goggles. "What are you planning to do with those?"

I gave him a little shrug. "I can't sleep, Dad. I thought maybe if I had Peter's goggles, I could play a game on my Flex-Phone without disturbing anyone." I hated to lie to my father, but what choice did I have? I certainly couldn't tell him the truth. He'd never let me go.

"Well, don't wake the rest of us," he said. "And how about getting into your P.J.s?" He threw me a kiss and turned away. I stared after him with bated breath as he returned to his room.

He'd noticed my clothes—all black—and that I wasn't wearing my pajamas. Plus the boots. Who would wear boots when it was bedtime? But he hadn't mentioned them. Nothing seemed to surprise my dad, especially since we'd been locked inside that hole. Just, "get into your P.J.s," and that was all.

Though my father had disappeared inside his bedroom, I still couldn't move, not until I was sure he'd fallen asleep. It wasn't long before the reassuring sound of a tired man's snores emanated from Dad's room.

I drew more air into my lungs and slid my bag out from under the bed. I arranged some pillows under my blanket, satisfied that they resembled a real person sleeping there. Hopefully, it would keep my parents from pestering me, at least until breakfast.

Backpack slung over my shoulder and goggles in hand, I stalked past my folks' cubicle, blew them a kiss, then sent another to my brother. Inside the sitting room, I stuffed my backpack with more snack bars and several bottles of water, plus a pack of dried fruit. I positioned Charlie's gun on top by the flap, where I could get to it easily. Satisfied that I'd thought of everything, I slipped out the front door and into the hall, easing the door behind me with a soft click.

I looked up and down the hall, saw no one, and made my way along the dimly lit corridors. I made a few turns until I reached the dining hall and beyond, the kitchen. The entire area had fallen into a creepy stillness. Only a few hours ago the big room rattled with the washing of dishes and the voices of people cleaning up after feeding a crowd. I looked anxiously from one end to the other. There was no sign of any night guards, no movement of any kind. It was like walking into one of those old graveyards I'd read about, where people from my grandparents' day were buried.

A deathly cold had settled where not long ago fires burned on stovetops and workers bustled about loading up trays of food. Picking up my pace, I searched the shelves and drawers for a knife that was small enough to fit in my bag but sharp enough to do some damage. I found a drawer full of them and picked one.

From there, I headed for the outside door. To my relief, it opened easily and soundlessly. I looked around—behind me, and outside to the left and to the right. So far, I hadn't encountered a single soul. No guards. No cleanup staff. Nobody. How clumsy of our leadership. How had they overlooked that one route of escape?

Carefully, I stepped across the threshold to the outside and eased the door shut behind me. I was free.

Chapter Eighteen

After I made it outside, I paused to get my bearings. Forest was all around, though the trees were only starting to come alive with new growth. For now, they looked like dark towers with long, spindly arms, knobby fingers, and only a scant hint of leaves. To my right a paved drive circled around the dome toward the entry road off the highway. To my left the woods grew even more dense. I wouldn't dream of going in that direction.

Crenshaw's drawing would take me to the right, where I could follow the paved highway close to the mine entrance. Once I got my bearings, I could veer off the road where I was certain Zaq and his buddies had likely set up their headquarters. My heart pounded with the thought of seeing him again.

I slipped on Peter's night vision goggles. It was as if someone had turned on a floodlight. The gnarled and eerie shapes now looked more like trees, with tiny buds appearing on the tips of their branches.

Moving with caution, I passed through the pile of trash, wove between the debris, ignored the black body bags, and made my way to the clearing. I held my breath against the stench and focused my attention on a path that followed the road to the east. I needed to stay alert to nocturnal scavengers that might be roaming around. The garbage heap must have drawn hungry critters close to the dome. Hungry bears came to mind. So did starving dogs and wolves. And I thought about that wounded baboon still limping around out there. Nothing was more vicious than a wounded animal.

I ran my hand along the fabric of my backpack and located the outline of Charlie's gun, already loaded and with the safety switched off. One quick tug on the zipper and it would fall into my hand, ready to fire.

I kept moving forward, away from the stench to a place beyond the tree line where I could take a breath of fresh air. With relief, I inhaled the scent of pine needles, dewy blades of grass, and moist earth. They reminded me of Grandpa's farm.

After being cooped up in the time capsule for more than a week, I was thrilled to be able to walk around outside. Peter's goggles illuminated my surroundings like broad daylight. The tinted lenses cast a subtle green film over everything and enhanced the lines of every rock, every fallen tree, every pebble on the path before me. Though my backpack was weighted down with the provisions I'd packed, I struggled on, secure in the thought that I might need every single item.

Once I got far enough away from the restricted communications of the time capsule, I took out my FlexPhone and held it to my lips. "Call Zaq," I whispered.

Once again, "Unavailable," popped onto the screen along with my boyfriend's smiling face. I gazed at him for a few seconds, and a chilling thought stabbed my conscience. *What if I couldn't find him? What if he was already dead?*

Suppressing that fear, I tucked away my phone and walked on. Maybe when I got closer to the mine I'd be able to reach Zaq. With that thought impelling me forward, I moved ahead a little faster and with more confidence.

A light breeze stirred the branches overhead. I scanned the trees and shrubbery for any sign of the baboon's glowing red eyes. Sensing danger, I unzipped my pack and let the gun fall into my hand. The stock fit nicely in my palm, like the weapon had been made for me. I felt a surge of confidence, and I thanked God that my dad had taken me target shooting a few times, before leadership took away his guns. Inwardly, I was disappointed that the man had given in to all of their demands.

I walked on with confidence, turning my head from side-to-side, my eyes sweeping the trees, the scrub grass, the undergrowth bordering the path I was on. The stillness unnerved me. It was too quiet, too still out there, and way too menacing.

I looked up at the sky. Not a star. The moon hid behind a sweep of clouds. The entire scene sent an ominous chill through my body. For the first time, I began to wonder if my escape had been a good idea after all.

Of course, it was too late to change my mind. I forced my thoughts back on my mission. I had to find Zaq. Then the two of us would locate President Brooks and alert him to the danger threatening the time capsules. Sounded simple enough. But I hadn't yet completed the first stage of my mission, and that was to find my boyfriend.

I mentally recalled the way my family had traveled from the location of the mine to the time capsule. The distance had to be no more than a couple miles. An hour passed. I was certain I had walked nearly three miles. Then I spotted the odd-shaped boulder where Zaq and I had paused for a break on our last outing together. I withdrew a bottle of water from my pack and took a sip. I shut my eyes and imagined my boyfriend standing in front of me like he did that day, his face clouded with concern, his lips mouthing a sad good-bye.

"Zaq, I'm almost there," I whispered. I was surprised by the flood of tears that surfaced, slid beneath the goggles, and now ran down my face. Using the back of my sleeve I wiped them away. Then I gulped a little more water, put the bottle away, and followed the path a little farther.

It happened without warning. A pair of strong hands grabbed my left arm and pulled me to the ground. I dropped the gun. My goggles fell off, but even without them I knew my attacker. The clouds above parted and a wedge of moon cast its glow on the furry creature hovering inches from my face. Angry red eyes glared at me, the mouth opened and white fangs glistened in the light of the moon.

I wriggled out of my backpack and swung the bundle between me and the beast, like a shield. With one hand I held onto the bag, with the other I searched the ground for the gun. I found it beside my head, lifted it, then lost my grip again. The baboon let out an ear-piercing shriek, followed by a vicious snarl.

I shifted from side-to-side trying to avoid its sharp fangs. The beast let out another shriek that sounded like laughter. And I knew, he was playing with me, taunting me, like a cat toying with a mouse before driving its teeth into its prey's neck.

I flailed about for the gun. The baboon beat me to it. He picked it up and tossed it into the brush. My heart pounded with another realization. The creature was far too intelligent. What kind of monstrosities were those scientists creating in that lab? And what did they intend to do with them once the war ended and we were all released?

The baboon grabbed onto my pack and tried to wrench it out of my hands. I felt helpless. Images of Zaq and my mom and dad, and Peter came before me. I thought of Mr. Crenshaw and his mission. If the beast killed me, I wouldn't be able to fulfill the plan he had set before me. I wouldn't be able to find Brooks and tell him what Crenshaw said.

The animal shrieked again and shifted his grip on my pack. He tossed it aside. Gone was my shield. I held my breath, closed my eyes, and waited for the prick of its teeth. It never came.

Instead, the baboon let out an anguished cry and lurched backward. He fell off my chest. I struggled to sit upright, then I scooted back off the trail and found refuge amidst the brush. I searched the ground for Peter's goggles, located them in the tall grass, and fumbled to put them on. As I began to focus, two images came into view. The baboon's shadow was clearly delineated in the moonlight. It was about the size of a large dog, dark and furry, with eyes and teeth that flashed in the silver glow from the sky.

On the other side of the beast moved a lone figure, dressed in black, and flying about like a Ninja warrior. They looked like a pair of dancers performing a choreographed number, lunging, leaping, arms flailing. Black on black, dodging, striking. Then a sharp blade flashed in the light of the waning moon. Blood splattered. An angry snarl erupted from the baboon, followed by a piercing shriek, and the animal collapsed to the ground. For only a few seconds, it writhed on the forest floor. With both hands, the dark figure raised the knife above his head and plunged it into the baboon's chest. Then the beast lay still.

I crawled around and found the handgun, raised it and pointed it at the dark figure, surprised to find he also was wearing night vision goggles. But his pair was a military version.

"You don't want to use that." My rescuer said, nodding toward the gun in my hand. "You're safe now." The voice was familiar. It stopped my heart.

"Zaq!"

He removed his goggles and grinned.

I couldn't believe it. I'd found my boyfriend—or rather, he'd found me. I leaped from the ground and rushed into his arms now spread in welcome.

"Zaq, I've been calling you on my FlexPhone. Why didn't you answer?"

He backed away but held onto my arms. "I didn't want to send out a signal and let the enemy troops find us."

He held out his hand, palm up, his eyes on the gun. I handed it to him. He bent over and lifted my backpack from the ground, then slipped the gun inside it. Without another word, he took my hand and led me into the brush, farther along the path, then veered off to the entrance of the mine.

I was in shock. I had just survived a wild baboon's attack. I ran my hands over my arms and legs feeling for injuries. Though I was badly shaken, I found no broken bones, no cuts, no teeth marks. Still, I couldn't stop trembling.

"I was almost at the mine when that beast jumped me," I told Zaq. "Almost there, only a few yards to go, and I nearly lost my life."

He paused on the path and searched my face. "Why did you come, Livie?" he said, and I couldn't help thinking how handsome he was, despite his frown. "Why did you leave the safety of the time capsule?"

"It's not as safe as you might think."

His frown deepened. "What do you mean?"

"Things have been happening in there, Zaq. Strange things. People have been dying. The power went out. Two of those mutant baboons got free. One tore up a few people inside the capsule, before he was killed. The other got away into the woods."

"You haven't answered my question yet. Why did you *leave*?"

"For two reasons. First, I wanted to find you. I'd been planning to escape from the minute I stepped inside that capsule. No, actually, from the moment I found out I was going there."

Zaq stopped walking. "You're gonna have to explain that one a little more," he said. "But, you can't stay here, Livie. This place isn't safe either. As I told you before, we have a fully equipped army. We're gonna fight. That alone will bring the battle right inside the mine."

"So, I'll fight with you."

He raised an eyebrow. "C'mon, Livie. I'll be so busy trying to protect you, it'll put my men in danger. You have to go back to the time capsule, where you'll be safe. It will only be for a little while. When it's over, I'll come for you. I promise."

I placed my hands on my hips and took a defiant stance. "I'm not going back." I crossed my arms. "By the way, Zaq. How did you know I was out here and in danger?"

He chuckled. "I knew because of Martino."

"Martino?"

"He's a member of our group, a nucleaputer tech. Wait till you see the contraption he put together using solar power. Those calls you made—though I couldn't answer, Martino was able to track your precise location. I knew exactly where you were at every given moment. When you got close, I came out to find you. Fortunately, I was armed."

"I'm not going back," I insisted with a stomp of my foot.

"You have to."

"No, Zaq. There's something else."

I told him about Mr. Crenshaw's request that we go to White Sulphur Springs and find Harmon Brooks. Zaq's eyebrows furrowed in confusion.

"Harmon Brooks? The President?"

"Yes, Mr. Crenshaw said he may be able to take back control and fix the mess America is in. There may not be any need for you and your friends to fight. Not if Harmon Brooks can get involved. He's done it before. He can do it again."

He blinked at me, then he frowned in thought. "I don't know, Livie. We're almost ready to move out."

"Please, let's just try this. If we can't find Brooks, then you can follow up with your plan."

He appeared to ponder this for a moment. "In that case, I guess we'll have to go," he said with a shrug. "If it means saving the country without having to fight, we should at least try. But, I'm going to need more information."

We had reached the mine entrance, but it appeared to be boarded up. I took a step back and looked around thinking there must be another way in.

"What's going on, Zaq?"

"Hold on." He let go of my hand and pressed his weight against the boards. They shifted to the right, exposing a large opening and beyond, only darkness. Grabbing my arm, he guided me inside. Then, he turned around and shifted the boards back in place, shutting us in and leaving the sounds of the forest outside.

I waited for the overwhelming rise of heat that usually engulfed me whenever I was caught inside anything smaller than a bathroom. It started with the pounding of my heart, followed by the shaking of my hands and the weakening of my knees. But none of those things happened. But I was with Zaq, and I knew I was safe, just like when he took me inside that cave many months before.

My eyes adjusted to the dim light. The mine was illuminated by torches attached to the wall. A set of tracks ran ahead of us, dipped down a long slope, and disappeared into darkness. An old mine cart stood idle on the tracks.

"Get in," Zaq told me.

I didn't hesitate, just climbed aboard, placed my pack on my lap and slid over to make room for Zaq. He squeezed in beside me, pulled the lever, and we were off, down the slope, around a curve, and down, down, down, like a miniature roller coaster, until we reached a large compartment at the bottom. I gathered my composure and looked around. The well-lit space looked like a hotel lobby, broad floor with sofas, small tables, and other furnishings. I began to breathe easier. Some of Zaq's team members were sitting at desks in front of computers. Others moved about, stacking guns, sorting through ammo, and arranging different sized knives on tables in the middle of the room. Several stopped what they were doing, nodded in our direction, then they went back to work.

I climbed out of the car and looked around. The stone walls were decorated with framed paintings and sconces bearing glowing candles. Somehow, Zaq and his guys had raided a hotel and had given their hideout a cozy feel. It could have been someone's office or the living room in a wealthy estate. I was amused. Zaq and his buddies must have started acquiring the furnishings months before the drone attacks. Yet, he never told me.

Dark tunnels ran off in all directions, leading to other parts of the giant hole in the ground. I could only imagine what else Zaq and his buddies had accomplished down there.

My boyfriend took my hand. I could hardly speak for the joy of being with him again. He led me down a tunnel to the right. We walked for maybe five minutes, with Zaq still holding me and my eyes focusing on the dimly lit trail ahead. The tunnel ended in a spacious room that had been furnished with beds, tables, seating areas, refrigeration units, and virtual monitors bracketed to the walls. It was like entering an underground apartment house, more than a hundred feet below the forest. The hum of the refrigerators alerted me to the possibility that somehow these young geniuses had found a way to supply power to their hideout.

Zaq's teammates were everywhere. Lying on the cots, sitting at the table, grouped together in tiny huddles. Zaq made introductions, but there was no way I'd remember all the names. Except for a few who stood out.

"This is our nucleaputer genius, Martino," said Zaq. "And this is Fabrizio, a former TV chef turned rebel. He makes sure we get fed. This is Carter, our weapons expert. He's amassed a whole air force of military drones. He must have several thousand now. All we need to do is equip them with explosives, and they can do our fighting for us. James is our cartographer. He lays out huge maps and keeps track of where the enemy troops are holed up. Most of the enemy's big honchos have settled into state capital buildings, what's left of the White House, and nearly every military fort in America. We're trying to come up with a way to blitz them all."

I looked around and made an immediate observation. "There are no females here. Only guys."

"That's right, Livie. We're keeping focused." Zaq blinked a smile at me, then his gaze filled with compassion. "You can't stay, honey. You have to go back to the time capsule and warn your parents. Just give me the old guy's instructions, and I'll take care of finding Brooks."

"Not a chance," I said, a pronounced stubbornness in my voice. "I'm here to stay, Zaq. I went through too much to get out of that place. I'm *not* going back."

He placed his hands on my shoulders and looked me in the eye. "Livie," he said, more serious than I'd ever seen him. "As much as I'd love to have you with me, it's not a good idea. You have to go back and let me do what I need to do."

"Are you aware of the leadership's plan?"

"What plan?"

"For me."

"No, what exactly do they have planned for you?"

"I'm a procreator, Zaq. A procreator. Do you know what that means? By the time I leave that place, I'll have had at least one child. Maybe two. But not with you. With someone else."

The reality sank in. His jaw dropped. Concern flooded into his eyes.

"That's why I can't go back. So tell me, is that what *you* want?" I challenged him.

He shook his head, slowly at first, then with more emphasis. "No. Of course not."

He wrapped both arms around me, and I snuggled against his chest.

"Okay for now, Livie. We can go together, find Harmon Brooks, and give him Crenshaw's message. Maybe you can stay there with Brooks, and I can come back here. We'll just have to face that decision when we get to it."

"I have one question, Zaq."

"What is it?"

"How are we gonna travel nearly 300 miles, and fast?"

He got a twinkle in his eye, and he smiled like he had a secret. "You'll see," was all he said.

Chapter Nineteen

For the time being, Zaq needed to meet with some of his *commandos,* as he liked to call the hodgepodge of warriors he'd amassed. I looked them over and laughed to myself. Some were outfitted in full military gear. They looked like they were about to conduct a raid. Others wore jeans and khakis, padded vests, and shirts of all designs and colors, kind of like the farmer's militia that rallied behind Paul Revere. But they were well-organized, with each group working on its own individual project.

Zaq appeared to be in charge. He gave directions to some, approved charts the cartographers had mapped out, and stood ready to answer questions whenever one of his *soldiers* approached him. I was impressed, even proud, to see how efficient Zaq's militia had become in only a matter of weeks.

He left me there, among the sofas and beds, so I could rest. But I couldn't sleep, so I pulled out my journal and dropped onto one of the corner chairs, away from all the activity. It was time for another entry.

May 4, 2058, 7 a.m.
I've left the time capsule, and after a harrowing night, nearly losing my life to the claws and teeth of a wild baboon, I made it to the mine with my boyfriend, Zaq. He's my hero. He rescued me from a monstrous baboon and brought me to this safe place.
Zaq's underground military facility is beyond awesome. There must be a hundred guys in his army. They work in groups,

some on individual projects, but without making much noise, except when they get one of their machines running, the cheers erupt all over the place and a brief celebration takes place with lots of back-slapping and praises.

The scent of fresh-ground coffee beans has drawn me to the little kitchen. Fabrizio made coffee and some type of fantastic fruit pastry. I don't know how they acquired all the food, but the kitchen shelves are stocked full. Fabrizio doesn't seem to mind my poking around his domain. I open cupboard doors, peek into the electromagnetic-powered refrigeration unit, and check the pantry. There's enough cold water to keep everyone hydrated for what could be a long siege. And the non-perishable stock appears to be more than sufficient for Zaq's hungry crew. They certainly aren't going to starve. In fact, they're probably eating better than we did in the time capsule. There are no freeze-dried package foods down here. Somehow, this little army has been able to acquire everything they need to survive for many months, if not years. I can only guess they must have emptied out one of the government-owned warehouses.

I move freely from the kitchen into other areas. Martino sits hunched over his nucleaputer, and I can't help but wonder what miracles he might perform. Genius may be the only word for him. At least Zaq thinks so.

With no women here, all the guys seem totally intent on their individual duties. An electric charge hovers, like they're ready to spring into action. Then there are the individual jobs. One young man is squatting in the corner oiling AK-47s, restoring Colt 45s, and adjusting laser guns. Many of their arms are remnants from past wars, but still usable. A gray-haired man is sitting at a table sorting ammo into categories. Another guy is mending torn uniforms and bullet-proof vests. And Zaq—my hero—is moving about the chamber overseeing each job and interacting with his men.

As young as he is, my boyfriend has taken on a major task. He especially seems proud of the military drones they've piled in a separate chamber. I find a little comfort knowing those tiny airships have to make up for the lack of actual soldiers. What chance will this tiny army have using outdated weapons against a well-equipped adversary? There are a lot of weapons typically used for hand-to-hand combat—knives, clubs, bayonets, and grenades. Like Zaq said, many of the battles are going to end up face-to-face with enemy troops. That makes me nervous because it means lives will be lost.

Zaq has agreed we need to follow Crenshaw's plan first. He wants to leave tomorrow evening for White Sulphur Springs, West Virginia. I have Mr. Crenshaw's map. Crude as it is, the old guy was careful to jot down specific landmarks to help us find our way. I have no idea how we'll be able to travel those 300 miles, but Zaq told me not to worry. He had this silly little grin on his face, which left me believing he'd already figured out some type of transportation, though I saw no sign of anything useful, except perhaps the mine tram. He assured me we won't be walking the distance.

Zaq wants to leave at sunset and travel throughout the night, eliminating the chance we'd be seen.

I set aside my journal and shut my eyes. There was so much activity in the cave I couldn't help but pick up on the excitement. But I became exhausted. I figured I'd be lucky to get a couple hours of sleep. All I could think about was the kind of mission that lay ahead of us. Zaq and I were going to head out in no-man's land. We had a map, a final destination, and—Zaq assured me—the right transportation. I had embarked on an adventure with no idea how it was going to end. Could we actually reach Harmon Brooks? Were we really going to meet the former President of the United States? Mr. Crenshaw thought so. The old guy had more confidence in me than I had in myself. I only knew if Zaq was with me I could tackle anything.

✝✝✝

Before I knew it, Zaq was shaking me awake. I stretched my arms and legs, yawned, and peered up into a pair of smiling brown eyes.

"C'mon, Livie, we need to get going." Zaq's whisper stirred me to life. He bent close and kissed me.

"It's 7 o'clock, Livie. It'll be dark soon. If we leave now we can reach White Sulphur Springs before 5 a.m."

I frowned at him. "That's not possible."

"We have transportation."

"If you say so," I pictured one of those obsolete gasoline-fueled trucks like my grandfather refused to give up. We could go maybe 50 miles in one of those dinosaurs. Certainly not 300 miles.

Zaq gave me time to freshen up. Their makeshift bathroom was equipped with a port-a-potty and a pitcher of water for washing. I emerged to find him leaning against a nearby wall, his hands in his pockets and one ankle crossed over the other. Dressed all in black, he looked more like a cat burglar than a rebel warrior. He grabbed my backpack and led me to the old mine car for another ride, this time back to the top. Coming downhill was one thing, but I doubted that dilapidated contraption could make the climb to the surface. Still, at Zaq's command, I climbed inside and braced for the jolt.

As soon as Zaq was seated beside me, he hit the lever, and the car lurched ahead and began a steady climb to the top with only a few jerks along the way. At one point, the track got steeper and we approached a curve. The car slowed to a crawl, then surprisingly, it picked up speed, then tackled the last rise and reached the end of the tunnel.

We left the mine shaft through the boarded up door, which easily slid back in place. The sun slid beyond the horizon and the gray of evening took hold. We both donned night-vision goggles—Zaq with his military version and me wearing Peter's toy set. I blinked my eyes, adjusted to the green film and took in the scenery.

"It's a good thing you brought that." Zaq tapped my goggles. "We're gonna be traveling through some dense forest. I'll need your help looking out for obstacles."

He took my arm and led me around the right side of the mine entrance to a large clump of shrubbery, and beyond an open field littered with handlebars and knobby wheels. With a fanfare, Zaq spread his arms.

"Ta-da!" he sang out.

He began to rummage through the piles of debris and came up with a fully-assembled motorcycle. I'd seen images of those things. They had become obsolete about ten years ago when powered skateboards rose in popularity. Being far smaller, those little boards could be stored anywhere. Just tuck one under your arm—then, when you're ready to travel, they're ready to go. They didn't need gasoline or maintenance of any kind. Fueled by electromagnetic charges their power held for days. I never had any desire to own one, but Peter had been asking.

Zaq selected a Harley, or so it said in big letters on the side. He pulled it into the clearing. The handlebars were bent, the seat cushion was frayed but it was long enough to accommodate two people. It had a broken mileage gauge, two shattered mirrors, a worn saddlebag, and badly deflated tires.

I burst out laughing. "You're kidding, right? Are we supposed to travel 300 miles on that thing?"

"Hey!" Zaq said with a mock frown. "Don't make fun of our transportation. It's got a full tank of gas, and aside from some cosmetics, it's a dependable form of transportation." He set about swapping parts from other bent and broken bikes, and was able to find a good set of tires. It took a little over an hour, but when he finished we had a perfectly functional motorcycle.

I shook my head in wonder. "Zaq, I think you can make any piece of junk into a treasure. But won't it run out of gas before we reach our destination?"

He shrugged. "Don't worry, Livie. We'll probably only have to fuel up once. We'll just keep an eye out for one of those defunct gas stations or an abandoned vehicle. If they have fuel, we can siphon it. That's what this hose is for." He dangled a length of rubber tubing in front of me, then coiled it up and stuffed it in the saddlebag.

Without another word, he rooted around the junk pile for two helmets, brushed off the cobwebs, and handed one to me. Wrinkling my nose, I gave it another polish, then turned it upside down and shook out bits of dirt and debris. Zaq donned his helmet and gave me an encouraging nod. Holding my breath, I placed the helmet on my head, adjusted the strap, and offered my boyfriend a big smile. Last of all, he grabbed my pack and shoved it inside the worn saddlebag on top of his siphoning hose.

Then Zaq gave me a wink and a crooked smile, swung a leg over the seat, and finally extended his hand, like a gentleman of the Victorian era, and helped me onto the seat behind him. He planted his feet firmly on either side and turned to look at me.

"Ready for the ride of your life, Livie?"

"Ready," I said, my voice weak. I slipped my arms around his waist. Being close to him like that, I felt a surge of confidence. I rested my head on his shoulder. He pressed his foot to the pedal and squeezed the handlebar controls. The engine emitted a series of clicks and pops. Zaq pumped his foot, pushed a button, and to my surprise the old bike rumbled to life. A slight roll backward, followed by a lurch forward, the front wheel lifted off the ground, and the back wheel kicked up a bunch of dirt and gravel. I tightened my hold on Zaq as we took off like we'd been shot out of a canon. Only one thought troubled me. The thing was so noisy, I didn't know how we were going to travel 300 miles without being seen or heard.

For a long time, we bounced over bumpy back roads, staying mostly within the shelter of the forest. We made a few sharp turns, veered on and off the paved highway, and scooted back into the brush. I found I had to dip my head now and then to avoid low-hanging branches, and I clenched my teeth whenever we hit ruts or bumps on the trail. Zaq drove like he'd been raised around motorcycles. He leaned with the turns and lifted off the seat whenever we approached a rise. I tried to do the same, glued to him as I was. I figured, as long as I bound myself to Zaq, I wouldn't get flung off. As for being a lookout, I'd already failed. But I'd acquired a little understanding of what my grandfather raved about when he talked about taking a cross-country trip on a Harley.

After a while, I began to relax and even found myself smiling. I was getting a taste of the freedom I'd so desperately wanted. I could hardly wait to tell Mr. Crenshaw about it.

At one point, I decided I should keep an eye out for obstacles. I raised my head and peered over Zaq's shoulder. The bike had no light but Peter's goggles gave me a good view of the trail ahead. I glanced at the gas gauge. If it wasn't broken, we still had plenty of fuel. Comforted, I rested my cheek against Zaq's shoulder and was reassured by his strong muscles. They flexed with every move of his arms and tightened whenever he needed to control the bike over uneven terrain. I didn't have to live in fear anymore. No matter what happened, I was with Zaq, and I felt safe.

† † †

We'd been on the trail for nearly three hours. We were totally alone, never saw one vehicle. Zaq had to stop twice at abandoned off-road gas stations. Using the hose he carried in the saddlebag, he tapped into a couple of the pumps and, by sucking on one end, he was able to fill our tank. With barely enough time to stretch my legs or clear my head, we took off again. My entire body ached from all the bumps and jostles and from straining to keep my balance as we rolled into every turn.

Another hour passed. Then another. "Can we stop for a bit, Zaq?" I called out. "I need to stretch my legs."

He turned toward me and smiled. The machine beneath us sputtered and then went silent. Zaq pulled off the trail onto an open pasture. A three-quarter moon cast a silver glow on the spread of grass. I slid off the seat. I staggered on rubbery legs to a soft place and dropped down with a sigh. Zaq joined me there, also heaving a sigh as he lowered his body to the ground. We removed our helmets and goggles and stretched out, both of us sighing with relief. Lying close to him with our shoulders touching, I stared up at the star-dappled sky and smiled. All the while, during my *incarceration*, I dreamed about being with Zaq again. I inhaled deeply of the fresh country air. Somehow, I felt far away from the war, from the regime that had taken over, from the confinement of the time capsule.

"I wish we could stay like this forever," I murmured.

Zaq breathed a long sigh. "Yeah, me too."

"Do you think we'll be able to find Harmon Brooks?" I ventured to ask. "And will he really be able to take over again?"

Zaq rolled onto his side and faced me. "Livie, I never try to second guess what's coming. I can only do my part and hope everyone else does too." He smiled sweetly and brushed a curl from my forehead. "Right now, all I care about is that I have you by my side. You gave up so much to be with me. You could be safe inside the time capsule, but you turned your back on a promising life, and you've committed your future to me—uncertain as it is."

I slid closer to him and placed a hand on his chest, found comfort in the pounding of his heart. "That wasn't security, Zaq. The time capsule was never a safe place for me. It was a prison. And that promising future? It promised me only heartbreak. I couldn't stand to think I'd be bearing another guy's child, and all the while I'd be missing you."

He leaned closer until our faces were only an inch apart. I closed my eyes and received his kiss, then waited for another, but he rose from the ground.

"We need to get moving," he said, brushing bits of grass from his clothes. "If we time this right, we'll be at our destination in about two hours, just before sunrise. Hopefully, we'll be able to complete our mission."

The next two hours went pretty much as before with the

bike bouncing over ruts in the trail and me holding onto Zaq. He located another abandoned gas station and siphoned a few more drops of precious fuel. The odor turned my stomach. So did the black exhaust that poured from the back of the bike when we started out again. I doubted people ever survived for very long back then without the clean energy we enjoyed. I'd heard about several deadly diseases that existed thirty years ago. Cancer, asthma, and all kinds of allergies. Each of them had been wiped out once people stopped smoking and got rid of harmful chemicals. Then there were the new medications, that powder that came from the surface of the moon, and other concoctions discovered by scientists in a lab.

Thanks to my dad, an alternative power had been developed. Now, as I choked on the puffs of exhaust from the bike, I appreciated my father's gift to the world even more. It's no wonder he was selected for the new build.

I leaned close to Zaq. "How much longer?" I shouted over the roar of the engine.

His shoulders lifted in a shrug. "Relax, Livie," he shouted back at me. "You wanted to come along. You're gonna have to relax and let me do the driving."

He turned slightly for only a second and took his eyes off the trail ahead. At that moment, we hit a huge tree root lying across the path. I hadn't seen it, and I'd distracted Zaq. The bike soared over the root, did a half-flip, and flung me into the brush. I dropped like an old rag doll. The bike and Zaq kept going. They tumbled head-over-heels farther down the trail and crashed in a tangled heap. The engine stopped roaring. Except for the crickets in the brush, there wasn't a sound.

I lay very still and mentally checked every part of my body— my arms, my legs, my back and neck. Except for a few minor aches, I was fine. Slowly, I raised myself to a sitting position and removed my helmet and goggles. I touch my cheek and found blood there. I pressed the wound to stop the flow, but it oozed freely around my fingers.

I checked Peter's goggles. The strap was torn, and there was a slight crack in the frame, but they appeared to be intact. I struggled to my feet and stared down the path in the direction of the crumpled bike. Frantic to find Zaq, I returned the goggles to my head and limped down the trail. I searched everywhere for any sign of my boyfriend. A groan rose from somewhere up ahead. I drew in a breath. Zaq was pinned underneath the bike.

I lunged forward. "Zaq, Zaq! Are you okay?" I bent close and tried to ease the bike off him. It was heavy and terribly cumbersome.

I searched around us for some type of lever. I spotted a broken tree limb, limped over to it, and dragged it toward the bike. Working with both hands, I jammed the limb under the heaviest part where the engine was, and I pressed down with all my might. The bike moved slightly. Zaq let out another moan. I placed all of my weight on the branch and gave it another push. The bike shifted. The branch split in half. And the pile of crumpled metal rolled off of Zaq's body. He lay very still.

Chapter Twenty

"Zaq!" A cold fear rushed through me. I leaned close, tried to find a pulse, pressed his wrist, touched his neck. I thought I felt something. "Answer me, Zaq. Please, be okay."

His eyes were closed. He didn't move. Didn't appear to be breathing. I held my own breath and kept an eye on his chest, hoping he would take a breath. Then, feeling utterly helpless, I collapsed on top of him and sobbed out another plea. "Please, wake up, Zaq. Breathe. Say something." I sobbed out my grief. "Don't leave me. I can't complete this journey without you. I can't complete *life* without you."

I leaned back on my heels and looked him over. Did his chest move, or had I imagined it? Was he breathing? I looked toward the sky and sent up a silent prayer.

Did God even hear me? I didn't pray all that much anymore. No one did. There were no Sunday morning services anymore. No prayer meetings. The leadership had gradually forced them out. Pastor Getz was one of the last to go, and I had no idea where he was. The change came quickly. Few people attended church anymore. They lived by their own rules. They depended on the leadership for everything.

I gazed up at the sky and sent up another prayer, weak as it was. "Please, God, if you're really there, please heal Zaq. Help us."

The world around us was turning from pitch black to a dull gray, revealing the first hints of morning light. I stared off past the brambles and the trees and looked to the east. With the rising of the sun our nighttime camouflage would be gone.

Activity would resume on the highway. The enemy would have no trouble spotting us. Zaq and I could be taken as prisoners or even killed.

I returned my attention to my boyfriend. He still hadn't moved. Tears spilled from my eyes. I collapsed in a sobbing heap and mumbled his name, "Zaq," though all hope was gone.

Out of the blue, I remembered the CPR course I took when I was 10 years old. Of course, we only practiced on a dummy. But, I figured, it's worth a try. I straddled Zaq and started chest compressions. I counted, one-two-three-four, then I leaned back and took a three second break. I repeated the cadence several times.

I couldn't believe when Zaq let out a groan. His chest rose and fell, without my help. I checked again for a pulse and found one.

"Zaq," I whispered.

His eyelashes fluttered open. He turned to face me, and though pain distorted his face, he managed to smile.

"What happened?" he mumbled.

"Zaq! We had an accident. The bike."

"Oh, yeah," he moaned. "I messed up."

"No, it was my fault. I distracted you, and we hit something on the trail."

He tried to lift his head, then fell back against the stony path. Grunting, he ran his hands over his arms and legs, then felt his rib cage. "I think I broke something."

"What, Zaq? What did you break?"

"I don't know. I'm in a lot of pain. Mostly my right leg and my side." He pressed his hands to his forehead. "My helmet. Where's my helmet? And my goggles?"

"I don't know, Zaq. They fell off, I guess."

"I remember now. The bike. I flew off the darn thing." He let out a another groan, then squinted at me in the waning darkness. "Livie, are you hurt too?"

"No, Zaq. I fell off, then you and the bike went down."

"You're sure?"

I nodded. "I'm sure. I'm fine, Zaq."

He breathed a sigh of relief. "You're gonna have to go on without me, Livie."

"No. I won't leave you."

"We're almost there. According to my calculations the bunker is only a couple of miles down the road. You can do it, Livie. But you're gonna have to go alone."

"No way, Zaq. I'm not going without you."

"The bike's useless. I don't know if I can make it on foot."

"You have to, Zaq. You have to try. Come on. Let me help you."

I placed a hand under his arm and gently tugged. He pushed away from the ground with his other hand. Slowly, grunting and groaning, he managed to get to a sitting position.

I looked him over. There were no protruding bones, no bloody scrapes. "Are you sure you broke something, Zaq?"

"I don't know, Livie. I ache all over, especially my right leg."

"Your leg?"

He stretched out, wiggled his feet, pulled his knees up and ran his hands down the length of his legs. Except for occasionally wincing, he shook his head.

"I think I'm okay," he said. "Give me a few more minutes."

I looked up at the sky. The trees stood out in black silhouettes against the graying background. Daylight was moving in fast.

"We need to get going," I said, near panic.

"I'll try," Zaq groaned.

"Wait," I said. "Just sit for a minute. It might save time if we take one more look at Crenshaw's map."

I crawled over to the bike, now just a mangled pile of metal. I pulled my pack from the saddlebag, then returned to Zaq's side with Crenshaw's map. I spread it open in front of him.

In the light of dawn, the lines on the map stood out like a giant spider web.

"Remember when we stopped a while ago to steal more gas?" Zaq said, excitement entering his voice.

"Yeah, I remember. You said it would be our last stop."

He nodded. "I noticed a couple of road signs back there. If I'm not mistaken, White Sulphur Springs should be about two miles down the road."

"Two miles? Can you walk two miles?"

"Maybe. I guess we'd better find out."

He struggled to his feet and forced an optimistic grin. I grabbed my pack and flung it over my shoulder. I located another broken limb and handed it to him.

"Here. This should make a good walking stick for you."

Grasping the branch in his right hand, Zaq rested his left arm on my shoulder. "Let's go," he said.

We limped together down the path in the direction of White Sulphur Springs. We left behind our helmets—no need for them now—but I hung onto Peter's night-vision goggles. We kept to the path, a short distance from the highway.

"Eventually, we're gonna have to move onto the main road," Zaq confessed. "It's the only way we can reach the bunker."

The farther we walked, the less dependent Zaq became on me. Though he continued to favor his right leg, he picked up his pace, and using the walking stick, he moved on ahead. I kept watching him, prepared to close the gap between us if needed.

After a half hour, we left the safety of the brush and stepped onto the main highway.

"Keep an eye out for traffic," Zaq cautioned. "Man or beast," he added.

My heart fluttered, but I kept walking.

The rumble of a vehicle sounded on the road behind us. Zaq tugged at my arm. We stumbled together behind the tree line out of sight. Moments later, a nuclear-powered Robotruck rolled over the rise and came into view. The sleek machine floated past us. Anxiety gripped my heart. The monstrous vehicle barreled down the road, stirring the air and causing shrubs to bend and trees to sway.

"Let's stay hidden," Zaq whispered, pulling me down.

I pressed my face against his chest, held my breath and waited until the monster grew smaller in the distance.

"You okay?" Zaq purred.

I nodded but couldn't speak.

"Try calling Harmon Brooks. I think we're close enough."

I pulled my FlexPhone out of my pack and cued in the contact information Crenshaw had printed on the map. An image came up of a man who was older than my father but younger than Crenshaw. I remembered the aging president, a balding man with magical green eyes. The word *Unavailable* appeared beside him.

"He's probably still in bed," Zaq said with a chuckle. "It's coming up on 6 a.m. Let's give it another half-hour and try again."

The world around us had fallen silent. Zaq and I made our way back onto the highway. We found the paved road far easier to navigate. Though he was moving easier, Zaq still favored his right leg. As for me, aside from a few aches and pains I didn't have any serious injuries. I pulled a water bottle from my pack, took a few sips and handed it to Zaq. He finished it off and tossed the empty into the woods. I huffed. At one time, I had joined an anti-littering campaign. Now such violations no longer troubled me. The bio-degradable bottle would one day disintegrate and become part of the forest, and even if it didn't, I had no desire to preserve the landscape for a government I didn't respect.

For the next fifteen minutes we didn't see another vehicle. But as we topped the next rise in the road we caught sight of our destination. The Greenbrier Resort. We drew closer and found the parking lot full of Robotrucks like the one that passed us on the highway. I paused to take in the entire scene. What once must have been a pristine setting with gently rolling hills and a well-kept lawn had fallen to ruin. Briars and brambles covered what once must have been a welcoming entryway. Out front of the hotel, patches of mud and weeds had replaced the flowerbeds, and closer to the front door stood large pots of burnt and brittle plants that may have stood tall and proud at one time. The walkways lay hidden beneath leaves and debris, and the front of the building looked anything but inviting.

The hotel was as wide as a city block. I imagined it once was quite majestic, but now it was hidden beneath a covering of soot and slime. Broken windows and cracked walls painted a rather eerie picture. And, like a specter of doom, fluttering from a tall pole in front of the resort's main entrance was China's national flag—a huge red rectangle with a big yellow star and a half-circle of four smaller stars.

I froze in my tracks, hardly able to breathe.

Zaq let out a disgusted grunt. "So, they've taken over what once was a magnificent hotel and turned it into a mausoleum." He shook his head. "Look how many Robotrucks surround the place. There must be a whole contingent of enemy soldiers inside. I guess that eliminates the inside entrance as a way for us to get into the bunker. We'll have to use the west side delivery door."

"I don't care," I said and headed toward the right side of the building. There was no path to speak of. I stepped carefully over deep ruts in the soil, and a variety of rocks and stones that now littered the once well-manicured lawn. Zaq limped by my side but kept a steady pace. Together we slunk between clusters of trees, most of them scorched to death by recent bombings. The last of their branches drooped low to the ground, and there was no sign of spring growth anywhere. By now, buds should have begun to show, and there should have been an expectation in the air that fruit would soon be available. The entire orchard appeared to be slowly dying. How sad that the Greenbrier Resort had lost its youth. Never again would it open its arms to guests, never again hear the tick of a golf ball or the pop of a celebratory cork.

A tear came to my eye, and I turned to face Zaq. "This is

what war is doing to America," I said, my voice breaking. "This is what the leadership has accomplished. The party that fought against Brooks is also destroying the rest of us." I couldn't restrain my bitterness. "What do you think, Zaq? Will Harmon Brooks actually be able to help? Will he have the resources to take back the country?" I nodded toward the parking lot. "Those Robotrucks tell me the enemy is far too strong."

He gave a little shrug. Doubt clouded his honey speckled eyes. "Didn't the old man tell you Brooks could do it?"

"Sure, but just like you said, Crenshaw is an old man. So is Brooks. What can they do against such power?"

We skirted the brick path that led to the front entry and circled around to the back. We hunched down within the decaying shrubbery and kept to the shelter of the tree line. I scanned the area for the green walls Crenshaw had described. Then I saw them, behind a copse of trees, running alongside a downward slope—two rows of twelve-foot-high panels painted an ugly green and partially hidden within clumps of shrubbery. The path continued down between the two walls. Crenshaw had been right. There was the *High Voltage* sign. I recalled he'd said it was fake, just a diversion to keep out unwelcome visitors.

At the end was the concrete door he'd mentioned. It nearly disappeared from view, for it had been constructed flush with the mountainside. The sun filtered its rays through a row of trees. I pulled out my FlexPhone. It was 6:30. Time to try Harmon Brooks again. This time, remembering Mr. Crenshaw's instructions, I texted the former president first—two simple words: Chess Match.

Then I called. Instead of the word, *Unavailable,* a holographic image of a balding man rose up before us, close enough for us to touch, if that were possible. He frowned in annoyance.

"State your business," he demanded, narrowing his eyes.

"President Brooks, I'm Olivia Jackson. I'm here with a friend, Zaq Myer. Mr. Crenshaw sent us."

The mention of Crenshaw's name set off a sparkle in those green eyes, and the frown on Harmon's forehead disappeared.

"Crenshaw?!" His eyes began to water. "Andrew Crenshaw?"

"Yes."

"How do I know he sent you? What proof do you have?"

I held up Crenshaw's ring. Brooks did the same with his own matching ring on the third finger of his right hand.

For a moment, Brooks lost his composure, seemingly overwhelmed with emotion. "I-I thought he was dead. Thought the leadership would have killed him by now, or maybe he died of an age-related illness, the old codger." He chuckled and his eyes misted over.

"He's very much alive," I said. "The leadership has been tapping into his vault of a brain. Mr. Crenshaw has been dictating a wealth of historic information, and I just write it all down. He's one of the chosen people living in a time capsule in Pennsylvania along with my family. He sent me to find you, to give you some information."

Brooks wiped a tear from his cheek and straightened, like he was attempting to regain his composure. "And where are the two of you?"

"We're at the delivery door on the west side of the bunker."

"Wait there."

Brooks' image shimmered and vanished. The connection was gone.

I put my FlexPhone away and moved closer to the big concrete wall. Moments later there was a loud crunch from the other side, and the door swung open.

"Come inside." Brooks waved us through the door. "And hurry." He kept watch on the area behind us.

It amazed me that by simply showing Crenshaw's ring and uttering his name, we were able to bypass any security measures. Here we were, visiting with the President, and there was no background check, no interrogation, simply "Come inside," and that was that.

Zaq and I stepped across the threshold, and two guards immediately shut the heavy door behind us. We stood before

Brooks and, to my surprise, my pastor, David Getz, was there beside him.

"Olivia Jackson?" Pastor Getz shouted. Then he rushed toward me and threw his arms around me. "You are a sight for sore eyes," he crowed. "So, your family made it into one of the time capsules?"

I backed away and nodded, my eyes glued to his face. I couldn't stop smiling at that wonderful man of God.

"I'm still trying to decide if qualifying for the time capsule was a good thing or a bad thing," I said with honesty. "Is your family here with you?" I asked him. "Martha and the children?"

He nodded. "So are Brooks' wife and kids."

Trembling, I peered past the two of them at the long tunnel before us. As though sensing my distress, Zaq grabbed my hand and gave it a reassuring squeeze. I drew closer to him and directed my attention back to the President and the pastor.

Brooks was a much shorter man than what newsreel images showed when he was President. But his welcoming green eyes and confident demeanor portrayed someone who wielded a great deal of power. He bore the aura reserved only for men who took control and handled it well.

"Follow me," he beckoned us, and he turned his back on us and started down the long tunnel. I looked around at the construction. Three large pipes ran the length of the tunnel. The walls were painted a cream color and were completely bare of decoration.

"These walls are made of two-foot-thick, reinforced concrete," he explained. "And those conduits run from a cooling tower outside the bunker. Though we'll be underground, you'll be able to breathe deeply of the outside air."

With long strides, he led the way farther into the bunker. We stayed close behind him and Getz. I looked at Zaq and found comfort in his smile. He was barely limping now as he walked beside me, still holding my hand protectively. He didn't have to say a word.

Before long we passed through a door to the decontamination

area. It was exactly how Crenshaw had described it. To one side was a bin where the politicians would have dropped their clothes, then a chamber where they could be cleansed of radiation, and a ledge on the other side where clean overalls and grooming kits appeared as welcoming gifts.

We didn't need to disrobe or go through the decontamination process. Brooks bypassed all those formalities, said they weren't necessary, and guided us into the bunker. Our first stop was the power plant. With obvious pride, Brooks described how the amazing system kept the bunker operating.

"We've converted the original diesel engines and auxiliary generators into nuclear powered motors, and we have a solar power backup," he boasted. "Everything—lights, refrigeration, cooling and heating units—are all powered by tiny micro-reactors embedded in the hills outside this facility." He gestured toward a wall of flickering lights. "These are all the components we need to keep this place going for many months and maybe years."

We next entered a large conference room with a podium and seating for more than 400 people. It was like entering the Capitol building, carpeting, plush seating, overhead lights, and it looked like a sound system had been erected on the stage. The walls were covered with murals depicting various scenes from the nation's capital, images that were once familiar to everyone. The Washington Monument, the Lincoln and Jefferson memorials, the Smithsonian Institute, the White House. Sadly, many of those structures didn't exist anymore, having been demolished after Ming Yu brought in China's military. During a battle with Russian forces, the capital was nearly razed to the ground.

Brooks led us down another hall to a dining room where 400 or 500 could be served at each sitting. Beyond was a restaurant equipped kitchen.

"My team members eat in shifts," Brooks said. "They also sleep in shifts," he added and led us down another hall with 18 dormitories with enough beds to sleep 1,100 people.

I stared at the levels of bunk beds and thought they looked

an awful lot like the cots in an Army barracks with little space between them and only the basics in pillows and bedding.

We ended our tour in the communications center. There was a small briefing room and a non-functioning AT&T telephone bank. On another wall a team of techs, both men and women, busied themselves at control panels. They looked up to acknowledge us, then delved back into their work. Others were seated at desks with portable tablets, their attention on images being streamed in from all over the world.

At last Brooks turned to me, his bushy eyebrows raised in question. "So, what did my old friend Crenshaw want you to tell me? I'm sure this wasn't meant to be a sightseeing expedition."

I loved Brooks' honesty.

"Mr. Crenshaw believes the people in the time capsule are in danger," I relayed the message. "He's certain saboteurs have found a way inside and are killing people, maybe by poison. And he fears someone may be planning to destroy the capsules and everyone in them."

Brooks nodded with understanding. "The question is who? The Chinese or the Russians? Either power could be behind the sabotage. So, who do you trust?"

"Mr. Crenshaw just wanted you to know what's going on," I told Brooks. "Whether these problems are caused by the new regime or not, the chosen ones need to expose and eliminate saboteurs in their time capsules across the land. Mr. Crenshaw believes the enemy is planning to destroy America's time capsules from within, that they want to get rid of the cream of our nation's intelligence. If any rebuilding is going to be done, they want their own people to do it."

Brooks' green eyes flashed with anger. He raised two fingers to his bottom lip, like he was pondering a response. He'd often done this when being interviewed by the press.

I held my breath and hoped for two outcomes. That he understood how dire the situation was; and that he could find a way to accomplish what Crenshaw was asking.

He heaved a sigh. "It may be too late," he said, dispelling my hopes. "Of more than three thousand time capsules around the world, fifty have been demolished already, and everyone inside has been killed."

I couldn't believe what I was hearing. "This can't be true, President Brooks."

He shook his head with sadness. "We assumed the attacks had come from the Chinese. They've always wanted complete power. Now, it seems, there's another possibility."

"What is that?" I needed to know.

"The Russians. I suspect they might resort to a type of kamikaze mission, sacrificing their own lives for the regime. There's no way to know for certain, of course, not until someone gets into the time capsule and exposes and eliminates the saboteur."

All I could think now was that I had left my own family inside the time capsule, and they were in danger. Already people had died of what looked to be food poisoning. Then there was the power failure. And the baboon attack. What else could an infiltrator be planning?

Chapter Twenty-One

While these thoughts were circling around in our heads, Brooks invited us to have breakfast with him. He first directed us to the washrooms. After freshening up, Zaq and I met with him for a light breakfast. I was surprised to find real scrambled eggs on my plate along with crisp bacon and buttered toast looking nothing like the reconstituted aberrations we'd been eating inside the time capsule. I gulped down a large glass of fresh-squeezed orange juice, and I didn't bother to ask where it came from. We were dining with the former President, so how could I expect less?

What an honor to be able to meet Harmon Brooks, and to discover he was a regular person. Brooks wasn't your typical politician. He didn't hit people with canned speeches, didn't mouth promises he couldn't keep. I had met the real President Brooks, not the one whose face used to be plastered on billboards and virtual ads, and I found I liked him very much.

Between bites of toast, Brooks asked me what life was like in the time capsule. I described the construction, repeating Charlie's explanation of the various levels and sections—the dining hall and kitchen, the exercise room, the chapel, the childcare quarters, the medical clinic where my mom stayed for several days, the layout of the apartments, and, last of all, the huge dome with its mysterious double-sided window. I told him about my escape through the back door of the kitchen and the gruesome sight I discovered out there. Brooks perked up even more when I described what I found on the bottom floor—the animal housing and the mutant baboons that escaped. Last of all, I talked about my visits with Crenshaw and my impression of the wonderful man of wisdom.

Brooks smiled at the mention of his old friend, then his smile faded to a pensive frown. "I haven't seen Andy in almost ten years," he mused. "He was like a second father to me. That man's brain holds a bundle of information about the way things used to be. He knows the scriptures like the back of his hand, and he knows how to relate God's word to current events and the threat of things to come. He's one man who can bring this nation back to normalcy if people will just trust him to do it."

My curiosity had been piqued. "Normalcy? Like what, President Brooks?"

"Like getting people outside the confines of their individual homes and away from their electronics," he said with a sneer. "We need to get back to face-to-face communications, the way things used to be. We need to open windows. Open doors. Welcome people inside. Go to a park for a day of fun. Take a walk past neighbors' houses and wave at people sitting on their front porches."

I recalled my Grandma saying much the same thing. Whenever she talked about the "good ol' days," she painted pictures of hometown life, barn dances, festivals, carnivals, neighbors helping neighbors. Grandma had me wishing I'd been born 50 years earlier. I sort of knew why things had changed, why people had gotten wrapped up in themselves with little chance of interaction. For one thing, the Covid epidemic sent everyone cowering indoors. Then an increase in electronics split family members from spending time together. Then more lethal viruses came along, and the cycle continued.

Like my grandma, Crenshaw remembered how it once was, and apparently Brooks remembered too. Perhaps that was one of the reasons he lost his presidency. He may have been trying to return the nation to what it used to be, and the new politicians were promising something else.

Brooks stared past me into nothingness, like he was remembering. When he spoke, it was with a nostalgic tone in his voice.

"Before I entered politics, Crenshaw and I met weekly to play chess and to hash over world affairs," he said. "His son, Johnny, was my best friend. But he didn't take an interest in what drew Andy and me together." Brooks grunted out a laugh. "I spent more time with Andy than I did with his son. But Johnny didn't mind. He went off and did his own thing, entered the military and got himself killed in Iran."

"Meanwhile, you enjoyed the best part of the 21st century," Zaq noted. "My granddad used to reminisce about his farm and Sunday drives and family get-togethers. He always said those were the days."

It didn't take much to get Brooks' green eyes moist. He nodded in agreement. "That era was too short-lived," he said with sadness. "Technology was beginnin' to catch on. Then it picked up speed and became a runaway train. It couldn't be stopped. Technology changed everything. It ended the warm get-togethers people once enjoyed in each other's company. It ended backyard barbecues, birthday parties, and all those meetings at the gym, the church, and the local park. Now, we've gone so virtual, all those pleasures of life are gone."

Zaq leaned toward Brooks, sympathetic lines creasing my boyfriend's forehead. "If you take back the presidency, will you be able to restore some of that or is it a hopeless cause?" he said, looking quite innocent.

Brooks chuckled. "What a wonderful, impossible thought, son. How I wish I could make it happen. But like you said, Zaq, it could be hopeless. I suspect there would be too much opposition. Too many people like the way things are going, everything automated and easy. Just have an android to it, that kind of thing."

"There must be others who miss the way things used to be," Zaq persisted. "Think about it, Mr. President. Some of us young folks heard all about that time from our grandparents. Lots of us would welcome a taste of it. I, for one, have been tied to my computer and FlexPhone for far too long. Except for Olivia and a couple friends, I've missed out on the kind of friendship you and Crenshaw had."

Brooks offered him a sad smile. Without saying another word about it, he released a sigh and rose from the table. "You kids must have traveled all night," he said. "Perhaps you'd like to take a nap. Afterward, there's something else I'd like to show you. It will blow your mind."

I had to acknowledge I was very tired, but Brooks had piqued my interest. Though I'd love to bypass the nap and see what he had in store for us, the long trip truly had worn me down, and the accident had left me sore and exhausted. Brooks signaled one of his aides who hurried over and showed Zaq and me to separate sleeping quarters. I was taken to the ladies' dorm where I chose a lower cot, sprawled on top, and pulled a fleecy blanket up to my chin. I couldn't help but think of Zaq inches away on the other side of the wall. Nevertheless, I didn't stay awake for very long.

It was late afternoon when I rose feeling refreshed and eager to find out what Brooks was going to show us. I found Zaq in the hall, holding a bath towel and waiting in line to get inside the men's shower. He'd stopped limping, a good sign the injury had healed. He smiled at me, and his brown eyes had a new sparkle.

"Meet me out here after you shower," he said. "We'll take a little walk."

A half-hour later, we were wandering freely throughout the bunker, retracing our steps and revisiting some of the places where Brooks had taken us. Zaq's face glowed with excitement as he peeked in doorways and focused again on the technical equipment.

"For somebody who misses the good ol' days, Brooks sure has a lot of high-tech stuff," Zaq enthused.

He left my side then and approached one of the techs. The two of them fell into deep conversation with Zaq pointing and asking questions, and the technician taking the time to explain. We spent the entire afternoon walking together, then split when something else caught Zaq's interest. It occurred to me that one of us would have liked to be born 50 years before, and I didn't think it was Zaq.

At suppertime, we connected with Brooks again. Getz also was there with his family. I spent a few minutes chatting with Martha, told her about Mom's brief illness, and explained a little about why we had come there. Her children sat wide-eyed, taking in everything I said.

I looked over the spread on our table and marveled over the gourmet meal Brooks' kitchen staff had laid out. There was canned ham and steamed vegetables, brown rice with sautéed mushrooms, baked crescent rolls, plenty of drinking water, and Brooks served each of us a glass of wine from a dusty bottle he took off the shelf. He didn't bother to ask my age, just splashed a little of the red liquid in a glass and placed it in front of me.

Again we discussed the strange occurrences that had taken place in the time capsule. Getz listened closely. "So Crenshaw believes the electrical failure was the work of a saboteur?"

"He is certain of it," I replied.

"And the baboons?"

"Failed experiment," I said. "The leadership dedicated an entire wing on the bottom floor to those animals. Those baboons were not normal. They seemed to be mutations, like someone had been performing tests on them. Why would anyone create such a monster? The time capsule wasn't simply another Noah's ark. Noah's animals were tame, and they were saved for a purpose—to repopulate the earth with their kind and to serve as food and sacrifices. But those creations inside the time capsule are mutations. The dogs didn't bark. They snarled. The cats didn't purr. They bared their claws and shrieked. What great purpose will they serve in the new world?"

"It doesn't make sense," said Brooks, shaking his head. "But the truth is, the Chinese don't conduct random experiments. They always have a purpose, and it's usually not good."

"Then there were those dead people," I moaned. "They didn't even get a decent burial. They were dumped in a trash pile like they had no value. Who would do such a thing?"

Pastor Getz appeared deep in thought. When he spoke, it was with intensity. "The Bible does say things would get worse and worse before the end. People calling good evil and evil good, that sort of thing. We can only hope there is a rainbow at the end of this terrible storm."

"But what else can we expect next?" I was near weeping. "It just keeps getting worse. And my parents and brother are still in there. I have a friend who's stuck there, too. His name is Matt Ellison. I've known him all my life. He even saved me once, pulled me out of an abandoned freezer when I was a little girl."

I glanced at Zaq and caught him staring at me.

"Matt's in there?" he said.

Is he jealous?

"Yes, Zaq, Matt's there. And he's been chosen for procreation. Like me."

Getz was frowning. "Procreation? Is that what they're puttin' on you kids now?"

He bowed his head, and I wondered if he was in prayer. When he raised his head there were tears in his eyes. "That's terrible, Olivia. You should not be forced to submit to such a barbaric method to increase the population. This isn't the Middle Ages. We don't arrange marriages anymore—if that's what this is."

"The problem is," Zaq interjected, "We may not know who's causing all the trouble in the time capsule. It could be the very leadership that's supposed to be protecting us. We need to figure out if we can save the innocent ones who are living there. Crenshaw is the only one who suspects someone is planning to destroy everyone."

Brooks sat frozen. He ran a hand over his bald head. His

emerald eyes had lost they're sparkle, and he seemed frozen, like he had not yet figured out what it was he could do.

"President Brooks?" I said, a quiver in my voice. "Do you have any ideas? Any way we can protect my family and stop the enemy from hurting anyone else?"

He blinked back to the present. "Yes, yes, of course we need to do *something*. I don't doubt the veracity of what Crenshaw has proposed. We can't alert the leadership, because we don't know if the leadership can be trusted. And there's another threat—a much greater one."

I stared at Brooks and caught my breath. Was he about to tell me something that would make me more terrified?

"Besides the threat to the time capsules—" he said slowly, like he was choosing his words carefully, "—China has taken over every major capitol building in the United States. They've moved into what was left of the White House and into most of the governors' mansions. A huge Chinese contingent has invaded the resort right above our heads." He pointed toward the ceiling. "They're armed and ready to strike. And more of their allies are pouring in every day. Picture the same thing happening all over America. And don't be fooled. They don't only want America. This is merely a starting point. They want to take over the whole world. When the dust settles, they will be in control of every living thing."

Zaq leaned toward Brooks. "Do you think they have any idea you're down here in the bunker?"

"No," Brooks said, his voice firm. "They can't possibly know. The old files, documents, and videos about this place were destroyed by my staff several years ago. The Greenbrier Bunker was a secret for the first thirty years of its existence. Most Americans under the age of seventy are not aware it was ever here."

"So what can we do?" Zaq pressed. "We've come this far. How can we help you win back America?" Once again, he sounded like a soldier ready for battle. I trembled at the thought. He was one guy. Eighteen years old and full of fire, but unaware of how small he was next to a giant like the Chinese army.

Brooks scrunched his lips, like my father sometimes did when solving a dilemma. He was older than my father, but younger than Crenshaw. Somewhere in between, I guess. And he had the wits and boldness of both generations.

"I want to help," Zaq insisted. "My men have amassed a huge pile of military drones—cast-offs from the last two conflicts. Can they be useful in some way?"

"Perhaps," Brooks replied, a spark of energy lighting up his eyes. "We have a large arsenal of explosives in this bunker, but no way to deliver them. They're powerful little pellets, the size of a gumball but able to level an entire complex of buildings with only one tossed in the midst. The problem is, we have no way of delivering them. With your drones, we might be able to transport those little pellets in a coordinated nationwide attack. We need to catch the enemy off guard. It could be a total surprise attack. Kind of like Israel's six-day war and the A-bomb devastation of Hiroshima and Nagasaki."

Zaq lurched to his feet. "Mr. President, I can help if you'll allow me to try." His voice bubbled with excitement. "My computer specialist is able to map out the attack sites in all 50 states. All we need to do is arm our drones with your pellets."

Brooks straightened and turned all of his attention on Zaq. My boyfriend was beaming. The President's green eyes appeared to be evaluating him. He looked him up and down, then nodded with confidence.

They stood and faced each other, then shook hands, like they had finalized an agreement.

"Are you certain your small contingent of militiamen might be able to destroy those strongholds?" Brooks questioned him.

Zaq balled up his fists and stood firm. "My guys have already modified those old drones. Once used for surveillance, they can now carry incendiary devices. They're small, palm-sized, but they're similar to the larger models made by Lockheed

Martin at the beginning of the 21st century. They run totally on solar power. It's like having a huge robotic air force at your fingertips, Mr. Brooks. They have the capability of traveling great distances unseen from the time they leave our control center until they complete their mission. All we need to do is attach your explosives. My guys can arm the drones and send them out in a sneak attack, without anyone on our side getting injured. It can all be done by long distance remote control."

Zaq smiled at Brooks. "You mentioned Nagasaki. Didn't the Enola Gay drop the bomb that pretty much ended World War II?"

Brooks grinned back at him. "That was before my time, but I believe it did."

"Well," Zaq went on. "This is the same thing, smaller attacks done on a much larger scale. It's just too bad we'll have to destroy the buildings that once housed American governors."

The glimmer in Brooks' eyes indicated he was already imagining the mission.

"You'll need coordinates for each location," Brooks noted.

"No problem," Zaq assured him.

"Come on." Brooks beckoned Zaq to follow him. "My communications department can supply everything you need." He led us down a separate hallway to a large well-lit room containing wall-to-wall computer screens, desks manned by hard-at-work technicians, and an array of maps on huge, lighted wall panels.

Approaching one of the desks, Brooks formed a huddle with Zaq and the technician. I stood back and studied my boyfriend, amazed that here he was standing shoulder-to-shoulder with the President, like one of the man's generals planning an invasion. Zaq was beaming. All too soon, he'd found his place in the world, and it was beyond anything I could ever hope for him.

An hour later, they separated, assured their plan was coming together. Zaq was holding computer printouts of the various checkpoints, and Brooks was outlining the mission in bold ink.

"You're going back to where you came from," Brooks said,

locking eyes with Zaq. "But this time, you're going to be carrying a truck full of explosives. You'll have to drive carefully. No speeding. No sharp turns. And definitely no crashes. I'm going to entrust the pellets to you and your men, Zaq, so don't let us down."

Zaq was nodding through Brooks' entire spiel. Then he said, "Will my main computer man, Martino, be able to communicate with your guys?"

Brooks nodded. He handed Zaq a computer chip. "These are my private numbers. Here's how Martino can get in touch with us. We need to coordinate this mission down to the last detail."

He turned toward me. "Olivia," Brooks said, his tone serious. "You need to ride back with Zaq, and I want you to reenter the time capsule and try to find out who is causing all the problems. But don't do anything that might endanger you or your family."

"I can't go back. I want to stay with Zaq."

"You want to save the people inside the time capsule, don't you?"

Of course, I had to go back. I responded with a weak nod. I needed to check on my parents and Peter. I needed to talk to Mr. Crenshaw. Together we might be able to find out who the saboteur was.

Zaq turned to Brooks. "How are we going to make that 300-mile trip and carry a load of explosives with us? We came here on a motorcycle, and it died a few miles back."

Brooks chuckled. "Don't worry, Zaq. I have just the right vehicle for you." The man's eyes sparkled like he was about to reveal a secret. "Some of our stealth trackers were able to confiscate a couple of the Chinese Robotrucks. They're powered by nuclear energy, and they're ready to go at a moment's notice." Then he raised his bushy eyebrows and looked at Zaq, and then at me. "You two kids are gonna get the ride of your life."

Chapter Twenty-Two

Brooks continued to fill us in on what lay ahead.

"Kids," he said, grinning like a toddler on Christmas, "we're going to load up the back of your Robotruck with our tiny incendiary devices. You won't be harmed by the explosives. They're not activated. Zaq, you'll take care of that once you get them loaded in the drones. Your Robotruck has a protective shield and spring action that gives a smooth, unhampered ride. You and your cargo will remain completely unseen. Not even high-tech X-ray machines can penetrate the walls and windows." He patted Zaq on the shoulder and rested his hand there, like a father might do before sending his son off to war.

"As for your journey," Brooks went on, "you don't have to be concerned about enemy vehicles you may encounter along the way. The Chinese troops will simply assume your truck is one of theirs on patrol. All you'll need to do is maintain a slow and steady speed. Don't draw attention to yourselves, and stay on the main roads. In other words, look as much like one of them as you possibly can."

I glanced at Zaq who was nearly coming out of his skin. *Right,* I thought. *Everything is one big adventure to him.* Over the last week, I'd had my fill of adventures, enough to last a lifetime. Getting out of the time capsule was the easiest of them. The first trauma came with the attack by a deranged baboon. Then, the hair-raising motorcycle ride to the Greenbrier Bunker. Meeting the President was a high point, and a pleasant one for sure. But now, the thought of riding in one of those nuclear-powered

Robotrucks while carrying a truckload of explosives got my head reeling. And now I was expected to rescue my family from danger, maybe expose a saboteur as well? The only good thing was, I'd be traveling with Zaq.

"We should probably leave around midnight," Zaq suggested. "It's the best time to travel undetected, right?" he looked at Brooks.

Giving a nod, Brooks waved for us to follow him. A few minutes later, we entered a part of the bunker we hadn't yet seen. Before us was a wall of metal, like the outside of one of those old airplane hangars. A worker raised a huge double door and we passed through into a large storage facility where two silver Robotrucks stood side-by-side. It was like looking at spaceships from another galaxy.

Zaq had been holding my hand. He dropped it, let out a whoop, and leaped ahead of me. By the time I reached his side, he was running his hand over the sleek exterior of one of the vehicles. There was no sign of a door. Windows were non-existent.

Brooks laughed and watched Zaq with an amused twinkle in his eyes.

"Wow!" Zaq yelled. "Wow!" He turned to face Brooks and began to pelt him with questions. "Is this the latest version? Is there a newer model than *this*?"

"Yes, it's the latest," the President said. "The original 2025 prototype evolved numerous times over the years until this one—"

"How fast will it go?" Zaq interrupted with another all-important question.

"You can expect to move from zero to eighty in three seconds. But I wouldn't recom—"

"What kind of range does it have?"

Brooks heaved a sigh. "This one is equipped with a tri-motor battery pack. It can travel at least 300 miles and back with no need to ref—"

For the moment, Zaq had settled down and appeared to be listening. The President moved closer and pressed his hand against the side of the vehicle. The door slid open. Without being invited, Zaq climbed inside. He glanced back at me, his face beaming. "Livie, look at this." He pointed toward the dash. "No gauges or controls. Only a touch-screen and a color-coded panel. It's better than an Air Force superjet!"

Like a kid with a new toy, Zaq disappeared inside amidst the colored lights and toggle switches. Brooks pulled me to one side and lowered his voice.

"Olivia, I want to apologize for sending you back to the time capsule, but I see no other way to warn the people inside that they may be in danger. But don't worry. I'm certain you'll be able to travel the distance without any interference. Our men have already been out in these vehicles, testing them. Passing drivers may flash their lights. Just flash back and keep going. And, by the way, these trucks are bullet-proof. The entire vehicle has a light-weight but highly durable stainless steel exterior. The windows are double pain safety glass. You can see out, but no one can see in. You'll be safe as long as you remain inside with the doors locked."

I tilted my head tremulously. "Are you certain we can't be taken prisoner or killed?"

He stroked his chin, like he was considering the right answer. "I could send one of my guards along with you. To keep you safe."

I shook my head. "Zaq has been training for combat. Give him whatever arms he needs, and he'll look after me." I said this with confidence, but inside I was tied up in knots.

Brooks turned to look at the Robotruck where Zaq was still familiarizing himself with the control panel. A scattering of lights came on at the front of the machine. They were so bright they wouldn't merely light up the highway ahead of us, they'd likely illuminate the entire landscape. Zaq must have done something or touched something, because the outside of the Robotruck lit up with long illuminations spanning both sides.

"Your boyfriend looks like he already has a handle on this,"

Brooks said. "He has the kind of technical know-how that makes him a perfect candidate for this mission. But, Olivia, it's going to be up to you to keep him focused. Don't let him stop for anything. Your main goal is to get back to your time capsule and help save the people you love. Once you get there, I'm certain Crenshaw will know what to do. He's a wise old coot. Trust his judgment, Olivia. He won't steer you wrong."

Zaq had exited the Robotruck, and was running his hands over every part. He breathed out little murmurs of approval, and turned his head now and then to smile at me. This was the guy who was about to take us home in one piece? I mumbled a silent prayer. Like my grandma always said, "Only by the grace of God."

We spent the next couple hours getting ready for the trip. Zaq and I packed my bag with snacks and drinks, and I hung onto Peter's night-vision-goggles. Then Zaq spent a good half-hour with a crewman learning how to work the controls. When they finished, I joined him in the passenger seat and left my door open.

I turned to Brooks who was standing a few feet away. "What would you like me to tell Mr. Crenshaw?"

He stepped closer. "Just tell him I expect to finish our last chess game, and it's my move. He'll know what I mean."

I would have liked nothing better than to get the two of them together again.

"Why don't you come with us, Mr. President?"

He hesitated, like he was considering. Then he blinked, his green eyes swimming in tears. "No, dear one. I can't. My place is here, with my staff. Somehow, we need to survive this war and restore our nation to its original glory. This handful of people—" he swept his hand toward the main part of the bunker—"except for a few who were in leadership roles, they're all I have left from my former administration. We must survive at any cost. In the name of Almighty God, we must restore things to what they once were, or the whole world will be doomed."

David Getz approached us and rested his hand on the side

of our vehicle. He leaned close enough to put his head inside my door. He rested his free hand on my arm.

"Father, bless these two brave souls. Bring them safely to their destination, and help them accomplish all they are setting out to do. In the name of your precious Son, Jesus Christ. Amen."

He moved back and prepared to shut my door. I closed my eyes and waited for the moment when Zaq and I were sealed up inside. My door clicked shut. I swallowed hard and fought against a rise of claustrophobia. When I opened my eyes, I was surprised that the two-way glass, while preventing people from seeing inside, like Brooks said, also allowed me a full 360-degree view of the outside. I breathed a sigh of relief. It was as if I was not shut up in a shell at all. I was in a well-fortified bubble of glass and steel, about to set off on a journey to end all journeys.

As planned, we left at midnight. Zaq activated the controls like a pro. The hangar door opened to the outside. We floated upward to a second door. There was a loud pop, and the door sprang open. We drove up a long tunnel toward the west side where a final door slid open. We passed through the opening and surfaced under the glow of a half-moon. To see the world at night like this, the landscape didn't seem quite as ominous as what it looked like during the day, dying amidst withered trees, scorched grass, and crumbling buildings. Everything looked—beautiful.

We traveled beneath a starlit sky, bound for a family reunion for me and the completion of a mission for Zaq. I didn't want to think about the consequences—what the leadership would say about my sudden reappearance, how my father might explain it away, or even if he had covered up the fact that I'd been gone for several days. Peter would surely rant over the little bit of damage I had done to his night-vision goggles. I pondered how I might explain my actions to my family. I only wanted to see them again, to warn them, to help them escape what promised to be a disaster. If I was unable to discover the saboteur, I could simply lead my family out the kitchen door to safety.

According to the tech's calculations, we could expect to arrive at the time capsule at around 4:30 in the morning while it was still dark. I could break in through the kitchen's garbage door long before the breakfast crew showed up. I'd have a lot of explaining to do when I arrived at our apartment, but I was certain my parents and Peter could be trusted to keep the whole thing a secret, if given the opportunity to tell them everything.

Meanwhile, after Zaq dropped me off, he had to head back to the mine and fill his crew in on everything that had transpired. The success of the mission depended on them being able to load the pellets on their supply of drones. Then, with Martino coordinating the drop zones, they could schedule a launch time.

My heart pounded with excitement. In a few hours, we'd be involved in a major quest to take back our country from the enemy. In the end, we hoped to restore Harmon Brooks to his rightful place as President of the United States of America. We needed to replace the Chinese flags with our own Stars and Stripes. As I pondered all that was about to transpire, a patriotic spirit surged within me. I was no longer a teenager whose one hope was to get out of a time capsule and live a normal life again. I had become a soldier of sorts, and I had embarked on a real mission.

✝✝✝

We'd been on the road for two hours and hadn't seen a single soul. Our Robotruck ran smoothly and soundlessly. I hardly knew we were moving, yet the green light on the dash said we were doing 60.

For a while, our conversation centered around all we had seen at the bunker, the amazing layout, the food, the people, the fact that David Getz and his family were there, and most of all, how pleasant the meeting with Harmon Brooks went. We were both excited about the mission we were on.

I took a moment to divvy out the snacks we'd brought. Then, another thought crossed my mind. While I had been grieving over my own family, I had failed to ask Zaq about his.

"Your folks and your sisters," I said. "Are they in a safe place?"

Zaq cast a sideways glance at me. The colored lights on the dash lit up his face and I saw him smile. "They went to my granddad's farm. He built a fallout shelter years ago, so I'm guessing they're safe and sound beneath the ground."

"I'm glad," I told him. "I know what it's like to worry about family members. Hopefully, you'll get to see them soon."

"Hopefully," he agreed.

At that moment, Zaq lost his smile. He straightened in his seat and glued his attention to the rearview mirror, which wasn't a mirror at all, but a wide-angle camera, I discovered.

"Those lights have been tailing us for the last 15 miles," he said.

I leaned closer to him so I could get a view of the lights. The illumination was like the scattering of lights I'd seen on the front of our own machine when Zaq was toying with the controls back at the bunker. They lit up the entire hangar.

The lights drew closer but didn't pass. Then I noticed, not one, but two vehicles had lined up behind us. They both had their lights full on, turning the world around us like daytime. They were so bright they lit up the interior of our truck.

"Can they see us? What are we gonna do, Zaq?" I began to tremble. He frowned and pressed his lips together, like he was preparing for a fight.

"Just sit tight," he said. "Remember what Brooks said. We have to act normal. Let's just wait and see what *they* do."

I returned my gaze to the rear-facing camera. My breathing increased along with my heart rate. I looked again at Zaq. Except for the concerned lines on his forehead, he appeared confident and controlled.

"I'm just gonna keep driving," he said with amazing calmness. He didn't speed up, and he didn't slow down—just kept going as if nothing was amiss.

With luck, our *friends* wouldn't suspect anything. How could they? How often did they come across

American citizens driving one of their own vehicles on roads they themselves commandeered?

But luck? How could I trust in luck? Hadn't my grandma taught me not to trust in luck or even in myself, but to pray about everything? Hadn't I done that in my younger years? But I had changed since she'd been gone. I'd grown into a self-assured, young woman. I'd been making my own decisions and handling problems on my own, without even asking God for guidance. But lately, with all that had been happening, I'd become less sure of myself. I didn't have as much control as I'd thought.

Now the new government had been controlling my life. Virtual classes—brainwashing sessions. The time capsule. The duties thrown upon me. Interviewing Mr. Crenshaw. Being a procreator. All part of a life I hadn't planned for myself.

And now this. I was in a life or death situation. I could lose Zaq, my entire family, everything I knew and loved.

My mind scrambled to recall some of those verses Grandma insisted I memorize. One in particular came to mind. *You will keep him in perfect peace whose mind is stayed on You, because he trusts in You. Isaiah 26:3.*

Without making a sound, I mouthed that verse three times. The two vehicles had drawn closer, one was almost on our rear bumper. I caught my breath, then I glanced at Zaq. He'd remained rigid, not a drop of perspiration on his forehead, his eyes glistening, his jaw firm, his back straight. I was amazed at how cool and calm he was.

The little boy that went nuts when he first set eyes on that Robotruck had morphed into a superhero, undaunted and capable of handling anything. Then the frown on his forehead eased. His lips parted in a tiny smile. His eyes turned to the road ahead, with only an occasional glance at the rearview camera.

He maintained a steady speed, like Brooks had advised, and he kept to the right side of the road. Slowly, one of the vehicles pulled out and came up alongside us. I trusted the tinted glass to keep us hidden from view. For all the driver knew, we could be Chinese soldiers.

Zaq kept driving, his eyes shifting from the road ahead to the rear-facing camera, to the vehicle on our left. The passing Robotruck slowly moved on and the second truck pulled up on our left. It seemed to take forever for truck number two to pass. That one flashed its lights. Zaq responded in kind. And the two moved on ahead, while Zaq held to the same speed. Soon, the passing taillights grew smaller and smaller in the distance. Then they were gone.

I let out the breath I'd been holding. My hands stopped shaking.

"That was a close one," I breathed.

Zaq turned and smiled at me. "We're okay," he said, his voice amazingly controlled. "You can relax now. In a little while we'll be at your time capsule."

"And you'll be back in the mine," I reminded him, with a touch of sadness. "This isn't what I had planned, Zaq. I wanted us to be together."

"We *will* be together. I promise. But we need to follow President Brooks' orders. He has a definite plan, and I want to play my part in that mission. Don't you?"

He turned to look at me, his eyebrows raised with the challenge.

"Of course," I confessed. "I just can't stand the thought that we'll be separated again."

"I'm not going anywhere but the mine," Zaq reminded me. "I have work to do. My buddies and I need to arm those drones and send them off. The entire mission should only take a couple of days. I'll monitor the attacks, trust Martino to figure out how to get in touch with Brooks, and when the job is finished I'll come looking for you."

My heart wasn't in it. I was behaving like a spoiled little girl, not getting what she wanted. Blinking back a rise of tears, I gazed at my boyfriend. He looked strong, focused, intent—nothing like the lovesick teenager who walked with me in the woods that day only a couple of weeks ago. That moment was gone. The two of us had been made to grow up awfully fast. Zaq obviously had succeeded, and though I'd felt a positive change in me, the little girl inside me still wanted her way. I needed to concentrate on the work Brooks had given me to do. I needed to discover the saboteur and get my family to safety.

Chapter Twenty-Three

Wwe arrived at the time capsule at 4:30 a.m., as expected, still under the cover of darkness. Zaq cut the engine and allowed our Robotruck to coast down a slight grade into the clearing behind the garbage dump.

The dome emitted a subtle aura, like a giant globe illuminated from the inside. It looked other-worldly from where I sat. To my relief, the time capsule appeared to be standing strong. No bomb had gone off. No destruction had occurred. Perhaps the saboteur had already been exposed and eliminated.

I reached for the door handle. Zaq's hand was instantly on my arm.

"Not so fast, Livie."

I turned toward him. "What's wrong, Zaq?"

He gazed at me with sadness. "I just wanted to hang onto you for one more minute," he said, his voice breaking.

I melted into his arms. "I know, Zaq. It's hard to say good-bye all over again."

"I'll be thinking about you the whole time," he vowed. "While I'm doing my job, I'll think about you doing yours."

"I wish we could work together."

"You know we can't. You have a job to do, and so do I." Zaq released me and set his dark eyes on mine. "You need to meet with that Crenshaw guy and try to find out who's doing the bad stuff in there. Meanwhile, I'm gonna take this truck to the mine. I'll immediately organize my guys to action. We have to arm those drones and get ready for a major attack. It'll take a while to set up our coordinates and initiate the strike, but once we launch those drones I'll be able to come for you."

"I'm afraid, Zaq."

He held up a hand. "It has to be this way, Livie. But remember. I won't be far away. As soon as I've done what I need to do, I'll come back for you and your family. I promise."

He kissed me and pulled me close to his chest, the safest place in the world, as far as I was concerned. Sobbing, I rested my forehead against his shoulder.

"You're right, of course. We both knew this had to be." I leaned back and searched his face. "How will you contact me when I'll be inside the capsule and you'll be in the mine?"

"Don't worry about it. Martino is a genius. He'll figure something out, maybe I'll use some of his equipment. One way or the other, I'll get a message to you."

"Okay, Zaq." I pulled away from his grasp, now resigned to our separation.

"Go on now," he said, gently pushing me toward the door. "Be brave, Livie. We'll be together again soon."

Zaq's boldness gave me a surge of confidence. I looked into his eyes. A real hero lurked inside those deep brown circles. He leaned toward me. We kissed again, then I grabbed my pack and slipped out the door.

I slid Peter's goggles on. The path ahead brightened under the green illumination. I made my way around the rotting debris and found the kitchen entrance. A foul-smelling haze drew my attention to a place about fifty yards away where trash smoldered and set off a rancid smell. I looked around at the piles of black bags, breathed in the rank odor of garbage and the sharp residue of smoldering ash, aware that along with the household debris, the bodies of the dead had added fuel to the fires. Thankfully, I didn't see any new corpses amongst the bags that littered the ground.

I reached the kitchen door, turned the latch, and was relieved when it opened without any alarms going off. As I slipped inside, I heard Zaq drive away, the Robotruck emitting a low rumble in the morning stillness.

Once again, Peter's goggles lit up the kitchen like it was lunchtime. I quickly left the area and made my way back to the elevators, descended one floor down and strode to our apartment like I'd only been gone for an evening stroll, nothing more. All the while, I tried to think of what I really should tell my parents. Once we got past the reprimands and the interrogation, hugs and tears were sure to follow. But at some point, I was going to have to explain where I'd been for the last four days. Ultimately, though, I needed to warn my folks about the danger that lurked inside the time capsule.

I pressed the security pad, pushed through the front door and shut it soundlessly behind me. Then I tiptoed to my cubicle. Though a shower would have felt great at that moment, I went straight to my room, collapsed on my bed, and fell into a much needed sleep.

✝✝✝

I don't know how long I lay there, but at some time early that morning, I awoke to a deep voice calling my name. Dad was hovering over me, his face lined with concern, though it could have been anger. Mom stood beside him, blubbering into a handkerchief. Peter was turning his goggles over and over in his hand, his eyes filled with disappointment. I looked from one familiar face to the other, then I shut my eyes in a last attempt to delay the inevitable.

"Olivia, I have one question for you and I want an answer *now*. Where have you been?" Dad's gruffness jolted me fully awake.

Peter lunged toward my bed. "You ruined by goggles, Ollie, you creep!"

"Quiet, Peter." Dad held up his hand, but fastened angry eyes on me. "You owe us an explanation, girl."

"Rave, let her talk." Mom's soft murmur was thick with

emotion. "Tell us the truth, Olivia. Where did you go? Were you hiding somewhere inside the capsule? Or did you find a way out? It's been four days, dear. Four days since we last saw you."

I pushed myself upright and rested on my elbows. I summoned as much courage as I could, hoping that, once they heard the truth, they would understand.

"Please," I pleaded. "So much has happened. You have to let me tell you everything, without interrupting me. I'll be truthful, I promise."

The lines on Dad's face remained rigid. Apart from clenching his jaw, he didn't move.

"What I have to tell you will sound fantastic," I said. "Most importantly, I want you to know, I met President Brooks."

Dad's jaw dropped, and his eyes widened with surprise. "What are you saying, Olivia? Where did you go?"

I plunged ahead and told him how I found Zaq, how he'd killed the escaped baboon, and how we set out on the mission Mr. Crenshaw had planned for us.

Sighs and gasps erupted from my mother and brother. But Dad frowned with displeasure.

"Crenshaw?" he fumed. "Why that—"

"No, don't blame him," I quickly interjected. "He knew I was planning to escape, and all he did was make good use of it."

"You said you met President Brooks. How did that come about?"

"We located him in the Greenbrier Bunker. Believe me, Dad, it was the time capsule to end all time capsules—ten times larger and equipped with everything Brooks needs to stay alive."

I went on to describe the bunker and Brooks' plan to arm the drones with tiny bombs.

Mom cried out. "What? You and Zaq?"

"I knew that boy was trouble," Dad barked.

"No, you're wrong. And I'm proud to be even a little involved in that mission." I looked from one to the other. "But it's Zaq and his men who will carry it out to the end. They're the true heroes." Then, because of the shocked expression on Dad's face, I added, "He may be the boy you wanted to reject, but he's doing a job most young men would run away from."

Mom hadn't stopped weeping the whole time I was talking. She kept dabbing her face with a limp handkerchief, released a sigh, and dropped onto the edge of my bed, like she'd lost every ounce of strength. Peter was staring wide-eyed at me, and I could tell his imagination was running wild as I described everything—the bunker, the President, the Robotruck, and our nerve-wracking encounter on the highway.

"This sounds too fantastic," Dad said, shaking his head. "It might have helped if you'd included me—I mean us—in this wild plan. Why did you and Crenshaw keep it a secret? We might have been able to help in some way. Instead, you simply disappeared. Do you know we hadn't stopped looking for you from the day you went missing? I tried to keep your disappearance a secret, hadn't told anyone else yet. I was just hoping you'd come back to us with a sensible excuse. As it turned out, you came up with a pretty good one." He rested a hand on my shoulder, like he was trying to make sure I was really there. Tears welled in his eyes. "Don't ever disappear like that again."

"I'm sorry, Dad. But this will turn out to be a good thing. Really."

"I can't believe you and Zaq drove 300 miles with those incendiary devices in the back of that vehicle. You could have been blown to smithereens."

"Not a chance. Brooks told us they were safe, that they needed to be armed first."

I went on to describe how Zaq and his men needed to attach the pellets to the drones and prepare them for an attack. This got a rise out of Peter, who let out a yell and started leaping about the small space that was my bedroom.

"There's something else," I said. "There's a real danger right here in the time capsule."

All eyes were on me. No one spoke. Even Peter stopped leaping.

"Mr. Crenshaw believes the time capsules may have been infiltrated by enemy spies, and President Brooks agrees with him. We need to find out if a foreign spy has snuck inside. Perhaps a Russian, or someone from North Korea. Brooks said we could be in great danger. If nothing else, we can leave the capsule the way I got out. But then, everyone else will be left here to die."

"And just how are we to spot an enemy spy?" Dad asked with good reason.

"I don't know, Dad. We'll need to keep our eyes open, maybe do some espionage work of our own."

Mom lunged toward me. "No, haven't you been in enough danger already? I won't stand for it."

"Mom," I soothed. I'll be fine. Dad will be with me this time.

"Me too!" shouted Peter. I'll keep 'em both safe." He donned his fraying goggles and did another fly about.

Dad was staring at me like he was seeing me for the first time. He responded in a serious tone. "You've been on quite an adventure, Olivia. But I agree with your mom. I don't want you in any more danger. Besides, during your absence, another problem arose."

"Dad, I was only gone a few days. What more could have happened?"

"We had a fire!" Peter shouted, coming to a stop in front of me.

"What? A fire?" An internal fire was perhaps the most dangerous scenario I could imagine. Trapped inside the time capsule with a fire? At the very least, there'd be smoke, chemicals, and no way of escape.

"Where was the fire?"

"A blaze started in the storeroom in the bottom level," Dad explained. "We lost some supplies. They put us on strict rations for a few days while they took inventory. Then a couple more people became ill and were taken to the infirmary. They never returned."

"They put the fire out," Peter piped up. "They have a really cool sprinkler system. The fire died down like it was nothing."

"It's no surprise to me the fire started," I said, my heart pounding. "Someone's trying to sabotage this place. Think about all the things that have happened since we arrived. Someone must have tampered with the electrical system, and then the baboons escaped. Then there were the mysterious food poisonings and the deaths of several people. Mr. Crenshaw is certain those incidents were no accident."

I looked from Dad to Mom and searched their faces for some sign of understanding. "I know what I've told you sounds like mere fantasy, but it's all the truth. I'm not lying."

Dad made a fist, and his face turned red with anger. "I *knew* something wasn't right in here. Too many things have gone wrong. If we're going to remain safe inside the time capsule for who knows how long, then we'd better do something, before things get any worse." The angry lines on his face begin to ease. "If Harmon Brooks wants us to do something about it, then we will. As far as I'm concerned, he's still President."

"He hasn't given up the fight, Dad. When he went into hiding he took with him a copy of the Constitution. He wants to restore the laws written within those pages. His followers are doing everything they can to keep him safe." I shook my head in wonder. "You'd be amazed, Dad. I wish you could see the bunker. I wish you could talk to Brooks yourself."

"If what you say is true—and I do believe you, Olivia—then we need to get organized. And we should include other people we've learned to trust."

"Like the Ellisons?" I said with a smirk.

"Yes, like the Ellisons," Dad said, his voice firm.

"I don't know, Dad. I trust Matt and his father, but I'm not so sure about Jeanine. She's been acting crazy."

"Okay, Olivia. I'll tell Charlie when I can get him alone, maybe while we're working on a design."

"There's more," I said.

"What do you mean, there's more?" Mom blurted out, concerned wrinkles gathering on her forehead.

"Brooks thinks the same thing is probably happening in all the time capsules in America," I told them. "He's certain enemy agents have been able to sneak inside every one of them, and they're destroying the people who live there."

"So what do we do?" Dad wanted to know. "We can't just sit here and wait for something else to go wrong."

"The main reason President Brooks sent me back here was so I could warn you about what's going on." I paused. "We need to find out if this time capsule has been invaded. Meanwhile, Zaq has a super tech guy named Martino, who may be able to figure out a way to contact people in the other time capsules and save their lives."

"So we start here," Dad agreed. "All four of us can keep an eye out." He looked from me to Mom and then to Peter. "All four of us," he repeated.

"We need to get with Mr. Crenshaw and decide what each one of us can do." I suggested. "He's a very wise man, Dad. All I know is, we've got to preserve the time capsule until Zaq and his guys complete their mission. It won't be long. They're going to coordinate the strikes so they happen simultaneously. Once they get started it could be over in a matter of minutes."

My father stroked his chin. "You say Brooks approved of this plan?"

"Yes, Dad. It was his idea."

"Then we have some work ahead of us."

"That's right. And Crenshaw might know how we can accomplish this without being obvious. He might even have an idea who's behind it all." I stared deeply into my father's eyes. "I trust him, Dad."

He gave a nod. "Okay, then. Invite him to our table tonight. Charlie needs to hear what the old man has to say."

My parents hadn't yet disciplined me for leaving. After all, what could they do? I was already grounded, had been ever since the first day I arrived in the time capsule. But something in our relationship had changed. We'd gone from parent and child to colleagues with a common goal. They had given me a chance to explain my absence, and they believed me. Maybe, through all of this, they also might see Zaq in a whole new light. No longer was he a reckless teenager who threatened to ruin their daughter. He'd turned into a strong and capable young man who'd set out to save America. A hero of sorts. Like those examples in my history lessons, long before the Chinese took over—brave souls like Paul Revere, Nathan Hale, George Washington, Abraham Lincoln. They, too, were impetuous young men at one time.

My mom hugged me, whimpered a little into my neck, then released her hold. Dad moved in and wrapped his arms around me, protectively. Even Peter got in on the act. He patted my head and thanked me for bringing his goggles back, despite the mess. Though I was exhausted from the previous day's journey, I could no longer sit back and let the time pass. I needed to freshen up in the bathroom and get with Mr. Crenshaw.

I savored the hot spray of a shower, splashed bath oils on my weary body, and dried off with a plush towel. The door to the Ellisons' side was locked. I could stay in there as long as I needed to. After a reasonable amount of time, however, I emerged with clean, apricot-scented hair and a generous dusting of aromatic bath power. Refreshed and exhilarated, I breathed deeply of the lingering mist from the shower.

There was much to be done. First thing after I dressed, I grabbed a power bar and a package of dried dates. I cued in Mr. Crenshaw's contact info and arranged to meet with him. For sure, he'd want to see me for an update. I pictured his wrinkled old face and watery blue eyes, and I couldn't help but smile. The man I had avoided in the beginning had become a dear friend. I could hardly wait to see him again.

Chapter Twenty-Four

When I arrived inside the dome, Crenshaw was already there, coffee in one hand, his FlexPhone in the other. He greeted me with a big, toothy smile. I leaned close and gave him a hug.

"Harmon Brooks sends his regards," I said, backing away. His smile grew wider. "He said to tell you it's his move, whatever *that* means." I leaned away from him and looked him in the eye. "Was he talking about a *real* chess game or was that code for something else?"

Crenshaw laughed like he had a secret. His eyes twinkling, he opened up to me. "It's a real chess game, one we started years ago, but was interrupted by a misguided nuclear missile," he moaned. "I'm sure my old friend is looking forward to finishing that game. After all, he *was* winning." He laughed again, and I caught a glimpse of the kind of friendship they had. The image stirred up a question.

"So you were close friends with the President of the United States?"

"Oh, as I told you before, I met Harmon Brooks long before he went into politics." Crenshaw settled back in his chair, like he was about to give me a long-winded account of their first meeting.

"You said he was best friends with your son," I reminded him.

He stared past the dome window into the wilderness outside the capsule. "Johnny and Harmon spent a lot of time together as kids. They played Little League ball when we still had such things. They went to the same school. Johnny came out with Bs and Cs. Harmon got straight A's." Crenshaw raised one hand, emphasizing Brooks' grades. Then he continued on, the same look of nostalgia returning to his face. "Harmon and I played chess on a regular schedule. Then the two of them went off to college, joined the chess club, and played on the soccer team. After graduation my son went in one direction. He joined the Marines. Johnny always was a tough kid, worked out like his life depended on him gettin' the biggest muscles in the crowd. Harmon, on the other hand, was a little on the wimpy side. He chose to go on to graduate school and earned his master's in law, then ran for Congress, and the rest is history."

"And you?" I prompted.

Crenshaw scratched his chin. "I stayed in touch with my son, of course. He had my heart, but my attention was on Harmon. I wanted that young man to succeed. And he did."

"So you were like a second father to him?"

"More like a first," Crenshaw said with an air of sadness. "His real father died shortly after he was born. I kind of filled in as a substitute, I suppose."

"How often did you connect with him after he left for the capital?"

"Once in a while he'd phone me, or I'd call him. He invited me to the White House one day, and that's when we started that last game, the one we never finished." Crenshaw chuckled. "I'd love to see my old buddy again, maybe reminisce about a time when life was easier, before a political upheaval made America one of the weakest nations in the world. If only our government leaders would have gotten along like Harmon and I did, things would be a lot different right now. Our nation would be stronger, and we could have fought off the enemy with a united force."

"Brooks never offered you a post in his administration?"

"Never did," he said with a shrug of his bony shoulders. "Not that I would have accepted. Such an honor would have been too far above me."

I marveled at his humility. Of all the people I knew inside and outside the time capsule, I could think of no one else I'd want to see in public office. This man was wise, kind, and yes, extremely humble. Wasn't that the kind of leadership we all needed?

He looked at me and offered a weak smile. The poor man had suffered through one disappointment after another. There was no telling what traumas he'd lived through in his 100-plus years. He'd been caught between life as he knew it and a political world where one of his dearest friends was attacked. He must have felt like he'd been pulled in two different directions.

The lines on Crenshaw's face deepened and a tearful sadness filled his eyes. I sensed a word of encouragement might bring him back.

"I have good news, Mr. Crenshaw." It was time to fill Crenshaw in on what I had discovered outside. I plunged into a monologue about the baboon attack and being rescued by Zaq. The troubled lines on Crenshaw's face told me how my story affected him. I quickly moved on and told him about Zaq's operation inside the mine. He raised his furry eyebrows in amazement. Then I gave him a full account of our trip to West Virginia on a beat-up, antique motorcycle, which brought chuckles and tears from the old man.

"Sounds like the joy ride of your life," Crenshaw commented, with a sparkle-eyed grin.

I giggled and continued to impress him with our tour of the Greenbrier Bunker, certain the telling of it must have activated some long ago memories. I gave my personal opinion of the place, using a variety of adjectives, like *astounding, incredible,* and *awesome.* He simply kept nodding.

He smiled when I told him Brooks' appearance hadn't changed much since he held the Presidency. "Same balding head, same shocking green eyes, but he's hunched over a little now, maybe from the weight that was put on his shoulders. It's amazing he held that office well into his 70s."

"Ain't 70 the new 40?" Crenshaw pointed out with a chuckle.

"I guess," I responded with a chuckle of my own. "The good new is, Brooks and my boyfriend were able to combine resources in a plan to defeat the invading armies." I experienced a surge of pride as I began to unveil their plan. "Brooks' crew provided us with incendiary devices—mere pellets, each one the size of a pea—which we transported in one of China's own Robotrucks. We came back here, and after dropping me off at the time capsule, Zaq and his men got to work inserting those devices in some old military drones they'd refurbished. It seems they're small enough to fly undetected at low altitudes, and capable of long-distance control from Zaq's communications center. Those little drones are being armed right now, as we speak, and will soon be launched in a coordinated strike against all enemy strongholds across the United States."

Crenshaw breathed a long sigh. "It's more than I could have dreamed," he murmured.

"It's all coming about because you sent us to the Greenbrier," I told him. "If this plan works, we'll be rid of the forces that overtook America. Our military will be able to reclaim our nation and reestablish our government, with Harmon Brooks in the top office once again. And you'll be glad to know, Brooks has been holding onto a copy of the Constitution. He wants to restore it the way it was originally written."

"That's wonderful," Crenshaw said, and his blue eyes danced with delight. "I was afraid the new administration had destroyed that document. Several Presidents before Brooks tried to either modify it or get rid of it completely."

"Mr. Crenshaw, my dad wants you to join us at our table tonight. He would like to discuss what we can do to protect the time capsule from an attack. We'll be dining with the couple who lives in the apartment next to us. Charlie Ellison and his family served as our welcoming committee when we first arrived."

"Ellison?" Crenshaw frowned as though troubled. "Ain't he the one you told me about? You know, the other half of your procreation project?"

I smirked. "You have too good a memory, Mr. Crenshaw."

"And you want me to come into the dining hall for my supper?"

"I know you're accustomed to eating in the dome," I offered. "But wouldn't you like to help us figure out a way to stop the threat inside the time capsule? We sure could use a word of wisdom from you."

He lifted a bony shoulder and followed with a shake of his head. "I already told you what I think, Olivia. This isn't the only time capsule under attack. I'm pretty sure every capsule in America is experiencing some sort of infiltration. The enemy is all around us."

"My dad and I are gonna keep our eyes open to anything suspicious. I'll watch people for clues. I can think of at least one person who seems a little strange. But then what do we do if we see something that doesn't look right? Do we run to the leadership? Are we sure we can trust them? To be honest, Mr. Crenshaw, other than my parents, you're the only other adult I trust in this whole place."

He set his coffee cup in the cup holder and took my hand in both of his. "You've given this old man a ray of hope, Olivia. I love watching your enthusiasm, your fire. It almost makes me leap out of this wheelchair and join your search. I've already told you what I think. I don't know what additional help I can give."

I found comfort in his wise old eyes. Again I urged him to join us for dinner. "Please, Mr. Crenshaw, will you come?"

He tilted his head to one side and released my hand. "I've always had my meals inside the dome," he insisted, and I thought that was the end of our conversation. Then he stared at my puckered lips and must have relented. "However," he added. "I see no reason why I can't break my own rules now and then. Okay, Livie, you win. I'll be there."

✝✝✝

I found Mr. Crenshaw to be a man of his word. At suppertime he hobbled in with a walker and came beside me at the soup station, where, with shaking hands, he ladled a vegetable concoction into a bowl. I reached for the ladle, finished scooping the hot liquid for him, and set his serving on my own tray. Together, we made it to our table, with Crenshaw tottering along beside me with his walker.

My family was already seated there along with Charlie and Jeanine and, of course, Matt. I sat beside my mom and placed Crenshaw on my left. I purposely avoided Matt's steady gaze from across the table. I refused to give him any encouragement.

As they often did when they got together, Charlie and Dad were already involved in an animated discussion about the work they planned to do once things opened up again. Charlie was pelting Dad with questions about the electromagnetic systems, and it seemed to me that he was getting more technical information than he needed for building the outer shells. His persistence sparked a suspicion in me. I needed to watch him closely. I wondered, was this how it was going to go from now on? Was I going to suspect everybody who said or did something out of the ordinary? How could I sort through all the clues and make sense of it all?

I glanced at Jeanine, and my former suspicions rose up. There she sat, looking smug in her skin-tight black pants and jacket with the rhinestone studded collar and cuffs.

I thought back to the days before we came to the time capsule. Didn't Jeanine visit Mom the day before her family left our neighborhood? Didn't she spend an unreal amount of time in our kitchen chatting about senseless things, kind of like Charlie was doing now? I tried to remember the scene. She'd come into our house with a small package in her hand, and she'd left without it. At the time, I didn't think twice about it. But it wasn't long after her visit—maybe a day or so—when Mom started acting strangely.

I began to remember other strange moments involving the Ellisons, and a cold chill ran down my spine. When we first arrived at the time capsule we left Mom alone with Jeanine in the entry. Mom's condition grew worse after that.

And what about the time the electrical systems went down,

and Charlie accompanied Dad outside to set up the probe? Charlie didn't help my father at all. In fact, when the baboon lunged out of the brush, he hesitated longer than he should have and never took a shot. If not for Walter the guard, my dad would have been attacked. Charlie was close enough to kill the beast, but he didn't even try.

Unaware that I was watching her, Jeanine grabbed Mom's coffee cup. "I'll get you a refill," she said sweetly, but her eyes flashed with arrogance. She rose from the table and walked to the coffee counter across the room, her spike heels clicking on the tile floor. I waited and kept my eyes on her. She spent an awful lot of time doctoring Mom's coffee. How long does it take to add a little cream and sugar? And what was that little bottle she'd pulled from her jacket pocket? It appeared she'd added something more to Mom's cup.

She returned to our table with the coffee cup filled to the brim, the light beige liquid nearly sloshing over the side. I reacted to my suspicions. I had to keep Mom from drinking whatever Jeanine had prepared for her. Visions of Mom back in the clinic on life support drove me into a panic. Even more distressing was the thought of her ending up in a black bag in the garbage heap.

As soon as Jeanine placed the cup on the table, I reached in front of Mom for a piece of her sweet roll and "accidently" overturned the cup, spilling coffee across the table onto Jeanine's lap. Jeanine shrieked and lurched out of her chair. She reached for a handful of napkins and began dabbing at her spangled pants.

"You idiot!" She snarled at me. Then she took a deep breath, aware that all eyes were on her. The glare disappeared from her coal black eyes, and she forced a smile. "Oh, it's okay. It was an accident." Without another word, she stood and stalked out of the dining hall.

Crenshaw and I exchanged glances. I couldn't decide if he'd seen what she'd done to Mom's coffee, or if my imagination had run wild. I needed to talk to the old man and get his take on it. I trusted Crenshaw. But I couldn't deny the clues. I began to suspect Jeanine and maybe Charlie were responsible for all the problems we'd been experiencing in the time capsule. After all, Charlie knew the construction better than anyone, except maybe the leadership. He'd described every part of it like he'd built it himself. He was an architect, so I imagined he'd be able to look beyond the surface, aware of things most of us didn't notice. And Jeanine? She'd left clues of her own. Her erratic behavior, her access to the coffee pots, her flirtation with my dad. Had she been in the dining hall the day those young people came into the clinic with food poisoning?

Crenshaw scooped the last bit of broth into his mouth, and dabbed his lips with a napkin. He sat back and passed a look from me to Dad and then to Charlie, like he was ready for a discussion.

My initial goal had been to talk about the things that had been happening in our time capsule. But now, with Charlie sitting across from us and Jeanine certain to come back at any moment, I wasn't sure they could be trusted.

Dad turned toward Crenshaw.

Fearing he might start the conversation, I leaped to my feet and reached for Mr. Crenshaw's hand. "I need to take a walk. Care to join me, Mr. Crenshaw?"

The old man frowned in puzzlement. Then he gazed into my eyes and caught my message. "A walk sounds nice," he said, and reaching for his walker, he rose from his chair.

Before anyone could object or even offer to join us, Crenshaw and I turned our backs to the table and shuffled toward the exit. Of course, our walk would have to be a short one, and it had to end in the dome where Crenshaw could sit and rest his tired bones and where we could talk without being heard. The old man and I had bonded, the very old and the very young, meeting on some level in between. I was comforted knowing I could tell him anything.

We sat together in a private corner of the dome. People

milled about, but nowhere near us. It was the usual scene. Nobody wanted to be closed up in an apartment for very long, so they went where they could at least get a glimpse of the outdoors. A walk after lunch had become a normal activity for most of the residents. Though the dome filled with bodies, they kept their distance. Some of them grouped into little cliques. A few stragglers simply enjoyed the alone time.

Settling back in my chair, I spilled my concerns about the Ellisons. I covered everything. Charlie's suspicious behavior, the unnecessary questions he asked my dad. Jeanine's threat to my mother. Then, I leaned closer to the old man and whispered, "Am I wrong?"

He pressed his lips together, like he was searching for the right words. "The Ellisons, huh?" He smiled and patted my hand. "When I served in the military, I learned not to trust anyone until I could confirm their loyalty. You may be on the right track, Olivia. I trust your intuition. But I hesitate to make a decision this soon. We haven't scoped out the rest of the residents."

I couldn't let it go. "I don't know what it is, Mr. Crenshaw, but I get a strange vibe from that family. Especially from Jeanine. Matt would like nothing better than to have a close relationship with me. I've kept my distance. And Charlie? Well, he's—I don't know—hard to read. He talks a lot but doesn't say much, except for how the time capsule was built and his plans for the new build. Lots of repetition but no new information. Know what I mean? It seems like he's more intent on gathering information than giving it."

Crenshaw nodded thoughtfully. "I've been watching Charlie for sometime now, myself. Sometimes he stands inside the dome and just stares out at the trees. I have to wonder what he's thinking. Or plotting."

"He let that baboon escape—I'm certain of it."

Crenshaw was staring at the spot where Charlie and Dad had been working outside the dome, like he was remembering the incident. "Yes, Olivia," he said, at last. "The whole thing seems strange to me as well. Charlie could have killed the beast. He had a direct shot, and he didn't take it. He waited far too long." Crenshaw frowned with suspicion. "Of course, he could have panicked."

"Do you suppose he's wondering if it's still out there? My friend Zaq killed it, but Charlie wouldn't know that."

"No, I don't think it's about the baboon. Charlie's been acting strangely from day one, almost like he's looking for something or maybe some*body*. I can't quite put my finger on it, but his behavior troubles me."

"So, he doesn't know you've been watching him?"

"Nope. And I want to keep it that way."

A sadness swept over me. "The Ellisons were our host family. They welcomed us in here. For years, they lived across the street from our house. Matt's been my friend since we were kids."

"Don't matter. When it comes down to survival of the fittest, friends tend to disappear."

I considered Crenshaw's remark, and stored it in the back of my mind. "So what do we do? How can I find out if the Ellisons are our friends or our enemies?"

"We need to get a hold of Charlie's identification chip." Once again, Crenshaw was asking the impossible. But all of his other ideas had found success. Zaq and I had followed his map and found the bunker. We'd connected with President Brooks. And we'd made it back to the time capsule unharmed.

I reconsidered Crenshaw's suggestion. "Charlie's apartment is next door to ours. We share the same bathroom. Maybe I can get inside their cubicle and do some searching when they're not home or when they're asleep."

Crenshaw's breathing grew heavier and louder, like my suggestion troubled him. "I don't know if I can let you do that, Olivia. It could be dangerous. Why don't you just tell the leadership and have them conduct a search?"

"No, we don't know if the leadership can be trusted. I can do this, Mr. Crenshaw. I'll be careful."

"Then at least tell your father."

"He'll never agree. Please, let me figure something out on my own. The less people know about this, the better. At least, for now."

I stroked his arm, just skin and bones beneath his polyester shirtsleeve. I couldn't help but pity the old guy. What was he like in his younger days? Probably a virile young man with muscular arms and a vibrant personality, I imagined. So this was what it meant to grow old. We could expect to just wither away gradually, like my grandparents had done and like Crenshaw was doing now. And like Brooks was doing too. I wondered, would he be up to taking the helm again when the time came? My heart nearly stopped beating with the thought that neither one of them—Brooks nor Crenshaw—had much longer to serve. I may have been one of the last people who was privileged to get that close to the old man who was sitting right there beside me, close enough to touch.

I found one ray of encouragement in all of it. Though Crenshaw's body was wasting away, his brain had remained youthful. He remembered more about the last 95 years than I had learned from my studies. The guy was amazing. I knew then that I could trust him with my very life.

"Don't worry about me," I consoled him. "I'll choose the right moment, when the Ellisons have left their apartment or maybe after they're all asleep. Then I'll meet with you again in the morning, right after breakfast, and I'll tell you everything."

Chapter Twenty-Five

If nothing else, our programmed meal times and sleeping schedule were going to help me know when the Ellisons left their apartment and when they returned. Before coming into that place, we depended on the usual cycle of daylight and nighttime hours to guide us. Now, unless we spent most of our time in the dome, we never knew whether it was day or night. The leadership signaled loud and clear when it was time to congregate in the dining hall. Bedtimes were strictly set. Everyone had to be in their apartments by 10 p.m.

After supper, Mom returned from her cleanup duties in the kitchen. My father left Charlie and was in our main sitting room watching the administration's daily report on the virtual screen.

I waited in my cubicle, flipped through pages of Grandma's Bible and paused to read the little notations she'd made in the margins.

Pay attention to this verse, she wrote, with an arrow pointing toward Psalm 91:1. And she'd drawn a big heart around Isaiah 40:28–31. *Mount up with wings as eagles?* With all the challenges I'd been facing, I needed wings.

Shortly after I read that passage, Mom and Dad retired to their bedroom and shut their door. Peter fell asleep while playing combat surveillance in his cubicle. He lay there, half on and half off his bed. I carefully moved his legs up and covered him with a quilt. Then I went to my cubicle to wait for the sounds of slumber to fill the air.

I kept checking my FlexPhone and noted the time. Around

midnight, I stepped quietly out of my room and headed for the bathroom we shared with the Ellisons. Inside the tiny cubicle I breathed easier, inhaled the scent of Jeanine's perfumed soaps, and the spill of minty toothpaste Matt must have left behind. The opposite door led to the Ellisons' apartment. Fortunately, the only locks were on the inside of the bathroom door. I reached out and carefully turned the handle. The door popped open. I held my breath and peered through the opening. The Ellison's main room lay in darkness. A deep rumble rose from the two bedrooms.

I opened the door, careful not to make a sound, and slipped inside the apartment. I didn't know exactly where to begin my search, but to my relief, Charlie's FlexPhone and ID chip were sitting in plain site on the dinette table. I was about to grab Charlie's ID chip, when a flickering red light drew my attention to a far corner of the room. Frowning with curiosity, I stepped toward the flashing red dot. It sparked from deep under a side table, partially hidden beneath a black cloth. I lifted the cloth and found a small metal box with a narrow point on one end and an on-and-off toggle switch at the other. It was set to red, the *Off* light. Beside it was a green bulb, but it wasn't lit. It was too dark for me to make out the letters, which appeared to be in a foreign language anyway. *Okay,* I figured. *They usually mean Stop and Go, or On and Off.* Three narrow tubes protruded from the top of the metal box and seemed to be attached with wires to another container with two small bottles holding a clear liquid. I turned on my FlexPhone and shined its light on the bottles, one at a time. Squinting, I read their labels. *Nitro-methane* and *ammonium nitrate.* I shot a series of pictures.

I frowned in thought. I would have to ask Mr. Crenshaw what those labels mean. I hurried back to the table to grab Charlie's chip. I was inches away, when a scraping sound rose from the opening to the family's sleeping quarters. I turned. A shadow had emerged from one of the bedrooms and was standing within 10 feet of me. The silhouette was familiar. Broad shoulders, scruffy hair, and about five feet, ten inches tall with muscular arms. Matt.

"What are you doing, Livie?" he whispered. "Why are you in my apartment?"

I edged closer to the table. "Hi, Matt."

I scrambled for an explanation, tried to come up with something he'd believe.

"I wanted to—to return your father's gun."

He looked me up and down and noted that my hands were empty. "Okay, so where is it?"

"It's in my backpack. I never used it." My response sounded lame, but he didn't flinch, just stood there, his eyes boring through me. "I'm sorry, Matt."

"I knew it was you who took my dad's gun. Just bring it back, and I won't ask you any questions."

"I will," I said. "If you'll wait a sec, I'll go and get it."

In the dim light I made out that he had crossed his arms, like he didn't trust me or was responding in anger. I chewed my bottom lip. If our friendship wasn't damaged before, it had to be now. Relationships are based on trust, right? He obviously no longer trusted me.

I spun away and retreated to my apartment, rummaged through my bag and returned with Charlie's gun and the box of ammo. My eyes darted to the dinette table. Charlie's FlexPhone and ID chip were still sitting there, in plain sight. I handed Matt the gun and the box of ammo, then I backed away, closer to the table.

"I'll keep it in my room and put it all back in the morning, after my parents leave for breakfast," he said, keeping his voice low. "You could have gotten me in a lot of trouble, Olivia."

He'd used my given name, a bad sign. No more *Livie*.

"I'm really sorry, Matt."

In the next second, when he turned his back on me, I grabbed Charlie's FlexPhone and ID chip. Then Matt spun around and took a couple steps toward me. "You know, I've had feelings for you for as long as I can remember," he said, and in the dim light I caught the hurt in his eyes. "But no more. You broke a trust with me that can't be repaired."

Here was the guy who once saved my life, the dear friend who'd pulled me out of an old freezer and kept me from suffocating to death. My chess partner, my neighbor, my friend for years. But he was right. A broken trust can't be repaired. Though he never would have admitted it, I'd been rejecting his advances from the beginning. I turned away, bent beneath an overwhelming sadness. If I hadn't met Zaq, I may have settled for Matt. *Settled. That's not love.* In any case, he couldn't even be my friend anymore.

I grasped the FlexPhone and Charlie's ID in the palm of my hand with small satisfaction. Once again, I'd deceived a good friend. But, the truth was, I had to find out if his father had fallen under enemy control. What if Charlie Ellison was the person who had infiltrated our time capsule and was causing all the problems, maybe even threatening to annihilate us? Maybe the metal box with the red light might be the very tool he was going to use.

I didn't look back. Didn't say another word, just passed through the bathroom door and headed straight for my cubicle.

I knew I should try to get some sleep, but I settled lotus-style on my bed, grabbed my virtual tablet and inserted Charlie's ID chip in the slot. Besides showing a very bad photo of Charlie, the screen displayed a complete history of the man's life, all the way back to his birth on January 27, 2016, making him 42 years old. I scrolled through his educational years, back when kids still rode big yellow buses to actual school buildings and they were only beginning to do virtual lessons at home. Then came his college education. He'd studied architecture, of course, and he did some online studies in three-dimensional printouts. He attended further training in a high-tech institution in Russia for four years. He won several awards for his designs, and once back in the United States, he landed a lucrative position with a firm that built high-rise office buildings.

It all seemed normal and even boring, except for one notation that caught my eye. It was his birth name. It wasn't Charles Ellison after all. It was Karl Semenov. My face went cold. *Semenov? Charlie has a Russian name?* The whole time he was living across the street from us, he may have been working for the enemy. He had to be the saboteur. I was certain of it. Everything suddenly made sense—how the Ellisons were the first to leave our neighborhood for the time capsule, Jeanine's strange visit to our house and Mom's unexplained drift from reality. Charlie bringing a gun into the time capsule, when it wasn't allowed. He'd claimed to have shot the baboon in the hall. Why did he let the other monster go free? I pondered all of this, but I couldn't come up with any answers. What could go wrong next? Was Charlie going to destroy the people who'd found shelter in the time capsule? My family too?

I removed Charlie's chip and turned my attention to his FlexPhone. The left screen displayed the usual prompts for communication and research. The right panel had only one icon, a small black box with a gold letter V in the middle. I tapped it with my finger, and a list of instructions popped up. Charlie had already checked off several items on the list. I cringed after each one, growing more and more anxious before reaching the bottom.

> *Find out all you can about Rave Jackson's work.* Check
> *Add rat poison to coffee urn.* Check.
> *Monitor number of dead.* Check.
> *Gather tools for incendiary device.* Check.
> *Begin to assemble explosives.* Check.
> *Disable electrical system.* Check.
> *Free the baboons.* Check.
> *Kill one for cover.* Check.
> *Let the other one escape with minor injuries.* Check.
> *Complete work on incendiary device.*
> *Set plan for family's escape.*

Annihilate capsule and everyone in it.

The last three items on the list hadn't yet been checked off.

I was certain I'd found the saboteur. Perhaps my grandma was looking down on me. Perhaps God had been guiding me all along. I was overwhelmed with sadness. This family—this man I had come to trust—they were the enemy. And what about Matt? Was he involved too?

I read again the last of Charlie's instructions, shaking my head in dismay.

Complete work on incendiary device. I thought about the metal box. As far as I could tell, it looked like it hadn't been armed. The red light was flashing.

Set plan for family's escape. That meant the Ellisons were planning to leave the capsule and find safety.

Annihilate capsule and everyone in it. As long as the Ellisons were still inside, there'd be no danger to the rest of us. This wasn't a kamikaze mission. It was murder.

My heart was beating in my throat. I couldn't breathe. I'd been right about Charlie. He was the saboteur. Poor Matt. Or was he in on it too? I had no doubt Jeanine was involved. But Matt?

So the Russians were killing us off—a few at a time—on the inside. In the end, they could set off the big blast, destroying everyone. I didn't know what was happening in the other time capsules. Probably they also were suffering from similar attacks. I hoped Martino had been able to send out a warning.

So the meeting of zone leaders had been a huge farce. America's allies were in danger. The leaders of China, Russia, Iran, and North Korea had not kept their word. They'd allowed the plan to continue knowing they were going to destroy the time capsules all over the world, except their own.

We'd been under the impression they were going to preserve a chosen few to help with the rebuild. They'd agreed that each country could preserve a remnant for repopulation and rebuilding after the war. It was obvious, the enemy had no intention of letting Americans succeed in work or in life.

What was it Brooks had said? More than fifty time capsules in Europe already had been destroyed, and all the people in them had died. It looked to me like we could be next. We needed to stop the Ellisons—or the Semenovs—or whatever their real name was.

I needed to talk with Crenshaw, needed him to figure out a plan and soon. Waves of nausea swept through me, and I felt like I was about to pass out. Like a therapist had taught me years ago, whenever I got into a stressful or close place, I needed to take a deep breath and let it out slowly. I did that now, several times. When I talked with Crenshaw in the morning, I'd have to make sure my dad was there. He also needed to know what I had discovered.

Overwhelmed and exhausted, I stashed Charlie's phone and ID chip in my backpack and lay back against my pillow. A thousand scenarios raced through my head. How was Charlie planning to attack? What exactly was that metal box in the corner? A bomb? Was he going to blow up the time capsule? If we wanted to stop him, we needed to know his plan. I'd gotten a few tips from his FlexPhone, but the information didn't provide enough details.

More questions surfaced. How did the Russians destroy the European time capsules? Was there a time frame, a deadline when Charlie had to get it done? Was he communicating with a main operation in Moscow? Did Iran's nuclear arsenal have anything to do with the final plan? So many questions but I had no answers.

I hit the light switch and reached for my Bible. Once more, I turned to the last book—Revelation—and I flipped to chapter twenty-one. *And I saw a new heaven and a new earth: for the first heaven and the first earth were passed away; and there was no more sea.* I pondered the verse. Was that the way the end would come? What about all those bowls and plagues and judgments mentioned in the previous chapters? I didn't recall any of those things taking place as yet.

I wished I had paid more attention to Pastor Getz's sermons. Wished I had read the books he recommended. Wished I had studied my grandma's Bible more thoroughly.

All I could do now was pray and hope God had not forsaken us, that we still had a chance to survive.

Chapter Twenty-Six

Morning didn't come fast enough. I must have gotten out of bed a half-dozen times during the night. Now, at 6 a.m., I went into the bathroom and listened for the Ellisons to depart. For a few minutes I could hear Charlie griping about having lost his FlexPhone. I heard scraping and rustling like a search was going on, then the three of them walked out in the hall and slammed the door behind them. They shuffled past our apartment, all three of them talking at once. After their voices faded down the hall, I felt it was safe to venture next door again.

I quickly transferred Charlie's list of duties to my own FlexPhone, then I passed through the bathroom door into their apartment. I returned Charlie's FlexPhone and ID chip to the table exactly where I had found them the night before. I giggled to myself and imagined Charlie's moment of confusion when he came home later and found everything right where he'd left them.

After that, I went about my day, as usual. First stop—the dining hall. I hurried through breakfast, chose a reconstituted Danish pastry and a cup of tea. I ignored Matt and his parents and found a seat at the other end of the room. Matt was glaring at me, like he hadn't gotten over our confrontation about his father's gun. I doubted our friendship would ever get back to what it once was. The Ellisons left the cafeteria without saying a word to me or my parents. My mom complained about all the work that was piling up in the kitchen. I sensed she was about to invite me to join her there and help. She kept staring at me, like she was trying to catch my attention. I avoided making eye contact with her.

I leaned close to Dad and whispered in his ear. "I have to talk to you, Dad. Let's get out of here. We can go to the dome and find Mr. Crenshaw."

"What about Peter?" he said.

"He'll want to follow us, Dad. We can't have that. He's got a big mouth, and what I have to share with you must remain secret for now."

Dad frowned pensively and rose from the table.

"Give Peter something to do, something he'll enjoy," I suggested. "You and Mr. Crenshaw need to know what I found last night. You're not gonna believe it."

"I'll get Peter settled in the workout room," Dad conceded. "There's enough toys in there to keep him busy for at least an hour. I'll meet you in the dome."

Mom had been watching us, but blinked away her interest and left for the kitchen.

I gave Dad a nod and hurried out of there. Minutes later I arrived in the dome to find Mr. Crenshaw waiting, as usual with a cup of steamy coffee in his hand. I pulled a chair up beside him and settled into it. Crenshaw took a sip of his coffee, then placed what was left in his chair's cup holder. He turned to look at me and his stark, blue eyes widened with interest.

"You've got news for me, don't ya?" he said, and the blue of his eyes sharpened.

I lifted out of my chair and leaned close enough to kiss his cheek. The intimacy had become acceptable to both of us, for the old guy had become a substitute grandfather to me. As I backed away, I caught him smiling.

"So your secret mission was a success?" he said, raising his eyebrows.

"It was. I have lots to tell you. But I can't say anything until my father gets here."

"We'll wait for your Dad," Crenshaw agreed.

We didn't have to wait long. Seconds later, my father entered the dome, acknowledged the old man with a pat on his shoulder, and pulled up a chair across from us. I smiled at the picture we must have made—a nice little circle of intimacy.

"Okay," Crenshaw said. "I've been patient long enough. Tell us what you've discovered, Olivia, and don't leave anything out."

Slowly and holding down my own emotions, I relived the events of the night before, how I ventured into the Ellisons' apartment, found Charlie's FlexPhone and ID chip and then encountered Matt.

Dad flushed with unease. "You took a terrible risk, Olivia. Why didn't you call me?"

I shrugged. "I don't know, Dad. I felt like I could handle it. You know, less noise. It turned out fine."

"Did you learn anything of importance?" Crenshaw asked, bringing our discussion back to the main point.

My sly grin brought a smile to the old man's lips. My dad also picked up my unspoken message and leaned closer.

"The best thing I can do is let you read it for yourselves." I opened my FlexPhone and showed them Charlie's checklist. Crenshaw kept shaking his head and chewing his lower lip.

My father scooted to the edge of his seat. "That list mentions everything that has gone wrong since we entered the time capsule. And they all point to a common end, Charlie's plan to blow this thing up." He straightened and looked at me. "But how?"

I told them about the metal box with the blinking red light. My description got both of them flushing with rage—a rage that intensified after I opened my photos and showed them the names of the two chemicals, *Nitro-methane* and *ammonium nitrate*. They also were able to see what I saw. The metal box and all the tubes and wires. Though the photos were a little dark, the images had enough detail to incite their concern.

Frown lines creased Dad's forehead. His cheeks turned a bright pink, and he made a fist. "There's no doubt about it.

Charlie's gonna blow us up," he said between clenched teeth. "I trusted that man, and he's a traitor, an enemy."

I caught my breath. "That's not all, his name isn't Charles Ellison, it's Karl Semenov. Dad, he's a Russian."

Crenshaw would have come out of his seat if he had the strength. "We have to do something," he fumed. "We can't let him get away with this."

I closed my FlexPhone with a loud snap, hiding the evidence but preserving it for later. The three of us fell into a deathlike silence. The only sound was the subtle click of the atmosphere filtering system turning on. I inhaled deeply of the cool burst of air. I looked at Dad. He appeared to be deep in thought. Crenshaw, too, was stroking his chin, nodding, and blinking his eyes. I only hoped they'd be able to figure out how to deal with Charlie Ellison.

Dad was the first to speak. "That object with the blinking red light. It sounds an awful lot like a homemade bomb."

I nodded. "I thought so too."

Crenshaw shifted slightly and bobbed his head. "It's definitely a bomb. A crude one at best. I've seen those contraptions before. Some of the components could be outdated, but they still work and are capable of putting out a blast that would annihilate this entire capsule if placed in the right location." He shook his head and the sparkle left his eyes. "I have to wonder how Charlie was able to smuggle all those parts in here past the guards."

"And a gun," I added.

Crenshaw gave a shrug. "Heck! They didn't even make us go through a screening process. Just let us all in, guns and bombs and whatever. No scanners. No searches. Just a big welcome. Looks to me like they were makin' us sittin' ducks right from the start."

Dad leaned closer toward Crenshaw and me. He lowered his voice. "In any case, we're gonna have to watch Charlie Ellison, but we'll have to be careful. We don't want him to suspect we're onto him. The thing is, that man isn't about to blow anything up with his wife and son still here. He's gonna want to get them to safety first."

"We should definitely keep an eye on them," I agreed. "There are times when you and Charlie get together, Dad, but you can't just follow him around. It would look suspicious."

"I can help," Mr. Crenshaw offered. "I can keep an eye out for Charlie and that wife of his whenever they come inside the dome. I've caught sight of them before—sometimes together but more often separately." He grunted a chuckle. "It's easy to keep track of that woman. The way she dresses would light up a dark room at a brothel. What strikes me is, she seems overly interested in the coffee urns."

Dad looked at me and blinked like he wanted to tell me something but didn't know how to say it.

"What, Dad? Do you think Mom is in danger?"

"I don't know, honey. I don't want her to get like she was, and if Jeanine had anything to do with her sickness we're gonna have to keep a good watch. We may have to fill Mom in on what's been going on. That way she'll be careful too." He paused and released a sigh. "We've got to keep our eyes on the whole family. Not just Charlie." He looked straight at me. "Much as I hate to say it, I think Matt could be inv—"

I caved. "I suppose I could hang around with him again."

Dad eyed me with compassion. "I don't want it to put you in danger."

"Matt's mad at me, Dad. But I know how to handle him. I'll just apologize and win his trust." I caught the look of concern on my dad's face. "I'll be fine. Really."

"The guy likes you, Olivia. I've seen it in his eyes, the way he stares at you through dinner. He hardly touches his food. That boy is definitely into you."

My face heated up. I must have turned a bright red. I sputtered out a nervous laugh. "You're not serious, Dad."

"Oh, yes I am. You don't have to make any promises, but it could help a lot if you spent a little time with him, preferably inside their apartment where you can keep track of that device."

"What if it *is* a bomb? Isn't that dangerous?"

Dad narrowed his eyes, like he knew something about explosives. "It doesn't sound like it's been armed. You said it had a flashing red light…"

I nodded. "Okay, I'll go over there, but I have to admit, I'm nervous about that thing. I may not be able to keep from staring toward that corner of the room, and Matt's sure to notice."

"One thing is certain," Dad said, turning his attention to Crenshaw. "We're gonna need to know when Charlie checks off the rest of his list. You may be the only one of us who will spot when that happens."

"I don't know," said Crenshaw. "You have a better chance of doing that when you're talking with him about the new build. Can you arrange more meetings with him?"

"I can, but I don't want to make him suspicious. As risky as it sounds, we have to catch him in the act of doing *something*."

Crenshaw's face was solemn. "For now I think it's best if we keep this information between the three of us. We don't know who we can trust."

"We need to get started," Dad said. "I'll try to meet with Charlie to go over some specs for the new build. I'll stick with him like glue until lunchtime." He turned to me. "Olivia, you get with Matt as soon as possible. Apologize to him, and sound like you mean it. Ask him to play a virtual game or something." He faced the old man. "Mr. Crenshaw, wherever you are you can just keep your eyes open. Watch for Jeanine to make an entrance. She'll never suspect that you're watching her." He stood and stretched. "We'll meet again after supper tonight, before we retire."

Crenshaw smiled in agreement, then he leaned back with a sigh. I nodded thoughtfully. Though I had reservations about being in the same room with that *bomb*, I felt pretty good about my role. I was beginning to feel more like a spy and less like a teenager. I couldn't help but smile. *Zaq would be proud of me.*

We had our marching orders. Dad left to find Charlie. Crenshaw remained in the dome, his eyes on the entry hall. And I headed out to look for Matt. I ventured into the weight room, the most likely place to find him an hour after breakfast. He was working out with a set of free weights. His muscular chest bulged beneath his sweat-stained tank shirt, and he accompanied every lift with a resounding grunt. He caught me watching from the doorway but he kept on pumping. His veins stuck out on his neck, and his face had turned the color of his copper hair.

I crossed my arms and leaned against the doorframe, prepared for a battle of wits. I couldn't believe Matt had turned bitter cold toward me. Somehow, I had to thaw the frost over his heart.

He finished the set and put the weights aside.

"Have you seen my brother, Peter?" I asked him. "My Dad thought he might have come in here after breakfast."

He gave a quick glance in my direction, didn't answer, just walked to the treadmill and began another workout. I wasn't about to wait twenty or thirty minutes for him to finish. I approached his treadmill and pressed the red cut-off button. The belt jerked to a stop. Matt glared at me, his blue eyes aflame.

"Please, Matt." I offered a friendly smile. "I didn't really come in here looking for Peter. I was looking for you. I wanted to apologize. Please, come and walk with me, so I can explain."

His frown slowly melted away. The flush subsided from his cheeks. He ran a hand through his damp hair, smirked, and stepped off the machine.

"Okay. I'll give you ten minutes." He said, his voice flat.

"That's all I'm asking for." I grabbed a towel off the shelf and held it out to him.

He took it, mopped his brow and underarms, then tossed it in a bin filled with dirty towels.

We left the gym and headed nowhere in particular, just meandered through the hallways, and ended up in the dome.

Crenshaw was watching the door like a hawk. I caught his nod of approval.

"I'm sorry I took your father's gun." I managed a sideways glance in an effort to catch his reaction. He was stone-faced.

"As you probably heard, I left the time capsule," I confessed. We stopped walking, and I moved in front of him, blocking his path.

He stared at me. No emotion. "I never heard," he said.

"You have to understand, Matt. I wanted to find Zaq. And you know, that baboon was still out there. I needed protection."

His frown deepened. "Okay, so did you find your *boyfriend?*" The emphasis on the last word sent a shiver down my spine. It was obvious Matt still cared about me, and he resented Zaq. But I could see a flicker of interest in the way his blue eyes searched my face. His voice had trembled when he spoke the word, *boyfriend.* All I needed to do was win back his trust. No promises. No denials. Just reestablish the friendship we once had.

I admitted only part of the truth. "Yes, I found him. Zaq wanted to stay with his buddies, and I came back here." I left out everything else. Matt didn't need to know about our trip to White Sulphur Springs, the meeting with Harmon Brooks, the Greenbrier Bunker, or our fantastic ride in the Robotruck. He definitely didn't need to know we had transported incendiary devices and that Zaq was mounting them on drones at that very moment. As long as Matt didn't ask any questions, I wouldn't have to lie to him. Just tell him enough to keep him interested. The main thing was, I needed to keep an eye on him, to make sure he wasn't planning to leave the time capsule any time soon. Once he did that, Charlie would be free to set off the bomb.

"Why don't we make up and start over?" I smiled sweetly and batted my eyelashes.

"Don't ever trick me like that again, Livie."

"I won't. It was one time, Matt. Really. We're still friends. We'll *always* be friends."

He released a long sigh. I saw disappointment in his eyes and in the pathetic way he looked away from me.

"Why don't we play some chess?" I suggested. "I might just beat you for real this time."

I didn't like deceiving him. I could almost feel guilty if I didn't have a bigger purpose in mind.

Matt sniffed his armpit. "I need to take a shower first. Do you want to wait in our sitting room?"

"Of course."

I couldn't think of anything better. With the sitting room lit up and Matt in the shower, I might be able to get a better look at that strange box in the corner.

I walked with Matt to his apartment. As we passed the door to our place I caught the sound of music pouring from our virtual set. I recognized the '90s hits and knew Mom was in there, humming along, like she used to do. It soothed my heart to have her back with us.

Besides watching Matt, I needed to keep an eye on my mother. Not only to protect her, but to make sure Jeanine didn't come around to our apartment. Though it wouldn't be easy, I needed to look for opportunities to follow her as well.

For the moment, I needed to put all of my attention on Matt. Winning back his trust had been easy. Keeping it was another story. If I made one mistake, I'd lose him for good.

For now, he was back to hovering over me like a lovesick calf. We entered his apartment. I settled into a chair in the sitting room, and he programmed one of his virtual games on the wall monitor.

"That'll keep you busy for a few minutes," he said. "See if you can beat my last score of 525."

Then he grabbed a bottle of water and disappeared inside the bathroom. As long as I could hear the shower running, I could snoop around at will. I headed right for the corner, lifted the edge of the tablecloth and lurched backward. The metal box was gone. So were the little tubes and wires that looked like the makings of a bomb. In their place was a pile of three-dimensional architectural components, most likely parts of a model for the new construction, maybe an apartment complex or a bunch of spec houses. There were no bottles of chemicals, no tubes, no wires, nothing like what I saw there yesterday.

I glanced around the room. Nothing out of the ordinary. Everything looked totally innocent, and I began to wonder if I'd seen a bomb in the first place.

The shower stopped running. I quickly peeked inside the bedrooms. No sign of any of those strange objects in there. They were definitely gone. But where?

Just before the bathroom door opened, I scooted over to the table and grabbed a seat. I turned my attention to the wall monitor, then lifted the remote and clicked it off. I would simply play chess with Matt and keep my eyes open.

Matt emerged from the shower looking refreshed and boyish. His blue eyes were sparkling. His wet hair was slicked back, and he wore a pair of shorts and a tight T-shirt that emphasized his chest muscles. Any girl would have been happy to call him her boyfriend. But he wasn't Zaq. My boyfriend was not as muscular, but he had a quiet strength that appealed to me. His brown eyes weren't as striking as Matt's blue ones. But when I looked into Zaq's eyes, I found comfort there, and peace. Matt had saved my life once, but it was Zaq who made me feel secure. Matt made me feel like I had to keep proving my friendship, and that was hard work.

Matt placed his chess board on the table between us. I smiled with amusement. In spite of all the technological advancements that had turned most board games into holographic exercises, Matt had hung onto his grandfather's wood-carved set. He gave me white, which also gave me the advantage. It meant I could move first. But I had to admit, nothing really gave me an advantage when I was playing with Matt. He'd held several championships for years.

I made my first move and sent a pawn forward. Matt

observed like a hawk, and I could almost see the wheels turning inside his head. He was already plotting his next four or five moves, while I was still deciding what my next move would be.

He was grinning with confidence like he used to do before we had our little spat. I might have felt sorry for him if I didn't find him utterly pathetic.

Chapter Twenty-Seven

While I tried to concentrate on the game, I couldn't help but wonder how things were going with Dad. Hopefully, he was having better luck with Charlie than I was having with Matt. In any case, we needed to stop the enemy's plan before it was too late. Since the strange device was no longer in Charlie's apartment, I assumed he'd placed it somewhere else inside the time capsule. But where?

Then there was the question of whether or not he'd finished putting the thing together. My dad had said the blinking red light meant the device had not yet been armed. Tubes and wires had lain to the side. Being a successful architect, Charlie could have put it together in minutes and then moved it to a place where it could do the most damage. As I pondered this, I tried to keep my hands from shaking. I didn't want Matt to see how stressed I'd become.

Our chess game had started slowly, but after six moves I had already lost my queen and both of my knights, and my king stood trapped in a corner. Matt had set a snare, and there was no escape. He leaned over the board, his chin in his hand, a sly glint in his eyes. I sighed with resignation, gently lay down my king and congratulated him with a handshake.

"Time for me to leave," I conceded. I rose from my chair and headed for the door.

"Hey, where are you going?" Matt called after me. "We have time to play another game." He winked. "Maybe you'll beat me this time."

"I need to take care of something." I left him sitting there, a stunned and curious look on his face.

I went straight to the dome and found Crenshaw in the exact spot where I'd left him. He'd reclined his wheelchair all the way back, almost like a bed, and his head lolled to one side. His empty coffee cup rested on its side on the floor. I had wanted to tell him the devise was gone, but he was sleeping so soundly, I chose not to awaken him.

A new plan rolled around in my head. I strolled around the perimeter of the dome and gazed through the glass. Like before, I pressed my hand against the pane, and like before, my fingers disappeared to the other side. I inserted my right foot. It also disappeared. I looked around. A few other people were there, but no one was paying any attention to me. Bravely, I stepped closer, penetrated the glass-like barrier with my whole leg, forced my head and arm in, but couldn't go any deeper. The glass wall was like a giant sponge, absorbing me only a little and then forcing me back inside the dome.

That settled one question. There was no escape through that artificial wall of glass and only two ways out of the capsule. The front entry door, which was securely locked, and the kitchen garbage door. Charlie must have carried the tubes and wires inside his suitcases when he first entered the capsule. Maybe he'd separated everything, placing a few items in his own suitcase and the rest hidden within his wife's underwear and his son's workout clothes. Then, in the privacy of his apartment, he'd assembled everything and now had moved it all to another place where he could either continue working on it or set it off. So why didn't the surveillance monitor catch his activities? Or had we been wrong in assuming we were being watched?

The odd thing was, everybody was there because they wanted to be there. No one was trying to escape, so there was one locked door in the front, maybe to keep other people out, and a garbage door that was never locked but no one seemed to care.

My heart raced, and for the first time since that day in the freezer, I broke out in a sweat. I imagined the destruction, the injuries, the deaths, the annihilation of what we all might face. We had assumed this was a safe place. I tried in vain to take a deep breath. My next thoughts turned to my need for survival. I had to get my mother and brother out of there. And Mr. Crenshaw too. But what about all the other innocent people who'd come to the time capsule under the guise that they would take part in the rebuild when the war ended? I wanted to warn them, but I didn't want to cause a panic. And I didn't want to tip off Charlie or anyone else involved in a plot to kill us all.

I looked around at the people who were milling about the dome, unaware that their lives could be in danger. There was the automobile magnate and his wife and daughter. There was the master chef and his fiancée. There were the mason, the artist, the seamstress, the medical doctor, the science professor. They had all been chosen because of their areas of expertise. But if Charlie's device blew the capsule to pieces, they would never get to use their talents in the new build.

And what about Charlie? He, too, had been chosen for his architectural skills. Jeanine had been a beautician at one time. And Matt? One of a dozen procreators.

At that moment, I realized I hadn't seen Matt since our chess game. Nor had I seen Jeanine since breakfast. And Charlie? I could only hope Dad was still with him.

I looked across the dome to where Crenshaw sat, now stirring from sleep. He pushed a button and raised the back of his chair upright. The power box hummed to life and clicked when the chair reached Crenshaw's desired position. The old man drew a handkerchief from his shirt pocket, mopped his mouth and forehead, and looked around the dome like he'd forgotten where he was for the moment. He spotted me watching him, grinned, and waved me over.

I went to his side, but stopped short of his chair. His eyes had a glassy, almost vacant stare, and he was trembling all over.

"What's wrong, Mr. Crenshaw?"

"Don't know." Then he lolled to one side, like he was having a seizure.

"We need to get you to the clinic."

He didn't argue with me. His spunk was gone. I stared in shock at this weak, helpless old man. In a panic, I hurried to the back of his chair, pressed the electronic button, and the chair lurched forward. Using the controls, I adjusted the speed and guided the chair down the hall, trotting along behind it. We went into the elevator, down to the fifth floor, past the entry guard, who shouted after us, and plowed through the double doors to the clinic. The antiseptic hit me the minute I stepped inside. I was instantly reminded of the day I went down there to check on my mom.

The same doctor came toward us. This time he was frowning.

"You should have checked in at the desk," he snarled.

"This is an emergency." I stared him in the eye, defying him. "Mr. Crenshaw needs help. And, he needs it *now!*"

The guard had followed us in and began to protest. Dr. Rand waved her away, then he approached Crenshaw. He bent close and checked the old man's wrist for a pulse. He shined a penlight in those old eyes, now dilated.

The frown on Rand's forehead deepened. "This man appears to be going into shock. You did right by bringing him in here."

I caught my breath. My arms went limp. I began to tremble. We couldn't lose Crenshaw. Not now.

Dr. Rand turned toward a side door. "Dorian! Come out here and give me a hand."

A young man in a white coat burst through the double doors. "Yes, Doctor."

"We've got another one," Rand said, almost in a panic.

"Another one?" I asked. "Another what?"

Ignoring my outburst, Rand beckoned the young intern to his side. "We need to get him into a bed and hook him up."

In less than a minute they had Crenshaw attached to a heart monitor and a host of other tubes and wires, plus an oxygen mask. Like my mother, his vitals set off a symphony of beeps and thumps on the nearby board, now aglow with multi-colored lights.

Rand got busy sorting through medicines. His intern went to a desk and began to enter information on their electronic file. He turned around and caught my attention.

"The patient's name?"

Andrew Crenshaw."

"Age?"

"I don't know. I think 100 or more."

"There were more questions. Some I could answer and some I could not. I was still standing there holding onto Crenshaw's empty wheelchair. My arms and legs felt like rubber. I feared I was about to lose one of my best friends. I thought back over the last day. Crenshaw had been the picture of health that morning. His eyes had lit up when we talked about spying on Charlie. It was like he had awakened from a long winter's nap and was ready for spring planting. So what had changed? Why did he appear full of life that morning and now looked to be at death's door?

I mentally retraced my steps back to the dome. His coffee cup flashed into my mind. It had been lying on the floor, drained of its contents. Then I remembered. Jeanine had spent an unusual amount of time puttering around the coffee urns that morning. What if she put—

"It's poison," I told the doctor. "I'm sure of it."

He lowered the vial he'd been holding and frowned in disbelief. Then his eyes sparked to life, and he barked an order at the young intern, who immediately rushed off and moments later returned with a large syringe and a tube.

Rand smirked at me. "Impossible."

"Do you remember the sickly young men who came in here last week when my mother was here? You suspected food poisoning then. I have reason to believe someone tampered with the coffee urns. And I believe Mr. Crenshaw drank coffee that may have been tainted a little while ago." I turned toward

Crenshaw, his eyelids half shut. Then I looked imploringly from the doctor to the intern. "Please, do something, doctor. Don't let him die." I must have sounded like an anxious relative, I didn't care what I sounded like, I wanted Crenshaw to live. I needed him. More than that, I loved the old guy.

Dr. Rand stared at me. "He does have many of the same symptoms of the others who came in," he conceded. "Shallow breathing, pale, damp skin, rapid heartbeat. And look at these sores around his mouth." He took a deep breath, then barked more orders at the intern, who inserted the tube through Crenshaw's nose and ran it down to his stomach. He began to pump the syringe. Slowly, a brown liquid ran along the translucent tube into the bowl.

I could hardly believe it. After all this time and all the advancements in medical technology, they were still using the same old method that worked on my grandfather when he got food poisoning from eating spoiled pork almost 40 years ago. It was amazing how far we'd come with some procedures and how far behind we remained with others.

The doctor glanced in my direction. "You need to leave," he said, and he returned to Crenshaw.

Reluctantly, I pushed Crenshaw's wheelchair to a corner, then I walked out the door, my heart pulsing. People were still getting sick. If Jeanine had done this, the Ellisons were doing a good job of eliminating residents. Once they left the time capsule, the device would go off, and the rest of us would all be blown to smithereens.

Now I had one goal. I had to find that bomb—if it *was* a bomb. I needed to check every floor, starting with the dome. I could make my way down each level to the bottom floor, if necessary. I needed to connect with my dad so we could finish the search together. But first, there was one more thing I needed to take care of.

I flew to the dome, hoping to find Crenshaw's coffee cup, so Dr. Rand could test it for poison. It wasn't there. I checked behind every piece of furniture—under and around the scattering of tables and chairs, behind the potted plants, and the free-standing lamps. His coffee cup was gone.

"What-cha lookin' for?" The squeaky voice belonged to my brother, Peter. I turned to face him. In his hand was Crenshaw's coffee cup, with the lip folded down like the old man liked it. A terrible fear coursed through me.

"What are you doing with that cup? You didn't drink from it, did you?"

Peter backed away and his eyes grew big and round. "I was just doin' my job," he whined. "I pick up garbage. This—" he thrust the cup at me, "is garbage."

"Gimme that." I whisked the cup out of his hand and left him standing there, puzzlement screwing up his face. I turned and ran out of the dome.

"I'm tellin' Dad!" he called after me.

I hurried back to the clinic and handed the cup to the doctor. "This is what he was drinking."

Rand took the cup. "Good job. We'll analyze the contents."

While there, I stole a the moment to peek in at Crenshaw. He was sleeping soundly. His color had returned. Comforted, I left the clinic and began my search for Dad.

I had no idea where he went. I returned to our apartment and grabbed my FlexPhone, took a quick look around, and noted that Mom wasn't there. No telling where she might have gone, but I couldn't imagine her spending time with Jeanine. I trusted that wherever she went she was safe.

I opened my phone and cued in Dad's contact info. I slipped inside the bathroom, confident I was apart from any surveillance bugs.

Dad answered on the first buzz. His life-size hologram appeared before me. He looked a little worn. His shirt hung on him like he'd thrown it on in a hurry, and he definitely needed a shave.

"Where are you?" I said.

"I finished going over the specs with Charlie. He just left.

"Something bad has happened, Dad. I had to take Mr. Crenshaw to the clinic. He was really sick. I think it was food poisoning, maybe something in his coffee. They had to pump his stomach."

"Is he alright?"

"He was when I left him there."

A few uncomfortable seconds passed. Dad released a long sigh. "Something else happened, Olivia. Your mom fainted in the kitchen this morning."

"What?" Panic began to set in all over again.

"She's fine. They put a cool cloth on her forehead and revived her. She didn't want to go back to the clinic, said she was okay. She's in the apartment now."

"No, she's not. I'm at the apartment. She was in here humming a little while ago. Now she's gone. Dad, something really screwy is going on."

"I thought you were supposed to be with Matt."

"I was, for a while. I played chess with him. But there's a problem. The box and all the wires and tubes has disappeared. I'm positive it was in the corner of Matt's apartment last night. While Matt was in the bathroom taking a shower, I had an opportunity to look around. I have to tell you, Dad, Charlie's little project is gone."

"Are you sure?"

"Positive. I looked everywhere. You know, that can only mean one thing."

"Right. Charlie's getting ready to check off the last few items on his list."

"We need to look for it, Dad. Time is running out."

"You're in the apartment now?"

"Yes, I'm still here."

"Wait for me there. We'll search the capsule together."

The trembling came back worse than ever. I was certain the walls were closing in on me. I couldn't breathe. Perspiration began to bead up on my forehead and the back of my neck. I burst out of the closeness of the bathroom and went to the sitting room to wait for Dad.

A myriad of questions ran through my brain. What could I expect if we found that device? Did Dad know how to disarm something like that? Worse yet, how much time did we have? And, where were the Ellisons? Somehow, we'd lost track of the whole family. For all we knew, they could have set a timer on that device and already left the capsule.

The door to our apartment flew open. In walked Peter. He was scowling at me.

"What's wrong with you, Ollie? Have you gone nuts?"

I swallowed my retort and gave Peter a pat on the head. "No, kid. I just have a lot on my mind. Sorry if I hurt your feelings."

He gave a little shrug. "That's okay. Mom told me there are times when girls get a little cranky."

I had to get rid of him. "Why don't you go to the virtual room and play some games?"

He stuck out his lower lip. "I thought I'd hang out with you for a while."

I couldn't have him following me and Dad. "You can't, Peter. I have something to do, and it isn't something for a little kid."

"I'm not a little kid. My work is finished until after lunch. Then I have to go around and pick up trash again. I'm bored."

"You won't be bored if you get into a virtual game with someone. Why don't you see if other kids might be there, and you can start a dual match?"

"Nah." Shaking his head, he plunked down on a chair and dared me to try and leave him behind.

"You have to leave, Peter. I'm waiting for Dad. We have something important to take care of."

He crossed his arms, and his lower lip jutted out. At that moment, Dad came through the door, spotted Peter sitting there and raised his eyebrows at me, questioning.

"He wants to go with us, Dad. I told him no."

Dad took one look at Peter. "Okay," he said with a shrug. "It won't hurt if he wants to go along."

"But, Dad," I mumbled, drawing closer to his side. "He can't know—"

"Don't worry about it, Olivia. Let him tag along. It may be for the best. We can keep an eye on him. We'll be together."

I let out a long sigh and led the way out of the apartment. We started our search on the first floor and stopped at the same familiar places I visited during my initial tour with Matt. The workout gym, the baby and toddler nursery, the virtual room, the cafeteria, the kitchen. We checked every hall, every nook and cranny, and we found nothing.

"What are we lookin' for?" Peter said, his face aglow with curiosity.

"We're looking for an odd-shaped box with lights," was all Dad told him.

Peter wrinkled his nose, but he trailed on behind us. Dad occasionally glanced back to make sure my brother was still following.

The next levels were filled with apartments. We traveled the halls, certain Charlie would not have access to anyone else's cubicle, so we spent very little time there. We headed down to the fifth level where the clinic was, but couldn't enter most of the areas because of restrictions. Chances were, Charlie couldn't get in there either.

Dad checked his watch. "It's almost time for lunch."

"We have one more level, Dad, the bottom floor." In my mind, the bottom floor was likely Charlie's best option. An explosion set off there would collapse the entire structure, including the dome.

"Sorry, I promised your mom I'd meet her in the cafeteria. Anyway, I want to make sure she's all right."

I had to agree. Despite the importance of our search, my mom meant more to me than anything. If it came time for us to leave, I wanted my whole family to get out with me. And I needed to check on Mr. Crenshaw. I lagged behind as Dad and Peter took the elevator up to the cafeteria, and I went back to the clinic.

I found Crenshaw still hooked up to a heart monitor and an oxygen mask.

"He's gonna be fine," the doctor whispered over the clicking of life-saving machines. "We found traces of brodifacoum in those coffee dregs."

"Brodi—huh?"

"Rat poison."

"Just as I thought. Doctor Rand, we've got to warn people not to drink the coffee."

"I've already taken care of it. The kitchen staff removed the urns. They brought me a sample, and sure enough, rat poison. They've cleaned out the urns and are filling them with the good stuff." He patted my shoulder and gave me a patronizing look. "They're gonna have someone stand right there dishing out the cups. No need to worry, but that was great how you spotted the problem."

"Is it possible to find out who tainted the coffee?" I was certain Jeanine had done it, but perhaps a thorough examination might help.

"I've alerted the guards. It's in their hands now."

"When will I be able to talk to Mr. Crenshaw?"

"Not sure. He's medicated. Check back this afternoon."

I left the infirmary and headed for the top floor and the cafeteria. Funny how the time capsule had seemed overwhelmingly complex the day we arrived but now had shrunk into a familiar grid of floors and rooms. I didn't feel quite as closed in since I'd learned my way around. Though I still wanted to get out of there, I was handling the confinement a lot better. Now I had one purpose. Find the device and get it turned off.

Chapter Twenty-Eight

It was supper time, and what a surprise! Charlie and his family were sitting at our usual table. I could relax for a while, knowing they hadn't left. Charlie certainly wouldn't let his wife and son hang around if he was about to set off a bomb. I grabbed a sandwich and a drink. As expected, the bread tasted like paper. The mayo gave a small amount of flavor. And the ham didn't look the least bit like real ham. Still, it was amazing what the cooks had been able to accomplish with the artificial ingredients. I thought back to the first meal we'd had in the capsule. It was like dining in a family restaurant. After that, everything we ate tasted fake and flavorless. After dining with Harmon Brooks, the time capsule food took another step down.

I missed the submarine sandwiches Grandma used to make from scratch. She piled the meat and cheese on and slathered all kinds of sweet dressings over it. What I was sinking my teeth into now had no flavor and no texture. I made a sour face and forced myself to take another bite. I'd already lost ten pounds in the last couple weeks. Couldn't afford to lose any more weight.

As expected, Matt tried to strike up a conversation. He chattered away about a wildlife show he watched on the virtual screen after I left his apartment. I listened with feigned interest and smiled politely, but I had nothing to contribute. I hadn't seen the show, and I wasn't really interested, not with all the strange happenings on my mind. In the last week I'd entered a whole other realm, one where spies lurked and people put together homemade bombs, and presidents made world-saving decisions.

Charlie had stuck his nose in his FlexPhone and seemed glued there. Jeanine fiddled with her hair and checked her fingernails. I signaled my Dad with a pronounced blink. He responded with a slight nod. Without saying a word, we left the table, disposed of our scraps, ready to continue our search. Thankfully, Mom appeared to be fine. Her face had color, and her eyes glistened with life. I was relieved when Mom sent Peter to pick up trash and she headed for the kitchen. Dad and I slipped out of the dining hall.

We headed straight down to the bottom floor. I should have succumbed to the effects of claustrophobia by now, but our mission had zapped me with so much adrenaline my head remained clear, and my focus was set on finding that box. I had a purpose, a job to do, and a strong will to complete it.

The air on the bottom floor carried the pungent odor of animal droppings mixed with some type of chemical—lye perhaps or maybe ammonia. Somewhere beyond the thick wall, dogs snarled, cats howled, and unseen beasts growled and rattled their cages.

"Let's split up," Dad suggested, and he left me standing there while he took off for the electrical compound at the far end. I began my own search among the boxes and crates in the storage area. I methodically checked all the shelves, moved containers from side to side, peered into the farthest corners, but found nothing. I pulled open flaps and looked inside the boxes but only unearthed an assortment of canned goods and packaged foods. I moved toward the refrigeration wall. There was no sign of the lighted device that had stood in the corner of the Ellisons' apartment. It had literally disappeared. I began to think I'd been mistaken. Maybe I only thought there were chemicals and tubes and wires. I'd been so wrapped up in the previous days' adventure, I wondered if my mind might have been playing tricks on me. I took a breath and recalled what I had seen in Charlie's apartment. And I decided. I wasn't imagining anything. The memory was too clear to be an illusion. It was real. The device was real. So were all the tubes and wires. It had to be somewhere down there on the bottom floor.

I completed my search and headed down the hall where Dad had gone. He'd been there a long time. I made my way back to the place where we had separated, then I traced his steps to the electrical compartment.

"Dad?" I called out. I surveyed the upper walls and corners, reasonably sure there were no cameras down there. In fact, I hadn't seen a whole lot of surveillance gadgets in the entire time capsule. Except for those two-way virtual screens in our apartments, it didn't appear the leadership had taken an interest in any of our activities. Could it be they trusted us? Or did they simply want us to *think* they trusted us. In either case, we'd been free to roam about the upper floors. For Dad and me to come all the way down to the lowest level seemed far more risky. Who else would want to come down there except for the kitchen staff and the veterinary crew who worked with the animals?

"Dad?" I called again, a little louder.

"In here."

I followed the sound of his voice, around a corner and through a doorway into a vast room with floor-to-ceiling electronic equipment. Lights flickered, gauges spun, bells and chimes rang. Insulated wires ran along the walls close to the ceiling and disappeared inside a conduit leading to the upper floors. Every piece of electronic equipment in the capsule depended on those controls. That was where Dad had gone to reactivate the power.

"This is what keeps everything going," Dad explained with a sweep of his hand. "Our heating-and-cooling system, our lights, the electric locks on the doors, our virtual screens, and all the equipment used by the kitchen people." He was describing everything like a man who was proud of his job. "This entire setup was so well-planned, little maintenance was needed. I never had to do much to keep things running. It's a nearly foolproof operation that can keep going for many years without a hitch."

"Except for that one time," I reminded him.

"Yes, except for that one time. Somebody must have been messing with the system for it to go down like it did."

"Charlie?"

"Maybe. Come to think of it, the first time we met we came down here. He hit me with an awful lot of questions about how the system worked. I thought we were going to discuss our plans for the rebuild. Instead, he wouldn't let up. Wanted to know how to turn it on and off, and what if there was a power failure—stuff like that."

"I'm sure he did something to it," I insisted. "And while he was down here he probably let those two baboons loose. Then he made a big production about trying to save everyone by shooting one of them."

A rage of heat flowed into my face. "All this time we were thinking Charlie was a good guy, a friend, a neighbor, when in reality, he was the one person we couldn't trust."

"Well, we can't do anything about that now, Olivia. If you're right about Charlie, he would have planted that bomb somewhere down here where it can do the most damage. Not only will it disable the entire electrical system, it'll start several fires throughout the capsule, and if the explosive is powerful enough, it'll demolish the entire facility in one major blowup."

I felt like I was going to faint, so afraid was I, not only for my own life but for the safety of my family and everyone else in the time capsule. Mr. Crenshaw. I would never see Zaq again, never again walk out of that claustrophobic place into the sunshine. And what about Peter? He was only beginning his life. I lost control and began to cry.

Dad wrapped his arms around me and pulled me close. I pressed my cheek against his chest. I could hear his heart beating through his rumpled shirt. The steady rhythm gave me comfort.

"Let's find that bomb," Dad said, releasing me. Again, we headed off in different directions. This time we stayed in the same room. I searched behind piles of extra parts. Dad went to the other side and peered inside cabinets and behind the electrical panels. He reached the far corner and started clearing the area, looking inside boxes, then tossing them aside. I laughed at the sight of him. He reminded me of Peter opening Christmas presents.

Suddenly, Dad froze. "Come here, Olivia. Is this what you discovered in the Ellisons' apartment?"

I ran toward him and looked where he was pointing.

There it was—a metal box, tubes and wires, exactly what I had seen in the apartment, only now everything appeared to be attached.

"Yes, that's it!" I drew closer. "It looks like he's hooked it all up. Look, Dad! The red light is out, the green light is blinking and it's making a beeping noise."

Dad latched onto my arm and drew me back.

I looked up at his face. Deep lines creased his forehead. He was no longer smiling.

"Is it armed, Dad? Does it have a timer?"

"I think so."

"Can you turn it off?"

"I don't know. I've never seen anything like it." He stepped closer, leaving me a few paces behind him.

Suddenly, a dark figure lunged from nowhere. A strong arm swatted me aside. I stumbled backward and fell to the floor. I landed with such force I struck my head against the hard pavement. A sharp pain ran down my neck. My eyes blurred. I blinked several times and tried to catch my breath. As my vision cleared, I made out the shape of a man. Small in stature, but with strong shoulders, and a balding head.

Charlie.

The overhead light illuminated something in his hand. It was partially metal. Looked like a hammer. He began to beat my dad with it. The glint of steel flashed amidst the flickering lights on the electrical control panel. The box against the wall continued to beep and the green light flashed.

I scooted to one side and searched the floor around me for

a weapon—anything to fight back. There were only boxes and wires, a stack of electrical components but nothing hard enough to cause any damage.

Dad was scrambling for a handhold, but Charlie kept bludgeoning him, never giving him a chance to get up and fight back.

I leapt to my feet, gasping from the pain in my shoulder. Then, I rushed back to the storage area and pulled two cans of beans from one of the boxes. I headed back to help my dad. Charlie was pulling my dad off the floor. Despite his compact size, the man had amazing control. More flashes rose from the hammer in his hand. He swung it mercilessly at my father. I heard the crack of bone, followed by a thud, then a guttural cry from Dad's throat.

I threw a can of beans at Charlie's head. It grazed his skull behind his left ear. I threw another, hitting him square in the back of his neck. He turned and glared at me. The kind face that had greeted us the day we moved into the time capsule had morphed into a monstrosity. His eyes flashed with evil. Sneering, he turned back to my dad and continued to swing the hammer. Charlie raised his arm high and was about to bring it down hard on Dad's head, a final blow to finish him off.

A fire raged through me, and without considering my own safety, I rushed in and lunged at Charlie's back, wrapped my arms around his neck, and threw him off balance. I scratched his face and neck, then tightened my grip and just hung on. He shifted his body, grabbed my upper arms, and flung me like a dishrag to the floor. He stood beside me and swung his leg back like he was about to kick me. Helpless, I waited for the crushing blow. It never came.

Instead, a shot rang out. Charlie stumbled away from me and fell to the floor. Blood oozed from his right shoulder. I looked past him and gasped with shock. Matt stood there, his feet planted firmly, his right hand gripping his father's gun.

His face riddled with remorse, he lowered the gun and stepped toward me, reached for my hand, and helped me to my feet. My head swam. My neck and shoulder throbbed, but I felt a great sense of relief. My dear friend had once again saved my life and my father's, too.

"Are you okay?" Matt said almost in a whisper.

"I will be," I said, and pressed one hand against the small of my back. "But my dad—"

I rushed to my father's side and examined the head wound where Charlie had struck him. A trickle of blood oozed onto my fingers. Dad let out a groan and slowly opened his eyes. He tried to push himself off the floor. But, weakened, he fell back in a heap.

I hovered beside him. "Don't get up, Dad. Give yourself a few minutes."

I turned to look at Matt. Tears were running down his face. He walked over to where Charlie lay.

"I suspected my dad was up to something," he said, crouching beside his father. A sob caught in his throat. "He told my mom we needed to move quickly. Said your father was poking his nose where it didn't belong. That machine he'd been working on had disappeared, so I figured he'd moved it somewhere." He looked about to crumble in defeat. "I knew something was up the first time I saw that thing. I asked my dad but he refused to talk about it. When he left in such a hurry, mumbling something about your father, I sensed it wasn't good. I went and got his gun and followed him here."

Matt's sad blue eyes gazed at me and then at my dad. "I'm so sorry, Livie."

He was back to calling me Livie.

I stood close to him and dared to ask, "Did you know your Dad was an enemy agent?"

Matt's face dropped. "There were clues, but I didn't want to believe it."

"Matt, we're gonna have to turn him in. Your mom too. I'm pretty sure she was involved and that she was tainting the coffee with rat poison."

More tears spilled out and ran down Matt's cheeks. "It's true then. There was a box of rat poison in our kitchen. I couldn't understand where it came from or why it was there."

I breathed a sigh. My heart went out to my friend. He'd just discovered his parents were enemy spies. I didn't know what to say. But one thing I knew for certain. Matt was innocent.

"You did the right thing, Matt," Dad said, slowly getting to his knees.

I reached out, took Dad's hand, and helped him stand. "Are you okay? I—I thought he killed you."

He touched the wound on his head, then wiped away a trickle of blood. "I'll be fine. But, we need to figure out how to disarm Charlie's bomb."

Matt handed the gun to my dad and moved toward the metal box. "I know how to do it," he said with confidence. "My dad taught me everything he knows about explosives. I thought he was grooming me for construction work. Now I know better." He straightened his back and looked me in the eye, then turned toward my dad. "I want you to know, I'm an American. I don't want to be anything else."

"It's okay, son. Just do whatever it is you can to disarm that thing."

Matt worked for several minutes, pulling wires and separating the fluid filled tubes from the rest of the components. His fingers moved with such dexterity I was reminded of the day he operated on the holographic patient. I was certain he was cut out for great things. Very soon, the green light stopped pulsing and the metal box stopped beeping. When Matt finished dismantling everything, he stood and lifted the box in one hand then yanked out the remaining wires. There was no green light, and no red light, for that matter. The devise had gone completely dark. And lifeless.

"We don't have to worry about that thing anymore," Matt said, his face flushed. My friend, the chess champ, had accomplished what must have been the greatest feat of his life.

He pressed a hand to Charlie's shoulder. The man groaned but didn't move. He turned sad eyes on his son. "Matt. Why?"

Matt brushed more tears from his face. "I love you, Dad, but I can't—"

Dad rested a hand on Matt's shoulder. "C'mon, son. Let's go and tell the guards. They'll come down here and get your dad."

"No," Matt said, pulling away. "I'll stay with him until you send someone. He's my father. Though I may not agree with his political beliefs, I need to stand beside him." He gestured toward the exit. "You guys need to get going." He stared at me with that same longing I'd seen multiple times, but there was a hint of resignation in his eyes this time.

He offered me a sad smile. "Good luck, Livie. I wish you and Zaq a good life."

His eyes had filled with tears. He quickly turned away from me, knelt beside Charlie, and pressed his hand against the flow of blood at his father's shoulder. Even as I walked away, a lump came to my throat. Matt was a loyal friend. He'd rescued me twice from certain death. Once from the freezer, and again from his own father's rage. Though I could see no future with him, I knew I would always remember him as the dearest friend I ever had.

✝✝✝

Dad and I hobbled off, wrapped in each other's arms. When we got to our apartment, Mom and Peter were waiting. Mom's expression went from anticipation to shocked disbelief. She gazed at Dad with concern etched on her face.

"Where have you been, Rave?" She drew close to him, pulled a handkerchief from her pocket, and gently dabbed the wound on his forehead. "My goodness, what happened?" She looked down. "And your shirt? Where did all this blood come from?"

Dad responded with a little laugh, though he must have been in extreme pain. "It's okay, Clarisse. I had a run-in with Charlie is all."

"Charlie?" She frowned and tilted her head. "He's our friend." She paused for only a second. "Isn't he?"

"Used to be," Dad said. "He *used to be* our friend. Charlie's not only an enemy to us, he's an enemy to our country." He pulled out his FlexPhone. "Hold on a second," he said, and punched in the codes for the guard desk. He reported what had happened with Charlie and let them know exactly where they would find him.

Mom kept blinking, like she was trying to make sense of what Dad was saying. "Rave, tell me what happened. I need to know. Believe me, I can take it." She turned her eyes on me, still questioning. "And Olivia, what happened to your cheek?"

"Yeah," Peter blurted out. "Looks like you been in a fight."

I reached up and felt the place where Charlie'd struck me. Mom guided me to the sitting room, and all four of us settled in chairs there. Dad and I took turns explaining everything to Mom, who moaned in disbelief, and Peter, who sat with his mouth open. The tension in our apartment built as Dad gave his account of what happened from the time he and I searched the bottom floor until we met up with Charlie. When he finished explaining everything, we fell together in the longest group hug our family had ever enjoyed.

Mom got up and went to the bathroom for a wash cloth and a first aid kit.

While she was doctoring Dad, my FlexPhone buzzed. I opened it and released a hologram of Zaq. He stood before us, his face beaming with pride.

"Our mission was a success," he announced. "We've demolished every enemy stronghold. Turn on your virtual screen, Livie. We've been liberated." He laughed and puffed out his chest, like he'd just won a medal. "The reports are coming in hourly," he went on. "American troops have come down out of the hills. All of the invading troops have begun a steady retreat away from American soil. They're leaving by boat, by plane, in every way possible. And guess what, Livie? The leadership in all the

American time capsules have unanimously declared Harmon Brooks President.”

“That’s wonderful, Zaq.” A thrill rushed through me. To think Zaq and I had played a part in saving America from total annihilation. And President Brooks would soon be back in office.

“Get ready,” Zaq went on. “’Cause I’m comin’ to get you. We’re going for another ride in the Robotruck. And this time, I want you to bring your family.”

Peter started clapping his hands and leaping about the room. “Really?! Me too?”

Dad patted Peter on the head. “Yes, son. You too. Okay, Zaq. We’re all going with you.” He turned to Mom. “Clarisse, you and the kids pack what you need. We’re getting out of here.”

We raced around the apartment, gathered our belongings, and met in the sitting room with our luggage. The virtual screen on the wall flashed with more information about the events that had transpired. Dad took a call from the guard desk. The guards had gone down to the bottom level and arrested Charlie, then they went looking for Jeanine.

I met up with Matt in the hall outside our apartment. He was carrying two bags and had a third tucked under his arm.

“Where are you going, Matt?”

“I intend to accompany my folks as far as I’m allowed to go.”

“Surely, they won’t arrest you too, will they? After all, you saved my life, and my dad’s. You stopped the explosives. You’re a hero, Matt.”

“Thanks, Livie. They know I’m innocent. I’ve been granted amnesty. And guess what? To prove my loyalty, I’m gonna join the Marines.”

I gave him a hug, then backed away. No longer did I see a lovesick fool. I was looking at a very brave young man. A hero. “I’m proud to have known you, Matt. I wish you well.”

Throwing his shoulders back, Matt strode off down the hall. Another lump came to my throat and tears welled up in my eyes, as I watched a dear friend walk out of my life forever.

My folks and Peter joined me in the hall, and we started for the time capsule's entry door.

"Wait!" I said, stopping short of the exit. "We need to take Mr. Crenshaw with us. He's in the medical clinic."

Dad looked into my eyes and must have seen the passion there. He melted with acceptance. "Okay, Olivia. Go get him. We'll wait here."

I left my bag with him and hurried to the clinic. It was my last trip down the elevator, to be sure, but I experienced no unease. I reached the clinic and halted in front of an empty bed.

Dr. Rand shrugged. "He left," the medic said. "That stubborn man woke up, got out of bed, and dared us to try to stop him. I imagine you'll find him in the dome, like always."

I raced to the dome, and, sure enough, there was Crenshaw, waiting with all of his baggage.

"Apparently, we're all being released," he said. "I sure want to know how."

I convinced him to stay in the wheelchair, and with his bags piled on his lap, I guided him to the front door where my family was waiting.

"You're going with us, Mr. Crenshaw," I told him. "And I'll explain everything when we get inside our transportation."

As promised, Zaq pulled up in the Robotruck. We helped Mr. Crenshaw into the rear seat. My Dad and Zaq stowed all of our bags in the back along with the old man's wheelchair. The sleek vehicle turned out to be more spacious than it appeared on the outside. There was room for all of us. I grabbed the front seat between Zaq and Dad. Mom and Peter slid in next to Crenshaw.

Zaq was at the controls. "I contacted the communications center at the bunker," he said, turning his head to look at us. "President Brooks is expecting us. Since the Chinese abandoned the Greenbrier Resort, Brooks and his team took over the entire facility and have begun to restore things the way they used to be. They tore down the Chinese flag and lifted a huge Stars-and-Stripes in its place."

I shouted with joy, and Peter let out a whoop.

Zaq started up the power, and we headed south. "It's gonna take some time to rebuild our country," he said. "But Brooks has already figured out a plan." He glanced at my father. "They want you to help, Mr. Jackson." Then Zaq eyed the old man in the back seat. "And by the way, Mr. Crenshaw, Brooks said to tell you he's got the chess board ready and waiting, whatever that means."

"It means he's gonna lose," Crenshaw said with a satisfied grin.

I sat back and relaxed, thrilled at the prospect of restoration coming years before we had expected. I looked at my mom. She was beaming. I took a deep breath for the first time in two weeks. No more confinement. No more wondering where Zaq was or if I'd ever see him again. I looked out the window and couldn't believe my eyes. The mist had disappeared from the landscape. The sun had climbed high in the sky. Off in the west arced the prettiest, biggest, double rainbow I'd ever seen.

Time Capsule is a complete work of fiction with fictitious people and fictitious events, except for some facts from history. For example, there really is a Greenbrier Bunker in White Sulphur Springs, West Virginia. Visit civildefensemuseum.org/greenbrier

Since 2021, people have been able to take an actual tour by making a reservation and traveling to the Greenbrier Resort in White Sulphur Springs. Cost at the time of this writing is $39 for adults; $20 for youth. For details Google Greenbrier Bunker Tours. Or, take a virtual tour at https://www.youtube.com/watch?v=g3kAcJruEOs.

The military uses drones for surveillance, and they can be armed with incendiary devices in case of war. Check out the tiny military drones at zdnet.com/article/us-military-equipped-with-tiny-spy-drones.

The Global Seed Vault is a real place on a remote island halfway between Norway and the North Pole, established to safeguard a great variety of crops.

And the Tesla company has created concepts for Robovans and Robotaxis, automatic multi-passenger vehicles of the future. Learn more at Tesla.com/en_in/we-robot.

Everything else—the time capsule, the Robotruck, the people, the story itself, are fabrications by the author.

Τhis has been a fun project to work on. It required lots of research and a chance to exercise my wild imagination.

I want to express my appreciation to my Beta readers, Joanna Jones and Elizabeth Saint Vicente for their insights and wise comments that made this manuscript more believable.

Many thanks to Mike Parker, my editor and publisher at WordCrafts Press, whose guidance and words of encouragement always make my work so much better. He believed in me when others didn't.

No writing project can make it to the finish line without the prompting of God's Holy Spirit who instilled in me a love of the written word, beginning with the Bible, and to God the Father who gifted a small child with a desire to tell stories, and to Jesus Christ, my Lord and Savior who doesn't allow me to quit.

I have a great respect and admiration for other fellow writers who work God's truths into their manuscripts and encourage me to do the same.

A Pulitzer Prize nominated journalist, Marian Rizzo has won numerous awards for her writing, including the *New York Times* Chairman's Award and first place in the 2014 Amy Foundation Writing Awards. She worked for the *Ocala Star-Banner* newspaper for 30 years. She also has written articles for the *Ocala Gazette*, *Ocala Style Magazine*, and Billy Graham's *Decision Magazine*.

Several of Marian's novels have won awards at Florida Christian Writers Association conferences and Word Weavers International retreats. In 2018, her suspense novel, *Muldovah*, was a finalist in the Genesis competition at the American Christian Fiction Writers Conference. Two of her novels have earned Amazon "Best Seller" status. Through her membership with Word Weavers International, she's been able to hone her craft through interaction with other members.

Marian lives and works in Ocala, Florida. She has two children, three grandchildren, and a yellow lab/mix named Buddy.

www.ingramcontent.com/pod-product-compliance
Lightning Source LLC
Chambersburg PA
CBHW021143310726
48971CB00002B/457